The Darkness Inside

Tam Hussein

The Darkness Inside by Tam Hussein
First published in 2022
© Tam Hussein

tamhussein.substack.com

About the Author

Tam Hussein is an award-winning investigative journalist with a particular focus on conflict. He is the contributing editor of *New Lines Magazine* and is the author of *To The Mountains: My Life in Jihad, from Algeria to Afghanistan* (Hurst) and *The Travels of Ibn Fudayl* (Darf Publishers). *The Darkness Inside* is his first novel.

To Mu'min

This novel is fiction, a work of imagination. Any similarity to actual persons, living or dead, or actual events, is purely coincidental.

Part 1

1. The Loop

At six forty-five Sid woke up to John Humphrys' familiar voice chirpily interrogating his guest on Radio Four. The two men were verbally jousting. It sounded like some game show, a charade. The radio presenter's voice was full of charm and wholesome wit and none of the cynicism that he should have as a journalist. He sounded like he didn't give a damn that the whole country would soon be hurled into the abyss. Sid had not yet discerned what the argument was about. His eyes were still sealed with the gunk of a full night's sleep and he had not fully shaken off its stupor.

He guessed that, as usual, the NHS was probably at breaking point, or that the country's politicians were behaving like they could just lay out their demands, and if they didn't get their way they would put out their black ships, and head towards Ilios and seize what they wanted. The *Today* programme ran those stories on every alternate day without fail, it was as if the editor had a rota: Monday was Brexit day, Tuesday meant NHS, obesity and cancer stories, Wednesday was the warnings about the economy, and so on – and yet despite the predictability Sid listened, intently, like a man listening out for seagulls on a quiet sea.

Outside, whilst the rosy tips of dawn took hold of the city, men disgorged its bins into the metal bellies of their dump trucks. Sid reached for his phone and brought it close to his eyes. He scanned the news feed in case there

The Darkness Inside

had been any breaking stories whilst his brain had been in darkness. His limbs slid off his double bed mattress onto the cold floor. He hadn't bothered to buy a bed frame. He started doing crunches alternated with press ups, all the while listening to Mishal Husain talking about the latest tweet by the president of the free world. After finishing he took the grey transistor radio into the shower. He shaved whilst listening to arguments over the country leaving the EU and the disastrous consequences and secretly loving all of it.

By ten past seven he was in a pair of chinos and a crisp white shirt, drinking coffee, all the time listening to the radio, even as he watched London moving out the window. In his hand burned a cigarette whose smoke slunk across his open-plan living room and kitchenette furnished with bland IKEA furniture. Sid had no particular urge to join the fast-paced Londoners from his eighth-floor flat – this was his time. The promise that dawn had made of sunshine had turned into a moody autumnal grey, just the way he liked it. Soon the nicotine and caffeine kicked in and coursed through him, and his brain started to finally wake up. The radio presenters' words began to swirl inside his mind, and were formulated into angles, ideas, news lines and perspectives. There was one idea that made a particular impression on him:

'The Mayor of London, Sadiq Khan,' said Humphrys, 'is accused of going easy on crime. This is the three hundredth murder on the streets of London in 2018 and there are fears that the Met have lost control of the streets.'

Sid's ears pricked up. He reached across the coffee

The Darkness Inside

table and raised the volume of the radio. He grabbed his phone and started typing: 'Mr Anis Ferjani dead on scene in Croydon'.

'The locals,' continued Humphrys, 'are demanding that the Mayor do something about what appears to be a gangland killing according to the Met. The Mayor's office has yet to issue a statement.'

Sid made another note: 'Mayor is avoiding responsibility, or is he going to blame it on the Tory cuts?' He reached for his muesli bar on the coffee table and took a chomp on it, thinking about the story, visualising all the elements that were required to make it interesting.

By seven forty-five Sid was gone, on the move. He was still listening to the *Today* programme on his headphones. By the time he reached Gants Hill station all the heavyweights were adding their two pence on the topic.

'It's atrocious,' said one with an exceedingly proud surname, 'how the Mayor can just sit by and allow this to happen.'

The other guest countered by saying, 'this of course wouldn't have happened if the Prime Minister didn't cut over thirty-five thousand police officers from our streets.'

And so it went like ping-pong; that typical technique where the producers take two guests with opposing views and set them against each other like hamsters in a cage where they thrash it out over the same issues – food, water or who gets to go on the wheel – but the cage, as always, remains the same. And then, just as things got heated, Humphrys chimed in: 'Well we're going to have to leave it there I'm afraid.' And on to the next topic, and still Sid listened.

The Darkness Inside

Having no signal on the tube compelled him to bring out his book: *Why Nations Fail* was this week's choice. He tried to read one book a week, hoping that it would give him an edge over all the others. But he had failed miserably. Some of the books he had read were just a blur. He had not allowed himself the time to digest the words. And all he could say about each book was that he had read it. This book, however, was far more important than the glance of a pretty stranger on the train. Sid probably didn't even see her, but then why would he? These girls, he thought, all had that same contour make-up look taken from that same YouTube video that made them look completely indistinguishable from each other. And yet, as he read intently, from the corner of his eye he noticed an old woman who could have been his mum with lines of time across her brown face. She leaned on a walking stick wearing soft-soled shoes. He stood up silently, and the old lady, realising that he intended the seat for her, sat down gratefully.

'Well,' she said in a kind patois accent – 'I see they still have gentlemen these days.'

He gave her a half-smile as if he was unsure whether she had meant it for him.

Sid got off at Liverpool Street and walked towards Shoreditch High Street, smoking his second cigarette of the day and thinking about how he should broach the topic with Martha. He took a side turn and walked towards the converted warehouse that had been turned into a snazzy media venture where everyone apart from the editor was below the age of thirty-five. Outside, a crowd of vapers, vegans, pescatarians and God knows what else had gathered.

The Darkness Inside

They were interns and people desperate for bylines, verified social media accounts and much, much more. They were all over-friendly and greeted each other with kisses on the cheek even if they had only met once; the sort of people who tweeted their feelings on their timeline and expected the whole world to give a shit. The sort of people who posted selfies with sayings from sages, saints and wise men in order to obtain that precious like on their Instagram page.

Sid walked into the *Loop's* offices, ignoring the receptionist, and went straight for the coffee machine. The place was already buzzing with news, rumours and gossip. The midnight staffers were yawning, ready to go home, having trawled the whole world for news ready for the new shift to update its audience. Editors were already on to their third coffee of the day. Sid made himself an Americano and walked towards a small hub of desks, the home bureau. His computer was nestled amongst six staffers and one intern whose sole job was to do the tasks that no one else wanted to do, like the hated Freedom of Information requests.

Martha was already at her desk, studying the staff rota and simultaneously looking at story pitches and ideas she would raise at the editorial meeting with Paul, the main editor. Today she didn't look that interested. Sid knew the signs when she was interested in a story – she would start to twist a pen into her frizzy red hair. Today there was none of that.

'Hey,' he said, putting his bag down. 'How's it going? You want a coffee?'

'Yes.'

'Here,' Sid said, handing her his cup, 'take mine.'

'That isn't coffee,' she said, abruptly turning around,

The Darkness Inside

'that's piss.'

'Oh, I forgot,' said Sid sarcastically, 'only you Italians know what coffee is. The rest of us have no clue.'

'Sid, you have finally understood how the world works.'

Sid held his cup to her as an offering, but she waved it away.

'I've got a bone to pick with you.'

'What?' Sid replied smiling, knowing full well what this would be about.

'Why didn't you return Tom's call?'

'You know why.'

'It's courtesy, Sid.'

'Come on, bad manners are fine amongst friends, and besides, I did message him to tell him I couldn't make it.'

'Yes, but it's rude, he'd bought two tickets.'

'I didn't ask him to – those tickets were for him and Amanda. He called me when she dropped out because she had to work late. He's expecting me to say yes. I don't even like jazz; it's shoe shop music that doesn't make sense. I don't know why he does that and then makes you feel guilty for not going along.'

'So why didn't you tell him on the phone?'

'Well, I knew if I answered he'd convince me – that's why you went in the end isn't it?' he laughed.

Martha knew it was true; Gardener had called her and made her feel so guilty that she couldn't get out of it.

'When Tom calls you he doesn't let go.'

'Well, you should call him and apologise.'

'No way,' Sid laughed. 'Once you apologise to him you'll be making up for it for the rest of your life. I'm still apologising for the time I borrowed his bicycle to go to a lecture and it got nicked.'

The Darkness Inside

'You stole it – he loved that bike.'

'I would have asked if he'd been there but I was running late. I replaced it.'

'With a shitty stolen bike.'

'I didn't know, did I?'

'You always fall on your feet.' Martha shook her head. Her attention was drawn to the papers, most of which, apart from the *Daily Star*, were dominated by Brexit. Noticing that her focus had now turned to work, Sid pounced on her with his pitch.

'Listen, Martha, lemme do this story.'

'Which one?' she replied, still turning the pages.

'The guy, what's-his-name.' He snapped his fingers as if it was on the tip of his tongue. 'The Anis Ferjani murder – the Croydon stabbing.'

'How comes?'

'Well, this story's about the Mayor isn't it? I mean, how long is he going to blame it on the cuts while all these kids are dying?'

'I know,' said Martha, laying her blue eyes on him. 'Paul wants Daniels to do it.'

Sid didn't want to hear that name. He sat down on his seat, frowning.

'What about you?'

He stared at her as if her reply was a test of loyalty.

'Let me see what happens after the editorial.'

'Daniels is useless. You might as well just print the press release.'

Martha smiled as if he had hit on something. 'Paul doesn't think so,' she said, getting up from her desk. She picked up her notepad and grabbed a pen.

The Darkness Inside

'Right, got to go. Speak later.' Sid watched her womanly figure head towards the meeting room. He hoped that she would fight for him. He turned on his computer and started to read up on everything there was about this new killing. Using an Excel sheet he started to compile names of family, friends, associates and, of course, official bodies that could be got at for a comment. He studied knife crime statistics and how the mayor had dealt with knife crime when he was an MP for Tooting. He worked thoroughly and systematically until Martha returned.

Sid knew before she even put her notepad on her desk what the outcome had been. She had always been a poor liar, ever since their student days. Whenever she filled in an extension form, he was the one who gave her the reason. He could tell by the pallor of her face and the fact that she avoided his gaze, but he had to ask.

'Well?'

'Paul,' she said, 'wants Daniels to have it.'

'Fuck! Fuck!'

He didn't even know why he swore – he already knew the outcome but for some reason he expected Fate to make an exception for him. Sid banged his desk, attracting strange looks from the other staffers on the bureau. He didn't really care what looks they gave him and each other. Who the fuck were they?

'Easy,' said Martha soothingly, 'he's a blue-tick verified journalist. Paul feels the story will get more exposure and traffic that way. Makes sense.'

'How many scoops,' replied Sid, 'has that blue-tick fucker got?'

'Not my decision, Sid.'

The Darkness Inside

'Did you push?' He searched her face.

Martha paused for a moment, as if she was offended. She looked wounded – what did she have to prove? Why did he always set up these hurdles?

'C'mon, Sid.' She stared at him, indignant. 'What's got into you?'

Sid got up from his desk.

'Sorry, I just need a bit of air.'

'Go on,' said Martha.

Sid felt even more pissed off as he headed towards the bathroom. He washed his face with cold water, just like they do in the movies. His head was burning with rage and he needed to cool down. Thinking no one was there, he stared at his own reflection, bashed the mirror with the palm of his hand and uttered that versatile monosyllable that can at once express surprise, anger and frustration.

'Fuck, fuck, fuck.'

He kept on saying it, hitting the mirror, and would have probably continued to do so had a timid man with oily skin not emerged from one of the cubicles, flushing first to announce his presence to Sid. He looked like an intern.

'Hello,' he said awkwardly, as if he was intruding. He went to the sink and scrubbed his hands quickly as if to say, 'Don't mind me, I'll be out of here in a flash.' But the more he tried to hurry things up, the more nervous he came across.

'You got a problem mate?' Sid said, annoyed at the young intern's nervousness.

'No, no, not at all,' said the young man, and he went out drying his hands on his jeans.

Sid stared him out of the toilet as if it was his personal

The Darkness Inside

fiefdom. Once the man was out, he bent down to see if there was anyone else in the other cubicles, in case another flustered guy came out equally apologetic and embarrassed at witnessing his fury.

By now he had cooled down enough to make his way out to the fire escape, which had, over time, become the place where all the smokers congregated. He had just started on his third cigarette when Daniels, wearing a smart brown suit and a hair cut that belonged to the sixties, joined him with one of those vaping contraptions.

'Hello Sid, how's it going?'

'Yeah, alright,' replied Sid glumly, 'you?'

'I have to go to this presser at the Met and then to the Mayor's, all because of this toerag.'

'Oh,' said Sid, feigning surprise, 'do you want me to go?'

'I think Paul would want me there. I'll tell you what, though – if you really want to help, could you go down to Croydon and sniff around there?'

'Why?' Sid asked, disinterested now that his hopes had been dashed.

'It would help a lot – I can dig around here and you over there.'

'What,' Sid said with a hint of sarcasm, 'digging at a press release? What will you get from that?'

'Quite a lot actually,' said Daniels, not spotting the subtle criticism. 'And you'll have a better in with the victim's family than I ever will.'

'Why?' asked Sid, fixing him with a penetrating stare. He had played it; he knew he had dealt Daniels the race card and Daniels was already wracking his brain as to how he should reply.

The Darkness Inside

'I mean…' replied Daniels, shifting from one leg to another, 'how can I put it?'

'You mean because we're both brown?'

'Oh, come off it man, you know I don't mean that. You can relate better to them. You're enterprising.'

'You arrogant little fuck.'

Sid threw his cigarette butt on the floor and stubbed it out. He went back to the office already regretting what he had said to Daniels. Daniels would no doubt let everyone know what Sid had called him. He could use it to counter the race card. Once, Daniels had been at a court case in Istanbul, and he had tweeted that the defendant had told him to fuck off. Later, Sid was told by a Turkish colleague who had also attended the court case that no such interaction had ever taken place. Daniels had gambled that no one from the British press would be present at the trial to contradict him. He had got away with it.

It was late afternoon when Martha pulled Sid up on his words. Sid was at his desk pretending to work.

'Sid, have you got a moment?'

'Yes,' said Sid, staring at the screen even though he felt her close to him. He could smell her perfume, some floral affair.

'You can't talk to people like that,' she said quietly. 'How many times have I told you?'

'He's an arrogant little fuck.'

'So what? Mention it in his appraisal or tell me. I can pass it on to Paul.'

'This guy automatically thinks that I should do these stories because I am "in" with the community. You know how he described me?' Sid swivelled his chair to face her. 'He called me enterprising.'

'What's wrong with that?'

'Fuck, Martha, open your Italian eyes – you think I'm some sort of Paki-Delboy flogging stories in Peckham? Only a prick would say that.'

'I don't know what you're talking about, but can you help him?'

'No, I fucking can't. You know what? Next time there's a story about Mexicans I'll ask you to cover it. You are Latin innit? Patronising prick thinks he can tell me what to do.'

'Finished?' said Martha, crossing her arms. She didn't accept Sid's interpretation of those comments – this was his paranoia coming through again. 'Daniels has a relationship with and contacts in the police, security and other places. He's been doing this for years.'

'He doesn't even want the story, did you know that? I have been begging you to put me on the foreign or politics gigs for years now. I bring you more scoops than Daniels year in year out. Has he ever got you an award?'

'No.'

'So why can't I get this chance?'

'You don't get the gig because you don't hold your shit together.'

'No, Martha, you know that isn't true. The reason I don't get the beat is because of this.'

Sid pointed to his brown skin.

'Really, Sid? Really?' Martha said, refusing to accept the race card Sid had just dealt her. 'Look around you. There's all sorts here. You can't hold your shit together, that's why.'

Sid didn't even look around the office. Martha was right

The Darkness Inside

– there were people of all colours and backgrounds.

'You know why Daniels got the gig?' Sid retorted. 'Because he went to Dulwich with Paul. We all know that.'

'You are way out of order!' Martha said quietly through gritted teeth, but she saw one or two glances from the staffers, so she calmed down. She moved closer. 'Sid, I know who my strikers are. Could you do this for me? And I will work on trying to see if there are other openings – I promise.'

For a moment Sid remained silent, immovable, like a sulking boy on the seafront who has dropped his ice cream.

'For me?' Martha said again.

Sid kissed his teeth and reached for his bag and jacket before leaving.

'Thank you,' said Martha, 'thank you.'

She breathed a sigh of relief. What would she have done had he refused?

2. Marrakech

Sid sat in Marrakech Cafe staring at Benny's English across the road, where pale journalists were sitting and staring into their phones. They had barely touched their food. Like him they were waiting for the rain to stop. Sid hated rainy dark days; they filled him with an intangible air of foreboding and dread. Martha was convinced that he suffered from Seasonal Affective Disorder and pressed him to take vitamin D tablets, but he dismissed it as a myth, one more alphabet disorder like ADHD and all the other pseudo-disorders that could easily be cured with a few slaps like in the good old days.

Sid could have joined them but he felt uncomfortable with the smell of crisp bacon lacing his clothes. Then there was cross-contamination – he always felt that staff barely cared if a bit of bacon fat got on his plate, even if he ordered a vegetarian English. He had seen how staff members, unversed in the rules of halal eating, would still use the same tong or cutlery to touch pork. He didn't blame them; why shouldn't they? He didn't understand the rules of kosher, so to expect them to do the same with halal wasn't fair.

Even though he wasn't particularly devout, the thought of pork nourishing his limbs was repulsive, so he sat in the cafe opposite watching cars go by and sulking about his shitty assignment. At least Marrakech Cafe smelled nicer with coffee brewing, onions frying, halal beef sausages

The Darkness Inside

cooking and friendly staff who seemed to care about its customers.

In fact, one of the friendly waiters, who also looked like he ran the place, approached him rubbing his hands. His expression looked disappointed when he noticed Sid's unloved and abandoned club sandwich.

'Was everything alright with the food, sir?'

'Yes, fine, thank you.'

'You haven't touched your club sandwich!' the waiter said as if it was a personal affront. It was as if he hadn't shown Sid due hospitality and wanted to make amends.

'Honestly,' replied Sid, trying to placate the waiter's sense of honour and shame, 'it's not you, it's me.'

'You sound like an old girlfriend,' he said with a wink. 'Can I get you anything else? We do some lovely desserts.'

Sid felt guilty.

'Yeah, go on then.'

'What can I get you?'

Sid pointed to a moist cake in the counter display cabinet that looked particularly appetising.

'Gimme that chocolate cake please.'

'Certainly, sir.'

The waiter went to the display cabinet and took out a slice of cake, put it on a plate and brought it to him.

'There you are.'

'Ta, mate.'

Whilst Sid sat eating his cake, he watched the waiter diligently inquiring into the needs and wants of all his customers. If the food wasn't up to scratch he took it personally. You could tell by his expression that each comment was taken to heart. Once Sid finished, the man

The Darkness Inside

returned and asked him how the cake was, as if to make amends for the previous failure. This time Sid told him it was lovely.

'Oh yeah?' said the stocky waiter. 'Then why the long face? I would have thought the chocolate should have done it.'

'No, it's not that.' Sid felt guilty again.

'What then?' said the waiter, who had such a reassuring face Sid felt he could confide in him. 'It's either going to be work or women, innit?'

'Well it's not women, I've forgotten what they look like.'

'Trust me, I'm trying to forget.'

Sid couldn't help but laugh at the South Londoner.

'Listen, are you local?'

'Grew up in Shrublands.'

'You know anything about this kid that got killed?'

The man stared at him suspiciously as if he was CID.

'Why?'

'I'm covering the story.'

'A journalist?'

Sid nodded.

'So why,' said the man, 'aren't you over there with the rest of the scum – I mean scrum?'

'Well they don't serve halal food do they?'

'You Muslim?'

'Yes.'

'Serious?' the man said as if he couldn't believe it. 'You don't see many of them in your line of work, do you?'

'Yeah I am. My name is Saeed. Sid for short.'

'Sorry bro,' said the man, shaking his hand. 'You don't meet a lot of Muslim journalists. I don't mean to be rude but the media has screwed us over so many times, sometimes

The Darkness Inside

you wonder if even the ones with Muslim names really are Muslim. And the Muslims that are in news are all coconuts. Know what I mean?'

'I understand.' He'd heard that argument so many times it didn't even hurt anymore.

'So do you know this kid?'

'Yeah, I know him. I mean I knew him.' He looked around him; there was a customer vying for his attention. 'I'm a bit busy at the moment but I close up for five. Could you come back to the shop later?'

'When? What's your name, akh?'

'Mo, and five-ish? Does that sound alright?'

'Yes, for sure.'

Even after Sid left the cafe, he waited around the corner, making sure no other journo he knew of went in there. He was worried the newspaper men, the ones that wore the shirts and ties, the proper scum, would go over there and steal the story from him. In a way, though, the fact that the media moguls were still old skool and wanted their staff to wear shirts and ties meant that they could easily be identified. But still, the newspaper men were the worst; they were humanity's equivalent of seagulls. They would just snatch morsels of food from your very hands. Many years back a *Sun* scumbo had followed him around nonchalantly as he knocked each and every door on a block of flats in Paddington, and then when he had finally hit the jackpot and found the guy he was looking for the scumbitch offered the guy a wad of cash and that scoop vanished in front of his very eyes, in less than a second. Had Martha not been there with him, he would have probably thrown the bastard down the waste shaft and buried him. From that day on he had learnt to protect

The Darkness Inside

his scoop, his game, the hard way and used all manner of ghetto strategies to achieve his objective.

At a quarter to five, he turned up at the cafe as Mo was pulling down the shutters, looking nervously across at Benny's English to see if there were any journalists who might recognise him.

'How comes you close so early?' Sid asked, trying to cover his nervousness.

'All the office workers go home,' replied Mo. 'No point in staying open. The locals are too poor to make it worthwhile, to be honest.'

Sid watched the cafe owner lock up. Mo told Sid to accompany him to his car.

'So what do you want to know?' Mo said as he trundled along.

'Well, is it true he was a gang member like the police say?'

'See,' Mo was already indignant, 'how the media twists things? This brother had nothing to do with gangs.'

'So correct it.' Sid realised that he had met a conspiracy theorist; the sort of guy who posted anti-vaccine websites and 7/7 conspiracies, illuminati, freemasons and everything else on Facebook. But Sid needed the guy so he let it roll.

'How?'

'Start by telling me what happened.'

'I don't know what happened.'

'So why is the police's press release wrong?'

'Coz he's a nice guy, that's why. Anis was never into gangs. He used to talk to kids about staying out of trouble. But how comes the media never says that?'

'It's a developing story.' Sid tried his hardest not to sound patronizing. 'We're still trying to build a picture of the

The Darkness Inside

brother. We're only as good as the information we get.'

'Come on,' said Mo, 'that ain't true.'

Sid tried his best not to get into a schooling session with him. He wasn't going to explain that there weren't a bunch of editors sitting round in some dark boiler room with a hook-nosed Fagin, brewing up stories to cause doom and destruction. He just wanted a few lines, some stills and film. They came up to Morland Road where Mo's Mercedes was parked. All things considered, thought Sid, he had done well working that little cafe.

'There's always an agenda,' continued Mo. 'If Anis was white it would be a different story. Did you see how they painted the killer of Jo Cox? You'd think the fucking Nazi belonged to Sesame Street!'

'That's the *Daily Mail* though!'

'Don't matter. They're all the same if you ask me.'

Luckily, no one was asking him, thought Sid.

'I promise you,' he said. 'I will tell the truth. I didn't get into this business to lie about my own community, you know. At the end of the day, I got a mum and a sister. You reckon I want to see their heads kicked in?'

'Alright,' said Mo. 'You might be different. But I'm just saying. Look at this.' He brought out his phone and played some videos. They showed the young victim, a twenty-something, standing there in his cafe. He had his thumbs up, with one arm around the cafe owner's shoulders.

'Marrakech serves the best English breakfast in Croydon!' he said. 'Those who know, know!'

'God have mercy on him,' Mo said, before showing Sid more stills of the young man enjoying coffee and croissants.

Sid started to look at the moving film and images. They

gave an insight into who the victim was. Clearly he wasn't some hoodlum jacking people's bags and phones and careering off on a moped.

'Have you given these to anyone?' Sid asked, being careful not to betray his interest in the photos in case the price for buying them suddenly shot up exponentially.

'It's on our Instagram page.'

'Can I have it?' Sid was hoping that Mo would just give it to him. No fees, nothing; that would have been the greatest triumph. A testimony to his ability to manipulate.

'Yeah, brother, if it was just for you, I would give it for free,' Mo replied. 'But since it's the media, I reckon they have a bit of spare change.'

'Yeah,' replied Sid. He had seen that coming. Mo was a socially 'woke' man who cared little for money; it was all about the destruction of the edifice that is mainstream media.

'How does fifty pounds sound?'

'Nah, it's a bit of an exclusive innit?'

Money had made that bond of faith, that Muslim brotherhood, disappear. They were businessmen negotiating.

'How much?'

'Two hundred.'

'Take it off Instagram now and I will pay for it. And you can't share it. Is that a deal?'

'Yeah.'

Sid then watched the cafe owner delete the pictures off his Instagram. He also got him to send him a message confirming that he wouldn't share the photos with anyone else. Of course, if he did, there might be little chance of pursuing him to the courts, but still Sid wanted to make him

The Darkness Inside

feel that there were repercussions for betrayal. Sid received the photos and, just to make sure he had got the information right, he asked, 'so you are a hundred percent sure he had no gang connections? Look at the way he got sliced around the neck. Doesn't look like an accident to me.'

'Hundred percent. The guy used to pray and everything. The only time I saw something weird was when he got into some argument with a Kurd. You know, one of those hardcore flag wavers who thinks the whole world was invented by Kurdistan?'

'No,' Sid said, 'can't say I do.'

'In Croydon you got loads, especially in West Croydon – those lot even reckon that the Prophet, sallallahu alaihi wa salaam, was a Kurd.'

'Really? Even the Prophet?'

'Yes! See to them Abraham was a Kurd and since the Prophet sallallahu alaihi wa salaam, descended from him, he's also a Kurd.'

'Nuts.'

'Tell me about it,' said Mo. 'You get all sorts these days – not just Polish schleps.'

'You reckon it could be one of them?'

'I don't think so; it was just an argument. Even though that Kurd was an arsehole anyway, it was Anis' fault. He had something against them Kurds in general. It's like every time he saw those guys with their skinny jeans and pooffy haircuts his face would just change. Don't blame him to be honest. They look like pricks. Listen, I need to pick up the kids.'

Mo offered him a lift to the cash machine and Sid jumped into the Mercedes to conclude the business deal.

3. The Scoop

Dawn emerged like a slab-grey corpse and imposed itself inside Sid's flat. Not even the colours purple or blue could be bothered to make an appearance; the whole place appeared clinical, lifeless and miserable. There was only one thing that appeared alive and vibrant in the salon – a vase that stood in the corner. It was made of Amalfi ceramic with a floral pattern of grapevines and lemons which embraced the Latin proverb *In vino veritas* – in wine there is truth. Martha had given it to him alongside a ceramic tile which depicted the splendour of Naples nestled under Vesuvius. Sid had hung the tile in the bathroom.

Sid sat on the settee smoking and listening to the radio whilst his eyes studied the residents opposite his flat scurrying to get their lives in order. Usually he paid little attention. It annoyed him that he could see people doing their everyday stuff right in front of his window just because some architect had a completely selfish idea or whim: to create a sense of space and light by making the outer walls of the building out of glass; no need for masses and masses of concrete. This selfish conception meant that people's private life had become Sid's theatre. It was *Love Island* twenty-four seven. Sid could see David rush to the bathroom every morning because, he presumed, David had a bowel problem so he couldn't hold his shit in for too long. Sid knew when David's girlfriend, Lisa, was pre-

The Darkness Inside

menstrual because she would have one of those teary moments for no particular reason and she might just binge watch *Friends* for several hours. He felt that sort of stuff should be kept behind thick net curtains.

He didn't need or want to have their lives imposed on him. But this intimate access to them had compelled him, in a moment of boredom and curiosity, to pull up their old addresses and their birth certificates. He even knew how many boyfriends Lisa had had. Most people, he had learnt, were promiscuous with their information. He could, given the time, find out everything about David and Lisa. Whenever he saw them walking their dog, or even kissing in the privacy of their living room, he felt embarrassed and looked away, freaked out by his own creepiness. They should make these new builds with windows instead of glass walls. When he wasn't feeling ordered, events in David and Lisa's life could unsettle him, disturb his equilibrium, but today was not one of those days.

Sid had woken up earlier than usual, at five, when the *Today* programme had started. Nick Robinson's hoarse voice announced that it was Tuesday: the country was heading for Brexit doom, Theresa May's cabinet was about to tumble, and the UK had entered into a state of near vassalage. And the sky, every last millimetre of it, was pitch black, with no stars in sight – dead. But neither the sky nor the future of the country had bothered him when he opened his eyes. Those things didn't interest him one bit, and neither did the muesli protein bar that had served as his breakfast for the last couple of years. His stomach was a knot of excitement.

The Darkness Inside

By dawn Sid's phone was already pinging off. He glanced at the incoming message – it was from Martha.

Paul was really happy. The papers ran with it too :)

Didn't hear it on the radio tho, Sid texted back.

Did you listen to BBC London? They are all over it. Heard Eddie Nestor is doing a big thing on it on drive time. Made METRO and Standard front page.

Did we watermark the stills? wrote Sid.

Yes, and the other papers are covering it on the other side too. Daily Mail? Did they pick it up?

They, Martha pinged back, *have the video too ;)*

Sid sent her a :) emoji.

See you later, she texted. *We should celebrate. X*

Sid stared at the 'X' for a moment, considering whether he should reply with an 'X' or with a more non-committal 'yes'. But in the end he put the phone down and kept on listening to the radio, leaving the text conversation to hang in the air without making any apologies. Little did he know that Martha would be waiting for that 'X' all morning.

Sid didn't notice the pregnant woman with the brown overcoat coming in and standing in front of him on the tube. He was too absorbed to notice her or another elderly lady standing a bit further down in the gangway. He had become that annoying passenger that reads across your shoulder, except he wore this curious broken smile as he read the headline.

Victim had no links to South London gangs.

He was experiencing a euphoria that came from seeing his story grab the attention of his colleagues and competitors. He received a text from the cafe owner

The Darkness Inside

congratulating him for 'showing the Truth' but, the truth was, the truth didn't matter.

It didn't matter that perhaps six million people on London's tubes may have come across his story as they shuttled and scuttled through the city's underground caverns and tunnels. What mattered was that his colleagues saw it, and asked, 'Who did that story?' And the reply would be: 'Sid'. And some guy would say: 'the cunt'. In fact, what would be even more pleasurable would be if the *Loop*'s competitors like *BuzzFeed*, *HuffPost* and others were forced to run the story, quoting the *Loop* – that was satisfaction. Stories like this meant you didn't need calling cards; you could mention it to an editor and he would remember it. Sid knew he was one step closer to that blue verified Twitter tick.

Sid's stop was fast approaching and as he got up to go, he couldn't help letting the young woman reading the *Metro* know.

'I broke that.'

The woman stared at him as if he was Harvey Weinstein or some other weirdo. He got off the tube self-satisfied whilst commuters walked past him, oblivious to his scoop.

When Sid entered the newsroom, he found Daniels standing with Martha, both holding mugs of coffee in their hands. Daniels was wearing toff clothes – browns, tweeds and brogues – one hand in his pocket. He was already telling Martha what angles the bureau should be pursuing. Martha listened to all the bullshit, spotted Sid and gave him a smile. Sid took off his jacket and sat down, hoping that Daniels wouldn't talk to him.

'Morning mate,' said Daniels, tapping him on the shoulder. 'Well done on the story, well done.'

'Thanks,' replied Sid, looking at the place where Daniels had placed his hand as if it had become dirty all of a sudden, as if it required disinfecting.

'So,' said Daniels chirpily, 'what are your plans today?'

Sid looked at him suspiciously and at Martha as if to ask what Daniels was scheming.

'Going back to Croydon to do some more digging. I think there's a few more lines to be had.'

'Like what?' Daniels asked.

'Well,' replied Sid, standing up, 'the guy had his throat slit. This wasn't some frantic panicked juk juk juk then run.'

Sid made several stabbing movements with the pen, which got Martha moving closer and listening more intently.

'It's like I came up from behind and sliced you. Execution-style. I don't know, the killing doesn't sit right.'

'What,' said Daniels, 'like an assassination?'

Sid sensed that his words were laced with sarcasm.

'Not saying that, just looks like a pro did it.'

'Like Jack the Ripper? Why didn't the Met say so?'

'Well,' said Martha before Sid took Daniels' bait, 'let's wait for the coroner's report, shall we?'

She turned to Sid.

'So how many stories do you think you have on this?'

'I don't know, but we can go to town on it like the *New York Times* piece on the Las Vegas shooting last year. Interactive digital, text, the lot. We can make it into a big investigation or a campaign, even, on knives. We can really own this!'

'Yes!' she said enthusiastically. 'We can make this into that Bellingcat investigation piece and really own it! And then we'll submit it to the British journalism awards this September. We didn't get anything last year – I swear to

The Darkness Inside

Jesus we will this year.'

'Well,' said Daniels, trying to dampen her enthusiasm, 'I'm not sure it can go that far. At the end of the day it's just another guy killed.'

'No,' replied Martha, 'it depends how you tell it. We can highlight so many issues in London using just that story.'

'Exactly,' Sid beamed, 'exactly!' She had seen the light.

'Let's go and win this!' she said.

'I promise you Marth, I will put my fucking being into this shit – I swear.'

'I know,' replied Martha. She knew that when Sid set his heart on something, he would see it through to the end. He reminded her of one of those dogs with lockjaw – once he bit he just wouldn't let go. There was almost this perverse loyalty about it. And her job was to be there when it was time to prise those jaws open and collect the prize, with a crowbar if she had to.

'Anyway,' said Daniels, unconvinced. 'I spoke to Paul, Sid.'

'Oh yeah?'

'He wants you to go to the Mayor of London's press briefing.'

'What?'

Sid couldn't believe his ears. He had just given birth to a story and now his newborn was being snatched away from him.

'That's what you wanted didn't you?' Daniels spoke as if he was doing him a favour. 'You're the best man for this story, that's what I told Paul.'

'What?! You are joking?' Sid began to turn red.

'No, not at all, he wants you to lead. I'll go to Croydon

The Darkness Inside

instead and you can hobnob with the Mayor's people. I just need the contact for the guy who gave you the film.'

'I can't believe I'm hearing this.' Sid was about to explode.

'What? What did I say?' Daniels asked.

Martha intervened and, turning to Daniels, said, 'I think you can go to the presser and Sid will go to Croydon.'

'But Paul wants him to…'

'Let me speak to Paul, it's my bureau,' Martha replied. 'I just think that Sid's making good progress on this.'

'Well… Paul…' bumbled Daniels, 'what am I going to say to him?'

'Don't worry about that', Martha reassured him. 'Leave it to me.'

'Okay. Fine.'

Daniels walked off in a huff. He hadn't got what he wanted. Sid stood there looking at Martha, nodding. It was a sign of gratitude.

'You need to get a blue tick, Sid,' she said. 'Let me know how it goes.'

'Yes, I fucking do!' Sid grabbed his jacket, smiled, and headed towards the door. For a moment he thought about replying to her message with an 'X', but then he thought better of it and headed out.

4. LIDL

It had started to rain when Sid arrived at the Lidl car park in West Croydon. The grey sky was spitting, taunting him like an impetuous Greek deity threatening to turn the wheels of fortune. But still somehow the rain and the greyness fit in with the general ambience of West Croydon. In fact, Sid couldn't imagine the place ever having sunshine. Over the course of his life, Sid had learnt to use his words judiciously – some, he had learnt early on, could result in unjustified beatings. Thus when Sid described West Croydon as a shithole, he meant it. It wasn't so much the shops – a combination of butchers, chicken and kebab shops and news agencies – but more the people he encountered, at least some of them, that made him come to this conclusion. There were a lot of alcoholics, nutcases and youngsters who looked like they hid scimitars inside their puffa jackets. As he passed they stared at him, daring him to stare back. Of course, that may just have been Sid's impression. Perhaps Sid was so far removed from the ordinary that he was describing a very normal street in the country. After all, he was living in a newsroom where journalists were discussing the eleven plus exams and whether their kids got into Dulwich College, Trinity and Whitgift – a stone's throw away from West Croydon – and perhaps Sid too would do so if and when he had his own brood.

The Darkness Inside

When Sid arrived at the spot in the car park where Anis had been killed, he found it had been turned into a shrine. Flowers of all colours, small candles and cuddly teddy bears, now soggy on account of the rain, sat there with the other teddies still smiling. There were cards and other objects that tried their best to remember the victim. Sid waited for a young, handsome journalist to finish off his news piece before he made his way over to look at the shrine. He also recognised Dev, the cameraman, who, as soon as he finished the interview, started to run around quickly, shooting the cutaways they would need to make the piece. Sid made his way down quietly, not wanting to disturb the veteran cameraman and the presenter. He could hear the young presenter speak to the news desk in a Scottish accent.

'Yes, I've added the new lines and we just need a few voxpops, then we're good to go for lunch time.'

Spotting Sid, the young Scot asked, 'Hello sir, are you local?'

'Yeah, I am,' replied Sid, adopting a working-class accent.

'Did you know him?'

'As a matter of fact,' replied Sid, seeing the hunger in the presenter's eyes, 'I did.'

'I am so sorry to hear that', the Scot replied, a little bit too enthusiastically. 'How did you know him?'

'We were lovers.'

'Really?'

By now the young man's eyes were like full-beam fog lights. He couldn't contain himself.

'That's strange, isn't it? I mean, Anis being, you know…'

'Muslim?'

'Yes. Do you think he was killed because of that?'

'Because of what?'

'Honour? Maybe that's why they slit his throat? Could it be an honour killing?'

'Well, he had a lot of lovers… I don't see why not?' Sid said thoughtfully, scratching his groin. 'I remember how he once fondled my balls just there where he died. It was an unforgettable moment.'

The journalist shifted about awkwardly as if Sid was giving him too much information.

'You can quote me on that,' Sid said.

By now, Dev had finished taking the shots and had put his tripod away and come up to them.

'Give it a rest, Sid,' said Dev in an accent that belonged to the eighties.

The young presenter looked at both men, laughed and gave a sigh of relief.

'Fook me!'

Sid laughed at the trainee journalist.

'Should have seen the look on your face.'

He turned to Dev.

'How's it going Dev? Long time. How's them horses?'

'They are running fine, just fine. Dorothy's getting a bit old in the tooth but otherwise can't complain.'

'You know what, Dev?' Sid replied. 'The way you look, I would never have guessed you were a cameraman.'

'Fuck off,' Dev replied, knowing full well that Sid meant quite the opposite. He looked exactly like that archetypal photographer you see on TV – khaki waistcoat with loads of pockets, a bandana, dirty jeans. He was a cross between a Rolling Stones guitarist and a crazy bastard.

The Darkness Inside

It got a laugh out of the trainee presenter.

'Listen,' said the trainee. 'I'm really sorry, I didn't mean to offend; I assumed…'

'All good, at least you didn't think I was an Uber driver. So what you got?'

The young journalist pointed to the cards. 'Nothing much really, except condolences.'

'The usual then,' Sid replied. 'You're an angel, the best dad, the best friend and such like.'

The presenter nodded.

'Listen,' he said cautiously. 'Could I ask you a question without sounding rude?'

'You've already shown great cultural awareness but yeah, go ahead.'

'Has the victim been to Afghanistan?'

Dev interrupted him as if he was getting tired with the calibre of this year's batch of trainee journalists.

'You are a muppet, aren't ya? When did the war in Afghanistan happen?'

'2003 to 2004?'

'No, they fought the Russians in 1979; you weren't even born then and neither was the victim.' Dev turned to Sid, shaking his head in disbelief. 'Where do they find these journos these days, Sid? Where? Fuck me.'

'So why,' said the presenter, 'do they describe him as belonging to the Mujahideen then?'

'Where?' asked Sid. 'Show me.'

The young trainee showed him a few condolence messages. Sid picked one of the messages up and read it.

'R.I.P. Bro. You are a true Mujahid.'

Sid looked at another message.

The Darkness Inside

'You fought like a lion'.

'For Muslims,' explained Sid, 'anyone who gets killed wrongfully gets called that.'

'Aye, out of respect?'

Sid nodded.

Dev interjected. 'It's like Thomas Becket, a fucking martyr, or to use a Scottish parallel, Mel Gibson in Braveheart.'

Sid laughed at the way Dev talked. He had done that to him too when he started off as a trainee but he soon realised that Dev's harshness was contrived. He was only that way because he didn't want to get too close to his trainees. He had lost some of his colleagues in Baghdad during the Gulf War and he didn't want to go through those bouts of inner darkness again. That was why his nose was so red, and likely his liver was about to cave in sometime soon. It could not filter the alcohol anymore.

'I'm sorry again if I offended,' said the young Scot, extending his hand. 'Anyway, it was nice meeting you. I'm Geoff.'

'Nice one,' Sid said, giving his hand a yank and a squeeze.

'Well mate,' said Dev, 'I'll call you when I need an Uber, we need to cut this film for lunch time.'

Dev turned to the trainee.

'Come on, otherwise I'm sending you back to Newsround.'

As the two trundled off to the van, Sid shouted, 'Don't worry, since I've known him he's always been a dickhead.'

'That's reassuring,' replied Geoff.

Once the men were out of sight, Sid started to meticulously go through each and every condolence message looking for clues, names, descriptions, memories, anything that could give information about the victim's demise. Those that he found interesting he took pictures of with a note. There were some that didn't make sense to him. In particular, one message caught his attention which read: 'Green birds, God willing'.

That evening Sid sat on the sofa binge-watching *House of Cards* on Netflix. He was trying his best not to think about the shrine and what it all meant. There were some things that just didn't make sense. But his brain was tired and his eyes were burning from too much screen time, so when he got home he had just jumped on the sofa, called Uber Eats and started season six. He ate through the pizza with ease and would have continued watching till late had his mobile phone not rang. He quickly glanced over to see who it was. It wasn't work but Reem, his sister, or half-sister to be more precise. He let the phone ring.

Reem seemed to know that he was holding the phone in his hand contemplating whether he should answer her call and started to ping off a stream of WhatsApp messages.

Salaams, how's things?
Just wanted to see if you have gone to visit dad?
When are you going to visit him? He doesn't have a long time.
:(

Sid didn't answer at all. Instead, he put his phone on vibrate and chucked it onto a soft rug by the bookshelf. It was as if he had had enough of her. What was more, he no longer wanted to continue watching the episode and it wasn't even half past nine. And so, little by little, the shrine and the messages in it started to creep into and roll around in his mind. He reached for his MacBook, which was hiding under the pizza box, and started to Google *ANIS FERJANI + CROYDON*. Nothing turned up. He did the same on Facebook; nothing. LinkedIn;

The Darkness Inside

nothing. Twitter; nothing. Instagram; nothing. Even archive. org; nothing. He continued thus for all the other social media platforms. Sid exhausted all the means at his disposal, typed the name in various ways – Anees, Anīs – even attempted the implausible spelling Aniis, but stopped short of Anes and Anus, which would just bring up the wrong sorts of results and images. It was two in the morning when Sid concluded that Mr Anis Ferjani was a ghost – this intrigued him. Since Facebook's inception, human nature had changed what men and women hid inside themselves – light and darkness. Those below the age of thirty had inverted their natures. That which was meant to be kept hidden was displayed for the whole world to gawk at, to like, to envy and to be repulsed by. It was as though their whole life was a spectacle. And whilst they lost something of themselves in this theatre, it had become Sid's playground. But how strange it was to find such a young man, who behaved as if he belonged to the ancients.

5. Wednesday at the Old Bailey

Tom Gardener stood outside the small entrance to the Old Bailey. There was no one there; not even the court officials had arrived. He huddled under the entrance frame looking up at the autumn sky and waiting to get in, his bag on the floor, his right hand holding a milky, thin cup of tea and his left a vape pen. Gardener wanted to get hold of the court papers first, finish off the job as early as possible, send it off to the *Times* and end it there. He could see how this case was going to play out. Papers loved cases involving terrorists, paedos, grooming gangs, wife-beating rapists and all the other dregs of the earth that went through the system. And all he had to do was just be there early and file the report and he'd be all good. Occasionally they'd ask him to go on a dig – he hated that. Gardener could dig; he was a natural mole. He'd knock on every single door on the street, rummage through dustbins to get that news line if need be, and the money was good. The papers all knew it, but most of the time, it was the fact that he turned up at the crease and stayed in the crease until the job was finished that gave him the edge. Hundred-not-out was his nickname. If there was a particularly difficult case he could bring his encyclopaedic knowledge and accurate court reporting to the table. And if he so wished, he could ever so discreetly call some of the parties involved. Over the years, as his hair had changed season, he had cultivated good relationships with barristers, lawyers, judges, coroners and police commissioners over late dinners, glasses of wine and cigars. With most he was on first-name terms. It meant that not only was he fulfilling the very purpose of court reporting, to make justice open to scrutiny and available to the public, but he was always in work. The truth was younger journalists weren't willing to sit through boring court rooms or inquiries day in, day out – they just didn't have the patience and neither was it glamorous enough for them to stick with it. Gardener could do that. And so, in his own little way, he had become a cornerstone, and what was more, it was a nice gig that he had honed to perfection. No running round, no breaking news, just come to the crease, score a century, raise the bat up – go home.

Gardener spilt his tea, when the phone rang so unexpectedly. He prayed that it wasn't his fiancée having been locked out again, forgetting her keys, but it wasn't.

'Hey buddy,' he said, answering Sid's call.

'Hey mate, how are you?'

'I was about to say the same; you sound tired. You know your sister messaged me last night, looking for you. Everything alright?'

'Yeah. What did she want?'

'Looking for you, but isn't everyone? She was saying you weren't answering her messages. I can believe that.'

'What did you do last night?'

'The fight. Remember the one I was trying to get you to watch with me?'

'Who won?'

'Honestly,' said Gardener, 'I fell asleep.'

'Great,' Sid said, disinterested. 'Got a question for you.

The Darkness Inside

You must come across this all the time.'

'Shoot.'

'If you got a guy who has absolutely no digital footprint, what would you think?'

'You tried all different variations in spelling and all that?'

'Course!' Sid sounded irritated.

'In that case, I'd think he's an old man, a luddite or a very smooth criminal.'

'Why criminal?'

'Well, look, when I've dug into cases I've always found some sort of digital footprint. These days it's impossible to hide – look at the Skripal case, the Russian intelligence officers tried their best to hide their identities but failed miserably.'

'Yeah, we know that.'

'You know in most T-cases, the guy convicts himself. The police just trawl through his social media accounts and find him holding a Kalashnikov. The ones that get off are the smarter ones not into taking selfies every ten minutes.'

'So you reckon Anis might be hiding something?'

'The stab victim from Croydon?'

'That's the one.'

'Maybe, or you're not searching properly. I mean the nearest thing I can think of is the Parsons Green bomber. He was impressive – for a seventeen-year-old kid he was a ghost. No digital footprint whatsoever. He was a pro.'

'Mate, could you do me a big favour?'

'It's going to cost you.'

'What?'

'Dinner next week.'

'Come on man, I hate that stuff.'

'Okay, suit yourself.' Gardener went silent.

The Darkness Inside

'Alright, alright,' agreed Sid. 'Could you ask your contacts whether he was on the radar of the security services?'

'That it?! You need to build up your own contacts.'

'Yeah.'

'Cool, give me a few days. Are you and Martha travelling up to Manchester?'

'For what?'

'Reunion.'

'She might – not me. Speak soon.'

Gardener put the phone down.

As estates go, Heath House wasn't bad. Even as darkness set in there were still some kids kicking a bit of leather about on the miserable patch of grass. They cussed each other's mums with such violence that in any other country it would have got them killed. A pale, waiflike mother stood smoking in the new-ish playground, which was soon to be attacked by vulgar graffiti. She watched her snotty toddler's attempt to walk up the slide. However much the toddler tried to reach its apex, he failed. Eventually he cried, giving up. The mother carried on smoking as if to say, that's life son.

Sid couldn't help holding his hands to his nose as he entered the lift on the council estate. It stank of piss and alcohol. When the lift opened on the third floor and he stood on the gangway, he looked round for exit routes, just in case things turned ugly. He took a deep breath; he didn't know who was behind that teak-coloured door. It could be some vicious Staffordshire bull terrier or the nicest old lady. Once he got to door number thirty-two, he listened quietly for a moment to see if anyone was in. He already had the letter ready with his contact details to pop through the letter box if they weren't. In a way he wished they weren't, but he needed face time with the family. He heard the faint sound of music coming from inside. He rang the doorbell. There was no response. Perhaps the doorbell wasn't loud enough. He went to the kitchen window and knocked, this time just a bit harder. The music stopped abruptly. He heard footsteps approaching the door and the door opened slightly. The latch chain, however, remained firmly in place.

An Arab-looking woman with brown frizzy hair and reddish eyes stared through the gap.

'Yes? We don't want anything.'

Sid countered her hesitation by giving her a Muslim greeting.

'Salaam alaikum, sister.'

'Wa alaikum salaam, brother,' the lady replied. He had obliged her to return his greeting of peace. This was a classic method that Sid employed in breaking down barriers. The only time you didn't return someone's greetings of peace was when you were angry, otherwise it was a religious obligation.

'Sister, I am sorry to disturb you at a time like this. My name is Saeed, I work for the *Loop*.'

'What's that? We don't need anything.'

'No, I don't think you understand, I'm a journalist.'

She paused for a moment.

'You're from the media? You are from the media?'

The tone of her voice became more nervous, maybe even verging on hysterical.

Sid nodded, all the while thinking: 'shit, shit, shit' – she was another one of those.

The Darkness Inside

The woman turned around and shouted down the hallway.

'Ayman! Ayman!'

Turning to Sid, she asked excitedly, 'How did you get my address? How did you find us?'

Sid was about to reply when a burly young man came to the door and undid the latch and stood over him. He had tufts of bum fluff on his chin and jaw. The woman moved behind him.

'You alright bruv?' he said. 'You troubling my sis?'

'Salaam alaikum bro.'

Sid's greeting of peace did not elicit the same reply. The man was silent. Sid knew who he was: Anis' brother, Ayman. Must have been, he was registered at that address; he was meant to be the younger brother, but the way he looked, he should have been the older one. Ayman stood in front of him, immovable, demanding a satisfactory answer. He just wasn't having any of it.

'I don't,' Sid replied, 'mean to disrespect your family or disturb you, but…'

'So how comes you found our address?'

The man stared at Sid as if he was expecting a better answer, or else.

'Look,' said Sid soothingly, 'you are on the electoral roll register so it's not hard to find you. All media organisations rely on these paid databases to trace people.'

'Okay.' The answer was good enough for Ayman. 'But what do you want?'

Behind him his sister was goading him.

'This is harassment, Ayman. See how the media chase you and destroy you?'

The Darkness Inside

'Sister,' Sid said, addressing the nervous woman, 'honestly that's not why I am here. If you want me to go away I will. All I want to do is to tell Anis' story so we can catch the killer.'

'No, no, no,' said the woman, working herself up. 'I know your game.' She squinted and pointed an accusing finger at him. 'All you lot do is demonise us. You'll probably depict him as a terrorist.'

'And just why would I do that?' replied Sid, astonished at the accusation and the curious response. In Sid's experience, usually victims of crime cooperated with the media to highlight their case so there was pressure on the authorities to act swiftly. 'He's a victim of crime. If anything, I want to put pressure on the Mayor of London. Don't you want to go down to City Hall and ask Sadiq Khan himself why your brother died?'

'Listen,' she said. She had stopped listening a long time ago; the game was lost. 'He's paid his debt to society; he's done his time. I don't want his past to be brought up.'

'Honestly, I'm confused,' replied Sid, disarmed.

'You can stay confused,' said Ayman, menacingly. 'We want to be left alone. Now, bop.'

'Okay, can I leave you my card?'

Sid extended his hand, offering his business card, but Ayman's forearms remained crossed.

'No worries,' continued Sid, 'just google me.'

'Walk. I ain't sayin' it again.'

Sid turned around and walked towards the lift, the woman's voice still on rant mode.

'They are all the same,' he heard her say, 'all the same. They twist everything to fit their agenda.'

The Darkness Inside

There were still some gains and positives to be had from the encounter, he thought as he walked out of the estate. The victim had a criminal record. He called Gardener asking him if he could find out who Anis' parole officer or lawyer might have been.

6. Promotion

What a waste of time. Martha was walking away from the kitchen after the company's 'green coordinator', Luther, had called a hasty meeting. He stood there with a disgusted expression underneath his perfectly oiled beard. Martha judged that the exquisitely curled mustachios must have been due to the eighteen-pound beeswax balm he had bought in Camden Market. The long-haired hipster stood there holding a yoghurt container as a small crowd gathered around him. They were apprehensive and somewhat unsure as to what heinous crime they had committed.

'Oh my God,' Luther said, holding up the yoghurt container and stroking his hazel-coloured beard. 'Can you imagine how many of these unrinsed containers clog up our recycling yards? Can you imagine the stench as they stay there for weeks and weeks?'

He basked in his own goodness and radiated righteous anger at all the staff members. Each and every one of them squirmed. None would meet his gaze for Luther was accusing them – all of them. No one could escape his wrath.

'Can you imagine the stench? Can you imagine the stench?'

Martha interjected. She had to stop him before it all went awry. 'Okay guys,' she said as he was about to launch into an environmental lecture which might end with a teary

The Darkness Inside

appeal. 'Make sure to rinse the containers and put them in the right bins please. Luther, you have three minutes. I want to speak to my team.'

Martha turned around and walked away, knowing that Luther was lost for words. Truth was, Martha would have probably let him continue if she wasn't so pissed. Luther could be funny, and Sid's impression of him was hilarious, verging on despicable. He could make her despise anyone, even decent men like Luther. No one was sacred; white, dead, eye-patched female correspondents were lampooned so hard it felt like blasphemy. Once he ripped into a *Times* article which did a piece on what a young journalist wore in a war zone.

'What the fuck?' Sid had said, reading the article. 'Is this the *Onion*? Who talks like that?!'

He then read the paragraph in a posh English accent that had Martha in stitches. 'The only drawback is that they're made of polyester, so if you get blown up, they'll stick to your skin. So in war zones I wear heavy cotton combats along with a belt that I can use as a tourniquet if anyone gets a limb blown off.'

She knew the journalist in question and there was a part of her that wanted to show solidarity with her against his cutting vitriol, but there was something about the way he read it that exposed its fakery. And, true enough, when she looked at the article there was the unmistakable picture of all the goods it had mentioned with the price tags attached.

Martha's planning for Christmas was dead. She had planned things so meticulously that if everything had gone well, she would have been able to take her leave during the festive season, spend Christmas and New Year with her

The Darkness Inside

parents in Molina and be back the first week of the new year. She had been looking forward to the baccalà, the salted cod traditionally eaten on Christmas Eve, the lamb ragu on Christmas Day, church, the choir, a stroll down to Salerno to see the lights. All of it was now dead in the water. The government looked like it was on the verge of collapse for the umpteenth time. The Prime Minister looked even more ragged, tired and on the verge of a nervous breakdown. Paul wanted to meet again to see what stories and ideas her bureau had in mind. She looked around for Sid – he was late.

He was only late when he was unsettled. When there was turmoil inside him. She became worried and was looking at her watch again when Sid came in. To her surprise he looked unperturbed; the only thing unusual was him drinking a Coke. He rarely drank soft drinks. He put his bag down on the floor and sat down. As Luther walked by, Sid threw the recyclable Coke can into the mixed bin next to her desk. Martha could have sworn Sid did it just to spite him. Luther glared indignantly. He was scandalised. Sid just stared at the young hipster as if to say, 'And what?' then turned to Martha. Martha was trying hard to suppress her laughter when Luther stormed off; he would bitch about Sid all day. She swore Sid had some sort of obsessive disorder.

'Sorry, my meeting overran,' he said.

'You're here,' she said, studying him and smiling, 'that's what matters. How's that going, by the way?'

'You know, the story gets weirder and weirder,' he said excitedly. 'Tom checked him out. He gave me Anis' case worker's details. We had a coffee together and she gave

The Darkness Inside

me an off-the-record briefing.'

'She?' Martha's smile disappeared for a moment.

'Yeah, what?' Sid said, unfazed by her reaction.

'And what did she say?'

'Well, turns out he was a tearaway, completely uncontrollable until he found religion. Then he just changed. She was super happy with him after that.'

'Was he radicalised?'

'Martha, listen, religion saved him.'

'Yes, I heard you; does special branch have anything on him?'

Sid shook his head.

'Nothing whatsoever. He's a ghost. He may have crossed the threshold to be put on a watchlist but if you keep your head low for a time, you get taken off.'

'Did you check?'

'Course!'

'That is strange, isn't it?'

'I know, that's why it's so weird,' Sid said. 'So what is it you wanted to see me about?'

'Let's go to a meeting room.'

They went into a private meeting room that was designed to 'stimulate creativity'.

'So,' Martha said, sitting down on the table. 'I wanted to talk about a promotion.'

'What sort of promotion?' Sid said, his dark eyes lighting up. Was this the moment? After all these years?

'Well,' Martha said, 'it's definitely more money and an opportunity to travel.'

'Great!' Sid punched the air. 'Is it foreign?'

'No, not quite,' said Martha nervously. 'Paul felt you

would be great as a sports correspondent. We're expanding, especially after the buyout.'

'Sports?!' Sid's shoulders dropped. 'Fucking sports?!'

'Now, now,' said Martha. 'I understand it's not what you wanted. But there's a lot of benefits to be had.'

'Why?'

'I pushed for it myself.'

Sid looked baffled, as if he had been stabbed in the back. He put his hands to his temples and rubbed them.

'Why would you do that, Martha? Why would you do that?'

'Because I remember how you did football and athletics at university. You still play and follow them, don't you? And since we don't have a politics or a foreign opening I thought, why not? You get to go to events that people only dream of and it's a stepping stone to foreign or the halls of Westminster. I know it looks counter-intuitive but believe me, it's a stepping stone to bigger and better things.'

'Oh yes, yet again Martha knows best,' replied Sid. 'Why didn't you give the position to Daniels?'

'What do you mean? He's a weed.'

'Why didn't you offer me a foreign bureau job or something else? Why does Daniels get to hang out in Westminster while I'm still tapping the keyboards here? I've got some of the biggest scoops this website has ever had! Why am I now sitting in a stadium? Why, Martha? Why?'

'Why,' said Martha, frustrated, 'is it always the same talk with you? We just don't have the opening.'

Sid stood up and leaned forward. 'How comes Daniels got a job in Moscow? Do you know why that fucker joined the *Loop*?'

The Darkness Inside

'Oh come on, Sid!' She rolled her eyes like she was listening to a conspiracy theorist. 'I've heard this before!'

'I have this from fucking Jim!'

'Who is Jim?'

'The photographer who went with him to Dadaab! The fucking wanker walks into the famine-stricken camp with a bag of sweets and chucks them on the ground so all those big-bellied Somali kids scramble for them in the dust, and he's shouting at the photographer to snap fucking photos saying, "Quick quick, before the *Times* get here." Some of them nearly died from that stunt. Sick! He's a sick man!'

'Give me facts, not anecdotes. That was never proven in the internal panel hearing.'

'Well,' Sid replied, in a tone of utter contempt. 'Maybe that's because Jim killed himself because he fucking lost faith in humanity? Why else would such a hotshot join such a shitty internet start-up instead of staying on at the paper?'

Martha was silent.

Sid sensed his advantage.

'How comes I can't be based in Moscow?' he continued. 'Why is it always about tired stereotypes? It's like me making it to the cricket team because I'm Asian but never to the football team even though I might have the talent of Messi. Isn't it?' Sid shook his head in disbelief. 'Same old shit Martha, same old shit.'

'It's not. This is an opportunity.'

'I must admit,' Sid said, 'after all these years, I had expected better from you to be honest. Marth, you and I both started around the same time, yeah?'

'Correct. I brought you in.'

The Darkness Inside

'So how comes you are an editor of the home bureau and I can't even go to a press release in Westminster? Why? Is it because I don't go for drinks with Paul? Didn't you go out with him a few times before you got the promotion? I'm not implying anything happened, I'm just saying.'

'Oh, you can keep your "just saying" shit to yourself!' Martha was red with fury. 'That is unfair, you know it. Do you know how much I pushed for this?'

'Oh! I see, I see! You want me to be grateful? You know what, I don't want it. I can deal with complex investigative stuff. You'll see. I promise.'

Sid got up and turned to leave.

'Where are you going? This meeting isn't over.'

'It is now. I am owed three weeks' holiday and HR has been on my case to take it. So I am going to take it as of now.'

'You're not going anywhere, Sid, you know that? You are just going to stew. How can you be so blind, Sid? Sid! This is the problem with you, your temperament. That's why you are still here. You're volatile. How can anyone work with you?'

Sid was gone. She watched him go over to HR and speak to Samantha; he leaned over as if to charm her, and then as Samantha put it through, he waved at Martha – it infuriated her. She could have him on a final warning or got him sacked for that sort of behaviour. But then he wouldn't be here, and she would be alone. Later on in the day when Samantha called her to see if it was okay for Sid to take his leave, she authorised it but, as if to reassert her authority, she only allowed him to take two weeks' holiday.

7. Coroner's Court

Two months had passed since Anis had died and Sid was no closer to finding out why the police had not managed to get hold of the killer or killers. Perhaps that was just life. There were people in the city who got killed or disappeared and no one gave a shit. All you had to do was walk up Victoria Street on the way to Parliament and you'd see the poor wretches huddling in doorways trying to stay warm, so why couldn't Anis be one of those unfortunate people that no one gave a shit about? Sid tried his best not to give a shit too. He tried to go on a holiday, bought a ticket to Tenerife in the hope that a bit of sun would make him feel better, but Anis just wouldn't let go of him. Ideas would come to him during the night. Anis would dance around his head like a rapper next to a pool surrounded by scantily clad ladies, as he lay on the sunbed trying to finish his assigned book. He was in a foreign country and yet everything seemed like a sunnier version of a northern seaside town. Every restaurant served paella but also English breakfast and German schnitzels. It was populated by inebriated Englishmen from Chavistan who drank beer for breakfast and probably voted for the likes of him to leave Britain. Some had the cheek to still look at him as a foreigner even on an island off the coast of Africa. It was weird staying in another Brexitland when an Englishman would ask him where he was from. And the worst thing was, where exactly

The Darkness Inside

would he find solace? In a German tourist? It was during such periods of alienation that Anis' ghost would float in. He would be next to Sid as he tried to snag a chavette. And the girl would sense Anis' presence.

'You are not with me,' the girl would say and leave him. Sid would be puzzled by the girl's actions. She had been so keen before. What had changed? He blamed Anis for sitting too close, looking over his shoulder and checking out her breasts. But it had nothing to do with Anis and everything to do with him; he was too clinical. The girl needed some small talk; there had to be some sort of mystery before she followed him to his room. Sid didn't understand that even for the most dissolute soul there had to be some sort of pretence. To her even this meaningless bestial act needed to be cloaked in meaning, however fake. Sid had stopped pretending because of Anis; he had given up on the small talk, the romance, the mystery and so she could not follow him. In Sid, the young woman had come face to face with the utter pointlessness of her own existence, and so she left his unbearable presence. In the end he thought about the case so much that he cut his holiday short and returned to work ready to attend the coroner's court just behind Chelsea Harbour to catch what the coroner said about Anis' death.

Sid stood outside the red-brick coroner's court taking a cigarette break when he spotted a middle-aged man wearing an awkward-looking suit and tie. The suit belonged to the eighties and the tie was an awful floral concoction fit for a Channel 4 News anchor. The man was red in the face and smoked nervously. Sid recognised him immediately from the press briefings. He was the lead investigating officer, Matt Parker, the bloke with the strong no-nonsense

The Darkness Inside

Mancunian accent. Sid swooped on him the way journalists do when they have the target all to themselves and know that the target was weak and helpless.

'Hi.' Sid put out a hand. 'Aren't you the lead officer who investigated the Anis Ferjani case?'

'Yes, I am,' replied Parker, as if caught by surprise. He guessed the slim man in front of him was a journalist. He looked around for any more of his kind. But the truth was, this story was as dead as Anis. There was no one to come to his aid.

'I'm Sid, I work for the *Loop*.'

'The *Loop*? Yes, yes, I read your stuff. Good reporting. The bosses weren't too happy about it. But to be honest we are so overstretched these days we rely on the papers. Off the record, of course.'

Parker was actually the sort of guy who put his hands to his mouth, whispering it, when he said 'off the record.'

Sid beamed at the recognition given by a seasoned investigator. 'Completely understand. Could I ask you a quick question, off the record?'

Sid mimicked the officer by putting his hand over his mouth when he said 'off the record'.

'Yeah, go on then.'

'Not to criticise your work but do you have a suspect?'

'Well... no,' Parker said, shuffling uneasily. 'Not yet.'

'Strange, don't you think?'

'Funny you should say that. I was talking to one of the officers the other day about just that.'

'How comes?'

'Well, usually you find them, easy. CCTV, or word comes out on the street. But this time, he's a phantom.'

The Darkness Inside

'Thanks.' Sid had heard enough. His hypothesis was getting confirmation from a seasoned pro. He threw his cigarette down. 'Right, I am going in.' Sid handed him his business card. 'Best of luck today.'

'I'll need it. I hate all this witness stuff.'

Gardener knew Sid was peering through the spyhole, looking at him. Sid was probably in his pyjamas looking dishevelled and unkempt. That was alright with Gardener; he would just continue to ring the bell.

'I'm not leaving anytime soon mate!' Gardener said. He was dressed for a night out.

He was right. Sid opened the door when he realised that Gardener was determined to see him. And he looked exactly as Gardener had predicted. 'What's wrong with you? You're still in your PJs? You owe me, Sid.'

Gardener walked in and slung his coat up on the coat rack. He took off his shoes and followed Sid into the living room, still waiting to hear his explanation. Sid paused for a moment as if he was concocting the excuse he was going to proffer.

'Sorry man, I was meant to call. How did you know I was here?'

'Where else?'

'I wasn't in the mood to be honest.'

Sid had opted for honesty.

'Bollocks.'

Gardener started to walk around the living room and kitchen, inspecting the mess.

'Strewth!' he scolded with a look of heartfelt concern. 'What happened to you? Look at you, you're out of

The Darkness Inside

shape. You're a mess, man. What's going on? Pull yourself together.'

Sid didn't fight him. It was true, he was a mess. He even had a little bump coming through his T-shirt. The bump was a sure sign he had stopped doing his morning exercises.

Thirsty, Gardener went to the fridge. As he opened the fridge door the waft of rotten food hit his nostrils. He grimaced, quickly grabbed a soft drink and closed the fridge door as quick as he could.

'Mate, see what happens?'

Sid looked at him, puzzled.

'What?'

'She just holds up your universe and you don't even know it.'

'Bro,' said Sid, visibly annoyed at the mention of Martha. 'It's got nothing to do with her.'

'Then what? Mate, you cannot call me at three o'clock asking me to look something up! I got work too you know!'

'Sorry, I should have texted.'

'No, no, Sid – I don't think you get it. You don't need to contact me at all. You need to sleep and leave it till the morning.'

'Okay, I get it.'

Gardener looked at Sid's crumpled figure. He looked like he had lost weight.

'Have you eaten anything?' Gardener asked. 'Do you ever cook anything here?'

He looked around the kitchen. The cutlery seemed unused.

'Is this even your home? Or just a place you sleep in? Come on, let's get some food.'

The Darkness Inside

The two men ended up at Alfredo's pizzeria in Hampstead. It had a wood-fired oven and was really cosy, with a rustic feel to it. Martha had taken them there for the first time. Although they couldn't tell the difference, Martha said that the arancini were cooked from frozen. Moreover, the place claimed to be a Neapolitan pizzeria but was far from it, according to her. After speaking to the manager she turned round and told them that the guy wasn't from Naples at all, or even from the South for that matter.

'You don't take pizzas from Northerners; you take polenta, meat dishes, whatever their regional delicacy is, but don't take their pizza.'

The pizzas were so bad she was outraged on behalf of all the clientele. She even thought about not paying, but to them the pizza tasted delicious and they kept coming back, and so did the rest of the punters. The place was packed with guests and busy waiters scurrying to take their orders.

'Leave this Alfredo alone,' they had said, and Martha had given them a look that seemed to pity them.

Sid cheered up once he had a few slices of pizza inside him. He hadn't eaten properly for days, relying on pot noodles, crisps and takeaways to sustain him. He knew that Gardener was studying him carefully, assessing his mood – that look on his friend's face was familiar. He might have got older but it had been there even when they shot pool at the student bar.

'How long,' asked Gardener, 'are you going to sulk with her for? She doesn't owe you anything. I mean, if it was me, I would have sacked you. That's how you know!'

'Know what?'

'Oh come on, man, you can't see it? You must be blind.'

The Darkness Inside

'Most of us are. So what now?'

'Go freelance.'

'That's not a good gig.'

Sid didn't like the idea of freelancing – he remembered the instability of the early days when he had to constantly pitch stories and do things on spec only to be rejected or paid a pittance. In his experience it was those bastards who banged on about rights and ethics that paid the lowest. And in a way he had a secret aversion to their moral righteousness. Sid didn't have much of an issue with the typical journalist at the *Daily Telegraph*. He was what he was, privileged with a double-barrelled middle name and private schooling; he chomped on caviar and drank champagne and because he had gone to Oxford felt that he could opine on absolutely everything even though he didn't know jack about the subject. That was fine, that was his background – you couldn't blame a man for that, if that was where God had placed him. But those bourgeois socialists who attended the same party but rattled off emotional lines about the famine in Yemen or zero-hour contracts pissed him off. There was something disgusting about their sugary ethics that would be thrown to the dogs once they were staggering home from the party and they needed Stavros or Ahmed the Uber driver on a zero-hour contract to take him home. Sid knew they were all about the 'retweet' and 'like'. It was those sorts of people who always seemed to know what was 'best' for him.

'I'll probably hook up with some of the guys that I know who run these news start-ups. Or if *Buzzfeed* or *Middle East Eye* pay me enough and give me an editorial position I

The Darkness Inside

might just take it. I would love to lead a team at the Bureau of Investigative Journalism. The *Loop* is dying – Femi called me the other day wanting a coffee.'

'Femi, didn't he work for the *Voice*? Is he still in business? I heard he moved to comms or something. My word, I haven't heard that name in ages. Give him my regards,' said Gardener. 'Still, though, I think you are writing off freelancing too quick if you ask me.' Gardener's view on freelancing was different. 'It works for me. But then again I only specialise in court reporting and crime. No one can be arsed to sit round the courtroom all day. So everyone calls me. But with politics and foreign, it's different. Everyone has a take on it. Everyone is outraged about Brexit, Trump, #metoo, so who are you? You have to be exceptional, callous and obsessive to succeed.'

'So what would you do?'

'I would go to Martha, get on my knees and beg her for the sports gig – that's a dream job. She did you a favour.'

'Too late. Turned it down.'

'What?' Gardener said, exasperated. 'You are a muppet.'

'Bro, I can't get this story out of my head. I'm telling you, I can't sleep without the bastard prancing around in my dream.'

'Ah... one of those,' Gardener said sympathetically. Every journalist has had one of those. 'I have developed tools to deal with that. Took me a long time but I did it. Stories are dead to me unless I get paid for them.'

'You are ruthless.'

'You have to be in this business.'

'You know what else?' Sid said. 'You know Anis was disabled? He had his femur smashed and his hip.'

The Darkness Inside

'Okay, how did he get that?'

'Car crash apparently.'

A pretty waitress came over to their table and asked if they needed anything and if the food was satisfactory. Gardener asked for a glass of wine whilst Sid requested another Coke. The young woman went off to get their order and Sid's eyes followed her figure as she went.

'There's just too many things that don't fit,' continued Sid. 'Why are the people who know him calling him a martyr and saying he's flying alongside green birds? Why isn't there a suspect? Why is the family behaving so weird? This guy was into some shit.'

Gardener hesitated for a moment, as if he was trying to find the right approach.

'Dude, I don't mean to offend, but can I be frank with you?'

Sid nodded.

'He sounds like a Jihadist. I had a case where one of these kids had died fighting in Somalia but the family said he had died in Lebanon in a "car accident".'

Gardener added quotation marks with his fingers.

'You reckon he might have been to Syria?'

'Check,' said Gardener, cautiously. He was always cautious about theories; he believed in facts. 'You got loads of 'em returning.'

Sid hadn't considered it from that angle but it was a plausible hypothesis. Even a cynical bastard like him had been moved to donate to Syria when the uprising broke out in March 2011. His sister would WhatsApp him mass appeals that announced that an aid convoy would be leaving with medicines and clothes for Syria.

The Darkness Inside

'If you have anything to give,' she would say, 'do it. You'll see the fruits of it on the Day of Judgement.'

She was so melodramatic. But one of these convoys had been collecting at his local mosque on Friday and he had thrown in a couple of hundred quid to alleviate his conscience. In truth, these convoys were naive, ineffective and a drop in the ocean but they gave a sense of catharsis for the distress that the community felt. Even he had felt helpless about it all. He had watched Syrians holding up placards peacefully, hoping that the wolf, Assad, would metamorphose into a cuddly puppy and give the people what they wanted: freedom and democracy; he had dared to hope and then kicked himself for his naivety. Power doesn't give up its seat without a fight. Instead Assad's goons had made the demonstrators disappear and his barrel bombs had fallen with sickening regularity. Like his colleagues Sid had retweeted and 'liked' the images of dusty, broken children and screaming women to highlight their plight, but in the secret recesses of his soul he had also done it to gain kudos and more followers. Human nature is such that soon enough, the uprising turned violent, young men started to get hold of weapons, foreigners came in and the papers at home reported that young British Muslims had gone to fight the great tyrant. Some commentators likened the jaunt to the Spanish Civil War when Brits went on a jolly to fight General Franco. But the analogy became unsustainable and by the end of 2013, whilst many young British Muslim fighters still sided with the Syrian activists, some of them had put a spanner in the uprising by overtly displaying signs that they were Jihadists of the al-Qaeda variety. It was an own goal that Assad capitalised on, and the press revelled in it. It gave security analysts shivers of secret

The Darkness Inside

pleasure. These Jihadists, it seemed, poisoned whatever they touched. They became factions; they mixed with the Syrian activists, tainting them. But then the Syrian rebels also had no excuse; they had had more than five years to come up with leadership, but they had failed miserably. In the end the centre ground was gone and all the strongest groups were Jihadists, al-Qaeda – or ISIS-affiliated. The latter had been born out of the university of insurgencies in Iraq. ISIS, unlike Assad who denied his crimes, killed and enslaved men so brazenly that it repulsed the world. Even though Assad killed more, it was ISIS who declared their enmity to humanity. It was then that the Syrian revolution died. Assad, it seemed, was doing what dictators and oppressors have done since time immemorial, but these foreigners had stabbed the Syrians in the back and Sid had little sympathy for them, aid worker or fighter or otherwise. Perhaps it was this disillusionment that had made him block the possibility out, but now Gardener had reopened the question and he began to look at the theory as a credible one.

'Why don't you work with me on it? I could do with the help.'

'With you? Yeah right!'

'Come on, I'll get Martha to pay you for it.'

'I've got too many cases on at the moment. And I got the Grenfell inquiry to deal with. But call me if you need any help.'

'You know what, earlier I searched him using them deep search engines. Paid a fortune for it.'

'That's why you didn't come out?'

Sid put his hands up, admitting his crime.

'I was worried about someone getting there before me.'

'No one cares about this case except you, Sid. Trust me, no one. It's a dead story. Did you come up with anything?'

'An email address.'

'Really?'

'Yep,' Sid replied, self-satisfied. 'That's a digital fingerprint to his life.'

'Amazing.' Gardener looked at his watch. 'Come on, let's go and watch the fight.'

Despite the presence of three large screens at the Fiery Dragon, Sid didn't watch the fight. Everyone else did – Joshua Buatsi was fighting. Whilst everyone cheered, primevally screaming at the screen, Sid was on his phone tapping away and surfing the web. Gardener didn't bother patting him on the shoulder or talking to him during the rounds; he knew Sid was on the trail like one of those hunting dogs on the scent of a fox. The fight went eight rounds and Sid didn't even notice that Buatsi had won and was walking about with that dignified glory that is so characteristic of the man. Gardener snatched his jacket and went out. Sid only noticed he was gone when he asked him a question and didn't get a reply. Sid put on his jacket and found Gardener waiting outside frowning like a jilted girlfriend.

'Bro,' Sid said apologetically, 'sorry.'

'You know what, Sid?'

'What?'

'If you don't give a shit about people who care for you, you'll grow old alone.'

Gardener's Uber approached before Sid could even formulate an excuse. Guilt struck him for a brief moment and he lowered his head as if mourning. Then he remembered his scoop and ordered an Uber.

Once home he immediately reached for his laptop. He did a deep search using his workplace's PPL account. He typed in ANISisaBIGMANN@hotmail.com. The search engine came up with a list of possible websites and people. Sid reached for his notebook and meticulously went through each and every search result, eliminating some and keeping the ones that needed further investigation. Most websites and search results were irrelevant, with no connection to Anis. Things appeared fruitless so he told himself to go to bed. 'No one cares about this,' said a voice inside him. But there was another voice reminding him that he wouldn't be able to sleep if he didn't get to the bottom of this search. So he persisted, giving himself an hour tops.

After two hours he came across one search result which gave him the breakthrough. He clicked on a Facebook group called 'BIKERS AND BITCHES', expecting it to be pictures of beautiful semi-nude girls with pneumatic breasts that gave the finger to gravity straddling slick motorcycles. The Facebook group name didn't lie; it delivered just that. However, Sid turned to look at the group members and, curiously, there was a picture of a younger version of Anis. His beard was shorter, his cheekbones higher; he appeared fresh-faced and youthful. The only discrepancy was that Anis' surname was spelt Forjani, not Ferjani. Sid clicked on his Facebook profile; there were only two friends, 'Abbas Rizwan' and 'Sami El-Masry'. He found their addresses on the 'GBG|CONNEXUS' database quite easily and started to build a profile on these associates. Sami El-Masry had a business address not too far from where Anis died. El-Masry Estates Ltd even had a Companies House address, 255

The Darkness Inside

London Road, and had submitted full accounts. It seemed to be doing well. Sami did have a social media presence, but curiously his Facebook profile had only been created in 2014. Abbas, however, had no trace whatsoever, which intrigued Sid. As he started to dig on Abbas his phone buzzed. He glanced over. It was Martha texting. Why would she text so late?

Hey, are you alright?

I am fine :) Sid texted back. Early on, Sid had discovered that throwing in lots of LOLs and smiley emojis saved him from giving real responses and having a meaningful conversation with someone.

You sure? Your sister got in touch with me.

:)

You can take a few days off to go and see him. Don't worry.

That's really sweet. Will head up there soon, Sid texted back.

You want to come over? To talk I mean.

I'm good tbh.

You want me to come over?

I'm gonna hit the sack. Knackered.

Liar.

Good night. LOL

X – Anytime you need to go, go.

THNX

8. Meat and property

Abbas finished trimming the fat off the meat. He threw the meat into the blue plastic bag; the fat went into the bin. It was a shame, really – he could have made a fortune just from selling the fat. If the old woman he was serving knew that in some parts of the world they hang the fat, separately in order for some inspired cook to rustle up a wonder she would have asked him to keep it. With the fat, she could make shakiriyeh, a yogurt dish with a lamb shank and fat, or she could put a fat cube on a metal skewer and then slide a piece of meat on, followed by an onion, followed by a kidney, then put it lovingly on the grill to cook.

He pitied the old Punjabi woman. She had no clue whether the meat was good or bad. He knew that the meat here wasn't the best but no one spotted it because punters, like her, were mostly South Asian. South Asian cooking could get away with using tired meat because the spices masked the tiredness. The old woman's inherited cooking philosophy was that spices not only added flavour but masked bad food in the absence of refrigeration and the hot climate. The South Asian palate, in any case, didn't like the taste of meat in its pure form. Back in the day he would baulk at the smell of meat but now he relished it. Arabs and other culinary cultures that enjoyed the unashamed flavour of meat would know not to shop here. Come to think of it, he probably wouldn't go here himself. Those who wanted the unadulterated taste of fresh meat went to the Algerian butchers across the road. But then they were more expensive, and that in these times meant a lot. He'd seen how West Croydon was getting even worse. The drug fiends and alcoholics were smoking their shit in the doorways, sharing their pipes whilst the police sped past answering a call from some young professional whose bike had been stolen from East Croydon station.

Abbas eventually finished cutting up the lamb, tied up the plastic bag, put it on a scale and stuck on the price. He gave the bag to the old woman and pointed for her to pay at the counter at the main entrance of the shop.

He was about to go back to chopping up some meat for the displays when the news flashed up on the television screen suspended above his head. He stopped and watched the images on the news. Every one of his colleagues paid little attention to the BBC; however, Abbas did, especially when news about Syria came up. That story in particular held his attention until the news presenter said confidently that there would be dire consequences for the Syrian president if chemical weapons were used. That's when he returned to his work, chopping up bits of red flesh with a contemptuous look on his face. He was sharpening his knife when one of his colleagues drew his attention to a customer who wanted to be served. He looked too good to come in here; either that or he didn't know his meat.

'Yes, my friend,' said Abbas. 'What can I do for you?'

'Well,' said the man, staring at the counter, unsure of what to buy, 'what meat is easy to cook?'

'Depends on what dish you want to cook.'

The man didn't even look at him; he seemed to be intimidated by all the various cuts of meat on offer.

The Darkness Inside

'Can you cook?'

The man stared at him, embarrassed, and shook his head. 'Not even to save my life.'

Okay, Abbas understood, the guy probably had his mum cook his food all his life and now having taken a job down south he was living on his own and he was absolutely clueless. He felt sorry for him.

'Mate, get some mince or go for the marinated boxes and you can stick it in the oven. All you need is an oven-proof container. Throw it in the oven and you'll be fine.

The man did exactly as he was told and went for the prepared marinated chicken.

'Thank you,' he said. 'Really, can't tell you how much I appreciate this. As you can tell I'm still trying to find my feet around here. London is so big and expensive. That's why I'm down here searching for a place to rent. Is Croydon any good?'

'Croydon isn't bad,' said Abbas. 'It's got everything here. Fifteen minutes into London as well.'

'That's handy. Do you know any good estate agencies that won't cost an arm and a leg?'

'Try El-Masry estates down the road.' Abbas signalled the direction to the estate agent. The man gave him an enigmatic smile as he left the shop, seemingly straightening up as if he knew exactly where he was heading.

Not too far from T's Butchers, Sami was sitting waiting for Mansur to finish off with his customer. He inspected his own appearance in the mirror while he waited. Overall, he was satisfied with what he saw; his suit looked crisp – he just needed to make sure his belly was tucked in – and his shoes looked sharp and polished, proper pimp-esque. He was in

The Darkness Inside

the process of inspecting his teeth, the money smile that had closed many a deal, to make sure there were no bits of food lodged in between when another barber who he hadn't seen before finished with his customer. After taking payment, he indicated for Sami to join him on the barber's chair. Judging by the previous client's haircut Sami could tell that this barber was accomplished, perhaps even superior to Mansur. He hesitated for a moment. He didn't wish to be disloyal to his usual barber's but the short Palestinian barber, who was still in the middle of shaving a customer, encouraged Sami to go with the other man.

'Bro,' said Mansur, 'just go with Elin, he'll look after you.'

Sami looked at the short pasty-faced feller, clean-shaven with one of those weird greasy haircuts you see the Afghans on the streets of West Croydon sporting. One side would be shaved and the other side spiky, and they'd accompany that cut with some skin-tight jeans that were shredded to pieces. Shit, why even wear trousers? If his boys wore those he'd beat them.

'Don't worry, brother,' said Elin, politely patting his chair as if to entice him to sit, 'my grandfather and my father were barbers.'

'Oh yeah?' Sami said, his interest piqued by the young man's politeness. 'Where?'

'Sulaymaniyeh.'

'Iraq?'

'Kurdistan,' replied the young barber, resolute in his politics. There was no Iraq to Elin; the land where the Kurds lived was called Kurdistan.

Sami sat back; that word, 'Kurdistan', had decided it for him. He looked at Elin apologetically.

The Darkness Inside

'If you don't mind, I will wait for Mansur.'

'No problem, sir,' replied Elin, unoffended, and sat down on the leather sofa. He started watching some singer pouting and dancing luridly to a song that sounded just like every other tune.

'What's the matter?' said Mansur, grinning. 'Don't trust a Kurd with a blade?'

All of them laughed.

'I wouldn't neither,' continued Mansur. 'Nutters. But they cut really good.'

Mansur took his time with his customer, but that was the good thing about him – he gave you first-class service every time. And if he ever cut you he wouldn't charge; he was an old skool barber that way.

Eventually, having finished with his customer, Mansur got the seat ready for Sami, and the large man sat down to relax. Mansur cut and trimmed him lovingly, even making sure the eyebrows were the right length and the hairs beginning to protrude out of his ears were waxed, and then he finished him off with a hot towel. When he finished Mansur would always announce it with 'nai'man!' as if it was a sort of 'voila!' uttered by a master chef. And Sami usually grinned, saying something like 'the missus is going to be happy – really happy'. Mansur always managed to get his slightly chubby face looking a little bit slimmer. He didn't know how, whether he got his beard line lower or because he cut the hair shorter, but it knocked a few pounds off him. He walked back to his office, singing to himself, his mind's eye playing out what might occur in the bedroom tonight as a consequence of his looking after himself.

Sami opened the shutters to his estate agency office and

The Darkness Inside

walked in, picking up the mail off the floor. It was the usual: promotions, offers and bills. There was one for Rob, his employee, and he put it on Rob's well-ordered desk. He dumped the rest of the letters in the bin and plonked himself down at his own untidy desk. He brought out his phone and called Rob.

'Rob? How long are you going to be? I'm alone here. Got a few appointments coming up.'

He was in the middle of talking to Rob when a potential client with a blue plastic bag appeared at the door. He cut Rob off and put on his charming salesman's smile.

'Hello, sir, how are you today?'

'Hello, I'm fine thanks. Are you Mr El-Masry?'

'Yes... I am,' replied Sami cautiously. He hated salesmen trying to sell him some trash. He noticed the blue bag in the man's hand – what could it be? 'Who is asking?'

'Sid, my name is Sid; I work for the *Loop*. Have you got a moment?' Sid handed him his business card. Sami took the card and studied it for a moment.

'Yeah, sure. Take a seat. The *Loop* you say? Never heard of it. What are you? A new property search engine?'

'No, we are like *BuzzFeed*.'

Sid hated mentioning the better-known rival.

'Oh, I see, you want to talk about Brexit or something? What it might to do local businesses? Trust me, it's going to be terrible. We might even have a recession, no one's going to have any money to spend...'

'Not quite,' Sid replied, but seeing that the estate agent was going off on one, he repeated 'not quite', a bit more forcefully.

'Oh, I see,' said Sami, surprised at being cut off mid-stride, and offered Sid a seat. He thought the wiry journalist stood

The Darkness Inside

there on account of his speech in Croydon town hall urging councillors to make contingency plans on business rates and MPs to stop this impending disaster in Parliament. He thought he had heard how his speech stirred up the room – he wasn't just angling for that chairmanship of the Croydon Business Association; he was trying to save the country from disaster. 'Can I get you something? Coffee, tea?'

'I'm fine, thanks,' Sid replied, sitting down.

'So how can I help?'

'Well, I have been working on Anis.'

Sid paused a moment to watch Sami's reaction at the mention of his name.

'You know him, right?'

'Anis? Anis?' Sid said as if baffled by the name, his face crunched up like he was trying to recall it from his memory. 'For the life of me... I'm sure that name sounds familiar but off the top of my head, I couldn't tell you.'

'Anis Ferjani, doesn't ring a bell?' Sid tried to jog his memory.

Sami shook his head as if he was mystified.

'You got a picture?'

Sid brought out his phone. He showed Sami a screen grab of the Facebook group, 'BIKERS AND BITCHES'.

Sid saw Sami's eyes widen for a second when he saw the picture of himself and Abbas. That was not just a look of recognition but panic, too.

'Oh, *Anees*!' Sami said as if his memory had somehow been found. 'You need to say it right. Yeah man, Allah have mercy on him. Terrible what happened. Terrible. Terrible.'

'Oh okay, well I'm writing a follow-up story on his death and I was wondering if you could help me?'

'How?'

'Give me the background to his story.'

Sami sat uncomfortably, brought out his vaporiser and started to vape in the office.

'Can I be anonymous? I have a business.'

'Yeah, for sure. As long as I can quote you.'

'Okay.' He leaned forwards even though no one was in the office. 'By the way, if my colleague comes in we are going to have to cut it short and rearrange.'

'Okay, no problem. We can always meet later.' Here Sid took a punt to test his hypothesis. 'So Anis and you went to Syria, right?'

'Well... what? Syria? I don't know how you came up with that.'

'I got contacts high up.'

'Oh okay, Anis did. Not me.'

'Well, see, most people, if you go through their Facebook, like my own, you can see that there is a consistent story or postings from the time of their first post up to now.'

'Yeah, and?'

'Well, Anis' Facebook profile disappears completely and you seem to have opened up another one in 2014. But the screen grab here, it shows me that you had a completely different Facebook account which you deleted. The dates match up with the coroner's report which says that Anis suffered a car crash whilst abroad in Morocco. Now this is just a guess but I suppose you went to "Morocco" too, didn't you?'

Sami stared at him in disbelief.

'Look mate, I pay loads of tax to HMRC. Just because someone went to Syria, don't mean that all of us are terrorists or something.'

'I'm not saying you are. You want to tell me what happened?'

'I've got nothing against this country, I'm from here, born in the heart of London. Yeah, I was there in Syria.'

As Sami was about to go into a long lecture that would most likely span Iraq, Afghanistan, Israel and Guantanamo, Rob, his employee walked in looking rather flustered.

'Hello everyone.'

Sami waved at the ginger employee.

'Well,' Sid said, changing his tone, 'let me see if there are any other properties that I'm interested in and I'll get back to you.'

Sid had transformed into a potential client again. He got up with Sami, who walked him out through the door onto the street.

'You know,' Sid said, 'a lot of my colleagues have been working on exposing the British Far Right following the death of Jo Cox.'

'Mate,' said Sami, understanding the threat, 'I'm paying so much tax it's unbelievable.'

'Well your tax liability might be reduced if I do a story on it. Help me and I will make sure you don't become the story.'

Sami fished out a handkerchief from somewhere and wiped his forehead and his nape. 'Okay, okay, gimme a few days.'

Sid walked away. Sami stood there nervously. He started to vape, took a few drags and then went into the office and decided not to bollock Rob for being late. He sat down and worried that his business might be ruined by a few words from an arsehole journalist.

9. Bowling

The bowling hall in Purley wasn't packed at all. It was Tuesday so the only youngsters that were out at this time were the roughnecks and strays who would probably occupy the cells of the prison service in the near future. The strong, distinct smell of skunk infused the air where a group of teenagers stood. A large bouncer with his ID strapped to his bicep was standing by the door watching them. He wanted them to know he was watching, so he stood there with arms crossed as if to say they were not welcome in the bowling hall and arcade. The boys looked at him and laughed a laughter full of contempt for the old. They didn't seem to be too scared of the big man. Why should they be? A zombie, katana, machete or kitchen knife could pierce him as well as it could pierce the next man. In fact, with their lithe bodies they could move quicker than him, and he had a large surface area to work on. Cut a major artery on his thigh and he'd bleed out quick.

When Sami passed him there were no issues at all. He parked up and gave him a smile and the bouncer stepped aside politely, still watching the group. They glared back and kept their hands warm by stashing them in their underwear, over which they wore skin-tight tracksuit bottoms that would intimidate no one, least of all the bouncer.

Sami found Abbas at the pool table. His beard looked

The Darkness Inside

magnificent and reminded Sami of those Assyrian kings he had seen in the British Museum when his wife had dragged him there. Abbas hadn't spotted him; he was concentrating on his shot. Then he jerked his right arm suddenly and potted the yellow ball, the white cue ball rolling up to his next target, and through this means Abbas quietly but confidently started to clear up the whole table. But Sami made his arrival at the table known. His cheesy smile meant that Abbas' cue ball did not arrive at the place he had intended, and the shot that presented itself to Abbas was difficult.

Sami stood there watching Abbas.

'I only,' Sami said, in an Arnold Schwarzenegger accent, 'shot five bullets, but when I shoot I only shoot to kill.'

Abbas laughed as if he was reminded of something that had passed between them in a bygone time.

'That was still a lame speech bruh,' Sami continued, switching to normal speech. 'You missed every single one of those targets; you were lame.'

'Shut up, man, lemme take my shot.'

Sami did another Arnold Schwarzenegger Terminator impression whilst Abbas prepared to take his shot.

'You know I told you I'd kill you last – I lied.'

Abbas missed and the white ball went into the pocket. It was disastrous but Abbas was laughing – that was a rare sight. The game being over, Sami gave Abbas a warm hug.

'What's going on, B?'

'Same old, same old,' replied Abbas. 'How's the family?'

'Bro, can't complain, Alhamdullilah.'

'Missus?'

'Complaining,' Sami said, 'that I am never there. I'm

The Darkness Inside

like, "Darling, we need the money." She's like, "But the kids need you." Yeah, I know but you know what, they'll be fine. It's not like there's some Sukhoi jets flying over our house.'

'True,' Abbas said with a wistful sigh, as if he wished that there were some Sukhois flying above them. He started to set up another game.

Sami grabbed the cue and chalked it. 'What's work saying?'

Abbas looked at him as if to say, don't even ask, it's awful.

'So come work for me!' Sami urged. 'My guy's always late. Ginger twat.'

Abbas put the cue ball on the line, inviting Sami to start.

'One: I can't be under you. Two: I'm not made for this stuff. That tie and suit shit kills me even more than cutting up lamb and cow bollocks.'

'Oh I forgot,' Sami said as he took the first shot, 'you're that "Get to the chopper!" guy.'

Abbas laughed at his impression of Shwarzenegger in *Predator*, watching the red and yellow balls scatter around the pool table as he took his first shot.

'Nah, nah,' said Abbas, 'you know who is good in that film, Billy! He's deep. He just takes it for the team when the Predator comes.'

'Proper martyr, innit.'

Abbas nodded.

'Remember when Abu Sulayman took it for the team?'

'Allah have mercy on him.'

As they were playing Sami broached the topic he had called on Abbas for.

'Listen, I got some guy coming in today? A journalist.

The Darkness Inside

Arrogant little prick.'

'Oh yeah? Asking about what?'

'Anis.'

'What's his name?'

'Sid or something. Got his business card. Got a Muslim surname. Clean-shaven though.'

'Google him,' Abbas instructed. 'Let's see how he looks.'

Sami googled him and brought up a picture of him. Abbas recognised him.

'The dirty little munafiq. A proper smooth pig! You know the guy came to see me today pretending he was looking for a place to rent? I sent him to you!'

'No! Oh man! Man!' Sami's face looked worried; he started to tug at his beard. 'Bro, this will kill my business. He's on it. I am finished. Just as I'm starting to do well. Man! Even the local paper did a piece on my success.'

Sami was getting increasingly agitated.

'Don't worry, he ain't got shit.' Abbas was calm. 'What did he say?'

'If I don't cooperate he will expose me. Like they been exposing Nazis and shit.'

'Oh okay, so he's a predator?'

'Yeah, that's right.'

'Then draw him in,' Abbas ordered. 'String him along with a bit of waffle. Most of these journos don't know shit about Syria or war. All he wants is probably some exclusive so he can buy his organic soya milk latte for five pounds – the prick. Give him that and he'll get off your back, trust me.'

'And if that doesn't work?'

'We'll get to that when we come to it. Find out what he

The Darkness Inside

knows and keep him close. It's minor.'

The South Bank was always beautiful during the festive season. Martha loved walking from one end to the other. Sometimes she hoped to bump into the young harp player outside the Globe playhouse; she would stand there for hours watching him caress and pluck those strings as if they were notes from heaven. Sometimes it even brought her to tears. Of course she never showed her emotions to Sid because he'd laugh at her soppiness but if she was walking there alone she felt no shame in shedding a few tears. That night, though, they had made up. They were always like that from university days. He was infuriating but the fact that he didn't care too much about what he would call an effete harp player was also the fascination.

There was something dark inside him that she had never been able to extract, however much she tried. There were moments she felt she was nearly there but then just as she thought she had grasped him and prised him open, he was gone. Far, far away. She wanted to take the darkness inside him and turn it into light. The pushback, however, always came with a phrase or two, 'you're not God' or 'you're not Jesus', and that was the signal for her to step back, otherwise he would disappear for a long time before allowing her to go near him again. He was like one of those distrustful dogs you might find in Battersea Dogs Home, or some dog made for fighting which didn't know anything else.

That night they had just visited Tate Modern and were heading towards the Christmas fair at the London Eye. There was a bar where they could sit around a communal fire; she would drink mulled wine and he would drink

The Darkness Inside

coffee. He never touched alcohol, surprisingly.

'So? What did you think?' Sid said as they strolled towards Waterloo, interlocking their arms. 'What? You didn't like it?' He studied her face, which was pale from the biting cold; her nostrils were red as if she had been blowing her nose with the inevitable arrival of winter flu.

'It was interesting,' she replied diplomatically.

'Whenever you say "interesting", that means it's dead. It's not going online.'

'I just find all this stuff so soulless you know. Like London. Look at the Tate, it's cold and ugly. Just reflects the inner state of the designer.'

'It's Brutalism – that's the point.'

'Is that what it's called? No wonder.'

'Yeah, I kind of like it. It's London. Brooding, mean. Don't give a shit.'

'Exactly, poor you. There was a time when you did.' It was a tentative attempt to prise him open once more. Sid didn't take the bait. 'You should go to Florence.'

'You always say that.'

'It's beautiful.'

He received a message on his phone. The estate agent had told him to come to the office the next day. Sid texted back confirming his willingness to meet. Martha watched his reaction; he had lit up.

'Good news?'

'Hopefully, you want to hear about it?'

'No, we are not at work.'

'Listen, I don't fancy going to the Christmas fair.'

He was so predictable. Martha had lost the Christmas fair as soon as he had received the text. The best she could

The Darkness Inside

do now was to salvage it in a different way.

'You want to go get some food at my place? I got some really nice bresaola my mum brought over.'

'No, no.' He hesitated awkwardly. 'I'm going to go home.'

She moved closer.

'We can eat at your place if you're tired?'

'Look, my place is a mess.'

Martha moved back and smiled.

'I don't get you.'

'Get what?'

'What are you afraid of?'

'I'm not afraid of anything,' he said as if he was beating his chest. 'No, I'm not. Trust me. I just got a lot of things on. You know, with my dad and stuff.'

'Liar. You haven't gone up to see him yet.'

'You're my boss, you know.'

'Oh, that's what it is,' Martha said, lacing her words with cynicism. 'Listen, I am going to shoot from here.'

She called an Uber. He was about to give her a peck on the cheek as the Uber pulled up, but as he moved closer, she gently rebuffed him, tutting.

'It's not appropriate, me being your boss and all.'

She winked and got into the car. Sid made his way home.

Sid was loitering around the corner from El-Masry offices when he received the text which gave the all clear from Sami. Sami's ginger had left the office. It was just in time; West Croydon was already dark and Sid's finger-tips were being nipped by the cold. He walked into the office and Sami was at the door wearing a grey shiny suit, a pink shirt and a god-awful yellow tie. He pointed to the seat in front of his desk.

The Darkness Inside

'Salaams bruv, come in, come in, grab a seat. Can I get you something? Coffee, tea?'

'Tea would be lovely,' Sid said, taking a seat and surprised that Sami was so easy-going considering how their last encounter had ended. He put his hands on the radiator next to him to revive his fingers and then brought out his notepad from his bag.

'How do you take it?'

'Milk, two sugars please.'

Sami went into the small kitchen at the back and prepared the tea and a coffee for himself. He brought out a tray of biscuits for Sid to chomp on and returned to the back. A moment later he brought out two cups and placed a cup of tea in front of his guest.

'Have a sip of that,' Sami said whilst taking one himself from the coffee. 'Don't have much time, my missus wants me to go to the shops so we got about an hour and a bit. Is that cool?'

'Yeah for sure,' Sid said, taking a biscuit and grabbing the warm tea. 'We can always continue some other time.'

'Listen, before we start, this can have a massive impact on my life. You understand that yeah?'

'For sure. As I said, this can be all anonymous.'

Sami held his gaze for a moment as if to emphasise how serious this was in respect to his life.

'So Anis and me got into this stuff by accident you know. Both our Dads are Libyan.'

'Oh, I didn't know. I thought he was Moroccan?'

'His mum is, but his old man is Libyan. Both of us are from the Warfalli tribe.'

'Political refugees?'

The Darkness Inside

'Exactly,' Sami nodded. 'Dad was always moving; paranoid that Gaddafi was going to send his goons after us.'

'Is that how you guys know each other?'

'We knew each other but we weren't too close.'

'How comes?'

'Anis was mad! Always hyper; getting into trouble in school. For climbing this and doing that. So obviously we didn't link much. We lost touch with each other until Libya kicked off and both our dads went back.'

10. Zawiya

Sami sat at the back of the pick-up truck. The truck had been painted beige. The colour had been slapped on roughly, intentionally almost. It had a dusty finish to it as if it was meant to merge with the desert landscape. Sami was squinting; the other brothers sitting next to him either had brought along some shades or wore caps to protect them from the bright white sun rays. Someone should have told him that Libya gets the most sunshine in the world. In fact, he didn't know that sometimes you could get sunburn just from the sun rays bouncing off the sand. It was a painful discovery – his neck was still sore. The two Libyans inside the pick-up were rocking their heads to some loud heavy metal music. For a moment he wished they wouldn't because as they were moving their heads, the barrels of their weapons, which they still had slung casually on their shoulders, were pointing in his direction. In the short while that he had been here Sami had already seen plenty of accidents. One guy, his cousin actually, had unintentionally shot off someone's toe in Benghazi – he had forgotten to secure his weapon.

Sami sat next to a religious Libyan with his customary long beard. He was reciting the Quran to himself, indifferent to the heavy metal. It was as if he was preparing himself for death. Opposite him sat another Libyan whom Sami understood only vaguely, not because he didn't understand his accent, but because he spoke real fast. The guy looked tanked up on something. Sami called him Abu Druggie in his head. He looked around him and took in the stark desert landscape, leaned forward and asked Abu Druggie where they were going in Arabic.

'What?' said Abu Druggie, taking his headphones off.

'I said where are we going?'

'Don't know,' he said, spotting the consternation on Sami's face. 'Don't worry, it'll be fine. Trust in God. Trust me, it'll be fine, it'll be alright – trust me.'

Abu Druggie flashed what was left of his teeth, the colour of disgusting teak, put his headphones back on and immersed himself in whatever music he was listening to.

Then the driver started up his four by four. Sami didn't know if it was because he had been ordered to move or if he did it of his own volition. He didn't know where they were heading but he knew it was in the direction of Tripoli.

After several hours of being jolted at the back, meeting the others like him going in the direction of Tripoli, he felt calmer. He wasn't in this alone. The religious brother was now sleeping on his shoulder even though they didn't know each other. If this was in London he would probably have pushed his head away but here he let him.

Zawiya sat along the sea, as most Libyan cities do. The place used to be a Sufi hermitage in days gone by and earned its name that way. Nowadays big oil-laden berths were loaded with black gold from huge cranes and then would leave for the shores of Italy and Europe. As such it was deemed an important port by the rebels. In better days the fishing was also good and you could go to the fish market and pick up succulent tuna and fresh anchovies when they were in season.

The Darkness Inside

Their huddle point was outside a warehouse which looked like it had something to do with scrap metal. The place was littered with gnarled and rusty metal car hulks everywhere. Sami sat down, looking lost amongst the hundred or so Libyans who were there. It struck him that these fighters seemed to know what they were doing; they moved around as if they were born to do this. Even the younger ones knew what to do, where to go, what to say. In the distance he could hear the noises of war; he didn't know the difference between the various calibre guns or planes but he could distinguish between gun and artillery and helicopter fire.

He looked around and saw a pick-up truck approaching. This one wasn't the Hilux type that he was sitting in. It seemed like one of those land cruisers with the exhaust running up the side of the driver's seat. Curiously, as it approached he swore he could faintly hear the cacophonous and unsettling sound of grime music. Four Libyans jumped out of the land cruiser. One of the fighters carried large plastic bags and shouted 'sandweech, sandweech' in Arabic. The word 'sandwich' was carried throughout the men and those who had the stomach for it moved towards the Libyan fighter, who started to hand them out. Sami didn't have the stomach to eat; his stomach was tight and yet at the same time he was breaking wind like an old man. Still, he was curious as to what sort of guy would be playing grime music in Zawiya, let alone getting the nuance of London road life expressed in the lyrics. As he moved to investigate he noticed Anis coming out of the driver's seat.

'Anis?!' he said, grinning with joy. 'Anis? Is that you?'

He looked different; he had this beige military baseball cap on, along with a military-style shirt, dark green combats with white Puma football boots and black socks. His hair had grown long and kinky and he sported a short beard. He looked altogether different; he looked like a man, not the boy Sami had known in London. Not that guy who appeared in YouTube videos with friends grime rapping about street life and how tough things were. None of that. Had war transformed him? Is that why men needed war? Would it transform him too? Anis stared at him as if he was trying to recall the face.

'It's me! Sami!'

'Sami wallah? Sami, it's you!'

Anis rushed to embrace him. They had not seen each other for years and yet for some strange reason war had brought them closer.

'Long time, bruh! Long time, when did you get here?'

'A few days ago! You?'

'When things kicked off. Old man came here straight away.'

'How's he doing, all good?'

'All good,' Anis said, looking concerned. 'Listen, do you know what you have to do?'

'No, no clue whatsoever.'

Anis called over to a thin Libyan with sunken cheeks and African hair that looked like it had been straightened and gelled back.

'This is Khaled,' said Anis. 'He's my boy.'

Khaled shook Sami's hand and exchanged pleasantries with him.

'Don't worry about anything,' Anis added. 'Just survive for the mo and stick to him and keep your head down. Make sure you do dua. Watch what Khaled is doing, that's it. You eaten?'

The Darkness Inside

'I have to be honest with you. My belly is messed up.'

'Don't worry,' Anis said, laughing. 'That's normal too. That's adrenalin. Just hold it together. Listen, let's link up later. Jump in with me.'

Anis drove his passengers in to about two kilometres away from the sea, until he came to an East-West axis where the rebels had positioned themselves by a tired-looking flyover of sorts.

'The whole point is to take that thing over there,' said Anis, pointing in the direction of a heavily fortified compound about five hundred metres from the road. Sami could see that behind its walls were several buildings and what seemed like a forest. He later found out it was called Joddayem forest.

'NATO has been pounding the compound but them bastards are still there. So we have to clean it out. That's it.'

Well that was a relief for Sami; it gave him some sense of purpose. At least now he knew what he was putting his life on the line for.

Anis drove the men close to the bridge, stuck his arm out the window and banged on the roof.

'Khaled,' he shouted in Arabic, 'look after him!'

Khaled gave a thumbs up; Anis gave Sami a nod to get out of the passenger seat and just like that he was off. Khaled, it seemed, knew exactly what to do. He crouched down low and indicated for Sami and the others who were with him to follow him to a small, scrappy building where they gathered. Khaled explained that there was a Russian Shilka gun mounted on a truck manned by two fighters. One was injured. The other was on the Shilka firing down the road from the bridge.

'We need to retrieve the injured brother,' Khaled said,

The Darkness Inside

'nothing crazy, nothing heroic.'

Then like a cat he moved and two men followed him towards the Shilka. By Sami's estimation it seemed like certain death. Moreover, mathematically at least, it didn't make sense. It felt like damn lunacy: four men sent in to get one injured brother from a large truck with a mounted heavy weapon. Exactly what was he doing here? Why was he following them? Why didn't he just stay back? But his legs carried him forward until they came to the ridge beside the road.

Khaled, still crouching, mumbled a prayer. Perhaps he was asking God to fortify him. Perhaps he was remembering all his past sins and misdemeanours and asking for forgiveness. But somehow Khaled didn't have the sort of face that asked for all those things. He just moved as if he knew it had been written in the holy scrolls that he was not going to die on that day. He seemed sure that nothing would hurt him except the bullet that had his name on it. And none of the enemy's bullets did; they were intended for the man on the Shilka.

Khaled paused, raised his fist, giving them the signal to stop, and indicated for the group to follow; then he moved. Sami didn't move; he pegged it. He could feel the bullets whistling past his head and surrounding him like a million angry bees. A raging sound seized his chest; it felt like the very soul that was contained within his body wanted to come out of his mouth, and yet he just kept on running, keeping himself as low as he possibly could. He looked to his left and saw the place thick with the haze of bullets the size of ketchup bottles. He felt as if the enemy was targeting him and him alone, and he suspected that all of the men

The Darkness Inside

probably felt exactly the same except Khaled. There was a lull in the fighting when the enemy reloaded and Khaled and the men scrambled across to the other side. They rested on the verge, catching their breaths as the enemy opened up on them again.

'Everyone okay?' Khaled said, breathing hard.

The group nodded.

'What did you do before you did this?' Sami asked.

Khaled showed him a gold canine.

'Used to make bread,' he said, smiling mischievously, then he moved and Sami followed alongside the verge until they came to the man firing the Shilka; he gave them a quick nod. The noise of the gun was deafening. The group were hot and the sun was so bright it hurt their eyes. As soon as they reached the truck, the four grabbed the injured man, who looked like he was sleeping and didn't care about the heat and the noise of this four-barrelled fire spouter. Sami, being the strongest, put him on his shoulders. He carried him along the low ridge next to the road until he came to a bombed-out building. There he handed him over to some medics who seemed to have appeared out of nowhere and took the fighter back to the medical point.

Sami felt like a chess piece. Khaled may have known what his unit was meant to do but that was it. There were two or three or four commanders who seemed to know exactly what they were doing and were ordering people to various places in the battle. Sami's part in the fighting seemed to be a lot about scrambling, farting, crouching, praying and moving slowly towards the compound in the eastern part of the city.

It took several days and evenings to get to their objective.

The Darkness Inside

The most memorable aspect for Sami was the red Nato tracer bullets meeting the Russian-made green ones and lighting up the night sky. It reminded him of a *Star Wars* battle. Eventually, when Sami's group had arrived at the heavily fortified base and took up positions they came under heavy fire. RPGs and Doshkas exchanged messages ending in bodies falling on the ground as if it was some World War II movie where soldiers storm the beach and drop dead not knowing their killer. Sami fired wildly at the base; whether anything he fired hit the enemy he would never know. There were about two hundred of them in rotation. When the men ran out of ammunition they would be reinforced by another group. It was the sheer pigheadedness of the rebels that made them stay despite the heavy defensive positions of the enemy.

It was only the hellfire missiles from Apaches that signalled the beginning of the end for the enemy base. One Apache emerged from the ashes and the smoke and unloaded its hive of wasps, which flew right over their heads. Sami cheered and cried 'God is most great!' when it struck the base bang on. For forty minutes or so the chopper fire continued and then it died down. And whilst Sami was hugging his friends, Khaled looked in the direction of the Apache and showed signs of consternation and worry, as if he didn't trust the chopper nor its pilot.

The enemy must have run low on ammunition because their return fire was not as intense. They seemed to be trying to conserve their ammunition. The order to take the base came and the mad dash began. Sami found himself running forwards; never had he been so proud of being a mad Libyan. He could have died that day and his joy would

The Darkness Inside

have been complete. He was surprised that they could take the fortifications so quickly; he disregarded the assistance rendered by the Apache and attributed this to God alone.

Even more bizarrely, Sami found himself fighting the enemy amongst the smoking wreckage in between trees that grew out of the sandy soil behind the fortifications. He heard their screams as their medics tried to patch them up and found discarded syringes in the soil. Khaled told him later that the enemy injected themselves with morphine when they were hurting.

'Everyone bleeds,' he said.

12. Invitation

'When Anis returned,' said Sami, 'he was so gassed that he started raising money for Syria. I mean it became an obsession. He was like them Jehovah's witnesses you see around here. Obsessed. Every Friday he's shaking buckets at the mosque. Every day he's setting up some fundraising page or posting something on Facebook. Sham this, Sham that.' Sami looked at his watch. 'Is that the time? I've been banging on for too long, my missus needs me to go to the butchers.'

'That's fine,' said Sid gratefully. 'You've been very helpful.'

'To be honest with you, it's kind of nice. Nice to get it off your chest, nice to talk about it to someone who gets it.'

'So when can we finish off?'

'Why don't you come round for dinner? My missus is a wonderful cook.'

Sami tapped his belly to illustrate.

'You look too scrawny to be married. How about next week?'

'I don't want to impose,' Sid said awkwardly. Dinner at someone's house, breaking bread and all, would oblige him to be nice; he didn't want to owe this man anything. Still, being invited to a man's house meant that the guy trusted him sufficiently to perhaps tell him more.

'Cool,' he said, 'you let me know what day is convenient. And if it's not convenient, we can always meet somewhere else.'

The Darkness Inside

Sid got up to leave, they shook hands, and soon he was out in the cold November night walking towards the station. As he was walking, Martha texted him – she worried too much.

Is everything okay?

Yes, went well, Sid texted back.

How well? She probed.

He's invited me to dinner. :)

Don't get too close.

Don't worry. At best this is going to be a great story at worst he'll be a good source. TC.

X. Let me know whenever you meet these guys.

Don't worry, texted Sid.

It's my job to worry – promise me. I am your editor remember.

Sid smiled as he walked towards the station. Maybe Gardener had a point; maybe she was a keeper. Sami was true to his word; he did call him up a few days later and told him to come round mid-week. And he wasn't exaggerating when he said that Layla was a great cook. Sami loved her bamiyeh, he loved her maqloubeh, he loved all the beautiful Palestinian dishes she just rustled up out of nowhere. And what was extraordinary was that she managed to do all of those wonderful things, run a home and raise two boys all at the same time.

On the day Sid came over she made kebseh, a rice and chicken dish that she knew Sami loved. Sami was convinced that this scrawny journalist would be so in love with her cooking that he would not be able to write anything bad about him or his family at all. He would point to his beautiful wife, show him how normal she looked, present his two good-looking boys and then let

The Darkness Inside

him see how self-evidently 'normal' he was.

Sami was sitting in his small living room on the settee. The twins, Ahmed and Eesa, were playing FIFA 19 on the Xbox. Eesa's team, Real Madrid, scored just as the full-time whistle went. Ahmed was upset by his loss. Sami grabbed the controller.

'Oi! My turn!'

'Dad,' Ahmed said, as if his love for the Xbox was an abnormality. Fathers shouldn't be so into computer games. This was, after all, not his domain.

'Step aside son,' Sami said, pushing his boy jokingly. 'Let Maradona teach you how it's done.'

'Who is Maradona, baba?'

'See you don't know nuttin',' Sami said, shaking his head. 'All you lot are about are the six packs of Ronaldo, but Maradona had a belly like mine.' He patted his belly and added, 'And he could still run rings around Ronaldo, Messi and Neymar combined. Those who know, know! Lemme show you how big poppa plays.'

He turned to Eesa and, still in a trash-talking tone, he asked, 'So who are you going to be?'

'You know who,' said Eesa quietly. Eesa, the younger one by six minutes, took that quiet confidence from his mother; he wasn't like Ahmed who could trash talk anyone and, as Sami heard from his teacher, could cuss like a mofo in the playground too. Instead, he just beavered away and by the time he finished with you, it was 5-2 full time. He'd tap you gently on the shoulder and say modestly: 'Next time, Dad. Good effort though.'

Eesa chose Chelsea this time; Sami chose Real Madrid. The game went unexpectedly well for Sami. That Welsh

The Darkness Inside

genius Gareth Bale scored and Benzema put a second one in the net very soon after. Sami got on the rug with his kids and celebrated on his knees like a proper footballer, pretending to take in the adulation of an imaginary crowd. Sami rapped a couplet from the late Biggie Smalls. Eesa frowned; he wasn't used to having two goals scored against him, seeing his father rap gibberish and Ahmed rubbing it in all at the same time. Sami, too, joined in; he always liked to see how much he could needle his boy before he got upset. 'We need to watch the replay. We need to watch the replay!' As they were watching the replay, the doorbell rang.

'Sami, the door!' shouted Layla from the kitchen. Sami got off the rug and clapped the kids around the head for them to follow him to the door to welcome their guest. Sami looked through the keyhole to make sure it was Sid – otherwise he wouldn't open. Sid was wearing a shirt and tie. Sami checked himself out. He was wearing tracksuit bottoms and felt self-conscious. He asked himself whether protocol required that they be dressed to the nines to receive his guest. His dad had always received his guests in his slippers and thobe, but then again the long flowing garment always had a certain dignity to it.

'Salaam,' Sid said, standing in the hallway with a box of petrol station flowers and chocolate. It wasn't the usual Quality Street or Tesco's Finest chocolate. His guest had put some thought into it and had actually chosen some decent Italian chocolates, and the roses had a woman's touch to them.

'Wasalaam,' said Sami, shaking his guest's hand, 'bro you shouldn't have! Come in.'

The Darkness Inside

Ahmed and Eesa shyly shook Sid's hands, gave him salaams and then rushed off to the living room. Layla came to the hallway in the middle of wrapping her head in a scarf.

'Salaam alaikum brother. How are you?'

'Fine, thank you. Here, I brought you this.'

Layla took the flowers and sweets.

'Really, you shouldn't have,' she said. 'Guests bring blessings to the home.'

'Let's hope,' replied Sid, 'this is part of God's blessing then.'

Sami directed him towards the small living room. He noticed that the place was very different from his own. Although it was in want of sunlight – most ex-council houses were – it was still a very lived-in living room. It had, of course, the usual framed Quranic verses; the Throne verse and Opening embroidered with gold thread and set in black velvet hung on the wall to protect the house from evil. The mantelpiece had pictures of the boys in various stages of their life. Someone's father, Sid didn't know whose, looked like he had passed away not long ago. Sid studied his picture; the old man sat on a sofa with several grandchildren surrounding him, and a smile that said he was ready to meet his Maker for his job was done. There were books on the property trade piled on the glass coffee table. The whole room became even more lived-in with the smell of delicious food wafting in from the kitchen.

Sid sat down at the edge of the sofa.

'Relax,' said Sami, aware of the formality. 'There's no proper way of behaving for guests in this house.'

Sid still sat there on the edge, as if he did not quite know

The Darkness Inside

what to do with himself yet. He watched the kids play on the Xbox.

'Do you play?' asked Sami.

'Only a little,' said Sid. 'You?'

'A little.'

Ahmed, whose ears were always open, added, 'Dad plays in the evening after we've gone to bed. Mum gets really mad.'

Sami gave him a jokey clap.

'Oi! Family secrets stay secret.'

He turned to Sid and asked, 'You got any of your own?'

'Nah.'

'Oh really? I assumed you did. How comes?'

Sid shrugged, thinking quickly as to what he should say and what he should reveal.

'Haven't met the right woman I suppose. I'm not sure this family thing is for me anyhow.'

'Well how do you know that?'

'Don't want to take the chance.'

'You must have had a bad experience or covered some horrible stories in your line of work to come to such a drastic decision.'

'Nah. Just saw some bad things with friends that put me off. I know it's not rational, but still, you need to go with your gut sometimes.'

'Like what?'

'Well,' Sid said, pausing for a moment. He didn't like the probing. Sami could have been a great journalist – he was like the late Sir David Frost, whose interviewing style was so subtle and made you feel so comfortable that you'd let your guard down and at that moment you'd drop a massive

The Darkness Inside

clanger like Tony Blair did over Iraq. Sami's expectant gaze wouldn't leave Sid.

'One of my closest friends found out he was the son of the other woman.'

'What do you mean?'

'My – I mean my friend's dad basically had an affair with his mum; she was the other woman. She didn't even know, thought she was the only one. The dad then broke up with her after the first wife gave him an ultimatum: either he leaves the woman for good or she goes. My mate's mum was heartbroken. Turned to drink. I had to work with him in a shopping mall as security trying to make a bit of extra money at uni, and I watched him having to throw his own mum out of the shopping centre. Imagine that? Your own mum?'

Sid was visibly shaken as he talked about the encounter.

'Sometimes when he couldn't do it because he was emotionally wrecked, I had to do it. That's when I thought, don't want to have a family.'

'You couldn't make it up could you? That's so messed up. But you know what, when you have kids you have to teach them what you believe in – what you stand for – and try to live up to it. So if you teach your kids to respect women, even if you don't at the time, you better up your game because they will soon find out.'

'Sami!' shouted Layla from the kitchen.

'Yes boss!'

Sami stood up rigidly like a soldier as if he was saluting a general. Sid laughed. When Sami clapped his hands Ahmed and Eesa switched off without pleading to finish off the game. They knew the rules. Sid got off the sofa and

The Darkness Inside

followed his host to the kitchen where Layla had prepared a wonderful dinner. There was tabbouleh, fattoush, kebseh, aubergine dips like mutabbal and lovely little pickles. Dinner at the El-Masry table was delicious. All the while as Sid ate, he was looking for signs he assumed would hint at something radical or extreme in the family but he couldn't find anything. Dinner table conversation consisted of an endless series of jokes made by Sami, with Layla reining him in and making sure they were within the bounds of propriety. By the time they had eaten, Layla was already sending the kids off to bed.

'Will you excuse me,' she said, 'if I don't have a dessert?'

'Sure,' replied Sid, 'I'm sorry to put you out.'

'No, not at all. It was a pleasure. Good night.' Layla left.

'More for us,' Sami said, clearing up the dinner table. He opened up a box of baklavas that he had stashed away in a cupboard and prepared some mint tea whilst Sid brought out his notebook.

'You know,' said Sami, taking a baklava, 'for a journalist you're not bad.'

'Thanks...'

13. Tripoli

Sami spent most of his time in Zawiya either with Anis or Khaled. They had been quartered in some Gaddafi officer's house and had taken over his games room as their own. They had 'requisitioned' his mattresses and blankets and had got more or less comfortable. Whilst they waited for the next rebel move, Anis didn't do much. Most of the time he organised and reorganised his rucksack. He cleaned his equipment regularly, made his bed and made sure that his men, seven in total, did the same. Sami didn't know why he had been given command of these men, and more importantly who had given him the command, but Anis took his responsibilities seriously. He kept them all well fed and whilst many of them lazed about, he was always off on an errand for someone or something. Sometimes he harangued them for their untidiness and sloth; he chided them to be cleaner and more organised. He reminded his men that Napoleon's army had been decimated by typhoid and dysentery – the men just laughed at him.

'Where did you read that?' they would ask him.

'Google,' he'd reply. Sami was surprised that he'd looked into it. He never thought that Anis was the type to even find out about such things.

The only memorable experience during his time in Zawiya was probably a week after the city had fallen. Khaled was sitting cross-legged on his mattress cleaning

The Darkness Inside

his weapon when an old man came into the room – he could barely stand except with the help of a walking stick. He wore a white kufi, shirt and trousers.

'Who is in charge?' he asked him. Sami pointed to Khaled.

'Yes Sheikh,' said Khaled, getting up and giving him a chair, 'how can I help you?'

The old man refused the chair and walked up to him and pulled him aside, whispering something in his ear. Sami strained to hear what they were talking about. Khaled appeared distressed by whatever the old man was saying. He hugged the old man and held him; it appeared as if both men were quivering. Khaled wiped his face, which looked red from the blood rushing to his head.

'Wait here,' he said to the old man. He went to the bed and grabbed his holster and was about to leave when Sami got up.

'Do you want some company?' He watched his friend, whose face was cold and impassive and had the sort of primeval savagery that resulted in two hundred- year-old vendettas, blood feuds, revenge, cruelty and bloody satisfaction once the object of one's rage was all but destroyed.

'No, it's okay,' he said, 'I'll tell you what you can do. Make the old man some tea while he's waiting.'

Khaled left Sami to look after the old man. He treated him like he was made of gold and kept him company.

'Is he capable?' the old man asked.

'Of course. Why?' Sami was puzzled by the curious question.

'Oh, nothing, my son, nothing.'

They sat talking for a while. Most of the time the old man

The Darkness Inside

rambled on and on about his daughters and how virtuous they were.

'The young one,' he said, 'I used to call her Mish Mish; she was like a kitten when she was a child.'

Khaled came back after several hours. The old man looked at him expectantly. Khaled's face was grim.

'It's fine now uncle, tell your daughters not to worry.'

The old man got up beaming and hugged Khaled; he made a long supplication to God for him and left. Sami never saw him again.

Sami had no idea what had transpired between Khaled and the old man except that over the course of several weeks, Anis kept having a go at Khaled. Sami had read that Western NGOs were kicking up a stink about how the rebels were mistreating prisoners locked up in Baraka Hotel, which had turned into a makeshift prison. Apparently, some of the younger prisoners had been strung up and their corpses used as target practice. Others had been pistol-whipped and taken to the desert, from where they never returned.

'You shouldn't have done it,' he said to Khaled one afternoon when the three were sitting in the bedroom taking refuge from the blazing sun.

'I don't give a shit as to what Amnesty thinks,' replied Khaled. 'These bastards lost their right to be considered human from the time they decided to murder and rape. These NGOs live in la la land. What innocence are you talking about when the fucker films himself raping your daughters in front of you? Since when did they become the judge of what's right and wrong? Fuck Human Rights Watch.'

The Darkness Inside

'Still don't make it right.'

'Listen, I'm Libyan, that's how we do it here. When you are in England we do it your way.'

Anis took issue with the comment.

'I put my blood on the line here just as much as you – my father is from here; that makes me from here.'

'Well, you don't sound like it, that's all I'm saying. If you did, you'd know about the honour of our women. You know pimps aren't allowed into paradise. If we aren't jealous about our women, then what are we?'

'Look, even the Shariah tells us to go through court; you can't just barge into a prison and deal with him!'

'Oh,' said Khaled angrily, 'next time I'll be like you, just watching that dog's soldiers deliver our girls to the camp so they can have their way with them through your binoculars.'

'You don't have a clue. We would have given the game away, you little shit! We were waiting for NATO air strikes! You think I didn't bleed when I saw those trucks drop them girls off?!'

'They weren't your women,' Khaled replied bitterly.

'You know,' said Anis, 'you can be a stubborn little shit sometimes.' He got up and left but for some reason Sami wanted him to stay and argue it out with Khaled. He felt that winning this argument was important. That even though Khaled may have had a point, Anis was right. It would have made him a better man. It would have shown him that one could not kill another without thought, without recourse to one's conscience. Anis should have stayed and fought with him – he should have laid down the law. If he didn't, the revolution would take a dark turn and eventually consume them all, till they too would be afflicted with the same darkness they had come here to remove. But Anis left and sulked, and in the evening things were back to normal again. They never raised the matter ever again.

Tripoli fell in a very straightforward fashion, crumbling from within. There remained pockets of resistance from the regime, most of which was comprised of blacks commanded by a Libyan officer who gave himself up at the slightest danger to his own person. It was pathetic to see how he had used these wretched men from some sub-Saharan backwater that Gaddafi had propped up with his gold. Some of the corpses had wads of cash in their pockets with the same serial number on each banknote.

'Duds, mate,' Anis said as he searched their pockets, 'they died for worthless duds. Subhan Allah how He humiliates the unrighteous.'

Sami never got to do much of the fighting in Tripoli. Most of the heavy fighting had been accomplished by the time they arrived, and it was now just a matter of cleaning up the dirt that had fallen between the cracks, which was done mostly by Anis and Khaled.

They would enter a block or an estate that was fortified with Gaddafi sympathisers who would pop out of the window taking potshots before disappearing to another window. It resembled an eighties computer game and continued throughout the day. Anis would number the buildings left to right, Khaled would stare through the binoculars and shout out coordinates like 'fourth building, third window, hundred and eighty metres' and then Anis would go into action. Three clicks for a hundred and fifty

The Darkness Inside

metres, raise the rifle slightly to give you the right range and then pull the trigger. Sometimes Anis would choose a spot where an RPG grenade had hit; from there he would go to the third or the fourth room away. He'd chisel through the two walls so the enemy couldn't spot him. Then he would drag in a desk and put up net curtains and all sorts of stuff that would camouflage him from the enemy, and there he would wait with Khaled. Whenever he hit someone he'd be joyous.

'Got the bastard.'

By the end of their whack-a-mole game both men had become pros at cleaning up the place. And by the time they had returned to London they were already thinking about marching on Damascus.

14. The Hollingshead

Amanda had always been told that she was beautiful in a classical sense. In fact, her boyfriend called her his 'Grecian beauty'. She didn't always believe him – she thought her chin jutted out a bit too much and her lips were a bit too thin – but when she did believe the assertion, she opted for subtlety when applying her make-up. Beauty had to look natural, not contrived; that was the philosophy that she followed. But then there was a shift in the paradigm. In the beginning it was almost imperceptible, but slowly around work she noticed that things became bolder: her colleagues had eyebrows that were more pronounced, thicker; bums were more curved and accentuated; clothes had to be loud and screaming; any attempt at being subtle had become grey and boring. She couldn't watch movies with her boyfriend because the action movies had so many sequences and cuts that she became dizzy when she watched them. Songs became more overt, lewder; it wasn't enough to shake your ass seductively, you needed to have a booty and twerk it like a porn star. The problem was that despite the loudness everything looked and felt the same. In the past, if friends wanted to raise money for charity they'd come up to her and ask: 'Hey Mandy, I'm raising some money for Save the Children, could you help?' Now it was: 'Hey Mandy, I'm raising some money for Save the Children by climbing Mount Kilimanjaro, would you sponsor me?' They'd still

The Darkness Inside

get the same amount, a fiver. It was a massive effort for ineffectual gains. Just like porn addicts who have to trawl through thousands of images just to jerk off pathetically. They all had to be extraordinary, unique and different and so ended up looking exactly the same. This of course applied to make-up too. And so Amanda had to spend an excessive amount of time in front of her vanity desk to apply what appeared to be the human equivalent of poly-filler on her face to have that contrary-to-nature look. Only then, when she looked like an alien, was she satisfied that she was beautiful.

Her boyfriend, Gardener, of course couldn't care less for that stuff. In fact, he found it off-putting and fake, but he didn't say anything. He knew she was very insecure about her looks.

When she saw him enter the bedroom she was surprised. She hadn't expected him so early.

'Hello darling,' she said, zipping up her evening dress. 'You're home early.'

'Thought I'd surprise you,' he said, giving her a kiss on her head. 'Thought we could have an early dinner.'

He brought out a concealed bottle of wine, and he looked at her red velvet dress, disappointed.

'I didn't know you were going out.'

'I told you, Laura is having farewell drinks at the Hollingshead. I mentioned it to you earlier this week.'

'Oh, sorry.' Gardener could have sworn she had not mentioned it. 'I must have forgot.'

He felt guilty.

'Yes,' she said, as if to reinforce it, 'or you didn't listen.'

She got up from her vanity desk and went into the en-suite

bathroom. Gardener sat down on the bed, undoing his tie, looking at her in the bathroom as she put on perfume. She was so elegant, especially the way she applied her perfume ever so delicately.

'Will you be late?'

'You know how Laura is, darling,' she said from the bathroom, 'once she starts on the Prosecco.'

'Quite.'

Amanda came out of the bathroom and stood in front of him. 'Well, how do I look?'

'Stunning.'

'You always say that.'

'I mean it.'

He never understood why she always questioned his sincerity. Amanda just brushed her lips against his, either to make him feel guilty, to express her disapproval, or because she did not want to smudge her red lipstick. She went to the hallway and put on her jacket and shoes.

'What will you eat, darling?'

'Probably go down to Bodrum,' Gardener said from the bedroom.

'You always have kebabs.'

'I don't like cooking for one, you know that.'

'Don't make me feel bad, darling.'

'I'm not.'

He felt guilty for making her feel guilty even though he had never wanted to make her feel that way.

'Bye, darling.'

The door slammed shut with a sense of finality. Gardener's guilt vanished and he went into the living room. He sat down on the settee and turned the television

The Darkness Inside

on. A ping went off on a mobile phone that was charging. It was Amanda's phone. She had forgotten it. Gardener glanced over at the phone and could see the WhatsApp message: *PETER: Darling, I am running late. Pick you up at the Hollingshead.*

There was a sound of keys jangling at the front door. Heels clacked on the wooden floor as they rushed into the living room. Amanda was back.

'Darling... darling,' she said, nervously staring at him, her immaculate make-up cracking, 'I forgot my phone.'

'I'll get it...' He reached for the phone.

'No! It's okay, I'll get it.'

Amanda rushed for the phone and got there before him. Phone safely in her hand, she went over and was about to kiss him, but Gardener stopped her.

'You'll smudge your lipstick,' he said coldly.

'Oh yes... thank you. Right, I need to go.'

'Have fun.' There was irony in the last word.

Amanda looked at him for a moment. Did he know? She closed the living room door. She never did that. The main door clicked shut, leaving Gardener to sit on the velvet sofa, alone.

Pollards Hill was barren this time of year – a patch in South London, Norbury, where you could look for the new crescent moon to determine if it was Eid or not. On sunny days you could have a quiet smoke alone enjoying the autumn colours or just have a think and take in the crisp air. But today was not that sort of day. The grass was patchy with clods of mud being kicked up. There was dog shit everywhere too. Sami was late again and tiptoed

The Darkness Inside

through the mud. He walked past an elderly Pakistani couple sitting with a black man wrapped up in a thick black coat on a park bench. Sami slowed down to listen in on the conversation. It seemed like the Pakistani dad was unconvinced that the black man would be a good son-in-law. On the opposite end was Abbas, sitting on another park bench. He was dressed like a tramp: heavy boots, builder's jeans, a dark green puffa jacket and a hat that looked like he'd killed a fox and stuck it on his head. It was clear that his main concern was keeping warm. He was staring into his phone. His lips were moving like one of those illiterates in school struggling with reading. Sami approached him and handed him a coffee in a polystyrene cup. Abbas took the coffee, still focused on reading the article on his phone. It didn't stop Sami from talking though.

'Man, why are you dressed so bad?'

Abbas looked at Sami for a moment as if he was annoyed and then returned to his reading.

'Man! I remember you used to take pride in the way you looked; Thursday night you'd go to the barbers, get perfumed up – you'd wear your best gear. You looked like a G! And now look at you! You've just let go of yourself. Don't you want to get a wife?'

'Man,' replied Abbas, 'looking at the state of your marriage, no. You don't seem to be wearing the trousers in your house. You know what they used to call guys like that innit? Tartoor!'

They laughed at the word, whose nearest English equivalent was probably 'cuckold'.

'You're right though, those were the days!' Sami said. 'We were kings them times! That's what these guys don't

The Darkness Inside

understand, we were kings. We might have been broke back then but no one could tell us nothing. You know what else I miss?'

Abbas had returned to reading and was completely ignoring him. It didn't matter to Sami; he was in a reverie, reminiscing. 'Madlu'a! Ah! Madlu'a!'

He missed that milk, cream, pistachio, semolina, all of it.

'Allah! Allah!' he cooed in appreciation, as if his belly had just remembered that delicious Syrian sweet.

'Madlu'a! London's got everything but they don't have that.'

'Acton,' Abbas said.

'Acton? What?' Sami said, surprised.

'There's a Syrian shop that makes it.'

'You mofo? You can't be bothered to get a haircut or clothes, or even attempt to find a wife, but you can go and find Madlu'a? How?'

'What do you expect me to do on my day off?'

'Acton, you say? You sure?'

'179 High Street. It's real. They're from Saraqeb.'

'Serious? I am there. Kids need a treat,' he said, patting his belly.

Abbas pointed to the phone.

'There is so much bullshit in this article I don't even know where to start.'

He glared at Sami accusingly.

'See, the trick here is to tell the lie which is closest to the truth.'

'Sun Zoo again? That's how you sell your properties, innit? Anis was sick in the head. You made him out to be

The Darkness Inside

some sort of superhero or something.'

'That's what you wanted. That's what you told me to do.'

'I didn't expect you to excel in your lying.'

'Listen,' Sami said, laughing. 'Let's go and get some Madlu'a now. Forget this. Remember how we'd go and get some at Abu Ali's? Or the bros would bring us some? You remember how we confiscated some from that FSA guy at the checkpoint?! He was pissed! We ate that with some hot tea. Best raise you ever made. You know! Come!'

'Nah man, allow it,' Abbas said.

'What,' Sami pressed, 'have you got anything else to do on your day off? I don't even know why I am hooking up with you! Come on you boring old fart, live.'

'Nah, I'm just not feeling it, it's my day off.'

'Come, let's go, I'll drop you off.'

Sami bugged Abbas until his resolve was worn out and they headed towards his car in search of this magical dessert.

15. Twitter

Sid sat at his desk staring at his Twitter feed. He had been expecting his article about Anis' adventures in Libya to do the rounds. The usual analysts would retweet the piece, 'like' it and congratulate him in order for them to get recognition for their own work. These analysts weren't trolls; they were the whores of Twitter. He was expecting that by the end of the week some nerdy analyst who had nothing better to do but translate some obscure text on Jihadism and was in all likelihood an involuntary celibate would add the hashtag #FF, 'Friday Follow', and add his Twitter handle, @sidnews87, and he would pick up a few followers, which would result in him coming one step closer to that blue tick verification.

Instead he watched his career being destroyed in real time. There was a tweet from @EDL4LIFE: 'You Jihadi apologist!'; another from @Jewhadi: 'Goatfucking Jihadi paedo'; and so it went on his Twitter timeline for an eternity. This is how it must have felt for Lucy Swanson, the columnist, when she wrote an article saying she had been 'ushered' out of a mosque in Stratford. The mosque was deluged with backlash and vitriol for days until it released CCTV footage showing that no such thing had ever happened. Ms Swanson claimed that there had been a misunderstanding; and all she got was a slap on the wrist and she kept her job. Sid surmised that he wouldn't keep his job even though he had done the story in good faith. He still remembered going through her timeline as memes of Usher kept on making the rounds. At the time he felt that she deserved everything she got. Here was this privileged white woman, public school educated, pontificating – and then getting away with a blatant lie! She needed to know how it felt to be on the other end. Now, he wasn't so sure she deserved it. Here he was watching Twitter explode, not knowing if he would have a job at the end of the day. He wondered what she had said that had allowed her to cling on to her job. Did she just deny, deny, deny? Did she say she had misspoken? Or was it an order from on top? He looked up to the heavens in supplication as another tweet landed like shrapnel on his feed and exploded with RTs and likes.

Martha came into the office upset; she had been at the editorial meeting. Her lips were tight, her hair fiery.

'Can I talk to you?'

Several staff members stared as if they knew that Sid was going to get a dressing down; that there was no excuse or wiggle room to be had, no excuse for his legendary tantrums. Some staff felt that he always got away with it; maybe she had a thing for him. After all, didn't they go way back?

'Yeah, for sure,' Sid said, pretending to be casual.

'In private?'

Sid got up and followed Martha to the conference room. He walked past Daniels, who gave him a knowing wave that bordered on glee. He went into the meeting room and closed the door.

'Have you seen this?' Martha said, showing him post

The Darkness Inside

after post of EDL and Britain First supporters uploading videos on Facebook showing Anis attending one of Anjem Choudary's demonstrations in Ilford, in East London. The most damning video was uploaded on YouTube in 2011; Anis was seen shouting abuse at the soldiers, waving a black flag and heard shouting, 'Your boys aren't heroes, they're in hell! Hell!' Several skinheads rushed at him, shouting abuse, and he responded in kind, kicking and punching before police officers separated them.

Sid read a post by Kevin McGrath, the Far Right leader: 'Do we need more proof that the liberal media are in bed with Jihadists? Join us for a Facebook live tonight at 7pm.'

Sid looked at how many views it had. 2.1 million views and rising. 'Fuck! Fuck! Fuck!' Sid started to shake; he put his hands on his temples and rubbed them. He couldn't comprehend the magnitude of this error bouncing around all over the world as he sat here in the conference room.

'Did you not check his story out? Did you not fact check him?'

'Well, no, not properly anyway.'

The only thing he could do was own his mistake.

Martha was upset.

'Why, Sid? Why? Christ! In this day and age? This is journalism 101!'

'I know, okay, I know! I fucked up. I believed him. See what happens when you do?'

Martha softened; he looked like he was having a breakdown. She moved a bit closer.

'You... you okay?'

He moved away.

'Yes, yes, I'm fine. I'm sorry I fucked up. Paul?'

The Darkness Inside

'He's upset,' she replied. 'The *Daily Mail* is running the YouTube video. But he invests in his staff. He's always done that.'

Sid breathed a sigh of relief. 'Does that mean I still have my job?'

She nodded. 'Just about.'

'You did that?'

She nodded again. He was about to hug her. But he stopped himself. It would be unprofessional. 'Thanks,' he said. 'I will fix this. I promise.'

'You better.'

That evening, as Sami was busy finishing off his paperwork for the day, Sid walked in. Sami spotted him and was about to smile, but he saw the grim look on his face.

'It's not Halloween, is it?' Sami said, trying to break the ice.

Sid was having none of it.

'Don't take me for a fool. When Libya was kicking off there's a YouTube clip of him in Ilford!'

'What you on about?' Sami said, acting as if he didn't know.

'You lied to me.'

'He was in Libya,' Sami stated. 'That clip was probably uploaded much later.'

'Liar!' shouted Sid. 'I am going to expose your lies. I am going to expose you as the Jihadist running a property management firm in Croydon. Sounds like a scoop.'

'You threatening me? I got kids, you know. You're willing to hang my wife and kids out to dry for an eight-hundred-word article?'

Sami's voice had turned imperceptibly menacing. The

The Darkness Inside

big friendly giant had become less friendly.

'I want the truth! That is all I want.'

Sami got up.

'Fuck off!' he said. 'You lot have no clue about the truth or about war. You sound like you'd sell your mother for a story.'

'Well, now that you say that, I did kick her out many a night at the shopping mall,' grinned Sid. There was something about him that said he had nothing to lose.

'So you were talking about yourself the other night? See, you lie too! You are a sick, sick bastard. You don't give a shit do you?'

'To show you I do care about the family, I'll give you a few days. Call me before the week is up.'

Sid left Sami standing behind his desk. Sami sat down and reached for his mobile phone; he tried to make a phone call to Abbas. There was no response. So he messaged him: 'Bro! I'm fucked!'

Abbas wrote back: 'Can't answer your call. Don't worry, call you later.'

Gardener was outside a McDonalds, not too far from Westminster Crown Court, having finished a sausage McMuffin. He didn't usually have breakfast outside – he usually had it at home – but things had changed recently and he was having more McMuffins and Bodrum kebabs. As a result of his fast breakfasts and dinners his slim frame had managed to protrude slightly at his stomach. He sparked a real cigarette instead of the vaping device Amanda had convinced him to adopt. Now that she was gone, he'd gone back to smoking real tobacco, and it was

The Darkness Inside

lovely. And what was more, he no longer felt guilty about it. There was no one to tell him what to do, how to feel, where to sit – nothing. He brought out his phone and called Sid, who picked up immediately. Sid had been waiting for him to call for a while.

'Hey mate, how's it going?'

'Fine, fine,' Sid replied impatiently. 'This story is killing me.'

'I can imagine,' said Gardener, pacing up and down the pavement and oblivious to the people who may be annoyed by it. 'Well, that's why I am ringing actually.'

'Give it to me.'

'Well, I'm covering this case in court. Completely unimportant and random. Some girl, Shayma, just got sent down for sending money to her husband fighting in Syria. Now here's the thing – there's an Anis Ferjani being mentioned in the court papers.'

'Really? How comes no one's picked up on it?'

'Probably because they transcribed his name wrong, Anees Forjani. I just thought it's got to be the same guy.'

'What does it say?'

'Anis was blackmailing her for money.'

'Really? It all makes sense. It all makes sense!' Sid's voice sounded excited.

'What makes sense?'

'Mate, could you do me a huge favour and get hold of the court paper for me or grab a snap?'

'Yes, for sure. What makes sense?'

'I'll tell you about it when I see you. Got to go.'

Gardener put the phone back in his pocket with an expression of puzzlement, but he knew Sid was on the scent like a bloodhound.

The Darkness Inside

Sid was nervous as he stood on Anis' windswept estate walkway puffing away on his cigarette. Lately, he had been smoking like a chimney. His skin was looking yellowish, as though he had some liver problem. That always happened whenever he smoked too much. The rain started to spit again and he flicked the cigarette butt down to the car park. He took a deep breath and knocked on Anis' family's door. He prayed that it wasn't Anis' sister who opened the door; if that hysterical medusa answered he might as well forget about talking to them. He would have to make a case for speaking to them in ten seconds or so. He listened. The steps that approached were unfamiliar to him. They were slow and trudging, as if the person was walking through heavy snowfall.

'Who is it?' inquired the voice behind the door.

'Salaam madam, I am Sid.'

'Sid? Who is Sid?'

'Saeed madam, I'm a journalist.'

'Journalist?'

The footsteps retreated to the recesses of the flat, then heavy-set footsteps approached. Sid guessed they were Ayman's. He cursed under his breath and took a step back. Just in case. The chain on the door was removed and an angry face glared at him. Ayman looked like one of those Japanese shoguns wearing a samurai mask, furious and ready to kill a dragon if need be.

'I thought I told you to never come here again?'

'I know.' Sid stood there completely still. Never show fear to a dangerous animal. They sense it. Hold your ground, he told himself.

The Darkness Inside

'So what you doing here?'

'Bro,' he said, raising his hands as if he wasn't hiding anything, 'I'm not here for a story.'

'Then,' said Ayman, stepping out of the door menacingly, 'why are you standin' in front of me?'

'I know who killed your brother.'

Ayman came up to his face. 'Are you fucking with me?'

Sid hesitated for a moment; he was about to get a kicking, but he took the gamble. 'I'm not. I am hundred percent sure. But if I am going to expose him I need your help.'

His confidence stopped Ayman in the course of action he was about to take. Ayman looked down both sides of the walkway and nodded for him to come inside, adding, 'I swear if this is a joke, you are dead. Mum's not well.'

Sid followed him into the flat. He took his shoes off and went into the sparse living room. It was designed in typical north African colours: blues and turquoise. The sofa was intricately carved and had beautiful latticework on it.

A lady in her mid-fifties came out of the kitchen. She had deep lines in her face with sad eyes.

'Hello,' said Umm Anis in an accented English.

'He's Muslim,' said Ayman.

'Salaam alaikum, my son. Sorry about earlier.'

'Walaikum salaam, aunty. I understand.'

'Listen,' said Ayman, 'Mum, sit down for a moment.'

Umm Anis sat down, watching Sid keenly.

'He thinks he knows who killed Akhoya,' Ayman said.

The old woman's mouth quivered as if she had been struck by a needle; she put her hands to it and stared

The Darkness Inside

out of the window surveying the grey landscape. Then she remembered something. 'Where are my manners? Ayman, make our guest some tea.'

Sid had an in. Ayman went into the kitchen to prepare mint tea.

'So, where's your husband, aunty?'

'He died a few years ago in Tripoli, God have mercy on him.'

'How did he die?'

'Heart attack.'

They sat in silence for a moment until Ayman returned carrying a tray with three small blue cups, a teapot and some biscuits. He poured the tea and served the crumbly biscuits to Sid, his mum and then himself. They sat quietly for a moment sipping the tea, taking in the sweet taste of sugar and fresh mint.

'The tea is lovely,' Sid complimented them.

Ayman ignored the compliment. 'So what's this you got about my brother?'

'Do you know Sami El-Masry?' Sid asked Umm Anis.

'Yes, of course.'

'Well, I think he killed Anis.'

'Wait,' said Umm Anis, upset. 'You come to my house to tell me this?'

'I'm a hundred percent, aunty.'

'Why?' She was almost outraged. 'I don't believe it. He's a good boy, from a good family. Nonsense.'

Ayman quieted her. 'Mum, that was then, people change.'

'I believe,' added Sid, 'he saw Anis as a threat to his growing business.'

'Why would he do that? They fought together.'

The Darkness Inside

Sid hesitated for a moment; speaking ill of the dead is never a good idea, especially to the deceased's mother. 'I don't mean any disrespect, but I believe Anis was blackmailing him.'

'My son, my son would never do that.' Umm Anis was agitated and upset at the accusation. 'He would never do that. He's a mujahid.'

'There's a court case where he's mentioned doing it to another person. Here, take a look.' Sid showed her a screen grab of the court documents that Gardener had sent over.

Umm Anis cried when she read the extract. 'May God have mercy!' She shook her head. Ayman looked at the screen grab, then got up, trying his best to control his rage.

'Mr El-Masry,' Sid said, 'didn't want to harm his business…'

'He popped him!' Ayman said, clenching his fist. 'I'm gonna kill him, I swear! I swear I'm going to do it now.' He was about to go for his jacket.

'Ayman!' shrieked Umm Anis, 'don't repay bad with bad. Listen to Saeed. He knows.'

'Look, I need your help. To expose him takes time, patience and conclusive evidence.'

'Let's just go to the police,' said Umm Anis. She got up, ready to go there and then.

'The police won't do anything,' said Ayman. 'They didn't do anything when he died and won't do anything now.'

'There is a way,' Sid said. 'Help me to help you.'

Ayman sat down, now willing to listen. After a moment he demanded, 'So what do you want to know?'

'Everything.' Sid brought out his notebook. 'I need to know everything.'

The Darkness Inside

'I don't like waffle,' said Ayman, 'so I'm gonna cut a long story short. This beef ting is between Talha and Radio in Syria. Talha was an Iraqi with a lot of experience fighting the Americans in Iraq. So when he joined our group everyone was gassed about it. He had experience in everything. I mean, they had actually tried to free him bare times from Abu Ghraib. They say he was close to the big man himself.'

'Big man?' Sid asked.

'Baghdadi,' replied Ayman. 'Keep up, I thought you said you were a journalist?'

'I am; this isn't my field of expertise. I didn't think Anis was linked to the big man.'

'It was all mixed up them times, all the different groups was mixing with everyone else. When Anis saw his experience, he sided with Talha. Because up to that time everyone was asking Abu Abdul Rahman to do operations and he was blowin' mans off with gun talk but no action.'

'Who's Abu Abdul Rahman?'

'Radio,' explained Ayman.

'Radio? That's a bit of a weird name for a Muslim isn't it?'

'He's a London man, but proper charismatic guy, y'get me? Spoke like five languages. I swear if he hadn't been born on road he'd be like an investment banker or somethin'. Anyway, when Talha comes in tension starts to build up between the two. Can't have two roosters in the same patch, even though they were meant to be part of the same Katiba, and under the same Shura council… we were in Reef Mohandiseen, North Aleppo when things kicked off proper…'

16. Reef Mohandiseen

Khaled sang along to the Arabic Jihadi nasheed he was playing in the pick-up. When the chorus came Anis joined in, almost shouting it: 'Ghuraba, Ghuraba, Ghuraba, Ghuraba…'

They kept singing along to the classic acapellas until they reached Reef Mohandiseen proper, a suburb of Aleppo. Khaled turned down the volume. Steel returned to both their faces.

'Don't worry,' Anis said in Arabic, 'keep on going.'

Soon they were driving uphill towards a set of large villas with their customary white and yellow stone which had been sourced from local quarries. These homes were for the big people; they had walls, verdant fig leaves that oozed their sticky sweetness and jasmine plants that infused the air. Anis pointed to one of the villas and Khaled pulled into the driveway and parked up by the gate.

Anis got out of the pick-up. Khaled watched him protectively, whilst at the same time trying to act as normal as possible. The villa had a number of pick-up trucks in camouflage colours with Russian Doshkas mounted on them. There was even a Russian truck with a Shilka gun parked up. But the actual courtyard-come-car-park which they wanted to gain entry to was gated and closed.

Anis confidently went up the steps of the villa that led to the main entrance. Khaled was about to follow him but

The Darkness Inside

Anis signalled for him to stay in the car. He removed his shoes and entered through the door without knocking. He walked into a large, spacious living room with tiled flooring and low mattresses laying alongside the wall.

'Shabaab,' he said, announcing his arrival.

Four bearded Syrians were sitting on the mattresses in their khakis and military fatigues with a pot of tea on the carpet and a bowl full of sunflower seeds. They looked bored but recognised him.

'Salaam alaikum, Ahlan! Welcome, Abu Hanzala' they said.

'Walaikum salaam, brothers.' Anis didn't recognise all of them, but one, Ahmed, a red-haired fighter, he recognised immediately. They had shared a few battles together. Ahmed got up, kissed Anis on both cheeks and hugged him.

'Where's Abu Abdul Rahman?' asked Anis, switching to Syrian dialect. He glanced furtively at each face in the room, measuring their level of allegiance to the commander.

'He's out,' replied Ahmed. 'Sit with us for a while and he'll be here soon.'

'When?'

'A few hours – give or take. Yalla! Sit with us!'

'No,' Anis said, looking at his watch, 'I don't have much time. I've just come to collect a few things.'

'Oh, okay. Not even tea?'

'Wallahi,' he replied, swearing an oath and touching his heart to signify his sincerity, 'I would love to but my time doesn't allow it. Can you open the gate for me?'

Ahmed called a short little Syrian from Deir Zour. 'Ali, could you open the gates?'

Ali got up immediately and shook Anis' hand. 'This

The Darkness Inside

brother,' said Ahmed to Ali, 'was with us in Taftanaz. How's Khaled?'

'Still alive, unfortunately. He's outside impatiently waiting.'

The men laughed at the morbid joke. Ali excused himself and went to get the keys to open the gate to the courtyard, leaving them.

'What else is going on? You look stressed,' Ahmed said.

'Oh you know, the usual,' said Anis, looking around the sparse room, his eye scanning every inch of it; a few Kalashnikovs rested against the walls and a hand gun in its holster hung on a coat hook. 'You know how things are. Anyway, enough about me, how's the family?'

'They're fine. Missus is pregnant.'

'Again?'

'Yes,' laughed Ahmed, 'again.'

'I can't keep up with you.'

'You English are stingy.'

'Correction, I'm Libyan.'

Ali came back into the salon. 'The gate is open.'

'Thank you,' said Anis.

Ali returned to the other fighters whilst Ahmed pointed the way to the courtyard. He asked Anis if there was anything else he needed. Anis touched his heart and told him to rejoin his friends and Ahmed did so.

'A married man,' said Anis cheekily as he left them, 'should take advantage of the freedom he is given.' It got a laugh from the men. He fetched his boots and then went into the courtyard at the back of the villa.

Khaled was already inside the courtyard with the pick-up. He was sweating on account of the midday sun, made worse by the white tiling on the floor which reflected the heat and

The Darkness Inside

brightness onto his eyes. He had a nervous, annoyed look about him and he had already turned the pick-up around so that it was facing the gate entrance.

Anis calmly went past the disused fountain at the centre of the courtyard and towards the storage depot at the back.

He opened up the depot and waved at Khaled to reverse the pick-up truck closer to him. Khaled reversed the car to the storage space and left the engine running, fixing his gaze on the gate. His friend opened up the back of the pick-up truck, brought out the boxes from the depot and loaded them hurriedly. The wooden grey and green boxes had Cyrillic script and that faint smell of munitions and weaponry. He was nearly done when Khaled banged the side of the pick-up truck to get his attention. Anis looked up, wiping the sweat off his brow.

In the far corner of the courtyard three men stood looking at them curiously, as if they were watching a strange spectacle. One of them, in the middle, had a long bushy beard and sunglasses. For a brief moment he took the shades off and looked at their activities a bit more intently, as if he was short-sighted. He rolled up his sleeves to show his powerful forearms, revealing his tattoos which Anis identified as London postcodes. The man signalled to the other men to go and take a closer look. Anis recognised them: Ilyas and Rami. Ilyas was an old-school rebel with two kids and Rami had only been sixteen when the whole thing kicked off in Syria.

'Salaam alaikum,' said the man with the shades. 'Abu Hanzala? Is that you?' He moved forward cautiously as he talked.

Khaled wiped the sweat off his brow and swallowed as

The Darkness Inside

if his throat had become instantly parched. Anis subtly checked that he still had his Beretta, his pride and joy, where it was meant to be at his back – concealed.

'Walaikum salaam brother Abbas,' Anis replied and switched to English: 'I didn't expect to see you here. I thought you were rolling with Radio?'

Abbas stopped. He didn't come too close, but stood there looking at the two men. 'What brings you here?'

'Oh,' Anis said casually, 'I've been sent to collect some of the ghanima.'

'By who?' Abbas asked suspiciously.

'Shura council.'

'Can't be, Radio would have told me about it.'

At this point Ilyas, who had some grasp of English, was mystified and asked Abbas almost comically, 'What? Which Radio told him? World Service? I don't understand. BBC? Shoo?'

'I just came,' said Anis, 'to collect what is Talha's fair share, that's all.'

'Talha doesn't have that authority; Radio is the Emir.'

'I didn't say he wasn't the Emir. I just came to collect what is Talha's right. He led the operation against them kafirs.'

'Well why doesn't he come and speak to Radio, man to man? I thought he was a big man?'

'Listen, don't worry about it. I got what I need. Let Talha and Radio deal with the issues at hand, okay? I'm just doing what I have been asked.'

'I'm afraid I can't let you do that, brother.'

'Why? If it goes in Radio's favour I'll return it.'

'It's trust. I don't betray people's trust. I'm responsible

The Darkness Inside

for those things there.' Abbas pointed to the depot.

'Then we have a problem,' Anis said coldly.

'Yes we do. As I see it, you are stealing.'

Rami and Ilyas wiped the sweat off their brows; they suddenly became aware of the scorching heat and the tension between the two men. Ahmed came out to see what was taking the men so long and found the two parties in what looked like a Mexican stand-off in a Western.

'Abu Hanzala! Abu Hanzala!' Ahmed shouted. 'Is everything okay?'

'Yes! Yes!' shouted Anis, but keeping his eyes on Abbas. 'All good.'

Ahmed wasn't satisfied with the answer and went in to call his friends, who emerged to watch the stand-off. 'What's going on guys?'

Khaled by now was soaking in sweat even though the air conditioning was on full blast. He was worried that there were too many of them.

Suddenly Anis pulled out his Beretta and pointed it at Ilyas, whose eyes widened.

'Hey, hey, what's going on?' he said, putting his arms up in the air. 'Calm down! Calm down, it's me, Abu Hanzala, it's me, Ilyas. Your friend, your brother! Are you mad?'

Abbas and Rami responded by pulling out their hand weapons and pointing them at Anis. Khaled, too, reached for his Kalashnikov and pointed it at the men. All that was needed was a bit of cowboy music from a spaghetti Western. The rest of the fighters with Ahmed were alarmed by the stand-off. They were shouting in the courtyard, urging everyone to put their weapons down.

'Calm down guys, calm down,' Ahmed shouted, 'we're

The Darkness Inside

brothers in Islam.'

'If I have wronged any one of you tell me,' added Ilyas, 'or we can go to a court to resolve this.'

Abbas stared at Anis. 'Shut up Ilyas!' he said, before turning to address Anis. 'Let's not go there, B. Let's not.'

By now Ahmed had decided where his loyalties lay and he ordered the men to get their weapons. The fighters went in to arm themselves.

'So,' Abbas asked, 'you are just gonna rob us like that?'

'I ain't robbing you,' replied Anis, 'just taking what belongs to him. I have been given someone's trust too, you know.'

'Do you really think you will make it out of here alive?'

Anis nodded calmly. 'Hundred percent. You don't want to start a war. More importantly, you don't want to orphan Ilyas' kids.'

'You're a sick bastard.'

'Everyone has some darkness inside,' replied Anis.

By now Ahmed's men had positioned themselves on the balcony overlooking the courtyard. Anis and Khaled felt the guns pointed at them. Abbas raised his hands; the men stood down and lowered their weapons.

'You're making a big mistake,' Abbas said.

'Mistakes make the man,' replied Anis. He moved slowly towards the car whilst still pointing his gun at Ilyas. He jumped into the back of the pick-up, still pointing his Beretta at Ilyas, whose hands were still raised in the air. Anis tapped the window of the pick-up truck and Khaled drove off. The rest of the men looked to Abbas for the order to shoot but he did not give it.

The Darkness Inside

Only when the car was out of the gates did Ilyas lower his hands and curse Anis.

Had it not been for the Shura council getting involved Radio and Talha would probably have gone to war.

17. Diabetes

Sid stood in the neat, carpeted hallway of an Edwardian apartment block, the sort of apartment block that ended with the word 'court'. He knocked on the door brazenly. Gardener hadn't opened the main entrance when he rang, so he called the flat upstairs and pretended to be a delivery man. He wasn't lying; the person he was delivering was himself. It always worked, as no one checked an Amazon delivery. He stood in front of Gardener's door banging away.

'Tom?! Tom!' he shouted.

The banging got a nice regal old lady to peer out from next door. She looked worried.

'Sorry about the noise,' he said to the woman. 'I'm just worried about my friend, have you seen him?'

'No,' she said cautiously, 'I'm afraid I haven't seen him for two days now.'

'Oh Lord!' he said, putting his hand melodramatically to his mouth. 'He's got diabetes!'

'Oh dear! Good God,' said the kindly woman, throwing caution to the wind. 'I wish I knew. Shall I call 999?'

'It's best if I do it; I know his condition. Let me see if I can get through to him. I am terribly sorry about the noise.'

'No, no, go ahead. Do what you have to do.'

The woman closed the door and gave Sid free rein to

The Darkness Inside

carry on doing what he was doing. Sid leaned close to Gardener's door.

'Tom! Tom!' he threatened. 'I'm going to bash through the door or call the ambulance if you don't open up.'

He paused for a moment. Gardener's footsteps could be heard approaching. The door opened and his friend stood there dishevelled, unshaven and in pyjamas with a ridiculous pair of pink rabbit slippers on his feet.

'Nice look,' Sid said, smiling. 'Nice.'

'Dickhead. I'm going to tell her I don't have diabetes. You are a manipulative bastard, you know that?'

'You taught me that.' Sid adopted Gardener's posh accent, seemingly quoting him. 'In this game one must adopt all manner of ghetto strategies to get what one wants.'

Gardener turned around and left the door open for Sid. Sid followed him into the living room where Gardener returned to playing his Xbox game, *Call of Duty*. The place was an absolute mess and smelled of pickled chillies, kebabs and garlic-flavoured farts.

'That bad, huh?' Sid said, watching his friend decimating the enemy.

'I didn't expect you,' Gardener said defensively. 'I'm fine.'

'Some of your mates called me, and then when Amanda called… and seeing that you're playing the Xbox. I know it's bad.'

Gardener paused his game. 'What did she say?'

'That you had gone your separate ways but remained loving friends or something like that.'

'Just that?'

'Just that. Reckon it was pretty dignified.'

'The little trollop.' Gardener's bitterness came through.

The Darkness Inside

'Five years gone, just like that. What the hell does that even mean? 'Loving friends' sounds like something Gwyneth Paltrow would say.'

'Come on, jump in the shower. Let's catch the game.'

Gardener didn't need much pushing. He got up and went into the bedroom. Sid attempted to tidy up the living room.

They went to a sports bar in Waterloo after a nice walk on the South Bank. Christmas spirit was in full swing down there but they didn't stop to admire the lights, the music and the sound of kids playing in the evening. Gardener had cheered up considerably with several glasses of mulled wine inside him. He was nice and warm and was now revealing all the secrets of each and every editor, sub-editor and reporter to his friend, who listened attentively. Sid never attended those kinds of parties alone. And those he did attend, he always went with Martha; she always knew what to do, what to say, when to laugh, when not to. It was as if she was the life jacket to that world and without her he was unable to stay afloat. When she excused herself to go to the bathroom, he stood there in the corner looking awkward and out of place, all the while wanting to know what it was that these people were talking about. Sid was always intrigued by the gossip, thinking that it would help him build up a profile of all the competition and their weaknesses. Just in case he needed it in the future. He took careful note of their coke habits, their penchant for youthful underwear models, male or female, their drunken antics, their fiddling of expenses and the sheer childishness of some reporters who had been so focused on their careers that they had sacrificed everything from getting married to having children or any other relationships that would

The Darkness Inside

make them into decent human beings, all for the sake of column inches or screen time. They may have reported on reality but they no longer knew what reality was. Food banks were a three-minute story. Move on. Syria was heartbreaking but it didn't stop one from asking whether instead of an old woman, one could find a young girl as a victim, perhaps? Yemen was awful, but could we find a girl less emaciated, because the reader might be put off by the horror. The world was filtered through the prism of these little gods; they could throw a tantrum at the waiter because their food was going cold and people would say nothing. If a child had done that, they would have been told off, disciplined, maybe even given a slap to teach them a lesson, but these correspondents and reporters were untouchable. They saw themselves as the representatives of the people, so they deserved to fly business class, they deserved to ask questions and have them answered, they deserved to snort coke due to the stress incurred by their jobs. They were the guardians of democracy, the fourth estate that held power to account. They never asked who held them to account and who questioned their assumptions. They walked around like they were intellectual giants when, actually, plenty of times the depth of their subject knowledge amounted to a Wikipedia article and a Google search; they were intellectually stunted.

The gossip continued in the sports bar even though Spurs were playing the Gunners. An attractive waitress wearing much too much make-up dropped off a bowl of Nachos. Gardener ordered another beer and Sid a Coke.

'Thanks,' said Sid after she had taken their order. 'I might

The Darkness Inside

need you later.'

'Sure,' said the waitress, not getting Sid's innuendo. 'Just shout.'

She went off whilst Sid's eye was still on her.

Gardener looked at him, disgusted.

'I don't get you, Sid.'

'What?'

'I really don't. Why are you even looking at her? You might as well go and pay for it.'

Sid looked both ways, as if he was searching for something or someone.

'Since when,' he said, 'did this country become Saudi fucking Arabia? And you the morality police? She's nice, what?' He shrugged his shoulders. 'And if I want to pay for it, what's it to you? It's clinical, no messy business. Speaking of which, you are free now.'

'Come on, mate,' said Gardener. 'You know I've always been looking for just that one, like me dad did. I thought Amanda was the one.'

'There's more man – plenty,' Sid replied, softening his tone. 'Don't worry. They are all the same. They keep you warm as long as you can manage their moods.'

'That's just it Sid, they aren't the same. You're lying to yourself.'

'No, I'm not.'

'Look mate, you can't tell me that this waitress is the same as Martha.'

'Yes.'

'Really, Sid?' Gardener stared at him like he was Sid's conscience. 'Really? You know Martha is someone you have kids with, someone you grow old with. When are you

The Darkness Inside

going to see that? Don't worry, you just go and play your sick little mind games with that little waitress and have your way with her. You'll probably break her heart and then she'll turn into you.'

'What's that then?' Sid sat up rigid, not expecting such a flurry of verbal punches.

'A miserable old cunt.'

That was a punch in the ribs. Sid paused for a moment. He wanted to lash out, hurt him back, maybe use Amanda's infidelity against him. He wanted to make him eat those words. Nay! He wanted to provoke the bitter tears of the jilted lover, trample on him like a great army does on the corpses it has butchered, and yet at the same time, deep within the recess of his heart, he knew Gardener was right. So the great rebel within stilled and he rested in quiet. Sid knew paying for it might be practical, something one had to do, to get the desire out. But he also knew the two were not the same, for if they were, why did he keep such things secret? If he went off home with the Nacho girl he might talk about it, but when he paid for it he mentioned it to no one, not even Gardener.

'I'm not so sure.' Sid proffered a defence. 'I remember when we were at graduation and she got so smashed I had to literally carry her home. That's when I realised we couldn't be together.'

'Man.' Gardener leaned forward, pointing his bottle of beer at him accusingly. 'That was years ago! People C-H-A-N-G-E. You're like Amanda, you remember everything. Trust her, for God's sake.'

'What? Like you did with Amanda?'

Sid regretted saying it before he even said it. He could

The Darkness Inside

see Gardener's wounded face. Well, at least they were quits. He couldn't let slights like that pass unanswered. People might take advantage.

'It hurts now,' Gardener replied, 'but I'll live through it. It doesn't mean I'm going to give up on finding that thing that my dad and mum had. I'm taking some time off to go and see them. Then, I swear to you, I am going to live.'

'Really?' Sid asked, sceptical.

'Yes,' Gardener replied forcefully. 'I might feel down now, but I'm not afraid of life, unlike you. I don't want to live such a threadbare life it's almost meaningless.'

18. BOX PARK

Even though it was chilly outside East Croydon station, Box Park was nice and warm on account of the outdoor gas heaters. Sid was already waiting inside looking at his phone. He was oblivious to the buzz inside this novel complex of eateries, tables and benches under one roof occupied by hip young Croydonites and Croydonistas. His cup of expensive coffee was untouched. He only spotted the flabby estate agent once he was through the entrance and down the steps and was practically standing a few metres away from him. Sid waved his hands to indicate where he was sitting.

Sami spotted him and made a face as if he had discovered something unpleasant; he walked towards him and sat down, businesslike. His face was morose.

Sid, wishing to avoid the chit-chat, went straight to the point: 'You thought about it?'

'What,' replied Sami, his voice tinged with sarcasm, 'do I even have a choice?'

'No, not really.' Sid's voice was uncaring.

'You know this can devastate my family?'

Sid yawned and nodded again; there was not even a hint that he gave a toss about the welfare of Sami's family. 'The truth,' he said, 'is more important than your family.'

'Since when did truth become important to yous lot?'

The Darkness Inside

Sami could taste the insincerity. He looked at Sid, trying to get a rise out of him, trying to stir his conscience into action. Sid didn't respond. 'Look,' said Sami, trying a different angle, 'don't tell him I told you but you need to go and see Abbas. Tell him it's about Anis.'

'What?' Sid looked at him suspiciously.

'Trust me, he's your man.'

'What and you're not? Anis wasn't blackmailing you?'

Sami looked nervous, as if acknowledging Sid's assertion. 'Just go to him. Don't tell him I told you though.'

'If you're playing me,' Sid said threateningly, 'I swear to God, I will write an article where you will be implicated in Anis' death. And you'll probably end up in jail.'

'But I didn't do it.'

'You can explain that to the feds while your business gets destroyed. I don't like doing this but you weren't straight with me. I hate liars.'

Sid got up and walked away, leaving Sami to ponder his words.

Reem was sitting in the empty hospital hallway. The whole place smelled of disinfectant and hospital. She held a polystyrene coffee cup in her hand – it hadn't been touched. She was holding it as if she was hoping to gain some sort of emotional warmth from it. But the coffee was turning grey, stale and cold, like a corpse. A cleaning lady went by with a trolley of cleaning products, then a doctor walked by and stopped briefly beside her. She immediately sat up straight and wiped her eyes, as if to retain something of her dignity.

The Darkness Inside

'I am sorry for your loss.'

'Thank you doctor,' she said, 'thanks for everything. I'm sure he's in a better place.'

'I'm sure he is,' said the consultant and left her alone. She put the cup aside and called her half-brother. She didn't know why she even bothered; he never replied. But she felt she had to, even if he pushed her away. She imagined it was what her father would have wanted. As usual the phone went to voicemail, so she texted him.

Where are you? she texted.

Surprisingly he responded, *Box Park – I'm in a meeting.*

He's gone to a better place. :(

I hope so. When?

This morning. Reem texted back.

Sorry to hear that.

He forgave you.

Forgave me for what? he wrote back.

Not being here to say good bye.

Good old Dad. Instead of asking me or my mum for forgiveness, he forgives me!

Reem responded but he was no longer engaging with her. She sensed that he would probably never engage with her again, so it was just her left now.

Martha was in the kitchen making some spaghetti. She had a profound desire to have spaghetti with raw garlic, fresh parsley, olive oil and parmesan cheese. The six o'clock news on Radio Four was on while she was preparing her dinner and she was looking forward to curling up later to watch something on Netflix. The phone rang as she was about to put the spaghetti in the boiling water but when she noticed

The Darkness Inside

it was Sid she did not put the pasta in, stopped everything and turned off the radio. She went into the living room and sat down on the sofa as if she was giving him all her attention.

'Hey?' she said softly.

'Hey,' he said, hesitating for a moment; there was a hint of uncertainty in his voice until it found its direction and purpose again. 'How's things? What you doing?'

'Making dinner – you want to come?'

'What you making?'

'Spaghetti with raw garlic, parsley and parmesan.'

'Sounds good. Who taught you to make that?'

'My father. So you want to come?'

'No, I can't today.'

'It tastes better than it sounds, believe me.'

'I believe you,' he said, his voice unusually gentle, 'and I would love to try it some other time.'

'Really?' Martha said, smiling from ear to ear.

'Yes, really, I mean it.'

'Well, that's a surprise,' she said, getting up from the sofa and pacing up and down. It felt like the excitement of a breaking news story.

'Yeah, well maybe I should have done it a long time ago.'

'Everything okay? How's your father?'

'Gone.'

'Sorry to hear that.' All she wanted to do at that moment was to hold him tenderly and not let him go. But she knew she would scare him. And he would run. So she didn't say anything.

'It's cool, it's in the past now.'

'When did he go?'

'Morning.'

'Do you need some time off?'

'No, he was dead to me the day he left my mum. This Saturday?'

'For sure.'

'Please, nothing fancy?'

'Okay.'

'Promise?'

'I promise,' she said.

19. Abbas

'Mr Rizwan?' Sid shouted. He had to shout; the noise of the electric saw was loud and high-pitched and the butcher was busy cutting through bone, tendon and flesh. Abbas finished with the saw and grabbed a knife to start trimming the meat when Sid shouted again: 'Mr Rizwan?'

This time the butcher heard him and turned around, brandishing his knife, looking at him for a moment and then calmly wiping the blade on his stained apron.

Abbas studied Sid's face for a moment. What a miserable bastard, he thought to himself. A beardless eunuch.

'Haven't I seen you before?' Abbas pretended.

'Have you got a moment?'

'Yeah, go ahead.'

'Can we talk in private?'

Abbas frowned and looked around the shop, which wasn't that busy; he tapped one of his colleagues to say he was going out for a moment. He put the knife down, rolled up his sleeves to display the postcodes tattooed on his forearm and walked past the Pakistani man on the till, saying in Urdu that he'd only be a moment.

Sid didn't realise what the butcher was doing until he was out of the shop. He promptly followed him as he strode along the main road until he came to the first side street. The butcher turned to Sid.

'Now, what do you want to talk about then?' It looked

The Darkness Inside

like he wanted to have a fight.

But Sid had steel inside him too. 'Well, I want to know about Anis' death and your involvement in it.'

'Wait,' said Abbas, knowing full well who he was, 'who are you?'

'I am an investigative journalist working for the *Loop*.'

'Never heard of you,' replied Abbas. 'Done?' He started to walk back towards the shop.

'Well just to let you know, soon your name will be mentioned alongside the death of Anis.'

Abbas stopped mid-stride and turned his broad frame to face Sid. 'I don't know anything about that, nothing.'

'I've been working on this story for months,' Sid said, adding a bluff: 'I have stood all of it up.'

'What do you mean, "stood up"? Talk English.'

'The work I've done has been cleared by the lawyers. It's good to go on the website. I just need to call the editors.'

Abbas stared into the ground as if he was torn. 'So when will it go online?'

'Whenever I tell the editor.' Sid sensed his advantage: 'Better get some good lawyers. Anyway, I don't have time for this. If you don't want to tell me it's not my problem.' Sid started to walk, knowing full well what would come next.

'Wait,' Abbas said, 'where you going?'

'Home.'

'Do you have a card? I just... I just need a few days. Gimme a few days.'

Sid gave him his card. 'You got one day.' He walked off knowing that Abbas was already in the bag.

Abbas told Sid to come to a twenty-four-hour Starbucks

on the Brighton Road. Sid met him late on a Friday night when the place was practically deserted. After all, who goes to a coffee shop on Friday night in Surrey? There were only two customers when Sid entered. They were taking a short break before continuing their journey. The barista, a girl who didn't want to be there, was busy on her phone while Abbas lurked in the shadows of the coffee shop drinking his chai latte. Her face expressed annoyance when Sid turned up and ordered a black Americano; that was the only drink he was confident she could make. She made the Americano and placed the takeaway cup on the counter. Sid took it and walked towards the corner where Abbas was waiting for him.

'A bit of a way out isn't it?' said Sid sitting down on the sofa opposite.

'Can't take too many chances. How'd you get here?'

'Uber.'

Abbas had his back to the wall, his arms stretched out as if he was in his lounge watching a movie. He looked relaxed, not at all nervous like he had been a few days ago. Sid got himself comfortable and stirred the sugar sachets into his coffee. Once the coffee was all ready Abbas leaned forward. 'Well,' he said, 'here I am. What do you want to know?'

'Do you mind if I record?' Sid said. He was surprised when Abbas consented.

'Go ahead. Got nothing to hide.'

Sid took out his recorder and started recording. 'So,' he began, 'you want to tell me why Anis was killed by Sami?'

Abbas laughed, 'Is that what you think?'

'Yes, I reckon Anis was blackmailing him. So Sami dealt

with it. He's a good actor.'

'See,' Abbas said, staring at Sid with disbelief, 'why no one believes the shit you lot write? And the lawyers cleared that?'

Sid nodded, knowing full well that the lawyers had not.

'Believe me,' Abbas said, disgusted, and took a swig of his tea as if he was washing away a bad taste in his mouth, 'Sami can barely fire an AK-47, let alone kill a man. I don't even think he killed anyone whilst he was there. You got this wrong.'

'So what's the truth then?'

'Anis got himself mixed up with one of those superstar Jihadis, one of dem man who think they're the dog's bollocks. Tall fucker called Talha. Anis had sided with him and was causing a lot of problems for all of us who were trying to do what we had been commanded to do.'

'What's that then?' Sid was surprised that a man with such a big beard could swear like a trooper.

'Fight in the way of God. This dickhead was treating us like cannon fodder. Good men died because of that prick…'

20. The Hospital

Days before the assault, Sami couldn't recall a time when the enemy had dropped so many barrel bombs in one area. He thought that the hospital in Owaija district, Aleppo, was the very incarnation of evil. That hospital had been perverted and used to garrison men, store munitions and extract confessions with pliers or with an unzipped fly if necessary. Due to its height the enemy directed artillery fire, MiGs, snipers and God knows what else against them. It was crucial to securing the East/West and North/South supply routes. It had to be taken out, whatever the cost.

The hospital was alienated from itself and resembled one of those miserable little council estates built during the seventies in Croydon. They looked like they were born from the same father. Both were located close to some brokeback area where the poorest citizens lived. If Owaija's people didn't have the tribe, family, honour and religion they would have carried on like those miserables in Croydon. They'd probably have ended up like Anis, standing on the roof somewhere billing up a spliff with some friends and looking down on passers-by, sending down some phlegm and watching it find its target. But these things were unheard of in Owaija.

Sami had learnt from an Algerian fighter who used to be a geography teacher with a penchant for weird facts that Gamal Abdel Nasser had built Kindi Hospital in the

The Darkness Inside

1950s when Syria had decided to unite with Egypt. It was built as a sign of the dictator's benevolence; to treat cancer patients with an iron fist. How and why the Algerian knew that the hospital had had two hundred and fifty doctors and six hundred and fifty nurses and was affiliated to the Aleppo Medical Hospital in its heyday was beyond Sami. Perhaps knowing random facts was a sign of intelligence.

Sami and Abbas trudged towards their car in Owaija when they came across some Jazrawis in fatigues, black woollen hats and fingerless gloves. They were climbing over the rubble where a barrel bomb had fallen only an hour ago and they were optimistically searching to see if there were any survivors. Abbas peered at Sami. 'No one's alive akhi,' he said and kept on walking. 'No one survives a three-storey house falling on top of them. If you can't put a plaster on a crushed face better treat them like an injured dog and take them out of their misery.'

'But shouldn't we just check?' said Sami. 'You know just in case?' He pulled at his long, magnificent beard; he did that whenever he was agitated. It was a habit from his school days. His lack of a chin meant his classmates nicknamed him 'chinless'. For five years he pulled at the chin as if he was willing it to grow, but no chin of note ever came, just spots. Sami's beard resolved all of that but the habit never left him. The long beard jutted out and gave the impression that he did have a chin. It was aesthetically pleasing.

'They are gone,' Abbas reiterated and he went on his way. Sami kept on staring at the efforts of the Saudis and reluctantly followed. His eyes still scoured for life beneath the rubble. But the Saudis hadn't given up; they were still removing rubble, peering through the twisted steel and concrete. In the distance he could hear the sirens and cars moving towards the site.

Sami's eyes fell on an old woman with tattoos on her face, wrapped in a shawl, wearing thick socks and sandals and sitting on the apex of the rubble clutching her black plastic bag with some vegetables and what looked like warm bread. Her hand was holding on to a tiny little finger that was either going blue from the winter cold or rigor mortis. She was talking gibberish, sometimes reciting the Quran, sometimes wailing, sometimes screaming: 'All I wanted was bread! Just that! That is all I wanted for my family and then you come along and Bashar takes three generations of my family! May God curse you!' In some ways she was right; the barrels were falling because the enemy knew something was afoot with the hospital.

That morning Sami had been cracking up as he overheard the radio conversations passing between the enemy. One of the soldiers was saying: 'I can see beards, I can see beards... I can see men wearing thobes... I can see men wearing thobes... over,' and the other guy was replying: 'They are al-Qaeda you idiot... they are al-Qaeda you idiot... what do you expect?!'

They left the Saudi Jazrawis for Sheikh Najjar and sat at a busy shawarma stall, heating themselves on a diesel stove, drinking warm tea and waiting for their order. Winter in Aleppo was colder than in London.

'I don't know how long this operation will last,' Sami said, rubbing his hands over the diesel heater. They had tried to take the hospital eleven times already and the enemy had become even more entrenched.

The Darkness Inside

'Eleven times!' said Abbas, exasperated. 'Why didn't they try to take the place with an Istishadi?'

'They did.'

'They did?' said Abbas, scratching his eye. 'What happened?'

'He blew himself up a bit too early,' Sami said, grinning.

'May God accept him,' said Abbas, laughing irreverently and shaking his head. 'Some of these guys are a bit too eager.'

No one could figure out how the enemy had held out for so long without the Liwa Tawheed rebel battalion knowing about it. The general consensus was that Liwa Tawheed boys must have been taking bribes and, in return, supplying the enemy with food, water, prostitutes and everything else they needed.

About three hundred rebels including Sami and Abbas were going to carry out the attack on the hospital. They had trickled in from all over the countryside during the build-up consisting of artillery fire. Radio was officially in charge of the operation – that was what the council had decided. Other boys were arriving from Homs, Hama and Lattakia. The Nusra boys and the North African battalion, Sham al-Islami, seemed to be the most organised and everyone apparently knew who was meant to do what, down to who made the tea. The Sham al-Islami boys reminded Sami of a football team. They were incredibly relaxed, jumping up and down, loosening up as if it was some sort of pre-match routine. It seemed as if they would just dodge and weave between the bullets like Keanu Reeves in *The Matrix*. The most disorganised battalion was Liwa Tawheed, consisting mostly of Syrians. Sami had been asked to be present for

The Darkness Inside

the photo opportunity and filming of the beginning of the operation. He was meant to film the declaration, full of bombast, rhetorical flourishes and so forth.

In the evening Sami turned up at the derelict little factory warehouse with a flimsy tripod and a small handheld camera. There, all the men were sitting in a large carpeted room with a furious diesel stove burning and teapots boiling. He yawned and rubbed his eyes, wanting to get this over and done with quickly. But he knew looking at the twenty or so men sitting and leaning against the flaky wall whispering to each other that this would be a long night.

'Ahlan! Sami! Shoo akhbarak?' said a stocky, powerfully built man, giving Sami a warm smile. Radio bade Sami to sit down. Abbas, who was pouring everyone some tea, handed Sami a small cup of red tea. Although there were twenty men in the room, only three or four were talking. And these men sat over a large map of the area.

'What's wrong with calling the attack Operation Tawheed?' said Saleh, a prematurely balding Syrian and leader of Liwa Tawheed. 'It tells the whole world what we all stand for and that we are all united in God's oneness.'

'Well,' said one, 'because it implies that the operation's participants all belong to Liwa Tawheed and that isn't right.'

'How about Operation Nusra?' said Radio, giving Abu Shaheed, the leader of Nusra, a sly glance as if he was soliciting his support. 'We all want victory.' He was right, of course; the word 'Nusra' means victory in Arabic.

'Yes,' replied Saleh, finishing his cup of tea and placing it down, 'but then we have the same problem; people will

The Darkness Inside

think that only Nusra did this. Unity is a higher ideal than merely victory.'

He had a point.

'Yes, yes you are right,' said Radio diplomatically, 'it is. But I think most people won't understand the concept; you know that the unity of God is hard to grasp. Think about it, what does Tawheed mean to the outside world who are still grappling with the trinity and all such polytheisms? All men understand "victory" – it has a more universal acceptance.'

'What's so hard about it?' said Talha, interrupting. The Iraqi said it with the politeness of a supermarket assistant working on New Year's Eve. 'Ask a farmer who's been shovelling shit all his life if he gets unity and he'll get it. Ask him about the oneness of God and you'll hear the testimony of faith immediately. What's so hard about it? I'm not here to pander to how the rest of the world sees us. I care about Muslims; they understand the oneness of God instinctively.'

It got a few titters from the others, especially from Anis, who had been lurking at the back watching the group. He seemed to be making his laugh more pronounced than the others were. So much so that Radio turned his head towards him to see who it was.

'Hmm,' said Radio philosophically, 'you know unity of God can be divided into three parts. No, no,' he said, dismissing the name with his hand, 'I just don't like it; it doesn't have a nice ring to it.'

'You don't like the word that talks about the unity of God?' said Talha in a tone which accused him of committing near blasphemy.

The Darkness Inside

One of the Emirs, Abu Ahmed, clapped his hands.

'Brothers,' he said with an impatient tone, 'can we focus?' He pointed to the map sprawled across the floor. 'We still haven't properly planned this operation; let us not get hung up over a name.'

'Right! That's decided then,' said Talha, clapping his hands as if it was final. 'Let's plan this Operation Tawheed of ours, yalla Radio.'

'Yes,' Radio said, glaring at Talha, 'I have a plan for Operation Nusra.'

'Right,' said Abu Ahmed, 'stop this childishness! We'll call it Operation One Heart, okay?!' He turned to Saleh, who considered it carefully whilst studying the face of Radio in case it could be perceived as a victory by him. Radio looked at Saleh and Talha to see whether it could be seen as a victory for the two others.

'Well? Can we move on?' pressed Abu Ahmed.

All the men nodded and focused their attention on the map. As they began, Talha added, 'Well, you know I was going to suggest it because one heart epitomises the oneness of God doesn't it?'

Radio let it go. But he didn't forget. As they discussed the plan there was further sniping between the Emirs. Sami excused himself and left. There would be no filming that night.

Eventually the Emirs thrashed out the plan. Saleh's Liwa Tawheed would bring three tanks, and Abu Shaheed's Nusra would bring five Doshkas as well as two tanks. Abu Ahmed would lead the attack after the six PKC points had been taken out by the Liwa Tawheed fighters. He would

The Darkness Inside

then secure the entrance to the hospital and the rest of them would follow. That, at least, was the plan.

On the eve of the attack the regime gave the rebels the biggest barrage of barrel bombs that Sami had ever experienced. They knew the attack was coming. He couldn't get a wink of sleep. There were moments when he was sitting inside a room of an abandoned factory on the south side of the hospital when he was seized by this immense primeval urge to curl up and return to his mother's womb, just waiting for the barrel to fall and deliver his end. The reinforced concrete roof would not bear the weight of the barrels. As they tumbled in the air, they made that mad BOOOW WOOOW WOOOW WOOOW WOOOW noise that seized him with terror. They landed so close that he made his peace with his Lord plenty of times during the night and just closed his eyes. And all the time he heard the desperate yells urging the gunners to get the barrels or the chopper or both. And then, when the barrels missed the intended target, Sami prayed for the clouds to come in and cover the days and nights with fog and darkness so no more barrels would fall. The only person who didn't seem to feel that way was Radio – it wasn't that he was showing off; he must have been born that way. Even the bravest fighters curled up like babies when they felt the noise of a barrel come that close. But Radio just kept on drinking his tea and refilling the empty or near-empty glasses, quietly supplicating to himself. It gave the men around him a degree of calmness.

The attack didn't start on time the next day. Usually operations started after the Fajr prayer, at dawn, so the rebels could solicit the blessings of God on the operation.

The Darkness Inside

But it was as if the whole operation had overslept on account of the barrel bombs falling the night before. When the men and materiel eventually mustered in the cold grey light of day, they came up short. Saleh's men, instead of bringing three tanks, brought only one. The Nusra boys brought one Doshka instead of the five they had promised. The men posted to ambush the retreating enemy's escape route were still having breakfast. The Liwa Tawheed boys failed to take out the six points that would resist Abu Ahmed's initial assault. In fact, the PKC points – the most crucial gunnery posts which had to be taken out, unless one wanted to die for the hell of it – were not taken. The hospital building took hits for sure and the noise was tremendous but the scarring was superficial and looked worse than it really was.

Abbas and his men had mustered in one of the buildings. They had punched a hole through one of the walls for them to constantly monitor what was going on using binoculars and Abbas' radio. He prepared his fourteen men, including Sami, making sure their guns were all in working order. By eleven o'clock the PKC guns had still not been taken out.

Abbas cursed quietly. 'Why,' he asked impatiently on the walkie talkie, 'haven't the PKC guns been taken out? Why haven't the PKC guns been taken out? Over.'

He did not receive a positive reply.

Instead Talha ordered him and his men to move in and attack the hospital entrance. Sami moved forward, waiting to obey the order, but Abbas halted him. 'Wait here. Wait.'

Despite Talha's order being repeated constantly, Abbas did not move from his place. When Abbas didn't reply, Talha's voice could be heard on the radio asking him why he hadn't started his attack. But Abbas ignored the order.

The Darkness Inside

'What's going on?' Sami asked. 'Why aren't we attacking? Why are we still sitting around here?'

'Brothers,' said Abbas, 'we are not going in unless those points are taken out because a hundred metres away is certain death – it will be for nothing. Let's retreat. Whoever hasn't slept could get some sleep. This isn't the way to fight a war.'

One of the men, a young Egyptian perhaps no more than nineteen, pleaded, 'Come on, let's just check if there's a way we can attack.'

Sami concurred. 'We should at least try, shouldn't we?'

'Why are you guys so eager to die for nothing?' Abbas said, shaking his head.

'Then at least tell the Emir!' Sami said, annoyed at the walkie talkie going off every few minutes. The voice was irate and angry.

'You are right,' said Abbas, and he responded to the Emir bluntly. 'Talha,' he said, 'I am not taking my boys on a suicide mission until the points have been taken out. Until then we are going to get some sleep. Over.'

A blur of swear words followed. But Abbas did not respond. The conversation was over. They returned to Sheikh Najjar to recuperate and, in a house alongside other men, to drink tea and wait, listening to the snipers conducting their own grudge match with their opposing counterparts. They heard their exchanges in the distance, but apart from the odd fazdika and the mortars sounding off it was a relatively quiet day for Abbas and his men.

In the evening, a Mitsubishi Pajero pulled up to the quarters. The door was slammed angrily shut. Talha strode in like he owned the place, and as soon as he entered he started to bark at Abbas.

'Why didn't you carry out the attack?' The huge Iraqi looked grim in his black hat and military camouflage.

'You are not the Emir,' Abbas replied firmly. He didn't fear this looming figure – Radio was the overall Emir.

Talha shouted, 'I am the operational Emir. What I say goes!'

'If you want to attack you can do it but I am following the plan that was outlined by our Emir,' Abbas said nonchalantly, putting emphasis on 'our', meaning Radio. 'I'm not taking good fighting men to their deaths just because you say so.'

'Didn't you come here for Jihad?'

'So?!' Abbas replied. 'I am not going to throw fourteen lives away on a suicide mission. You may not have any but they have mothers and fathers.'

It was a nice little snipe at Talha's pedigree and the Iraqi felt it for sure.

'I don't care how many lives get lost,' said the Iraqi angrily, pushing his weight around. He looked like he was on a Baghdad street arguing with a taxi driver. 'They will get martyrdom and they will get their reward!'

Abbas was unmoved by his aggressive gestures. He kept on stroking his beard which infuriated Talha even more.

'You can get martyred,' replied Abbas. 'I pray that you are soon.' There was laughter from his boys. 'I am not taking my boys until those points are taken out. Do you understand?'

Talha started to swear, curse and froth at the mouth.

'You finished?' Abbas asked. He turned to his men and told them to get up and follow him out to another location away from Talha, who continued to glare at him.

The Darkness Inside

After they had found a new location to spend the night, Abbas made sure that all the men had eaten and were nice and warm. He also called Radio and notified him of Talha's behaviour. It resulted in Talha receiving numerous phone calls from seniors reprimanding him. Radio and several members of the Shura council went down to Talha's headquarters. No niceties or pleasantries were exchanged as they studied the ordnance map of the district.

'I've noticed a weak point in one of the entrances,' Radio said, pointing to the map. 'You will attack it when the guards change their shift.'

Talha showed Radio the weaknesses of his plan but Radio, as if to reassert his authority, replied, 'The risk is acceptable. It's the best idea we have had so far.'

'Very well,' said Talha; he couldn't argue with him in front of the executive Shura council.

'It will only work,' said Radio, 'if your men give our boys covering fire as a distraction. I will ask Abbas to lead the attack personally.'

'Can you do it now? I am having trouble getting through to him.'

Radio called Abbas and gave him the instructions.

Abbas and his men awoke to the shrill, high-pitched sound of an enemy fazdika. It kept the unit on edge for the whole day. At least with tank shells or mortars there was a warning. The first bang was the launch of the projectile and then the elegant whirr followed; this allowed one to gauge where it would fall. If you heard the explosion that meant you were alive; not so with fazdikas. There were no signs of tiredness in the men. The shrill noise of the fazdika had scared tiredness and slumber away. All that was left was a bitter anger towards

The Darkness Inside

the hospital that stood there like a stubborn wart. It didn't matter what you threw at it; it just wouldn't cave in and brazenly kept on returning fire.

Abbas had been thinking about the operation all night – it wasn't a bad idea. By afternoon, he had ordered several of his men to bring the large guns as close as possible to the entry point, drawing heavy fire from the guards. Then three fighters from the Sham al-Islami battalion did the usual pre-match warm up, checking their guns and loosening up their limbs, and off they went towards the hospital. The three men headed towards a big rock under heavy enemy fire as if it was a stroll in the park. Once they reached the block of concrete they rested whilst the bullets bounced off it. The first fighter, a Moroccan, just casually stuck his head out to take a look. He signalled and moved forward. Abbas could hear the TAK TAK TAK and he prayed that they would make it to the next rock. And they did. Abbas shook his head in disbelief. 'Nutters!' he said to himself. But seventeen meters on and the Moroccans were cut down by enemy fire. Only the first one was alive, but he was injured; he screamed in agony and held his stomach in pain. The enemy left him there waiting for someone to try to retrieve him; he was the worm – the bait. That is when Abbas remembered.

'Where is the distracting covering fire?' Abbas shouted down the wireless whilst watching everything on his small binoculars. 'Talha! Where is it?! Are you trying to get us killed?' There was no response. Abbas used so many expletives about Talha's family that even as the Moroccan fighter was bleeding to death some of the men couldn't help but laugh.

The Darkness Inside

A young Egyptian was killed as he took the bait to retrieve him. He went against Abbas' orders. Abbas and his men stayed with them till their last even though they did not venture out to retrieve their bodies.

21. The Operation

Following the failure of the operation, Talha was now in charge. He had convinced the leadership that Radio was no longer up for the job. 'He cannot deliver victory,' he had said. 'The men are complaining; they are unwilling to follow him.'

And so Radio received the phone call from the Shura council in the evening. Abbas had been there when Radio had taken the phone call.

'You are to follow through with brother Talha's plan and make every effort to help him realise it.'

'Certainly,' Radio replied.

Abbas felt for his friend, as he now had to watch all the preening and swagger that emanated from the Iraqi as he outlined his attack. In a similar meeting to the countless other ones they had attended, the new Emir had presented his plan. It was very simple. A truck would be filled with explosives, tons of them. It would then be driven towards the hospital entrance and be exploded remotely. It would take a few days to prepare before it could be dispatched. Abbas was assigned the task of preparing the truck; it was as if Talha wanted to humiliate him. After all, that sort of job was done by a grunt, not by someone of Abbas' calibre. But Abbas carried it out without complaint and sometimes when he did the work he even had an enigmatic smile on his face.

The Darkness Inside

On the day of the truck's departure, Abbas and Sami watched it through their binoculars as it snaked its way towards its target. Sami was praying to God, urging it to reach the hospital. It was already drawing heavy fire from the enemy, but then it suddenly stopped. It was as if the hospital had thrown a spell on it, for it couldn't move. A truck filled with two tons of explosives was just sitting there in between a few trees and wouldn't start or respond. The driver tried to get it going but once it looked like the truck had given up, he made his way back.

Abbas was smiling as he heard Talha over the walkie talkie screaming to find out why it had not reached its target.

'Abbas! Abbas!' he said frantically, 'Why is it not moving? Did you check the truck when you organised it?'

'Yes, I'm sure,' Abbas replied, 'I'm sure everything was in working order. Maybe it was sabotage or the cold weather.'

Talha started to mouth off. Abbas just turned off the walkie talkie.

'He's going to have to explain,' said Abbas, turning to Sami, 'how he's wasted two tons of explosives tonight.' There was a hint of glee in his voice. 'Pretty costly that.'

'Look!' said Sami, pointing to two figures approaching the truck, 'I can't believe it! Legends.'

Abbas' lips tightened and he raised the binoculars again. He had to admit that was insanely brave. 'Radio would never send his boys to do that.'

The two figures, Anis and Khaled, went up to the truck trying to start it up manually, but it simply refused to budge like a stubborn metal donkey. The enemy realised what was going on, and why the rebels were trying to get the reinforced truck going. They started to send RPGs in their direction whilst the men worked frantically to get it to start. Sami couldn't look, as he was expecting them to be smoked into oblivion at any moment. In the end the men gave up and the two tons of explosives went up in a loud mushroom cloud when an RPG finally struck them full on.

The failure infuriated Talha no end. Someone – he did not know who, although he had his suspicions – started a petition against him that claimed that he was being too careless with their lives. There was nothing he could do to stop the petition from reaching the leadership, but before that got submitted he was going to ensure that his plan was implemented. He had learnt early on that there was nothing that could mitigate discontent except success. He supervised the job personally; he made sure to reinforce the two trucks with armour and loaded them with two tons of explosives himself. There was to be no sabotage. He ensured that the men gave the trucks heavy cover when they began their run to the sound of 'God is most great'. His diligence paid off when two great mushroom clouds emerged from the hospital, shattering every window on the industrial estate that the rebels were quartered in. After the two explosions the barrel bombs stopped, mortars were no longer launched and the MiGs did not come – they had given up. Above all, no returning fire was coming from the hospital. The game was up. Talha's men all but strolled into the building, receiving no fire whatsoever. Talha had men waiting to ambush the enemy, and one or two enemy soldiers were caught escaping.

The resistance in the enemy had been bombed out of them. There were seventy or so soldiers inside; they were

The Darkness Inside

severely dazed and some were badly injured. Some had had their brains splattered on the floor as if the sheer force of the blast had taken their heads away. In one room they found men in different states of injury: shrapnel, crush and bullet wounds. Some of them had even had their faces blown apart; others were bleeding out slowly. There seemed to be no difference between the dead and the injured and the smell, a combination of blood, shit and sweat made the place unbearable. None of the men received any treatment to end their groaning, only insults, kicks and curses.

Talha and his men went through the building and found plenty of ammunitions, arms and food, which Talha immediately sequestered. They must have bribed some of the rebels to get this through.

In other rooms there were letters, phones, messages to loved ones, to brothers, sisters, nephews, mothers and fathers. They found bottles of alcohol but they also found prayer mats.

When Sami arrived he found that the ragged and dazed prisoners had already been dragged out of the hospital. Anis, Khaled and Talha's other men had placed them in various craters that had been created by fallen barrel bombs and artillery. Judging by the growth of the prisoner's beards they had stayed in the building a long time and were never relieved. Sami could have mistaken them for one of their own boys. Most of them seemed like poor country boys. He counted about thirty men already in the craters; there were other prisoners coming out and being corralled past the six-foot Iraqi commander in his black woolly hat. He laughed grimly and slapped their hams

The Darkness Inside

and backs as if they were cattle going to the slaughter. He was still taunting them cruelly when an armoured pick-up truck arrived at the site and parked up.

Radio and Abbas emerged out of the car and walked up to Talha. They all shook hands. Congratulations were exchanged and praise was given to God. It seemed to Sami that they were trying to outdo each other in the praise of God. Radio praised God to remind Talha that he had nothing to do with the victory. And Talha praised God to let Radio know that victory was granted to him because he was the chosen one, the most pious and forgiving.

'I thought you would let us know when you were storming the building.'

'Oh, I'm sorry,' said the Iraqi apologetically. His self-satisfied politeness had returned. 'I most certainly was going to, but things were moving so quick and my walkie talkie was playing up – technical difficulties.'

'Really? How is it working now?'

'Perfectly.'

'Couldn't you have sent someone to tell us?'

'I didn't want to risk our men; the snipers were ferocious. There's a petition,' he said, looking at Abbas meaningfully, 'claiming that I am careless with my men's lives. I didn't want to give that impression.'

'I see,' said Radio, staring at Talha.

'No matter,' said Talha. 'Here, have the honour.' He gave Radio one of his daggers, inviting him to murder: 'Choose any one you like.' It was as if the commander was hosting a banquet in honour of the gods. The prisoners were mere yearlings or heifers chosen for the sacrifice.

'Keep it, I have my own.' He walked up to one poor soul,

The Darkness Inside

took out his Turkish hand gun and pointed it at the man, who seemed completely indifferent and just stared straight ahead. Radio blew his brains out. The act was clinical. The condemned, who had once been known for being a generous host, who loved to drink iced mulberry juice in the Old City after Friday prayer, fell to the ground and dark blood poured out. Radio stepped aside, not even staring at the man he had just killed. The nameless man left the world with his only legacy being a question for his mother, who sought to answer it to the end of her days: how, where and more importantly why did her beloved child die?

'God is most great,' shouted Talha as if this was the beginning of some macabre ritual. His men started the slaughter. 'Who is filming this?' he shouted. One of his men waved the camera at him. 'Good! Good!'

Khaled slit the throat of a young-looking soldier who begged him to have mercy, but it was too late. He struggled a bit and had to put his boot on the soldier's body, as he severed his head. His friend, Anis, was far more creative. He didn't cut his victim; he brought out a cord and slipped it over him like one might throw a scarf around a loved one on a cold winter's day. As the blindfolded man realised what was happening he began to struggle like a fish on land. His arms tied behind his back, he arched and kicked out with his legs. But Anis held him fast, putting his knee on his spine like he had done this act a hundred times. He tightened the garrotte slowly and steadily. There was almost a tenderness to his garrotting. Soon the body went limp and a foul stink emanated from the corpse; as he gave up the ghost his bowels gave way and voided whatever was inside. Anis let him lie and he moved on to the second man. He

The Darkness Inside

unsheathed a knife he had attached to his belt and stabbed him in the heart casually. The man did not even know what had entered him until it was too late.

Talha turned to Abbas, who was standing watching the scene, and waved at him, inviting him to take part. Abbas drew out his own dagger and found an exhausted man on his knees, not looking at the slaughter, waiting for his turn obediently. This was war, his body seemed to say. Sami thought he was the bravest man he had ever seen. Abbas walked up to him from behind and effortlessly, smoothly, dare one say elegantly, slit his throat. There was no noise, just a wheezing from the man; Abbas put him gently down to the ground as if he was a goat or a dumb animal and let him bleed out. He turned to Sami and offered his knife. Sami shook his head and turned to walk away.

'Where are you going?' Abbas shouted.

'The battle is finished, the fun is over.' Sami waved and left.

22. Abbas

'See, my mum,' said Abbas, keeping an eye on the bored barista in case she was listening, 'always used to tell me about an old Pakistani proverb: the thief always has the word "police" ringing in his heart. I guess Anis was like that.'

'I don't get it,' Sid said, jotting the proverb down.

'You never heard of that proverb? What sort of Pakistani are you?'

'Mate.' Sid wasn't intimidated by the accusation. 'I've never been to Pakistan. So explain what you mean.'

'Well Anis even blamed us for what happened to him in Atmah during Ramadan.'

'Atmah? The refugee camp?'

Abbas nodded.

'So what happened?'

'I'm not fully sure; Sami could probably tell you the story better. Anis and Khaled and some European fighters from Sweden and France and other places were sitting down in some house in Atmah about to break their fast. They were sitting on the floor when some pick-up trucks with mounted Doshkas pulled up very quietly and just opened fire on the house. Sami told me they made huge holes in the walls. Anis was badly wounded and Khaled died in his arms. The guy went mental after that; Sami said he cried for days after Khaled was killed. To be honest with you, if it were me I'd consider myself lucky because the gunman was about to finish him off too. Anis was in the living room about to get sprayed when the trucks received returning fire and they ran. God's decree!'

'So where were you?' Sid said, abruptly interrogating his version of events.

'I wasn't there, if that's what you mean,' Abbas replied defensively. He shifted his eyes to the girl again to check whether she was close to them.

'Is there anyone who can confirm where you were?'

'Sami, he was there.'

'Someone apart from him?'

Abbas shook his head. 'No.'

'So, where were you then?'

'I'd been invited for Iftar in Hraytan with Radio.'

'So who do you think did it?'

'Kurds of course, who else?' replied Abbas as if the answer was self-evident.

'Why?'

'It's the sort of shit they do, innit? I mean, who would do that? On the first day of Ramadan when everyone's breaking their fast? Come on. Even Talha wouldn't do that. You have to be one of them Godless PKK bastards to do that. They even put their daughters on the frontline, they blow up mosques, why not this shit?'

'So what happened next?'

'There was a massive kick off,' said Abbas. 'Instead of going after the Kurds, which Radio would have done, Talha blamed Radio and accused us of being behind it. Can you believe it? He always had it in for him and was looking for any excuse to kick off. And things would have kicked off. All the Europeans surrounded Radio's house while all Radio

The Darkness Inside

was thinking about was getting Anis over to Turkey for treatment. Remember this is the guy who had stolen from him! Anis went back to the UK with metals and screws in his body, pissed at the whole world and us. He dedicated his whole life to destroying us when we had done him nothing but good. After that, only me and Sami were left, so we became really tight. What happened in Syria happened in Syria. I'm not sure Anis understood that.'

Abbas took the last sip from his cup and looked at his watch.

But Sid wasn't quite finished; he expected more. It was as though the tale was incomplete.

'Is that it?'

'Yes,' Abbas said, perplexed. 'You tell me. I thought you knew who had the smoking gun? I've given you what I know. What else do you want from me?'

'So Anis wasn't blackmailing Sami?'

'He might have been - Anis was angry at the whole world, especially after him being disabled and stuff. All that pain, while we are in London without a scratch, living life.'

'So Anis lashed out?'

'Exactly. Like I said, most of us were like: what happened in Syria stays in Syria. But not Anis; he was cut up about it. And he was going to take everyone down with him.'

'So that's why Sami killed him?'

'Nah! No! Is that the quality of your detective work?!' Abbas said, disappointed. 'After all I've told you? Sami could never do that. Look, Sami was in a war, he tried his best to kill the enemy, and however much he tried he couldn't. He's useless – why do you think we got him to do the filming? He was scared shitless. He's a teddy bear – a big friendly giant.'

The Darkness Inside

'So who?'

'You know, sometimes God intervenes. It was just a coincidence that he was killed. May God have mercy on the brother. Listen, I need to go to work tomorrow. If I were you I'd let this one go. Trust me. That's what got Anis killed. He just couldn't let the past go.'

'I find letting go of the past hard.'

'So you won't let it go?'

'Nope,' replied Sid, 'I need to know what happened.'

'Suit yourself,' Abbas said, getting up with a sigh. 'I can see you're one of those obsessive types.'

Sid nodded. Abbas put on his hood and his leather gloves and watched the journalist trying to process his story. He looked weary and tired.

'Come,' said Abbas, 'let me give you a lift back.'

'I think I'll get an Uber.'

'Fine, at least let me drop you to Croydon. There's not many Ubers out here in the sticks. You'll have to wait a long time before one of those bastards will pick up a job from around here.'

'Okay then.' Sid got up, buttoned up his jacket and put his phone in his pocket whilst Abbas went to use the bathroom.

Abbas came out of the cafe and found Sid smoking a cigarette outside.

'You should stop smoking' said Abbas, 'it can kill you.'

'Everything can kill you,' replied Sid; his breath was steaming, full of vitality despite the freezing cold.

'True.' Abbas, pointed to the dark side of the road. 'I'm parked over there,' he said and started to walk in the direction of his car. Sid followed, still smoking.

Both men turned a sharp bend on the road, which went

The Darkness Inside

up the hill. It looked like a country lane with a ditch on the side.

'Nearly there,' said Abbas as he crossed the road. Sid followed; he was in the middle of the road when the bright white LED lights of a black Range Rover turned on and blinded him. He was caught in its full beam as it piled into him hard, its nudge bars crushing bone and flesh, throwing him down to the ground. His head landed awkwardly on the road; he felt cold tarmac as he lay on the ground groaning, semi-conscious. A hazy vision of Martha appeared in his mind's eye as he felt the car reverse over him; Martha kissed him as the car drove over him yet again, cracking his ribs, the bones piercing his lungs. He heard the Range Rover drive perhaps twenty yards further on and stop on the side. He heard Abbas' footsteps approach.

'Bro? Bro? You alright?'

He smelt Abbas' beard, perfumed with musk, coming close to his face to check if he was breathing. A liquid was building up somewhere within him. He couldn't scream. Then he felt leather gloves over his mouth and nose. It all went dark.

Sid wasn't breathing anymore. Abbas checked the journalist's pocket, took his phone and bag. He calmly dragged the man into a ditch and flung him in there like he was a sack of rice in a warehouse or a lamb carcass. The body fell into the brambles with a rustle. Satisfied with his handiwork, he walked towards the waiting Range Rover. It still had the engine running. He got into the car and the driver, a slightly older man, powerfully built with strands of ash grey in his beard, looked at him; he had eyes that laughed a lot, perhaps when he played with his children

The Darkness Inside

after picking them up from school, perhaps with his friends.

'Done?'

'Yes,' Abbas nodded.

'You sure?'

'No one survives that, trust me.'

'Okay, put your seat belt on habibi, it's the law,' he said with a hint of irony.

'Khalas,' said Abbas, 'go, this isn't the time for jokes.'

'Sometimes, akhi,' said Radio, looking in the rear view mirror pityingly as he pulled off, 'you need to let dead dogs lie. That's what people don't get. There's a price you have to pay to come home.'

'As they say,' said Abbas, 'the cat doesn't chase the mouse for the sake of God.'

'Oi! That's my line.'

Martha had plenty of time to choose the dress she was going to wear for their dinner. She was off for the weekend, which meant that in the morning she could really spend time thinking about the pros and cons of each dress. She knew it was silly; he wasn't the sort of person who noticed. She tried to tell herself that it was just a dinner. Just a dinner. But she knew him – this time he appeared more serious than ever. She just sensed it in his voice.

She would never have done that for any other person: trying out various combinations of clothes just to appear effortlessly elegant and casual, if that was even a thing.

She messaged him late morning just confirming that they were still on for dinner. She thought about the wording of the message more than some of her journalists did when they strung sentences together. She

The Darkness Inside

didn't receive an immediate reply – that was normal. She knew that sometimes Sid wouldn't reply for a few hours so the two grey ticks appearing on WhatsApp did not mean that he hadn't seen the message. She didn't worry herself too much but she couldn't help looking to her phone from time to time to see whether the two grey ticks had turned blue. They never turned blue. She went to the supermarket and bought the ingredients she wanted for their dinner. It would always be a three-course dinner. Simple but good food. Italian food relied on good ingredients.

Around five o'clock she messaged him again. When she didn't receive a response she called him. It went straight to voicemail. He's probably forgotten his charger, she told herself. That is probably why he hasn't responded all day. Content with her reasoning, she started to cook. She was going to make him a parmigiana the way her grandmother made it. There was going to be gnocchi with homemade pesto and of course a fennel salad. By nine she knew he wouldn't be there. She didn't feel very hungry. She wasn't angry at him; she had sent over twenty messages and none of the ticks had turned blue. This wasn't like him. She wanted to cry, but there was a knot in her stomach that didn't let her do that just yet. So she went to bed. She cried and she imagined herself giving him a kiss and smothering him with her love.

Sami came into the kitchen, which was already alive with noise. He kissed his wife, who was rushing to make the twins their packed lunch whilst also trying to have her own breakfast. Ahmed and Eesa were eating Frosties and Rice Crispies respectively. One of them was trying to convince the other to swap a football card. None of this seemed to concern Sami; he nonchalantly grabbed some toast, poured a coffee from the percolator and sat down with the kids, turning on BBC London. Eesa was so engrossed in trying to close the deal that he had forgotten to eat his breakfast.

'Eesa, hurry up and finish your breakfast!' Layla said. 'We don't have time for fooling around.'

'Mum, I am eating as fast as I can.'

'You said that five minutes ago and you haven't touched your food.'

'Yeah,' added Ahmed encouraging her, 'tell him mum.'

It provoked a kick from Eesa underneath the table and Sami had to just raise his voice a decibel until order was restored. 'Boys,' he said, 'trying to listen to the news here.'

'An unidentified man,' said the newsreader, 'is in a critical condition fighting for his life in what the police suspect is a hit and run incident in Surrey. The man was found in a ditch by a dog walker. Police are appealing for witnesses.'

'No, no, no!' Sami muttered to himself, his usual cheerfulness gone. He seemed to zone out. It was only his wife's voice of sanity that brought him back.

'Hello, hello? Are you with us today?'

'Sorry, sorry,' said Sami, returning. 'Yes, what is it?'

'Could you drop the kids off?' said Layla. She noticed his sudden change in expression.

'Are you alright?' She moved closer, as if she wanted to check his temperature.

The Darkness Inside

'Yes, yes, I am fine. Don't worry about it.'

'You sure? You look like a ghost. It's just that I'm running late.'

'Yes,' he said, putting his clenched fist down on the table, 'I told you, I am fine. Really I'm fine. I'll drop them off.'

'Okay, okay darling, just asking.'

'Oh, I'm sorry,' Sami said, catching himself, 'something's happened at work and it wasn't meant to have happened that way.'

'I'm sure it'll turn out fine. If you need me, I'm here.' She gave him a peck on the cheek and started to harangue and cajole the boys into getting dressed.

Part 2

23. Natale

Martha watched dawn spreading her yellow robe over the ancient aqueduct and chapel in front of her father's house. She drank an espresso outside, wrapped up in a warm woollen sweater, taking in the silence. There was a lazy cigarette burning in an ashtray waiting to be picked up and enjoyed. She listened to the rushing sound of the river that coursed past the converted paper factory which had been her home. The rivulet would eventually end up in the town of Vietri.

This place had so many dark secrets. During the humid summer holidays she had had ample time to explore it. Once, in search of a one-eyed tabby cat, she had discovered a secret subterranean passage in the chapel that took you all the way to Salerno, if you had the courage, and back to Cava de' Tirreni. Dad said that Ferdinand I, the King of Naples, had used the passage that went right past his warehouse. She even discovered that the aqueduct whose craggy feet were planted on her father's land had been sketched by Turner, who had passed by on the way to Paestum.

This morning would be the only quiet period she could enjoy before chaos ensued. She knew that Dad would be running the day's errands before the Christmas vigil dinner. There was nothing to be stressed about, he would say, itching at his throat which showed all the signs of developing into a considerable turkey neck in his old age. Mum would be rushing around frantically – this was, according to Dad, all of

The Darkness Inside

her own making. She always did it, because she could never say 'no'. So she said 'yes' to looking after the grandkids, 'yes' to making the gnocchi, 'yes' to a quick coffee at a bar, 'yes' to picking up such and such person, and it would mean that none of those things happened at all, or all were badly done. All that could be said of the gnocchi was that it was, in the words of Martha's Dad, 'well meaning'. Unless he relieved her of the burden, she would be a nervous wreck, or the food would be inedible even though she was a fantastic cook in normal times. Martha wanted so badly to spend time with her, just to play Burraco or Machiavelli, but in these times she was no good.

Dad believed it was because she was from Sapri. They were just crazy, he said. Had he known she was from there he would have stayed clear away. But unfortunately for him it was too late; he had already fallen in love with the girl he thought was from Naples. And in some ways it was true – her mother had grown up in Naples and that's where they met. In many ways, she was very Neapolitan, but in other ways she was as bat crazy as those people from Sapri. And Martha's father always brought it up jokingly, so much so that it had become a ritual. Everyone in the family knew that Carlo Pisacane, the great nationalist, had landed in Sapri with his two hundred or so men hoping to unify Italy. He lived by the motto 'deeds create ideas'. Unfortunately for him, his deed resulted in his death. When he landed on the beach at Sapri, the locals attacked him thinking him a gypsy trying to steal their food; they killed him and that was the end of his adventure.

Martha went inside. Everyone would be up soon and would need their coffees. She put the moka on the stove

The Darkness Inside

and began preparing the meal for the vigil. She started on the broccoli, taking off the bad bits, working diligently with the occasional cigarette and coffee break. By noon Martha had quietly worked through the gnocchi, boiling a ton of potatoes, smashing them, kneading them and shaping them. She managed it without any help from her mother. Her mother had come through intermittently, and had got it into her head to start slow-cooking the peppers but then rushed off to help an old neighbour who needed something doing (it would be a most unchristian thing if she didn't), so Martha finished them off for her. She didn't ask whether her daughter was okay or why she wasn't as chatty as she usually was.

Martha had been quiet ever since she had arrived in Molina a few days before Christmas. She was wracked with worry about Sid and a company investigation that was being carried out to see whether she and her editor Paul had been recklessly negligent. Had they failed in their duty of care towards a staff member? It would culminate in a panel hearing where the judgement would be presented. That could be her finished – that could be her Brexit. But Mum, of course, hadn't noticed her worry, busy as she was with the Christmas preparations. Dad, though, had asked if everything was alright as soon as he picked her up from Naples Airport. 'Yes, of course,' she had said, 'what makes you think that?'

'Your eyes,' he'd said, 'look as if you suffer from hay fever.'

Usually they looked like clear blue ink circles surrounded by milk white, but now they appeared reddish at the edges.

'It's the pollution in London,' she had replied.

'Should have stayed here with me,' he had said and

hugged her, not pressing her with more probing questions. If he knew his daughter it would come out soon enough. Over the following days he had treated her gently, as if she was wounded. Despite the busy period he managed to fit in long walks alongside the Salerno corniche, father and daughter, chatting, strolling with his hands behind his back like he owned the whole place: King of Campania. So when it came to preparing dinner for the vigil he was there beside her, quietly doing what was required. He had already done all the shopping. He brought over the salt cod, the baccalà, which she turned into a nice salad with olives. He helped her fry up the battered cod and eels whilst she made a lovely sauce for the vongole. She made the stringy broccoli to perfection, did the escarole stuffed with pine nuts and breadcrumbs and cooked it for three hours. By the time she had finished she had managed to complete all the dishes to serve fifteen hungry mouths and a Russian salad to boot; she wasn't even stressing.

To Martha, preparing Christmas dinner was akin to a breaking news story. There had to be someone who held the place together while everyone was scrambling trying to catch up with the guys who had dropped the story; that anchor was her. When the Westminster terror attack happened everyone, including her editor, was screaming down the phone saying that Channel 4 News was going to name the attacker. She knew from not one but three lawyers that the suspect they were naming was behind bars. She refused to go with the name; it didn't matter who said it, she had it on three lawyers' authority that the man was inside and she wasn't going to budge even if the editor himself was shouting down the line. In the end she was proven

The Darkness Inside

right, and the correspondent had to climb down live on TV. Whilst rival journalists looked at new lines that *BuzzFeed*, *Daily Mail* and Sky were putting out there and scoured the very frontiers of the Twittersphere coming up with titbits of information, she came up with a clear strategy for her team to follow. She gave her journalists names, addresses, leads and story direction, moving from the attack to victims, to the killer and so forth. She always had the big picture in her mind's eye; whilst everyone was focusing on the micro she was looking at the macro level. When her team became too immersed in the fine details she could put the story down on the head of a pin and say: 'But Sid, this is the story.' Or she might turn around and say, 'Sid, I think you need the day off.' Christmas dinner was a breaking news story with only one element that needed managing – Mum – during the cooking and so it was much easier to deal with. Moreover, Dad sent Mum away on an errand whilst he organised the tables, plastic plates, napkins and drinks. He moved the furniture around in the cosy living room to accommodate the dining table and seats and put the logs in the fireplace as a finishing touch. Everything was thought through – he had been doing this since the time she wore pigtails and pretty little Minnie Mouse dresses.

When the guests arrived, it was perfect. Of course the aunties brought their dishes, the struffoli laced with liqueur, the drinks, the wine and the homemade specialities, but Martha could say that it was a job well done and it was nice to serve them. It was lovely to see her cousins behave like complete buffoons as in old times, complimenting her food and singing comic arias to her in appreciation

The Darkness Inside

of her cooking. She loved feeding her cousins, especially Lulu; he always cheered her up. He was from the north with a pronounced northern accent which jarred when he elongated the last vowel. If Lulu was her favourite, her least favourite was Andreas, and yet he intrigued her. Andreas reminded her of a wounded animal; he was tough due to mistreatment, not because he couldn't love.

He was the youngest of her cousins – Dad called him a little shit, just like the way she called Sid a little shit. Many Christmases ago, when Andreas had asked if Santa had brought him any more presents, he had nicked one of her nephew's shit-laden nappies and wrapped it up in a Christmas wrapper, put a green tassel on it and told Andreas that Babbo Natale had reserved a present just for him. The look on his face when he opened it was priceless. But when she looked at Andreas now at pimply eighteen, moody as hell and sitting far, far away from where his father and his stepmother sat, she understood that there was something that didn't sit quite right with him. His closely cropped hair reminded her of Sid, along with his efforts to keep conversations generic; his calling his stepmother by her first name was something that made her want to hold him, comfort him and yet also keep away from him. He also had a certain grown-up way of talking that people liked listening to precisely because it was odd coming from the mouth of an eighteen-year-old. That Christmas he, to her amazement, asked her about the Brexit conundrum and whether the people preferred a hard Brexit or a referendum.

'But how do you know this stuff?' Martha said, astonished, as they sat together eating some struffoli.

'I follow the news.' Andreas looked at her as if she was

The Darkness Inside

stupid – wasn't it obvious?

'Really?' She turned to Andreas' father and instructed him to take him out more.

Andreas' father complained that he was stuck in his room all day listening to the radio. Andreas frowned at his father undermining him.

'Why?' Martha asked Andreas.

'Well,' he replied, 'I want to be a journalist like you.'

'Why?'

'So I can leave this place,' he said, looking at his father who was whispering something in the ear of his stepmother, a pretty Polish lady, 'and see the world. There's nothing for me here.'

'Oh, but leaving here means abandoning all the good food!' Martha said, trying to cheer him up, but his mood suddenly darkened.

'I can live without it. Anyway, not a big fan of Polish cooking.'

'So,' she said, 'what did you think of my cooking?'

'Alright, I guess,' Andreas said, not quite aware of how offensive he sounded. 'The spaghetti wasn't al dente.'

Martha got up. She looked visibly distressed.

'I'm sorry,' said Andreas, alarmed, flashing a look at his father to see if he had noticed his indiscretion. 'I didn't mean to offend.' He was at an age where he hadn't realised that no one likes absolute honesty. Only God loves that.

'It's okay,' Martha said, touching his shoulder as she left, 'it's not you, but you need to learn how to talk to people if you want to be a journalist.'

She excused herself from the dining table and went to her room, which looked exactly as she had left it when she

195

The Darkness Inside

was twenty, and sat there silently. She could hear Mum entertaining the family with one of her stories in the living room and laughter as she delivered the punchline.

After twenty minutes there was a gentle knock on the door.

'Is everything alright, teso?' said Dad tenderly. 'Can I come in?'

'Yes,' she said, wiping her eyes and making them look even redder.

Dad came in wearing a purple jumper.

'You're missed, my love. You are going to have Mum burn the bloody incense for averting the evil eye.'

Martha laughed at those Neapolitan habits.

'Not everything has to be perfect, you know,' he said, sitting down on the bed next to her. 'I mean the food is never going to be as good as mine, is it?'

'No,' Martha replied – it never would be, that was a fact. Dad was a connoisseur and had a passion for cooking.

'So what is it?'

'Nothing,' replied Martha, 'it's nothing.'

'You know you can be strong and cry; it doesn't mean you're weak.'

'Do you?'

'Yes, when Naples lost the cup.'

'It's not the same.'

'Seriously,' Dad said, touching her, 'there's been plenty of times, not just over football.'

'When?' Martha pressed him. 'When?'

'When mum miscarried at six months. I had been waiting for her. I had felt her.'

Martha had heard vaguely about this older sister she

The Darkness Inside

would have had but who never came. Dad rarely talked about her. But clearly she had an existence to him.

'And sometimes,' he added as if he was talking about himself, 'you can cry even if you're not strong, when your heart is broken and you can't go on. It's fine, my love. Having a hard heart is no good.'

She hugged him and he held her. And finally they came, the tears flowed freely; she shook as she let go, and yet as she cried, she worried that her tears would make her Dad's jumper wet. She tried to move away but he held her there and she cried some more. Mum popped her head in to see what was going on but Dad just signalled for her to leave them alone.

'I just wish I could have done more,' Martha said.

'Could you have done more?'

'I wish I did. I miss him.'

'Oh, I thought you said he's a little shit.'

'Yes, but I still miss him. I can't bear him being alone in that state whilst I am here feasting.'

'I see he's one of those.'

In a way, even though he knew it was unchristian, he wished he had died. Those men were the ones Dads all over the world prayed their daughters never met, let alone brought home. And it was God's law that daughters of the world always fell in love with men like that. Andreas was one of those shits in the making and there was nothing Dads United could do about it.

'What do the doctors say?'

'He'll probably be in an intensive care unit for at least a few months.'

'That long?'

The Darkness Inside

She nodded.

'He still can't breathe properly so they're cleaning his lungs and stomach out. The doctors are keeping him asleep so they can change him. His sister says he's picking up a lot of infections. Honestly the NHS is getting worse. No one seems to know anything!'

Dad laughed.

'At least they're not stealing his organs whilst he's asleep.'

In Dad's view, the health service in Britain was heaven in comparison to the health service in the South. He looked at his daughter's face – it had that look that reminded him of the hills around Molina in autumn after the rain.

'My love, there is nothing you could have done.'

'Papà, of course I could have done more. That's why they are putting me in front of a panel. They are checking whether he was working or not. If he was, then I had a duty of care towards him.'

'Was he down on the rota?'

'Dad, it doesn't work like that.'

'Just answer me. Was he down on the rota?'

'No, he wasn't down to work. But as his editor, I should know my staff. They expect me to know my staff, and he works all the time. He's like one of those Lagotto dogs searching for truffles.'

'Look, your boss is trying to save his ass, or the company's ass. It's normal all sorts of questions will be asked. So all you need to do is sit back for this month while they do what they have to do. You didn't know he was working that day. He wasn't down to work on the rota. Don't worry.'

'I wouldn't be worth my salt if I proffered such a lame excuse.'

The Darkness Inside

'Enough. Come on, let's go back. People are going to ask.'

'You go; I'll be out in a moment. I need to put my game face back on.'

'Okay, amore.' He kissed her on the forehead. 'And if you still can't come to terms with it inside then get to the bottom of it. You need to be able to look yourself in the mirror always.'

'Can you?'

'Of course.'

24. Reem

The buzzer rang. Reem went to the intercom and buzzed her guests in. After a few moments the doorbell rang. She reached for her headscarf, wrapped and adjusted it in a flash and opened the door. Martha and Gardener were at the door, smiling at her tenderly. Martha stood there in a black coat with her red curly hair lighting up the hallway. Gardener, also in a black coat, had turned silver. He had slimmed down since she last saw him. Martha hugged her warmly and Gardener shook her hand.

'Come in,' Reem said, and took them into the kitchen.

They could smell the cardamom and cinnamon in the kitchen area. Reem had been boiling the doodpatti for about an hour. She knew that they loved its bastardised version of a chai latte, that milky tea with cardamom and cinnamon. She brought out a Spanish cheesecake she had baked and presented it to them on the kitchen top, then poured the doodpatti into oddly matched tea cups and offered it to her guests. 'I'm sorry,' she said in a pronounced Mancunian accent. 'Sid doesn't much care for cutlery; I haven't had a chance to go to **IKEA** to turn this place into a home yet... '

They laughed quietly at that – it sounded exactly like him.

'You've got a fight on your hands,' said Gardener. 'He always told me that too good a living makes you lose your edge. Makes you soft.'

'Soft for what?' Reem asked.

The Darkness Inside

'For the fight, I suppose.'

Reem thought about Gardener's words for a moment. 'Is that a reason for giving up living? What's the point of living in the basement all your life when you have a conservatory, a second floor and even an attic?'

'That is living to some journos,' Gardener explained.

'Don't worry, hacks don't make sense,' Martha reassured her. 'So,' she said, looking around her Spartan surroundings, 'how are you keeping?'

'So so,' replied Reem. 'One day at a time. How about you?'

'One day at a time. The wait is killing me. I'd rather have my day in court, as they say.' Her eyes searched Sid's living room, looking for the Amalfi vase that usually sat in the corner and for the tile depicting Naples. These two objects, made of Amalfi soil, sun and sweat, had lit up Sid's flat, but like Sid they were nowhere to be seen. Where were they? She wanted to ask but was scared that it would come across as insensitive. Perhaps Sid had given them away after their last fight. He could do that – all sweetness could vanish in a flash of anger.

'When is it?' Reem asked.

'Mid-February.'

'That's in a few days' time. So soon.' Reem reached for her hand and squeezed it in solidarity. 'I'm not saying this to make you feel better; there is nothing you could've done.'

'Thank you,' Martha replied. 'That means a lot.'

'We are in God's hands,' Reem said, resigned. Then, turning to Gardener, she asked, 'How are you, Tom?'

'I'm fine,' replied Gardener, 'spent a bit of time with Mum and Dad over Christmas. Ready to face the world again. It gets better, believe me.'

'That's nice to know,' said Reem.

'This tea is fantastic,' Gardener said. 'So how is he doing?'

'Grumpy – they've moved him out to a normal ward now.'

'Can we see him?'

'I wouldn't, not yet anyways. He's finding it hard to come to terms with it all.'

'So what's he doing?'

'In bed, mostly sulking.'

Gardener rolled his eyes. 'What does he expect? Suddenly to get on to a story, when he was in that ditch for that long before he was found? I wouldn't complain.'

'He's strong. He'll get over it. I think he's worried he'll lose his job.'

'I don't think that will happen,' Martha replied. 'That would reflect really badly on the company. Word has spread in the industry, so I would tell him not to worry about it. And as long as I am there, I will make sure he gets as much time as he needs. I want to sack him myself!'

'Oh, that's a relief,' replied Reem, laughing at her quip. She turned to Gardener. 'Did you have any luck with the police on this?'

'No,' said Gardener, 'I think they just want to close this. Busy I suppose with this serial cat killer terrorising owners in Croydon.'

'Seriously?!'

'I'm serious.'

'What is this country coming to?'

'So what now?' Martha asked.

'I don't know,' said Reem, sipping her tea, 'how I'm going

to manage all this with work. Sid and I are still in the middle of sorting out our dad's estate.'

'Is there anything we can do?' Martha understood her – this was the reason Reem had called them over to the flat.

'Yes, I was hoping to recruit you,' Reem replied. 'I would really appreciate it if you two could keep an eye on the place. I can't come down as often as I would like. Even if it's just dropping by at the hospital, watering the plants, opening the mail and the like. Please tell me if it's too difficult?'

'No, no, not at all,' said Martha. 'Really, it's the least we can do.'

'Really, leave it to us,' Gardener said.

Reem beamed and thanked them profusely. 'You know,' she said, 'Sid loves you both very much.'

Martha and Gardener looked at each other as if Reem was describing someone altogether different.

'Is Sid capable of that word?' Gardener said, half serious and half joking.

'I believe so.'

'How do you know?' Gardener asked.

'Sid rarely mentioned anyone when he called but he mentioned you often.'

'Honoured,' Gardener said, laughing.

'And me?' Martha asked, in jest but more serious than she had ever been.

'You were his boss,' said Reem smiling, 'but I got the feeling that he looked at you as more than that.'

'You are a paraculo,' said Martha joking.

'Paraculo?'

'We use this word when someone is protecting their ass from getting a beating.'

The Darkness Inside

Reem repeated the word a few times. 'I'll remember that. But I wouldn't call you two if you weren't special to him. He trusts very few people.'

'I don't know why,' said Gardener, 'but he is special to us too. He's loyal.'

Martha and Reem laughed at that because it was true.

'God heal my brother,' said Reem.

'Amen,' said Martha and Gardener in unison.

Martha and Gardener left Sid's flat with a set of keys, having promised that they would check up on him and water the plants at least once a week. Reem left for Manchester with the burden weighing less heavily on her shoulders.

25. The Panel

Martha wasn't worried that things might fall apart. She had been thinking about this panel hearing for a while. She could rent out the two spare rooms in her flat until she found something else, or she could rent the whole flat out, move back to Italy and live off the rent, take it easy for a while and then take it from there. Since Sid's accident she had begun to question her professional instincts. She was more unsure of herself. Recklessness and 'game' were good in this line of business but had she been too cavalier when it came to Sid? Had she just let him run riot without any oversight? Had she trusted him too much and not taken into account his recklessness? Had she even encouraged him to go one step too far? Had there not been times when she had overlooked his dustbin raiding or Amazon 'delivering'? Maybe she needed to go slow for a bit. Enjoy good company, good food and family. Feel like a normal human being who didn't see a story in every tragedy. In any case, if she felt the itch, she could always go freelance in Italy; ANSA and other agencies were always looking for capable journalists.

With these feelings in mind, she had already put out an advert on Gumtree and received inquiries daily. So she wasn't worried anymore about the outcome of the panel hearing when she turned up at the office; all she cared about was to give a good account of herself. She was resigned to all outcomes. She had asked Hardcastle, the duty lawyer who had always backed her, to be with her at the hearing. He had agreed without a moment's thought. It was a testament to his innate decency. She was in the bathroom when she received a text from Gardener, an emoji of a flexed bicep: stay strong.

She looked at herself – minimal make-up, just some lipstick; she looked dignified. She adjusted her trouser suit. For a moment she contemplated putting on a more vampish lipstick as if to say whatever your decision I don't give a shit, but she thought better of it. She imagined herself in front of the panel, arguing with them on editorial issues, but in the end the rouge lipstick would come across as too cocky. Pastel red was fine.

She walked into the private meeting room at the back of her workplace. The room was stale and untrendy; tables and chairs were set out in a circular manner. The usual tea, coffee, water and wrapped biscuits set up was at the back. Paul was already there in a navy blue suit. He was clenching and unclenching his fist, as he did when there was a breaking story and he had drunk too much coffee. There was no one beside him; he had decided to represent himself. Hardcastle was there next to him too, waiting for her. He got up when she came in, he grabbed her hand and squeezed it. 'Is there anything you need?' he asked. 'Remember, if there is anything you object to, tell me and I will raise it.'

At quarter past nine the three members of the panel came into the room: Thompson, Jane and Delilah. All were consummate professionals. They had all served as former news editors, had picked up awards and were brilliant and well respected in their profession. Martha admired them all. The only person who could be said to be non-independent

The Darkness Inside

was Mr Thompson, a silver-haired top dog in the news group who curiously fasted on Tuesdays, allowing himself only green tea. The other two came with Reuters, AP, *Times* and *Washington Post* credentials – they had been brought in from outside to lead the investigation.

Since Sid's accident Jane and Delilah had interviewed all involved with his case. They had scrutinised the decision-making processes amongst the editorial team. They had looked into how they carried out investigations, what the safety procedures were. They had even checked the flak jackets and found them to be in good nick. They had sat with the legal team and the head of high-risk security, Patrick, and reviewed their policies and procedures. No one, apart from Martha, would have known of Sid's activities to have assigned him security. There was nothing untoward or suspicious about the way they went about their business. They had been brought in precisely because they had lost people – friends in Iraq and Mali. Delilah had sent a cameraman, Shukri, and the local Iraqi fixer, Ibrahim, to report on an operation by a Shia militia when they ran into the militia at a checkpoint. Shukri lost his life and Ibrahim remained wheelchair-bound to that day. It was these tough editors who were there to ensure that the corporation would be fair to both of them.

After a bumbling but thankfully brief introduction by the chair, Mr Thompson, the proceedings began. Mr Thompson clearly didn't want to be there or to subject his staff members to such an ordeal, but the logic of the faceless corporation could not be denied. Everyone had by now read the report and knew what the issues were. The details were laid out as coldly as a coroner's report.

The Darkness Inside

The only thing that was not included in the report was the judgement.

'So,' said Thompson, adjusting his silver-rimmed spectacles, 'we feel after careful scrutiny of the facts that Mr Robeson should have been more aware of the events during the news gathering process given the fact that Mr Khan was a maverick. However, the panel feels that it was the nature of the relationship between Mr Khan and Ms Fillippo that lead to Mr Robeson not being aware of what was happening until it was too late for all involved.'

'Mr Thompson, could I stop you?' Martha interjected. 'What do you mean by "nature of the relationship"?'

'Well,' Mr Thompson coughed uncomfortably, 'the impression we have is that you and Sid had, shall we say, a "history". Is that right?'

'We were at university together – we are very good friends.'

'So there wasn't anything more than that going on?' Mr Thompson stared at her quizzically, as if he knew better. 'You weren't romantically inclined towards each other?'

She blushed. 'I resent that suggestion.'

Hardcastle coughed and adjusted his seat. He leaned over to her. 'Martha,' he whispered in her ear, 'do you want me to take over? I think he's pushing it.'

'No, I can answer for myself, thank you.'

'Are you sure? This is why I am here.'

She touched his hand in thanks. 'Really, I am fine.' Paul looked at her as if to say: 'Take his advice, take it and shut up.'

Hardcastle leaned back. His phone vibrated; he had received a message. He leaned over to Martha. 'I'm just going to go out and get a letter that has just been delivered.

The Darkness Inside

It's urgent apparently.'

Martha nodded. 'Don't worry, go.' He left the room discreetly.

The chair coughed politely to get Martha's attention.

'Very well, that is duly noted. In any case, due to this personal connection, not all processes were observed, which meant that Saeed, or Sid, was left to his own devices. Had Ms Fillippo been aware of who he was seeing that night he could have been assigned a backwatcher or provided with additional security. Now, there doesn't seem to be anything suspicious about his accident that can be linked to his work according to the police. Had all the steps been observed it is likely that he would still have been running after a story instead of being bedridden. The panel feels that the blame therefore lies partly with Mr Robeson, who was perhaps a tad too over-reliant on the home editor. We cannot but conclude that the editor should be put on a final warning and the home editor dismissed due to her severe neglect. Is there anything anyone would like to add?' He looked over to the other panellists who shook their heads, avoiding eye contact with Paul and Martha.

Paul coughed as if he wanted to say something.

'Mr Robeson?' the chair said. 'Would you like to add something?'

Paul rose, adjusting his tie before speaking.

'Whilst,' he argued, 'I accept my part in this sad affair and accept totally the final warning, I would like to add that the decision to dismiss Martha is unfair. Martha's support, diligence, skill and ingenuity has led to our organisation winning awards for our world-class journalism. To be dismissed for something that was not in her control – that

The Darkness Inside

Sid, who all of us knew was a maverick – seems a bit harsh. Knowing her the way I do, I know that she feels the pain of our colleague, not to mention her dear friend, daily. And I would urge the panel to reconsider its position. I need her on my team. She remains a valuable asset to the company.'

Martha was deeply moved by the editor's support. She hadn't expected that from him. But that is why he commanded such loyalty in the newsroom.

'And you? Ms Fillippo?' the chair asked. 'Do you have anything to add?'

'Yes, I do. There's not a single day,' she added, 'that I don't examine how I should have been on top of this investigation. And I am truly sorry to the panel and most importantly to my friend, Sid, for this failure. So I will also accept whatever the panel decides as being fair. I only ask that I be given an opportunity to resign rather than being dismissed.'

The door opened. Hardcastle had returned with an opened envelope. He looked at Martha as if she was mad; she was meant to fight – not give up. He was there to stick up for her, but instead she had admitted guilt. He leaned towards her as she sat facing the panel of three. Martha just patted him on his hand as if to say it was all under control.

Hardcastle coughed to get the panel's attention. 'I am very sorry to do this, Mr Chairman, but I have just received a letter.' He held the letter up and showed it to all and sundry as if it was a document of historic importance. 'It is a brief letter. But it is from Mr Khan. May I read it out?' He looked at Martha, who had turned red.

Mr Thompson was pleasantly surprised. 'Please, do.'

'Dear all,' said Hardcastle, reading the letter aloud. 'I am

The Darkness Inside

not quite sure what happened on the night in question; I don't remember everything. But when I woke up, my sister told me that Ms Fillippo has a hearing with regards to my actions. This seems wholly unfair. Whilst things are still not clear as to what occurred on that terrible night, I know that I wasn't working. I was there to meet a friend; he did not turn up. And I ended up finishing my coffee and walking to the bus stop when I was supposedly struck. Signed, Sid Khan.' Hardcastle folded the letter, got up and gave it to the panel chairman.

'Oh,' said Mr Thompson, 'this, it seems, changes everything. We will need some time to confer. Let's break for half an hour and we will reconvene.'

Martha, Paul and Hardcastle went outside to a coffee bar. They ordered several coffees. Martha hugged Paul and Hardcastle.

'Thanks Paul,' she said. 'That was really sweet.' She knew he had put his job on the line before Hardcastle read the letter out. He had two kids, one of them in public school, and had a pretty substantial mortgage to pay off. He could have just kept his head down when the panel spoke, but he didn't.

'I need you on my team,' he said, smiling. 'You better win me some awards.'

'Let's see what the outcome of their conferring is,' Hardcastle said, still worried. 'I would have thought that it was common sense to have a panel hearing after Sid was out of hospital and we could ascertain all the facts before dragging everyone through this awful process.'

The panel reconvened. 'In the light of what has been added,' said the chair with an embarrassed look on his

The Darkness Inside

face, 'we feel that Ms Fillippo should not be dismissed and this panel hearing should be annulled with no fault on any party.'

A wave of relief surged through Martha; she grabbed Hardcastle's hand and squeezed it in thanks.

'What did I do?' he asked.

'You were there,' she replied. 'That is enough. I need to see Sid.'

'He still doesn't want any visitors, he said so in the notes.'

She wanted to do the same with Paul, but looking at his expression she realised that he still had his game face on; the matter remained a serious one, but the features of his face had softened. She sent Gardener an emoji, a dancing lady, to let him know what the outcome of the panel was.

He replied with an emoji of celebrations and confetti.

As she left the office, having already booked her holidays in preparation, she felt that somehow she was getting off way too easy. Something within her, the editor within, who held her staff to a higher standard, told her that perhaps the panel should have verified Sid's claims. How many times had she come across a friend or family member who was lying to protect their nearest and dearest? Perhaps Sid was doing the same?

Martha went to Sid's flat, although she didn't need to. Reem had given his plants a good drink before leaving. She went to the bedroom and found the vase she had given him in the corner next to the mattress. The Amalfi tile she found in the bathroom, facing the toilet. She didn't know how to take it that Sid took a dump staring at the Amalfi coastline – not exactly where she would have put it. After watering the plants again she started looking for the customary shiny

The Darkness Inside

notepads that they had in the office cupboard. Sid never kept his notepads or anything in the office. He was so paranoid that he didn't even use their official emails unless he had to. In the past Sid had seen management shutting out staff members from accessing their online contacts and materials once they had left the company; it meant that the corporation had all those contacts and the employee none. So he made it his business to keep all his contacts to himself. Not only did he regularly back up his work computer but his notepads he kept at home. Martha went to the living room, looked at the low-lying bookshelf and found what she was looking for. The black notepads and some that he had bought were all there, each with a sticker with a year written on it. The notebooks spanned back several years. Martha went back to the bedroom, looked in one of the built-in closets and found what she was looking for: Sid's worn sports bag that he sometimes brought to work. It was into that that she unloaded the notepads to take them home.

It took Martha several days to sift through his notes. She told Gardener she was going through them because she still had a few days left of her vacation and it was cold and dark outside, 'so why not?'

'Yeah right,' Gardener said cynically. He surmised that perhaps opening that box would allow her to come to terms with her guilt. She had initially started off with verification in mind; objectivity was paramount. But as she sifted through the notepads, increasingly she found herself studying them like religious devotional codexes. She poured over them like the devotee who asks her prophet whether God has made mention of her in the heavens. Each scribble,

The Darkness Inside

each word was studied and considered; what did it reveal to her about his feelings for her? Would she finally find out the mystery? Had she opened him? Had she captured him? For days she worked on those notes, like a journalist, like a priest, like a Rabbi, like an exegete, to answer these questions. In the end she was defeated; most of his notes were as incomprehensible as those ancient texts found on the banks of Nineveh designed for God's eyes only. He had doctor's writing which was hard to decrypt. Her name did crop up but usually in the form of reminders: 'check with Martha', 'call M', 'deadline for M-Boss' and so on. Such mentions revealed little about his feelings for her, however she might spin them. Those notes spanning several years back didn't bring anything of significance apart from memories of what they had said and done when they had worked on stories. They evoked remembrances of them sitting inside a car, waiting for a story to come out of the door. Of them scheming, plotting and planning strategies; of headlines, of awards, of late-night chats. They brought forth tears and smiles but as to his feelings for her: nothing.

Once she got to the more recent notebooks, objectivity began to return. There were things of interest which intrigued her. As her holiday came to a close, she became a journalist again and she admired his extensive notes, mindmaps and to-do lists, alongside names and addresses that were hastily scribbled down. There were rough outlines of stories. Sometimes one name cropped up and it would be circled or have an exclamation mark by it or a question mark. Martha guessed Sid had experienced some sort of epiphany and she could see him having it all by himself. She had seen it in the office; it was delightful, almost childlike.

The Darkness Inside

When it happened, she would stop him, saying, 'What is it? What is it?' And he would be unable to explain anything but it would make perfect sense to him.

'You get it?' he would say. She would shake her head. 'Don't worry. Bear with me.' He was delightful in those days.

Gardener was also helpful and filled her in on some of the theories Sid was working on. One of the final questions Sid had posed in the last notebook was this: Did Sami kill Anis because Anis was blackmailing him? That, to her, seemed to have some promise. She knew that Sami had also been killed and though it might have been coincidence, it may also not have been.

When Reem came down for the weekend Martha persuaded her to take her to see Sid. The hospital was creaking like the human beings within – stressed nurses or pale geriatric men walking like zombies, accompanied by a drip, having a fag outside, their veins blue as they took a drag. The ash fell like snow on their yellow toenails and no one cared. However, the corporation had provided Sid with a well-lit private room with fresh flowers.

Reem went in first whilst Martha lurked outside his room, listening.

'Salaams,' said Reem, coming up to Sid and giving him a kiss on the head. 'I have someone here to see you.'

She could hear Sid was annoyed. 'Why? I don't want anyone to see me like this.'

'Too late now, they are outside,' she said with the authority of a no-nonsense Mancunian who knew what was what. 'You need to face the world and stop feeling sorry for yourself.'

The Darkness Inside

'Who is it?'

'Martha.'

'What?'

'Oh come off it, you big berk. Martha, come in.'

Martha found Sid sitting up in a blue gown, leg in a plaster, watching the news with one eye on his Twitter timeline, which was moving up hypnotically. He had an expression which seemed to say that he could see the world moving in his hand and he was stuck here in a shitty hospital. He was trying to remain dignified. He greeted Martha as she walked in with a large bunch of flowers and chocolates which Reem took off her hands.

'Thank you for the flowers and the chocolates,' Sid managed to say, embarrassed at the way he looked.

'No problem at all,' said Martha, touching his shoulder tenderly. 'How are you?'

'Oh you know, getting there.' He nodded to her and asked her to take a seat.

'Well,' said Reem as Martha sat down, 'I'll fetch us some teas.' She left the room.

'Thank you,' Martha said.

'For what?'

'The panel.'

'Don't worry about it,' Sid said, waving it away, still with his eyes on the TV. 'It's the truth.'

He had a shock of blackish hair with brown in it. His stubbly face, despite having had a few months to recover, still showed the scabs from the brambles. This had probably been due to Sid picking at them impatiently so he could look normal. There was also an ugly scar running above his eyebrow. He seemed to be moving his jaw up and down as

The Darkness Inside

if he was exercising it; as if it caused him discomfort, the way it might if you had been punched there. Physically he was thinner – the muscles, from lack of exercise, were less taut.

While she studied him he kept looking away; he didn't want her here, studying him, but he couldn't be rude to her.

'This will make you laugh,' Martha said. 'You know Daniels booked a holiday? Then used a Green Tomato taxi to take his girlfriend off to Hampstead Heath and proposed to her?'

Sid's eyes lit up. 'Did management find out?'

Martha nodded.

'Who found out? How?'

'I don't know, but when you're on holiday and you use the corporate taxi account and you post the evidence on Instagram, you're going to be found out, right?'

'You follow him don't you?'

Martha grinned.

'It was you!' Sid laughed, 'I know it was you!' He was still laughing when Reem walked in with the teas.

'I told you,' she said, 'Martha would cheer you up.' Turning to Martha she said, 'This is the first time I've seen him laugh in months.'

'He thrives on other people's misery,' replied Martha.

'Not true,' Sid said, 'not true.'

They sat there drinking their tea and chitchatting before Martha excused herself. As she got up from the chair Sid asked her, 'Will you come and see me again?'

'Do you want me to?'

Sid nodded. 'Yes, I would like that very much. Maybe Tom can come and visit too.'

The Darkness Inside

She left the hospital with Reem accompanying her to the entrance. Martha thanked her for taking her to see Sid and Reem thanked her for breaking his despondency.

26. Work

When Martha returned to work, she was hungry and eager to get her teeth into a big story. So far the home bureau hadn't produced any stories or investigations that were really worthy of consideration for any press awards. They would submit stories but she knew that the judges would soon chuck them out. *BuzzFeed*, *Guardian* and the *Times* had done some really strong investigations this year, but they hadn't. There were things about Sid's statement and story that didn't sit easy with her. She had long learnt that you had to listen to your gut. If something didn't 'feel' right after all the work put in, then there was something that needed doing to make the gut feel whole again. So Martha did something. After work she went to the place where Sid had been struck and she stood by the muddy verge, peering into the brambles where they had found him. She tried to put herself in his shoes, she looked around, she started talking to him.

'Why on earth would you come here? Sid, you would never come here.' She walked along the empty road.

'What were you doing here? You must have been working! That's the only reason you would come here. Am I right, Sid? Am I right?' She walked back to the main road. Brighton Road was in front of her; there was a dull field with a dusting of snow behind it and trees partially obscuring it. She turned and stared at the Starbucks cafe that was pretending to be a Tudor building. Her pale face lit up. She peered at it again; it was a twenty-four-hour Starbucks. She walked towards it, feeling the opening. He was meeting someone. That part of his statement was true. But how often do you meet friends in an obscure Starbucks in a suburb called Horley?

'Why didn't you let me know, Sid? Please tell me this wasn't a Tinder date? Please tell me this wasn't a one night stand? Sid!' Martha scolded him.

She went into the Starbucks. Two members of staff were serving customers some sickly flat whites. One of them, a blonde girl with an unnatural-looking white smile, asked her how she could help.

Martha told her that she was a journalist and wondered if she recognised Sid. She flashed a picture on her phone.

The girl said, 'Yes, but I think you should speak to the manager first.'

'Honestly, there's really no need,' said Martha. The shutdown was beginning.

'Look, we have already told the police everything. Let me get the manager.'

Before Martha could talk her out of it, the blonde girl went to the back office and fetched the manager. The manager, a professional Eastern European lady, told her matter-of-factly that the member of staff had told everything she knew to the police and that any other requests had to go through head office. The shutdown was complete. Martha thanked the lady and left.

At least she had got confirmation that Sid had been here and met someone. Shutdowns were never nice but when

The Darkness Inside

an organisation shut down journalists like Martha, that was an open challenge to her. She had uncovered many a scandal that way. Here, though, it was clear why they were doing it; they were protecting their staff from unwanted media attention. She knew that the police would tell her nothing. This knockback wouldn't stop her from beavering away at other leads over the week. Whilst everything continued on as normal at work her mind began to tinker away at the mystery of Sid's accident.

Sami's wife, Layla, didn't give her any titbits. In fact, the only reason she had even managed to get an 'in' with her was due to her knocking on the door and offering condolences, and even then did the widow leave the latch on. Layla thought Martha was her late husband's friend or client and, out of courtesy, entertained her for a moment. Martha went along with her assumption until Layla asked her who she was. Only then did Martha come clean and identify herself as a journalist. She was walking an ethical tightrope. She could hear Layla sniffling behind the door.

'How did you know my husband had been killed?'

'I'm a journalist, madam,' replied Martha. 'It's my job and one of my friends was hurt whilst working on a story that Sami was involved in.'

'You're a friend of that journalist?'

'Yes, Sid is his name.'

'Look,' Layla said, suddenly deciding that she was being drawn into a trap. 'I don't know anything about anything.'

'Wait! Please, just a few questions. Just give me a minute.'

Layla granted it, but her responses were either: 'I don't know,' or, 'the security services are dealing with it.'

'But why?' Martha asked; she was really tempted to put

The Darkness Inside

her foot in the gap so Layla couldn't close the door. 'Why would the security services be involved?'

'I don't know,' Layla replied wearily. 'Look, I need to help my children with their homework. Do you mind not calling here again? Just don't want the media attention.'

Martha nodded.

'Here, can I give you my card, for if you change your mind?'

'I won't,' she said, but she took it anyway and closed the door on Martha.

Well, at least Layla had her card. That was a start. If Layla called her then she could tell her about the work she had done on uncovering South London gangs trafficking people in Calais. She might like the work she had done on the way one of the Gulf human rights directors was trying to cover up a work-related death in his palace. Yes, she could show her those award-winning scoops including all the work she did on the Panama papers. That might change her mind, Martha thought optimistically. Still, that special branch had got involved was interesting. As she walked home, she called Gardener, who was also intrigued.

'I'd imagine,' Gardener speculated, 'probably because it might be Syria-related. If that is the case SO15 might get involved. Not sure though. Let me ring around or drop round their offices in Hammersmith.'

'Listen,' she said, 'you want to do something this weekend?'

'Yeah sure, do you have anything in mind?'

'No, but it would be nice to catch up.'

'Let's fix a time closer to the end of the week. Take care.'

Martha got a different response when she turned up at

The Darkness Inside

Anis' family's flat in Thornton Heath – as soon as the woman heard that she was Sid's fiancée she hugged her as though she was one of their own. There was no need for her to show the press card, no need for the spiel explaining all the intricacies. There was no need to tell her that Sid was recovering. Ayesha bundled her into the house and hugged her again warmly.

'My poor darling,' she said, 'the likes of him are rare.'

She led Martha into the living room, sat her down, made mint tea and served it in tiny blue cups decorated with stars and fed her Moroccan sweets. Martha felt awkward; what had she done to deserve such compassion and love? She was an impostor after all.

'If you don't mind me asking,' said the kindly woman with black mascara, 'when were you going to get married?'

'A year from now,' said Martha without hesitation. 'We were in the planning stages, just organising our finances. See, my family would have to come over.'

She started to tear up.

'I'm sorry,' said Ayesha, 'I didn't mean to cause you pain.'
'Really, it's fine.'

She reached for some tissues on the table and blew her nose.

'So where did you meet?'

'University of Manchester, I came here on an Erasmus programme. I didn't know anyone here and Sid took me under his wing. He just showed me what to do, how to do things. He was very sweet that way. Always there. Wouldn't let anyone laugh at me when I pronounced the words wrong. Later on, when I came back to do a postgrad, he was still there.'

The Darkness Inside

'Yes, he was very kind. I could tell he had a good heart. My brother, Ayman, wanted to kill him when he knocked on our door but I stopped him. So are you a Muslim?'

'No.'

'Inchallah,' Ayesha said, praying that God decreed it thus; 'never mind, you are from the People of the Book. Never mind.'

Martha wanted to ask why it mattered but she stopped herself. She had got this far – why rock the boat?

'So when did he propose to you?'

'Last year – we were strolling on the Strand and he popped the question.'

'You see, God always takes the best ones. That is God's way, may He have mercy on him. He was the only one who tried to help us you know. The only one.'

'Really?'

'Yes, of course, my mother prayed for him when she found out. He was going after the people who had killed my brother. So they went for him.'

'They? Who?' Martha sat up.

Ayesha put her hands to her mouth and stared wide-eyed at her. 'You mean no one told you?'

'Told me what?'

'See what a good man he is? He probably didn't want to worry you.'

Martha's blood started to boil. She wanted to shake the woman, tell her to slow down and stop the melodrama. Something within her switched on and she smoothly transitioned into breaking news mode; calm and composed.

'What was it,' she said, 'that he was working on?'

'Well he told my brother exactly who killed Anis. Ayman

wanted to go after him but Sid stopped him.'

What a fool, thought Martha. He had overstepped the line for the sake of a story. Her face went red with anger.

'When Sid went after Anis' killers they tried to kill him. So my Ayman took revenge.'

'That's why he killed Sami?'

Ayesha nodded. 'May the bastard rot in hell.'

Martha wanted to expose Sid's lies there and then; he had no right to accuse Sami that way. He knew, as she did, that unless they had the smoking gun, he should never accuse someone of such a crime that way. People had had their lives ruined because of his stupid brinksmanship. She restrained herself; the story was intriguing and Sid was onto something – she could feel it.

'Where is your brother now?'

'Feltham Young Offenders, but he's due to be moved as soon as he turns twenty-one.'

'Is there any way I can get in touch with him?'

'Yes, if I call him he will move mountains for you. My brother is like that.'

27. Sid

Sid was in the middle of reading a paper titled: 'The Non-State Militant Landscape in Syria' published in 2013. At that time there seemed to be about fifteen rebel organisations in Syria. These were of different political persuasions and some of the factions differed significantly from each other – from the FSA, Free Syrian Army, who wanted a secular democracy to hardcore Jihadists who wanted a caliph at their head. As he was getting his head around the various factions and their intricacies, there was a knock on the door.

'Come in!'

A nurse came in. 'Mr Khan, you have a visitor.'

He looked up from his phone and it was Martha standing outside. Her face looked serious. Lips pursed, as if determined to have it out. 'Come in, Martha,' he said, pretending not to notice, 'how nice of you to pop by. Take a seat.'

She came in and sat down, waiting for the nurse to leave. She looked in an irrational mood. 'Could you, plump my pillows up,' Sid asked her. 'I got these bed sores.' Martha got up from her seat and plumped the pillows. 'Thank you. Soon I'll start physio.'

'You can stop it right there, Sid.'

'Stop what?'

'I know what you are doing.'

'What?'

The Darkness Inside

'Stop the bullshit.'

'What?' The more he said the word, the more she got angry. These Italians were easy to rile up.

'Be sincere, Sid.'

'Sincere?' He had noticed that when you got them riled up, they started switching to Italianisms – Sid had learnt that from experience. Sincere meant: 'tell me the truth'.

'I don't understand.'

'Stop bullshitting, Sid, just stop it! I know your game.' Martha was angry; she was whispering a scream at him, so her neck was sinewy instead of delicate.

'Look,' Sid said forlornly, 'there are things I can't remember. When I was sleeping all I could think about was our dinner. That I hadn't called you. That I want to get at the truth.'

Martha's rage stopped. She hugged him. 'I'm sorry, I didn't realise.'

'My memory is patchy. Can you fill me in?'

She did her best to, mentioning various names to see if they jogged his memory. When he found out about Sami, he held his hands in his unkempt hair. 'What about his kids?'

'They'll survive.'

'Who did this?'

'Ayman. He went to avenge his brother and you.'

There was another pang of guilt. 'Why?'

'Well,' she said, trying hard to control her anger, 'I don't know if you remember but you told Ayman that Sami killed his brother. You shouldn't have done it. You pushed the story too far.'

'No, I would never do that! Ayman's sister is very manipulative,' he paused for a moment as if confused, 'I

The Darkness Inside

did? I don't remember.'

Martha nodded. 'If I am honest, had I found out you wouldn't have been working for us anymore, or in this business ever again.'

Sid stared out of the window. 'I understand. I'm sorry.'

'Me too,' Martha said.

'You know,' Sid said, his tone ruminative and laborious, 'all I ever wanted was to prove myself to you, that I was a journalist worth my salt, you know? I remember you always saying that I should get that verified tick on Twitter and then I'd see. I guess I took it too far.' He studied her face. Martha had her hand to her mouth; she looked like she was wracked with guilt. 'I knew one day, if I was a blue tick, had awards, the lot, you'd be super proud of me. I am so sorry, Martha, to let you down.'

He watched her, as guilt travelled through her.

'Look,' she said, standing up as though re-energised, 'let's go after them.'

'No, no,' Sid replied shaking his head, depressed, 'enough is enough. I put you through too much already.'

'We have to!' she said, jacking up the enthusiasm to lift them both. 'It's a great story.'

'You think?'

'Of course. Award-winning even.'

'How?'

'Come on Sid, what starts out as a simple knife story turns out to be Syria-related and linked to Jihadists. In light of Paris, Brussels, Istanbul, Westminster and London Bridge, do I need to go on? It's massive, especially if we see arrests as a result of our investigation. Come on Sid, you know this!'

The Darkness Inside

'You're right.' Sid watched her intently, studying her face. 'We can't let Paul know though. Otherwise it will all come out.'

'Exactly, so this will help you and keep you occupied while you are recuperating. You could do all the back-office work. The standing up, the checking before we approach the lawyers – this,' she added with a wink, 'can be our little secret.'

'Well,' Sid said, unsure, 'I suppose it will give me something to do. But, Martha, I can't face Ayman. It would tear me apart. You will have to do the legwork.'

'Leave it to me.'

'Why are you doing this?'

'Don't know. Guilt, I guess.'

'You understand that it's a massive undertaking?'

'Sid, I know, I'm your editor. I know the legal threshold is high.' In truth, that was an understatement. Rarely did newspapers accuse people of murder, but that was exactly what she was proposing. Essentially, short of a smoking gun, the evidence had to be immense. When *New York Times* reported on the Assad regime's secret network of prisons, Anne Barnard and her team had worked on it for seven years. So for two people to work on a story that involved massacres, murder and more was difficult, not to mention dangerous. Testimonies had to be collated, confirmed, checked. A confession or overwhelming evidence was required to ensure that the lawyers who would have to approve the work – for this piece would be highly libellous – would not refuse.

'Yes, of course, the more evidence the better. But it's dangerous. You sure you want to do this? Look at me. You're doing this without a backwatcher.'

The Darkness Inside

'Please,' Martha said, 'don't patronise me. I know what I'm getting myself into.'

'Didn't mean to offend you. I care for you, that's all.' Sid reclined on the pillow. Martha squeezed his hand. She could see the lucidity of Sid's mind returning. He sat and talked as if he was healing in her very presence, as if he had been thinking about this for a long time even when he was immersed in the darkness of unconsciousness.

'In order to get to Radio,' he directed, 'you need to get to Abbas Rizwan; he's the key. He's told me a lot. I still remember what he told me that night. It's crystal clear in my mind. I have already tried to stand up those details. I guess he relied on me dying so told me everything; that's not evidence, that's hearsay. He destroyed all the evidence when he took my phone and my bag with my notes and recorder inside. Go to my place and grab my spare Marantz recorder; it's small but powerful. Trust me.'

28. Abbas

Abbas' mobile phone kept on ringing – he knew exactly who it was. He pulled the warm duvet cover that smelled of sweat and socks over his head and stayed there. He had slept for eight hours, probably more, and still felt tired. He just didn't want to get out of bed. He reached for the phone and saw the message. It was from the boss: *What the hell are you playing at? Where are you?* Another message said: *How long are you going to be "sick"?*

Abbas wrote to him saying he was still 'very very sick'. The boss wrote back then: *Then get me a medical certificate.*

He wanted to write back: *If you want to play it official, why don't you give me a payslip instead of cash in hand?* But he didn't want to push it. He got up and put his bare feet down on the cold floor. One part of him wanted to wrap himself up in his single bed and sleep a bit more.

He sat there shivering, unwilling to get out of his sparsely furnished single room, with peeling wallpaper and a faint smell of mould, to turn on the boiler. Then he remembered the boiler had caved in on him. It was too old. The gas man had given him some electric heaters; one of them was under the bed. He reached for it and turned it on. It warmed his chunky feet for a while. He wondered why he always felt so depressed in winter. Everything seemed so pointless. It must be the lack of sunlight. He had never felt depressed in Syria, even on the coldest of days. At least if Sami was around he would cheer him up, but he wasn't around anymore. He grimaced at his memory, asked God to have mercy on him, and swore revenge on the bastard who had stabbed him – it was just a matter of time. He pushed Sami's image away from his mind's eye.

Eventually he mustered up enough courage to put on a coat and make himself some tea. Somewhere amongst the messy kitchen he found a tea cup and dug up a pack of biscuits – Jammie Dodgers – threw a teabag in milk and boiling water and didn't even bother letting the bag brew. He took a swig and grimaced as if he had tasted piss.

He cleared up the chicken boxes that had accumulated on the dirty coffee table and sat down on an old green sofa which was beyond salvation. Then he turned on the TV and started to channel-flick. He went between CNN, NBC, Bloomberg, Al Jazeera, Sky News, BBC News and RT. That cycle of watching endless news continued on till lunch.

At around one o'clock he felt hungry. He put on his coat, went across the road and ordered some fried chicken and chips from the TFC. When he returned he found a text message from Radio: *Salaam alaikum, Yasser is telling me U r pissing about.*

I'm sick, he wrote back.

Make sure U C a doctor. Get a certificate too.

Okay, Abbas wrote back.

God heal you, drink some hot turmeric with honey, I swear it works wonders.

Okay.

The Darkness Inside

Abbas started to tuck into his wings and chips. For some reason, even though he had chicken or burgers every day, he never got tired of them. He swore that the bossman added coke or some other narcotic opiate to have people like him hooked on them. After he had finished he received another text from Radio.

Booked you in for 3 o'clock with Dr Siddiqui.

Abbas was upset; he wanted to write back that Radio wasn't his mum. He may have been his Emir back then, but now Abbas was his own man. On reflection, that's how Radio had always been. He always ensured that his men were looked after; that's why they would put their lives on the line for him. So he was just doing things that were in his nature. If he didn't go, he guessed that Radio would be knocking on his door scolding him for turning into a fat bastard, paying for a cleaner and maybe even making him some chicken soup whilst cussing him all the while. There was nothing for it.

The only other guy who would take the time out to look after him had been Sami – his wife would send him the nicest things. Surprising how much he missed him when he had been so annoying whilst alive.

At two thirty he received a text message from Radio to make sure that he was out of the house and walking towards the GP. He knew that if he didn't go, Radio would be there with his car. So he got ready and went. He didn't really care what he put on. Main priority for him was warmth, and so he wrapped himself up in fleeces, a coat, mufflers and double odd socks as he made his way through the grey world of Croydon in February. He walked past the tired hospital, past the Indian sweet shop and the dosa

The Darkness Inside

cafe that smelled so good, although he would never spend his money there. Abbas worried about places like that; even though he had never had much contact with Hindus he was convinced that these fellows kept a spray bottle of cow urine around and blessed their food by spraying it. And so, despite the temptation of tucking into a tasty dosa, he refrained from eating those thin South Indian lentil pancakes accompanied with various dips.

He passed the African nurses standing outside the surgery drinking tea and smoking cigarettes, keeping the NHS afloat, and went to reception. The receptionist, in Abbas' estimation, was an effeminate, possibly gay little kafir, who had the cheek to be visibly repulsed by his presence. Nevertheless, he was polite enough to call him 'sir'.

'Take a seat, sir and Dr Siddiqui will be with you in a moment.'

The 'moment' lasted for about half an hour before he heard a door open and a Pakistani-accented voice call his surname: 'Rizwan, Mr Rizwan.'

Abbas turned in the direction from which he heard his surname and hauled himself to the room. Dr Siddiqui looked exactly how you would expect a Pakistani doctor to look: black framed glasses, a long beard like the cricketer Moeen Ali, a white coat and a shirt. 'Assalamu alaikum,' he said when Abbas entered, 'what can I do for you?'

'Walaikum salaam. Well,' said Abbas, unsure of exactly why he was sitting in front of a man who was scrutinising him, 'I... I need a medical certificate.'

'Right, what is wrong with you?'

'I don't feel very well.'

The GP must have seen cases like his all the time; without

The Darkness Inside

even asking Abbas for permission he started to take his blood pressure, going through the routine of putting the stethoscope on the patient's chest. 'You seem healthy,' Dr Siddiqui said. 'Maybe you need to be a bit more active and watch your weight, but you're fine.'

'Look, all I do is sleep, I feel tired all the time. The more I sleep the more tired I feel. And I don't know why.'

'I see,' said Dr Siddiqui thoughtfully. 'When you're sleeping, do you have nightmares or anxiety?'

'Sometimes, not the anxiety bit though,' Abbas said, as if it was a weakness in him. 'No, I could never get that.'

'What about the nightmares?' Dr Siddiqui waited for his patient to reveal what they were. But his patient was looking down on the floor like a shy schoolboy. 'Do you want to tell me what they are?'

'I don't remember them.'

'I see,' said the GP, jotting it down. 'Has anything happened over the past three months, maybe a bereavement or a family member passing away?'

'No, no family has passed away, thank God.'

'But someone has passed away?'

'Yes, a friend.'

'Want to tell me about it?'

Abbas looked at the doctor. What a nosy git, typical Pakistani uncle prying. 'What's this about?' he said, his tone of voice slightly louder. 'What is there to tell? He's dead. End of story. Got stabbed outside his shop.' He frowned; just who the hell did he think he was? What the hell did he want to know? That he was drinking tea, warming his hands on the radiator after having unloaded some sheep carcasses? That Sami had sat down to a nice cuppa when

The Darkness Inside

the bastard came in and sliced him to bits? What did he want to know? The guy was dead. How was that going to help him?

'Sorry, I didn't mean to pry,' replied the doctor, but to Abbas' annoyance he was still jotting things down on his notepad.

Abbas didn't like the fact that he was still noting things down. Leave it bredrin, just leave it doctor, before I plant my fist in your beardo face. 'What you writing about me?'

'Oh, just some observations.'

'Better not be bad.' Abbas raised his voice a decibel louder.

'Well,' said the doctor, unafraid, 'you want the medical certificate don't you?'

That response calmed Abbas right down. So it was just procedure.

'You know, if this continues, then maybe we need to try something else.'

'Like what?'

'Counselling or a Pakistani solution,' smiled Dr Siddiqui, cheekily unfazed by Abbas feeling offended.

'I'm not going to no psychologist, they are nuts. What's the other solution?'

'Are you married, Mr Rizwan?'

'No.'

'Where are your parents from?'

'Sialkot.'

'You know, in Pakistan we would say that your problem is a spiritual one. Maybe you need to get married.'

'That's a headache.'

'Maybe, but I think it is better than Prozac and other

drugs. They are very strong.'

'I don't need any of that. I think once the sun is out I will be fine, but my boss needs me to get him a medical certificate or I lose my job.'

Perhaps Dr Siddiqui didn't want to subject his patient to drugs that only suppressed an issue or a question in the human soul that one could not avoid. Often his patients focused on the puddle of water on the floor, desperately trying to mop it up rather than plugging the leak in the ceiling and finding the source for the problem. Many of these mental health issues that afflicted his patients, he concluded, were to do with the spirit, but medical books would never tell you that; only a saint would. Maybe it was because he felt an obligation to his countryman, or because he knew what the solution was, that he wrote out a medical certificate for him. Handing it over, he said, 'You would do well to get married.' And as if to add the poetical flourish so typical of those steeped in Persianate culture, he added, 'Every man needs his Leila.'

'Well,' said Abbas, frowning sceptically, 'I don't trust these bloody Leilas if you ask me.' He took the medical certificate before the offer was retracted and left. He didn't thank the doctor because he wanted medicines, not spiritual advice about the state of his heart.

Abbas returned to work after a week. He made sure it was Friday so he could pick up his pay cheque, get some time off to go and pray the Jummah prayer and start a bit later on the weekend. The weather was turning brighter; there seemed to be more sunlight. He gave the medical certificate to Yasser, a barrel-chested Afghan who could probably grow a full beard in half an hour. It didn't placate his boss – Yasser still looked at him suspiciously.

'You seem fine to me,' he said, in his green puffa jacket and mock fur-lined hood. 'What's wrong with you? Come on, man.'

'I don't know, read what it says. I'm not a doctor.' Abbas knew full well that the Afghan was semi-literate and wouldn't bother reading the scribble on the certificate. Yasser threw it straight in the bin.

Abbas turned to the tasks at hand. He noted, however, that there was a coldness in the way he was treated by the other workers. Yasser must have been talking shit about him all week and making them work harder, blaming it on his laziness. So it was no wonder that he suffered their looks of annoyance all day.

After closing time and cleaning the shop, Abbas and the workers all went downstairs to collect their two hundred and fifty or so pounds. Abbas stood in line expecting to get paid. Yasser sat on the worn sofa in the small staff room with its over-used tea kettle, small table and fridge, handing out envelopes to his staff. When it was Abbas' turn Yasser didn't have an envelope for him.

'If you don't work, you don't get paid,' Yasser said as if it was final.

'What,' Abbas said, 'you never heard of sick pay? It's the law.'

'You are getting cash in hand for a reason. Because we don't do those things.'

'Are you sure? I might just make a phone call to HMRC.'

'Are you sure? I might just make a phone call to the anti-terror hotline.' Yasser gave him a knowing grin. It was an evil-looking grin.

The Darkness Inside

'You are a fucking bastard.'

Yasser flared up – you can insult an Afghan but there is one thing you should never do: insult his honour by insulting his womenfolk. He was furious. Several of Abbas' Afghan colleagues stepped in between the men. They realised that Yasser should have paid him; after all, they had been sick before and they had received the week's wages in full, so why the exception? But Abbas shouldn't have called Yasser's honour into question. He was wrong.

Before they could calm the situation down Abbas' arm made a looping arch so that his fist went over the men and landed plum on Yasser's jaw. Yasser's eyes widened as they registered the fist and then his face burned bright with anger. Abbas had that feeling he got as he went into combat. He nearly grinned; at once he became full of vitality. He threw his fist again, straight through the men – it was like a hammer or spear piercing bronze armour or a siege engine hitting a wooden door. Abbas had crossed the boundaries. The staff members now sided with their boss; violence was not necessary. But it was fine, this was Abbas' resignation letter. Abbas kept on fighting, his only goal being the destruction of this Afghan tyrant. The staff members now attempted to push him back with more violence, but the more they pushed him the more he came for them in the room. One of the staff members, a young Afghan, decided that this was the point he should go for help, followed by a second. They ran out of the staff room. Abbas and Yasser were now tussling on the floor. Yasser head-butted Abbas on the nose, which started to bleed. Abbas tasted that salty taste of blood as he punched, clawed and hurt his boss, repaying him for all the slights and oppressions he had

The Darkness Inside

inflicted on his honour over the years, and as he did so, he called him a bastard. This only made Yasser angrier. By the time the young Afghans returned with their friends Abbas had knocked Yasser spark out.

'Abbas jan' they said politely, 'baradar, that's enough.'

Abbas suddenly snapped out of it. He looked around him; he was back in a small staff room which looked like it had experienced a tornado. Yasser lay sprawled on the floor, tongue out as if he was sleeping. Abbas spat on him and then kicked him as hard as he could in his balls. He wanted to make sure Yasser would never have any children. He then grabbed a knife and cut him on his cheek. He wanted him to be reminded of his defeat every day, three hundred and sixty five days a year. Only then, when he had done all that, did he stand in front of his work mates, who cleared a way for him to leave. He left no longer tired nor depressed, even if he didn't have a job anymore.

It wasn't long before he received the phone call. Radio called him the next day while he was still in bed. He was irate.

'What the hell did you do to him? Are you crazy?!'

'No,' he said grinning, 'he wouldn't pay me.'

'So that means you can just beat up my friend? Are you out of your mind? I could have paid you! Do you know what I had to do to get you that job? And what I am having to do so this doesn't escalate? These bloody Pathans don't take this shit lying down. When they start blood feuds they last for centuries. What's got into you?'

'Nothing, he was just disrespecting me. Every man has a right to respond to that, doesn't he?'

Radio was quiet for a moment. 'Look, come work at the car wash. I need someone who can manage it right. Do all the paperwork and stuff.'

'When?'

'Take a few days off. Piss off to somewhere and then come find me.'

'Look, I need to pay the landlord.'

'I'll sort it.'

'Okay.'

29. Feltham

It took Martha two hours to get to the Feltham Young Offenders prison on the following Saturday. All week she had been busy dealing with Brexit intrigues and her Saturday was being spent seeing this inmate. She hoped Ayman would be forthcoming. She arrived at the visitor centre and went through the security process: the ID, the search and all of those things that many people she was with did regularly. There was the young sixteen-year-old telling her screaming infant to 'shut the fuck up', the haggard-looking cockney mum from Southend with some biscuits and the churchgoing Windrush grandmother going to visit her grandson or nephew and hoping that Jesus would save him from the devil's path. Martha looked like an anomaly in her elegant beige coat and brown boots. Some probably assumed she was a solicitor and the prison officers softened their tone towards her when they addressed her.

Ayman was better looking than she expected when she met him in the large visiting hall. He had gentle grey eyes – a far cry from the mugshot that made him look like one of those Saracens that her grandmother had warned her about when they visited Vietri or Amalfi or even the island of Capri in Naples. In the paintings they were always rough-looking fellows dragging some beautiful poor damsel away into their ship. In fact, her

The Darkness Inside

grandmother said that St Andrew, the patron saint of Amalfi, had prevented the Turkish admiral Barbarossa from landing there with his Saracens. The same St Andrew had also saved her from American B-52 bombers as they approached Vesuvius to drop their payload on Naples. Martha grew up with those stories; her grandma sang about Abdallah and fakirs in the camper when they went on holiday during the summer months. She would be singing whilst grandad or dad would take turns driving the camper:

Quatto quatto, lemme lemme
viene da Gerusalemme
il fachiro Casimiro
che ipnotizza la città.
cumbala cumbala cum ba lla!
cumbala cumbala cum ba lla!
O Abdullà me so incantato 'sto braccio qua.
O Abdullà me so incantato.'

But Ayman was tall and handsome. He had a buzz cut with a short beard; his grey eyes matched the grey jumper he was wearing. There was a gentle toughness to him. He gave her a smile, flashing a gold canine. She offered her hand, saying, 'Hello, thank you for seeing me.'

'No problem,' he said. 'I am sorry. I hope you don't mind; I don't shake hands with ladies who aren't my wife.'

Martha didn't like it, of course – shaking her hands wouldn't mean she would pounce on him and seduce him, but at least his wife could trust him.

'Not at all,' she said, taking a seat opposite him.

The Darkness Inside

He sat down, leaning forward and looking side to side.

'Can I get you something?' Ayman said.

Martha noticed that he was looking at her red tresses as he talked to her. 'No, I should get you something.'

'I'm fine, really. So my sister asked me to help you. She said you might be able to reduce my sentence, even.'

'Well,' she said, 'I don't want to get your hopes up. But I will certainly try. Knowing the background may help in sentence reduction.' She brought out her notebook. 'So should we get to it?'

He gave her a thumbs up. 'Shoot.'

'Well let's start with the obvious: who hurt your brother and' – she paused for a moment as if she was pained – 'my fiancé?'

'Oh! I'm so sorry, I really am. I know how it feels. But the answer is easy: Sami, Radio and probably Abbas had something to do with it.'

'Radio? That is a strange name.'

'Well his name is Abu Abdul Rahman.'

'So why is he called Radio?'

'I don't know. Some say he was a roadman back in the day and that's what they used to call him. Others say he was one of them guys who lived a low life and then discovered Islam. Next thing you know he's on Speakers' Corner with a megaphone preaching twenty-four-seven. So they started calling him Radio. In Syria the Arabs never called him that, it was just us.'

'Was he a leader?'

Ayman nodded.

'Why?'

Ayman shrugged as if he wasn't sure. 'They say he

The Darkness Inside

was in Afghanistan in the late nineties or noughties but I'm not so sure. But he seemed to know what he was on about.'

'So you don't know him?'

'I only met him in Syria.'

'What was he like in Syria?'

'He was a wolf. A nasty piece of work and so was his crew. You could be sure that wherever he'd pissed Abbas wouldn't be too far away.'

'So why didn't you go after him as well?'

'He hides. He's got his fingers in too many pies too. I even heard he's got associates in here.' Ayman looked around the visiting hall to see if he could point out one or two. 'I wouldn't be surprised if they were watching us now.'

'So what do you know about him?'

'Not a lot to be honest. I heard he moved around Hanwell ends with some Somalis, holding little circles in some tiny little ghetto mosque run by some Somali guy. Heard he was running VAT scams, rental insurance scams; his boys were lashing bags, cards, anything and everything. Then he went to Syria, returned via Dubai and now he's some sort of legit businessman with two or three wives and loads of kids. Still doing the same shit on a bigger scale.' Ayman shook his head. 'I don't get these guys at all.'

'How can he get away with all that stuff?'

'I don't know, but you need to prove it don't you? With him you can't prove nothing.'

'No, I mean how does he justify it religiously?'

'Those lot? They have no honour. They'll rape a girl and then claim she's a slave girl. To them this country is at war

The Darkness Inside

with Islam so anything goes. They will steal, rob, rape, loot, but ensure that some of that wealth goes to the Muslims. You see it even here. Scummy guys who convert to Islam to get on the halal list and then try to sell drugs to inmates saying that they live in the house of war.' Ayman shook his head. 'Fake Islam if you ask me.'

'Will you help me to expose him?'

'For sure, I don't fear no one but God. You tell me what I have to do. And I'll do it.'

Martha couldn't be bothered trying to grab a bus from the prison to Hatton Cross and then homeward bound. She had already got up early to get to Ayman for nine thirty and she wasn't about to spend the rest of her Saturday on transport, being jostled by travellers coming from Heathrow Airport. She didn't want to stand; her feet were already killing her. So she took an Uber straight home – at least she could sit and relax while the driver took care of everything else.

Providing the driver was not the chatty type, she would be able to brief Sid and he could fill in bits and bobs that didn't make sense. So she sat there hunched up in the back, messaging away, whilst Sid filled her in on everything she needed to know. When she got home, sleep was already catching up with her. So she had a quick rucola salad and some mozzarella and fell asleep on the couch. She woke up two hours later with five text messages from Sid asking her to send over pictures of her notes so he could transcribe them. She sent them over.

30. Dinner

'Excuse me,' said Gardener, looking at the man with the broken face on the till. 'Does Mr Rizwan work here?'

'What?' said the man with the plaster on his nose, bruised eye and stitches. The noise of the saw cutting meat was loud.

'Does Abbas work here?' Gardener asked, a decibel louder.

The man glared at him. 'He doesn't work here anymore.'

'I see,' said Gardener. 'When did he leave?'

'A few weeks ago.'

'Strange, why did he leave?'

'I fired him,' Yasser said, eyeing him suspiciously. 'He's got a screw loose.'

'Do you know how I can get hold of him?'

'Who wants to know?' replied Yasser, rubbing his hairy chin. 'You don't look like a friend of his.' He flashed him an ugly grin. 'You smell like police to me.'

'Well,' replied Gardener, 'I'm a bailiff actually.'

'Oh! What a shame,' said Yasser. 'Had you told me you were police I would have driven you to him myself. I don't like bailiffs; they are a pain in the arse.'

'Yes, that's what we are meant to be.'

'He's a nasty piece of work that haramzada, nasty.'

'I'll take my chances.'

'Well, if you insist,' said Yasser, 'he's at Optimum Car

The Darkness Inside

Wash down the London Road, that black ugly little building. You'll find him there.'

'Thanks.'

'My pleasure. Make sure you clean him out, okay?'

Gardener left the ugly man on the till. He walked through Croydon town centre with its tatty shop fronts, three fried chicken shops and a combination of buskers, shoppers and beggars and into East Croydon Station. From there it was one train to Victoria Station and then the Tube to Camden.

He arrived at Martha's flat by late afternoon. He had picked up some nice Scottish shortbread and a bottle of Drambuie. It was already getting dark and cold and a warm dram would be nice after Sunday dinner. Gardener always knew he was on her floor because it smelled of freshly made coffee. He had texted her to say that he was five minutes away and that she should put the moka on, and she had done so. As he rang the doorbell she was already on the door looking delightful in a white woolly jumper and jeans. She kissed him on both cheeks as they did back home, and he went in, presenting her with the offerings he had brought her.

She gratefully accepted his gifts and led him into the cosy living room whose centrepiece was a beige leather sofa facing a tiled cityscape of Campania that she had put up. It started with Amalfi and Salerno and went all the way to Naples with Vesuvius caressing the city. It had the blue colour mixed in with the Amalfi lemon. Below the tiled cityscape was a blocked fireplace with an electric faux-log fire. On the mantelpiece were figurines from Pulcinella, a laughing Berlusconi and the traditional Christmas figurines,

The Darkness Inside

presepe, that depicted the nativity scene. She should have put them away until next year – after all, it was nearing the end of March and the Christmas tree had been discarded like an old lover – but she had kept the Christmas figurines that reminded her of home.

'How are you keeping?' she asked him.

'Oh, you know, keeping busy,' he replied, looking at the disgusting figure of the former Italian Prime Minister Silvio Berlusconi, who was smiling and showing his bum cheeks to the world; each cheek had the words 'bunga bunga' written on it. It was a reference to Berlusconi's Bunga Bunga sex parties that had caused a major political scandal in Italy. Martha went into the kitchen, poured him some coffee and put some hot milk in a small container. Gardener, though he loved the aroma of Italian coffee, found its strength overbearing, so he needed to tone it down with a bit of milk. She also opened up the Scottish shortbreads, put them on a small plate and brought it to the living room.

'So how did it go?' she asked, before grabbing a biscuit and taking a bite.

'Well,' replied Gardener, 'this Abbas guy has left his workplace.'

'Okay,' said Martha, sitting up, her curiosity awakened.

'He got fired. My hunch is that he beat the guy black and blue.'

'Why do you say that?'

'The guy seemed really pissed off and his face was a mess. So I am just putting two and two together.'

'I see. Did he tell you where he went?'

'Yep,' replied Gardener. 'Optimum Car Wash on the London Road.'

The Darkness Inside

'Great! Thank you for this. What about this Radio?'

'Honestly nothing, there's no birth certificate, nothing.'

'Could have been born outside the UK; you said he was North African right?'

'Not on the electoral roll neither. No marriage certificate – nothing.'

'Hold up,' said Martha. She brought out her phone and texted Sid.

'What you doing?' Gardener asked.

'I'm just texting Sid your findings and some queries about Radio.'

'Did he put you up to this?'

'No, no, I'm just picking up the reins myself,' she replied whilst her fingers deftly texted away.

'Well,' he said, unsure of her adopting such an unorthodox approach, 'as long as you've got the boss backing you…'

Martha wasn't listening; Sid had responded. He didn't have much to do in hospital after all.

'So,' she said, paraphrasing Sid's message. 'This Radio guy might not believe in democracy. For them its tantamount to infidelity and so he might never have voted, or if he's dodgy he might have changed his name by deed. As for marriage certificate, apparently all you need is two witnesses for an Islamic marriage so there wouldn't be a record of that at the registry.'

'Sid's a bit of a machine, isn't he?' Gardener said. 'Up to speed on that elusive little bastard?'

Martha nodded whilst looking at her screen as Sid was typing. 'Look,' she said, reading his message out loud, 'see if there are any pictures of him on Speakers' Corner and get Ayman to stand it up.'

The Darkness Inside

'Might work,' Gardener said. 'Might just work, you know. I expected Sid to be depressed. There's none of that, you know. I even asked him, why don't you have any angst about it? Aren't you going to turn some prayer beads or open that Quran of yours and have one of those life-changing moments you see in the movies when the hero is frustrated by his circumstances? You know what he said? "What you going to do? It was meant to be this way. Journalists get killed every day, life doesn't care if you're hurt, or in pain, or if you've been run over and still pissing out blood. Who gives a shit? Move on. All that matters is winning."'

'Machine,' Martha said, shaking her head, but there was grudging admiration for his dedication. 'A hack to the core.'

'You know he's turned his room into an office? You've given him a purpose.'

'Well at least it keeps him busy in between physio.'

They drank their coffee in silence for a moment. Martha watched her screen; Sid was typing.

'Guess who the director of the car wash is?' she said when his first message came through.

'Who?'

'According to Companies House Abbas Rizwan has been the director now for several months.'

'Oh,' said Gardener, genuinely interested, 'imagine that! From being your everyday butcher, you become the director of a business. Just like that. Who was the previous owner?'

Martha already had the answer. 'Prior to that it was a certain Abdul Rahman Khan? But interestingly enough

251

The Darkness Inside

Sid can't find a home address for the guy.'

'Also known as Radio?'

'Possibly!' Martha beamed with excitement. She looked at her watch. 'What do you say to fried aubergines, cheese and pasta?'

'Sounds good to me.'

'Me too!'

She got up from the living room and went into the kitchen. He followed her. She cut up the aubergines into tiny cubes and then soaked them in salt water. She then got Gardener to squeeze the salt water out of the aubergines until the cubes looked like the wrinkled skin of an old woman. She fried the aubergine cubes until they were dark while he cut up some provola cheese into large chunks.

From start to finish it took them about an hour and a half to prepare a three-course meal, and it was enjoyable. Gardener had seen his mum and dad do this when he was young and had wished to do the same with his fiancée but it never happened.

As they sat eating the pasta he asked her, 'Martha, we've known each other for a long time, right?'

'Right,' said Martha.

'Would you tell me the truth? If I asked you?'

'Of course.'

'Am I ugly?'

'No, not at all. Whatever gave you that idea?'

'Am I too nice?'

'What do you mean "too nice"?' Martha said, laughing.

'Look, sometimes I wonder whether I should be a bastard, you know. Maybe Amanda left me because I was "too nice". And now I can hardly meet a half-decent person to settle

The Darkness Inside

down with. I am in my mid-thirties and I want to find that person to spend the rest of my life with, to have kids, and I am in a desert. It seems either I am not an attractive prospect or the times are a changin'. Maybe no one wants to settle down anymore.'

'Or maybe you're looking in the wrong places?'

'Where? You tell me. Can I ask you something?'

'Yes, for sure.'

'Look, we both love Sid right?'

Martha went silent for a moment.

'Don't worry,' Gardener said, 'it's obvious to everyone but Sid.'

Martha laughed. 'That obvious!'

'I told him not to let you slip through his grasp.'

Martha was surprised. 'You did?' She was touched by that. She reached out and squeezed his hands.

'Always. But you know he's a bastard.'

'Yes, a proper bastardino.'

'So if you knew that, why on earth did you stick with him? Why don't girls like you, who know how to look after their man, go for men like me? Do I need to change into a bastardino?' There was no awkwardness in Gardener's questioning; they were far too close for that. He just wanted an honest answer.

'No, no, please don't think like that; we just reflect our own diseases onto each other. Look, sometimes I think Sid is God's punishment on me. You know, when I was growing up, Mum and Dad used to give us very little money so we could just about have a pizza and a drink outside. They probably knew what the world outside was like so they purposely kept us on a shoestring budget. Once we grew

The Darkness Inside

up and they knew we wouldn't go crazy with drugs and such like, they worried about boys – and for me it was boys who caused me heartache. Once your heart has been broken it's hard for it to be repaired and restored, and then you replay that cycle yourself again and again. I remember I had a really, really good boyfriend called Carlo; he was handsome, polite and studying medicine. My parents thought he was a good match. But you know what I did? I two-timed him with a crazy boy with a motorcycle. Honestly, I still ask God to forgive me for that to this day. He didn't deserve that and I pray that he's with a saint of a woman now instead of someone like me.'

'Why?'

'I don't know, I just felt that Carlo would agree with everything I said and wanted to do. If I wanted to go somewhere he'd say okay. He'd never argue with me. He would smother me with affection till I had to push him away. And then I lay my eyes on Sid and it was completely the opposite. I knew he was a wounded animal from the first day I met him. I knew he had love in him, but I also knew he was a wolf. And maybe God sent him to punish me, I don't know. But don't let Amanda turn you into him. I am sure God will give you an incredible woman. Just be patient.'

'And you?'

'I think he's not finished with me yet. I still need to pay the price.'

31. Abbas

Abbas was still a bit upset at the way Radio had treated him. 'Do something,' he had scolded, 'look at you! You're turning into jelly! Man, I remember you were built like an ox.'

Just because he had given him a job didn't mean that he had to give him life advice as well. It was true, Abbas still had some of the vestiges of the bull about him; his chest was still broad, his arms were still strong, his hands could still wring a man's neck with ease. The only problem was his belly – it was growing at an exponential rate. He could no longer see his toes, nor for that matter anything else below. But the problem was Texas Fried Chicken across the road and the fact that his job entailed sitting around all day in a portakabin watching his staff do the work while he took a few bookings and wrote up some receipts and invoices as and when he needed to. Otherwise it was mostly war films on Netflix.

He was in the middle of watching a movie when there was a mighty racket outside in the yard. It startled him and he belched. He looked through the window where Zia, a young Afghan, was standing looking at a red Punto 1.2. He looked sheepish and worried as a redhead was telling him off. Abbas could hear him.

'But miss,' said Zia apologetically, 'I think, I think that you are mistaken.'

The Darkness Inside

'Mistaken? Me?'

'Yes, miss.'

'Where is the manager? I don't want to talk to you,' she said, looking for someone more important and completely ignoring Zia.

Zia looked lost and in need of saving. Abbas got up from his seat, let out another belch, opened the portakabin and went out. She was really an extraordinary-looking woman. She had lovely curly tresses that went all the way down to her shoulders and beyond. Women these days didn't have that. Her eyes were deep blue and her skin was very pale with tiny faint freckles on her face like distant stars in the night sky. She wore a green coat and what looked like brown riding boots.

'Hello madam,' said Abbas, 'is there a problem?' He found himself giving her a grin, something he had not intended to do.

'Well, I hope you can help me,' said the woman, 'look!' She pointed to the panel on the front wheel. There was a long scratch on it.

'Looks like it's been scratched,' said Abbas, coming closer and inspecting it.

'I am glad we can agree on that. Your boys did it. I dropped off my car today and I come back and it's scratched.'

'No, no, no,' said Zia, interjecting. 'We didn't do it!' he protested.

Abbas knew Zia to be an honest illegal, with kids to feed back home as well. He wasn't in the business of trying to lose his job.

'So are you saying I did it?' the woman asked Zia. She stared at him.

The Darkness Inside

All Zia could do was shy away; he wasn't used to women staring at him so directly. 'No, miss! No! I don't know what happened.'

The customer looked at him. 'So what are you going to do about the damage?'

'Well we didn't do it, miss,' Abbas said.

'Okay,' Martha said, rubbing her hands like she was scheming, 'I am wondering how many illegals you employ here?'

'None,' Abbas replied, taken aback by her abruptness. 'But we don't need that sort of attention and trouble. Why don't you come in and let me make you some tea and see what I can do?'

'Now that's progress!' said the woman, seemingly placated. Abbas led the way to the portakabin and told her to wait outside for a moment. He went in to tidy the place up, make it fit for guests, when he became aware of the smell of fried chicken, body odour and wind that had accumulated in the portakabin over several weeks; that was probably why Radio had grimaced and scolded him when he had come to the office in the morning. He opened up the window and sprayed the place with a bit of sickly air freshener. He got rid of chicken boxes and stuffed them in the rubbish bin hurriedly. He panicked. 'What will she think of me?' his face seemed to say.

Then when he felt that it was semi-presentable he opened the door again cautiously.

'Sorry about the mess,' he said, noticing how her pretty nostrils flared up as they came in contact with the pungent, musty odour. He bade her sit down on a chair next to his work desk and he turned on the electric kettle on a small

The Darkness Inside

table in the corner.

'Tea or coffee?'

'Tea,' she said shifting uncomfortably, looking at her surroundings as if she was trying to get the measure of the person who sat in this portakabin office.

He made her a nice cup of tea then sat down facing her. Removing the nervousness from his mind he focused on the task at hand.

'Do you know, madam,' Abbas said confidently, 'that you are the first customer who has accused my staff of scratching their car? Customers have accused us of many things but not scratching a car. We have been here for years. You are the first.'

'So what are you saying?'

'I am saying you are mistaken.' He leaned forward and watched her as she started to turn fiery again. 'But I want to make sure that we all leave happy. I don't need the hassle; I know I am honest. So leave the car with me and I will have the scratch sorted in a few days' time. Just give me your details and I will be in touch.'

The woman didn't like it, he could tell by her expression, but he wasn't in the business of being conned or played by some woman. 'Do you have any form of ID?' She handed over her driving licence. 'Martha Flippo, is that right?'

'Fillippo,' she said, correcting him. 'Are you going to leave it with that guy?'

'No, I will take care of it myself.'

'I appreciate it.' She stuck out her hand for a shake.

Instead of reaching for her hand Abbas put his hand on his heart. 'I am really sorry,' he said, 'but my religion doesn't allow me to shake a woman's hand. Please don't be

The Darkness Inside

offended.'

'Not at all,' Martha replied, but it was clear she was offended.

When she returned a few days later Abbas had cleared and tidied up his portakabin. He had even managed to go out and get some everlasting plastic flowers from a pound shop in Croydon town centre. In fact, he had gone the extra mile and had the whole area where the cars were washed given an all-over clean up. The barrels were gone, the tyres neatly stacked and the cones nicely lined up. Radio was certainly pleased by the makeover when he handed him a bag of mobile phones to get rid of.

Abbas watched her coming into the car wash, scoping the place out. For a second he had a slight doubt about her, that she might be immigration or even police. He could usually smell them from miles away. Perhaps she was just curious about the operation, the valet service and all the nice cars that came here to get cleaned up even at this early hour.

She knocked and stepped into the portakabin and Abbas stood up to welcome his guest.

'Hello Martha,' he said, 'how are you?' She wore this zesty perfume made out of lemon rinds or something like that. It smelt wonderful.

'Hello,' she said, putting out her hand awkwardly but then, realising that he didn't shake hands, puttng it down again.

Abbas stood there apologising. He felt like a fool. Don't be apologetic, he kept telling himself, but the more he told himself the more he did apologise. 'Tea?' Abbas asked her just to break the cycle of his pathetic apologising.

The Darkness Inside

'That would be a nice apology,' she replied, smiling. She didn't seem so harsh after all. He made her a cup and handed it to her. She took it gratefully in her hands, touching his hands for a brief second. He fished out some donuts from a small fridge.

'I shouldn't,' she said, looking at him as if he was a criminal.

Abbas hesitated for a moment. 'They are Krispy Kremes,' he added.

'Go on then,' she said and grabbed one. 'Aren't you going to have one?'

'I shouldn't,' he said.

She stopped, waiting for him to take one, as if to say that she wouldn't have one either unless both had committed destruction together. He reached for one, grateful that there was someone who would be complicit in the crime. He took a chomp.

'So why don't you shake hands with women?' she asked, drinking her tea. 'You are forgiven by the way, the tea is wonderful.'

He wasn't used to being interrogated this way. 'Well... it's a bit complicated.'

'Are we impure? Or too tempting?'

'No... I mean...' Abbas was having to think; he didn't expect to proselytise about Islam this early, let alone to a woman.

'Go on,' she said, softening, 'take your time.'

'We believe that the Prophet, peace be upon him, was the best of creation, right? For us. So we follow his example all the time. He didn't shake hands with women. The only women he touched were the members of his family.'

The Darkness Inside

'But is that because we are impure?'

'No,' he said, 'not impure, it's just that the Prophet didn't want to open the door to fornication and adultery between men and women. In Islam we stop things at their root. So we don't drink alcohol because it can lead to so many problems.'

'I see,' she said, seeming interested, 'I didn't know that. I thought we were impure.'

'That's a Christian thing I think. No, women to us,' he said, thinking about the right words, 'they're like those pearls in the oceans.' He used an analogy he had read in a pamphlet. 'We protect them with our lives.'

'So you think we need protection?'

Abbas looked at her curiously. He wasn't an educated man – he had never been to college let alone university – and though he did not understand terms such as 'patriarchy' or the feminist theory taught at universities all over the country, he believed that it was just a natural state of affairs. 'There are a lot of wolves and beasts out there,' he said.

'Can't we protect ourselves?'

'Well,' Abbas said thoughtfully, 'honestly?'

She nodded her assent.

'No. We are stronger and everything rests on that.'

'Rests on what?'

'Force is power.'

'So you think that's how the world works?'

He nodded. 'Isn't it?' In his experience men did the fighting and he had never fought any women in his life. Only Kurds employed women snipers but if you caught them, they were as good as dead. He never came across

The Darkness Inside

a women's fighting battalion; men bled to protect them. They enforced their will; they protected the flock from tyrants, hordes and crusaders. That was how it always had been and always would be. In fact, he reckoned that the only reason that women had so much equality now was because it had been granted by men. Women's rights were an illusion, for when the fighting started, it would be back to the primordial state of affairs. He looked at her. She stared back at him. If he wanted, for all her attitude, his hands could snap her neck with one quick twist. Threatened with that, all those theories would be out of her head and she'd beg him to spare her.

She got up. 'Thanks for the tea.' She placed the cup on the desk as if to assert her independence.

He handed her the car key. It had been labelled with her surname, 'Fillippo'. That proselytisation went well, he told himself sarcastically. Educated women were a pain in the arse. He could tell she didn't like what he was saying. But the truth was the truth.

He got up and took her out where his workers were already washing, buffing and hoovering the cars. The air was filled with the spray of the water jets used to clean the vehicles. He took her behind the portakabin; the red Punto was at the back. It looked brand new. She inspected the scratch.

'Fixed,' he said. 'All the scratches are gone.'

'Yes. That is very nice of you. Look,' she said, 'I am going to do a bit of reading about Islam. If I have any questions can I call you?'

Abbas' eyes lit up; what exactly was she saying? 'How?' he blubbered in a response.

The Darkness Inside

'Give me your number,' she laughed.

'Oh? Yes! Of course.' He ran back to the portakabin as if she might disappear before he returned with his business card. She was already inside with the engine on when he came out. He handed her the business card, breathing heavily. As he did so, her fingers brushed his hand ever so lightly again.

'Sorry,' she said apologetically.

'It's okay,' he said as she drove off. What a beautiful red Punto, he thought.

32. Abbas

He was surprised that she had even texted. After all, how could you trust someone to keep their word to Man when they did not keep their covenant to God? He was just being stoic about it, but when she did text it gave him secret pleasure. Perhaps she didn't know about the covenant? It was just a basic 'hello'. He received it when he was closing up shop and didn't respond. Usually, if he didn't recognise the number he didn't reply. Then later when he was at home watching the football she wrote again. He didn't bother reading the message; Klopp was having a god awful time of it with Manchester City. But when his eyes fell on the message – *Hi, I don't know if you remember me but this is Martha, you fixed the scratch on my car* – Mo Salah's genius was totally forgotten. Abbas took his feet down from the coffee table and looked at the message again, just to double check that it was really her. He stared at it for a while; what could she mean by that? His mind turned it over.

Hello, Abbas texted back, *U alright? Hope there weren't any issues with the Punto?*

It's fine.

Gr8, he texted back and added a thumbs up emoji.

So, she said. *I have been looking into Islam a bit, and was wondering if you could help?*

Sure. How?

The Darkness Inside

I have been googling a lot.

That's no good, he texted back, *a lot of misinformation.*

Yes, that's what I noticed. Hard to navigate through it all. I was wondering if you knew any women who could answer my questions?

TBH with you I don't know many sisters.

What about your wife?

I'm not married.

Really?!

Why? Abbas was flattered and a bit offended.

Nothing, I just assumed you were taken. I mean married.

No, I am not.

If I have any questions could I drop by?

I don't know how I can be of help, but if you think I can be of use then for sure.

Thank you :), she texted, *TC.*

Abbas couldn't help thinking that :) and the TC were a very nice gesture coming from her and he thought about it for the rest of the game. He wasn't even too upset when Manchester City scored and clinched the victory.

He didn't expect her to turn up but on the off chance that she might he made sure that his office was presentable. To the great surprise of the workers he even went out to buy himself some clothes. They were mostly woollen jumpers of a dark green, blue and grey variety and with his leather boots and jeans he looked like a woodcutter or a tough sailor who belonged on the Pequod. When Zia wondered why the boss had splashed out Abbas simply replied 'sales' and closed the door behind him. Initially Zia was satisfied with the answer, walking back to the workers, but then he realised that the sales had ended a

The Darkness Inside

long time ago.

'What's going on with the boss?' he asked some of the Pakistani workers, busy washing the car. They were all puzzled. All sorts of theories both simple and complex were bandied about, especially by some of the Punjabis, whose reputation for the lurid and vulgar was world famous.

'Yaar,' said one, 'I heard the boss told him if he didn't shower he would fire him?'

'Really?' said Zia and laughed. 'May God give you martyrdom soon! Amen.'

'Zia, what do you mean? You want me to say Amen?!'

'Yes of course. I want you to die so you don't speak so much bullshit.'

'Yaar, I'm telling you, I have heard he hasn't had a proper wash, I mean proper shower, for thirty-three days and he has pubes as bushy as an Indian saddu!'

There were other theories bandied about too, but when Martha turned up again in her red Punto the mystery was solved.

'Larki! Hay hay! It's his Punto Yaar. It hasn't been squeezed or milked in a long time.' The other workers laughed at the dirty innuendo.

'Larki?!' said Zia. 'That is not a girl, that is a demon, a churel?'

'Look, if she looks like that who cares if she's a demon or not? Zia, why are you so melodramatic man?'

'I didn't know Abbas saab even had a heart.'

'Zia, it's got nothing to do with his heart, look at her! It's to do with his lann.'

'Abbas saab prays, he doesn't think like that.'

'What?! Those people who pray don't have a lann? Zia

The Darkness Inside

you are a fool Yaar. Have you seen how many kids those mawlanas and mullahs have? They probably think about it while reading the Quran. And those ones in Mecca and Medina, I'm telling you their lann is tingling even as we speak! Kasme – I swear it will tingle until they die, that fire will never go out. Zia, she's looking at you, don't just let her stand there. Go!'

'I seek refuge in God from the evil devil. You go!'

'No Yaar! Zia bhai you are the supervisor, you speak to her.'

Zia shivered and the staff didn't know if it was on account of the cold weather or her presence.

Zia didn't speak to her though; keeping his gaze firmly lowered he went straight to the Portakabin and knocked on the door.

'Abbas saab that crazy woman is here,' he said, panicked.

Abbas came out of the door, adjusting his collar.

'She's not crazy,' he replied. 'Let me handle it.'

Abbas noticed she had straightened her hair since the last time. She looked autumnal in her dark olive jacket, brown trousers and knee-high boots. It was entirely appropriate for such a dull day.

'Hello,' Abbas said.

'Hi, how are you?'

'Fine, thanks.'

'Can I have the car cleaned, please?' she said, handing the keys to Zia who was standing nearby nervously. Zia looked at Abbas who nodded for him to carry out her request.

'Boss,' said Zia nervously, 'could you take a look at the

The Darkness Inside

car?'

Abbas was a bit upset at Zia's reluctance but he looked over the car.

'Are there any scratches?' Zia asked.

'No,' replied Abbas.

'Okay, madam,' said Zia, turning to Martha, 'I clean your car, but no scratches on the car okay?'

She nodded. Abbas could tell she was about to laugh. It made him happy.

Zia took the car to the group of workers, who watched the spectacle with keen interest.

Martha brought out a container. 'Here,' she said, handing it to Abbas.

'What is it?'

'Tiramisù.'

'Why?'

'Well I figured I should at least make it worth your while.'

'Oh no,' Abbas said, offended, 'I am not like that.'

'You are too serious; we can have it with the lovely tea you make.'

He blushed. 'You shouldn't have, really.'

'It's okay,' she said, walking towards the portakabin, 'I made sure there was no alcohol in it either.'

Abbas followed her into the portakabin. As he entered the office, he shouted to Zia, 'Give it a full valet service!' Inside the portakabin he turned on the heater and made her the tea the way she liked it. He brought out the fan heater from the cupboard so she didn't feel cold. She was grateful for the kindness. 'Are you still cold?' he asked. 'Because I have a cover if you want.'

The Darkness Inside

'No, I'm fine.'

Abbas sat down on a two-seat sofa opposite her and asked, 'So why do you want to know about Islam? It's quite strange.'

'Well,' she said, 'it's the fastest-growing religion amongst women; I find that strange.'

'The Truth is the Truth.'

'Perhaps. Also where I am from we have all these strange traditions linked to Islam.'

'Where are you from?'

'Italy.'

'I didn't know you were Italian.'

'No? Why not?'

'Well, well,' he said apologetically, 'when you think of Italians you don't think of gingers – I mean, red-haired women.'

'That is true, but there are plenty of us, even in the South where I am from. Anyway, Salerno has one of the oldest medical schools in Europe because some sailors brought over Arabic books on medicine from Tunisia. Salerno was also a centre for ivory carving and glass making, which was because of the Saracens.'

'I didn't know that,' said Abbas with a sense of pride, as if his very own forefathers had brought the chest over.

'Yes, you know, when I was a girl I remember my father telling me that Sicily had been occupied by the Arabs, and he gave me a Saracen head keyring. You know what the Saracen head was about?'

'No?'

'Well there was this beautiful girl who fell in love with a handsome moor and started a love affair with him.

The Darkness Inside

When she found out that he already had a wife and child she chopped his head off and used it as a vase to grow flowers in. They bloomed so wonderfully that people started making ceramic vases to copy her.'

'Yes, polygamy can be difficult for women to accept.'

'My dad also used to say, "If Mahomet doesn't come to the mountain, the mountain will come to him." So it got me thinking about Islam a lot.'

'I see.' Abbas was impressed by her intellect. 'So what can I do?'

'Well I was hoping you could help me navigate through Google and tell me what I should look at and what I shouldn't.'

'I personally would avoid a lot of that stuff on Google and YouTube. Most of those people on YouTube are weird. You have to be careful; either they're Sufis, Ahmadis or some scholars for dollars.'

'Scholars for dollars?'

'I mean they are mouthpieces for tyrannical rulers who pay them.'

'What about Sufis?'

'They're deviants.'

'Ahmadis?'

'They look like Muslims but they aren't Muslims.'

She seemed frustrated. 'Don't you have a church or an organisation that can give a correct position on Islam?'

'No, we don't need it because Islam is simple. All you need is the Quran and Sunnah. We don't need priests, we can just talk to God directly.' He got up, went to the cupboard and searched around. Brought out a book. 'Here, this is a translation of the Quran. Take it.'

The Darkness Inside

'Really? Can I give you some money for it?'

'No, this is a gift from me to you.'

'That's really very kind of you.'

'I hope you find the answers there. He whom God guides no one can misguide and he whom God misguides no one can guide.'

'What about the Sunnah?'

'Well these are the sayings and actions of the Prophet.'

'Are there many?'

'Thousands,' replied Abbas authoritatively.

'Must be difficult to make sense of it all.'

'Not as difficult as you think.'

'Which books should I start with?'

Abbas thought for a moment. 'Give me a few days and I will sort it out for you. Don't worry.'

The conversation lasted for a good hour before she left. And that very day after Abbas finished work he took the train into London and went to Regent's Mosque, where they had a bookshop. He bought her several books on the sayings of the Prophet. He even bought her books on science and a book titled *Evolution Deceit*, hoping to hit home the truth of Islam. It was truly the work of the Prophets. He also bought himself some perfume to wear because, as the Prophet said, wearing perfume was charity.

In the following days when she came over she stayed longer than usual and Zia gave Abbas a knowing smile whenever she went in. He left the door slightly ajar so the guys didn't get ideas that he was up to some dishonourable things with her. While the workers outside discussed whether his was a case of love or lust, he presented her

The Darkness Inside

with the books he had bought her. She seemed genuinely touched. She wanted to pay for the books but he would have none of it. She left his portakabin office calling him an 'honourable man' and he said it to himself a few times, just rolling it around his tongue to get used to the sound of it. After all, was he not an honourable man?

33. Meal

Abbas did his best not to check his phone messages but the truth was every time his phone pinged or vibrated he would bring it out and see if she had sent him any questions. As for him, apart from some aphorisms he did not send her any text messages. If he received an emoji from her his face lit up and if he didn't receive a response to his aphorisms it would put him in a dark mood. But she did not ignore him; she texted once in a while asking how he was and saying that she had a lot of work pressure and deadlines.

He knew his mood swings were stupid and irrational and he became angry with himself. How could a few texts, or the lack of them, make him feel so high or so low? How base, how superficial was that? So he devised various strategies to keep himself busy before her next anticipated visit. He had started to go to the twenty-four-hour gym on George Street.

Training was great. For a long time after he had returned, he felt that he had let himself go physically. There were few who understood him. Radio didn't see him as much; having two wives and kids was hard work so they couldn't spend as much time together. And in any case, Radio was always busy. He was taking on more wives to such an extent that Abbas couldn't keep up with the number of women he had married and subsequently divorced. He even refused to be the go-to witness for Radio's numerous marriages any longer, after a woman, another one of his mental cases, turned up one day at the portakabin screaming and making a fuss about maintenance. Radio had dismissed her complaints: 'Some women, akhi,' he said, 'have angels cursing them till the Day of Judgement. All I'm trying to do is help them and this is how they pay me back.'

Still, Abbas heard about his seed cropping up all over South London and he wondered whether his two wives even knew about all the other kids and wives he had. Sometimes they would call the office and ask where Radio was, and he would have to inform them that Radio had left the country for a few days.

'Where has he gone?'

'I don't know, sister, I thought you could tell me.'

And just as mysteriously as he'd disappeared he'd pop up unannounced at the portakabin with a bag of something that needed getting rid of.

With Radio's mysterious absences Abbas had started to lean on Sami more and more, but now that Sami was gone, he had let himself go completely. He had little to do in the evening so he started to work out at the gym every day. Sometimes he went really late, when there were none of those women who wore such tight clothes that they left nothing to the imagination. You could see their camel-toe, and whether they had an innie or an outie, or a gap! As he saw it, they were nothing but whores.

The gym was a good distraction and due to his new-found devotion and the fact that he had trained in the past, the changes were visible within three to four weeks. His body responded easily to the pressure of metal; his limbs

The Darkness Inside

remembered how it felt to be combat-ready. And he liked the fact that he was probably one of the strongest guys at the gym, excluding the steroid takers and the bodybuilders who couldn't even scratch their backs. But he didn't really view the bodybuilders as men; they were too vain for his liking. Too obsessed with the way they looked, insecure human beings totally focused on posting stuff on social media – he would eat those narcissists alive if he faced them man to man. He knew it and somehow they knew it too. For they would not look at him as he grimaced and roared when he pushed the weights. They looked away as he huffed from the exertion. They knew who the king of the jungle was and if need be, he could prove it.

She came back in mid-April, unannounced. The rain was of the misty type, as if the air was filled with car wash spray. She asked to have her car given a once-over and valet and handed Zia the keys. It was lunch time and she caught Abbas just about to go out to get some food. He couldn't help but wonder if she had intended to look pretty or if she just was pretty. He wondered whether she had just thrown a woolly jumper and a pair of jeans on and just looked delightful in the rain or whether she had put some thought into it. Did she care that his eyes needed something pleasing to look at? Her hair looked so soft, so red, he could put his face in it and be immersed in it forever. He must have been staring at her for a long time because she stood there looking bemused, waiting for him to say something.

'Hello,' she said.

'Oh hello, it's you.'

'Is this a good time?'

'No, no problem!' Abbas said, not wishing her to slip

The Darkness Inside

away. 'I was just going out to get some food. Do you mind if I let you in while I go get it?'

'I haven't eaten either.'

'I see,' he replied, unsure of himself; he hadn't gone to lunch with a woman for a long time. 'Shall I get you something?'

'Where were you going to eat?'

'Kebabkhana,' he said, 'it's a dirty place but it's really good.'

She laughed. 'My father always says that the dirtiest places are the best.'

'It's spicy,' he said as if trying to dissuade her. He was embarrassed that he ate there at all.

'I love spicy food. Should we go?'

'Are we going to argue over who is going to pay? Because I don't do Amreeki.'

'What's Amreeki?'

'Splitting the bill the way Americans do. I know these days women insist on that stuff. But I am not really into it.'

'Where I am from,' she said, 'when a man takes out a lady, he pays.'

'Oh, okay,' Abbas indicated to Zia that he would be about an hour and to call him if there was an issue. Then he turned to her. 'Do you mind if I ask you a question?'

'Depends what it is. Single or married, that type of question?'

'No, not that type of question, but now that you ask, are you married?'

She paused for a brief moment. 'Widowed.'

'I am so sorry.'

'It's okay, time heals. So what did you want to ask me?'

The Darkness Inside

'What is a bidet?'

'What?' She burst out laughing. 'What sort of question is that?'

'Well,' Abbas said, a bit embarrassed, 'you know sometimes you sit there googling? I wondered if your people are like the English and the bidet came up.'

'If the answer is whether we use water after a number two – the answer is yes. Strange question though!'

'Honestly that's a discovery. I thought it was only us Muslims who used water after going to the toilet.'

'I feel you have a new respect for us.'

Abbas laughed. She had divined his thoughts. They went to Kebabkhana, probably the dirtiest kebab joint in the Cronx. The grill was already busy with kebabs and chickens on it, whilst the display was heaving with Pakistan's finest dishes, fresh and steaming hot. The tables and chairs which occupied most of the shop were already filled up with punters and Uncle Feisal and company were busy serving them.

What surprised many was the fact that even though the *Croydon Advertiser* had named and shamed the joint as one of the dirtiest places in the area, Pakistanis still bought their kebabs there; that meant they were good. The food was cooked by people who seemed to have been made for that role; when God created everything and he ordered the pen of destiny to write all that would come to pass, a footnote was added to say that Uncle Feisal would make kebabs excellently for the rest of his life on earth and would receive a heavenly reward for such a godly task.

But even Uncle Feisal and company were surprised to see Abbas with such a beautiful woman in tow and tried to

The Darkness Inside

temper her choices. In fact, Uncle Feisal was so kind that he personally cautioned and advised her on what dishes were mild and what dishes were hot, and which ones she should stay away from. When she pointed at the halim, Uncle Feisal's eyes widened and his mustachio bristled. 'No, no, no, no!' he said, shaking his hands, 'it's too hot for you, my dear.' Halim, a combination of lentils, rice, meat, fried onions and green chillies, for the uninitiated could cause such combustion in the stomach that it would result in a burning ass for days. During Ramadan this dish caused huge problems at the Tarawih prayers, with men belching away whilst the Imam was trying to recite the Quran; the air was infused with the tasty dish.

But Martha insisted on eating the dishes he warned her against, and what was more she chose hot, spicy and mild ones and ate them with relish. Abbas and Uncle Feisal watched amazed that the pale lady could actually hold the spicyness without much difficulty.

'We have hot food in the south of Italy too, you know,' she said as she tucked into her kebab.

'I thought you people only had pizza and pasta,' said Abbas.

'Have you ever been?'

'No,' said Abbas, 'never.'

'You should visit; you would love it. You know a pizzaiolo can sometimes earn more money than a junior engineer in Naples? They are superstars.'

'What's so special about them?'

'It's the way they make the pizza dough. Also if you look at the ovens, they use wood. When wood burns, the water that remains in the wood, that sweet scent, gets into

The Darkness Inside

the dough, and then there's the climate and everything else. Nothing like a few fiocchi di neve and Neopolitan coffee – believe me. You should go.'

'Maybe one day.'

The hour's lunch break ended up going on for another two hours. When they returned they found a black Range Rover parked up. The portakabin was open and Radio was sitting down at his desk looking at some paperwork. Radio saw Abbas come in and the stocky man with a rough beard got up and gave up the seat to him.

'Wow, man! Gone a few weeks and look at you! You look like an animal.' He hugged him. 'Akhi, where have you been?' He shook his hands.

'Sorry, I just popped out to lunch,' said Abbas awkwardly. 'It took a bit longer than usual.'

'Not to worry man, I keep telling you to take some air during your breaks. You're cooped up here all day.' Radio suddenly spotted Abbas' guest, who seemed busy with her phone messaging and had followed them both in. 'Who is this?' Radio asked.

'This is Martha.'

Turning to Martha, Radio said, 'Sorry I didn't introduce myself – Abdul Rahman, but they call me Radio – don't ask me why!' He stuck out his hard calloused hands, which Martha shook after a moment's hesitation. She looked at Abbas as if to say: 'How comes he can shake my hands and not you?'

'Nice to meet you, I'm Martha.'

'This is the lady with the red Punto,' Abbas said.

'Oh, Ms Fillippo? I hope there weren't any issues with the car?'

The Darkness Inside

'All sorted,' Abbas replied.

'I am glad,' Radio said, staring at her as if he was studying her. 'My boys got working on it straight away.'

'So Ms Fillippo,' he added, remaining ever so polite, 'what is it that you do? You seem very familiar.'

'Please call me Martha. I work in publishing.'

'I see, must be really interesting. So what brings you here to Croydon?'

'I work around here.'

'Where?'

'I have some clients here in East Croydon.' She seemed nervous and distracted.

Abbas found Radio's way of looking at her strange. It was not a pervy look, more like the sort of look he gave when he scrutinised something or someone. Like one of those barbers who stared into your eyes as he shaved you. His hands stroked his bristly beard downwards like he was some sort of philosopher contemplating an important question. And then, as if he had reached the conclusion of his pondering, he said, 'Anyway, I have to go.' He turned to Abbas, giving him a knowing look. 'Look, I got a bag for you here.' He patted the bag resting on the desk. 'My kids need picking up. Well, it was nice meeting you Martha.' He gave her a big grin that seemed insincere.

'Pleasure,' Martha said, still on her phone and not looking at him.

He hugged Abbas. 'Call me later big man.'

He left them in the portakabin. Abbas stood there awkwardly watching his boss jump into the Range Rover and driving off.

'He's a bit creepy,' Martha said.

The Darkness Inside

'No, he's intense, that's all,' Abbas replied. 'One of the best. When he's with you he's with you. He's a good man.'

'Anyway, thanks for lunch.'

'No problem.'

'Maybe one day, I can buy you some dinner.'

Abbas laughed as if his honour would never allow a woman to buy him dinner, whatever the circumstances.

34. Santores

For Martha, one of the things that she missed about Italy was its culinary culture. London had many things but it did not understand food or, more precisely, quality food. How could it? London was for the transient being, like Pontecagnano in Salerno, a posting stage in life, where you work for a while but from which you move on if you don't make it in terms of money. How could such transience appreciate quality? Something that can't be quantified and does not obey time nor what London demands, something that you recognise only when you see or taste it? But what irked her was London's fakery, its coffee for instance. Not the Starbucks and Prets, no, they didn't pretend to be anything else but pure merda. But Nero's coffee was an abomination; it evoked nothing but contempt. That charlatan of a drink wouldn't be consumed in Milan, let alone Naples. The roasting was so long it tasted acidic – like battery acid. And it was this crime of a beverage that claimed to be Italian. It made her furious every time she walked past one of those chains. But even Martha had to admit that what Londoners lacked in culinary sophistication they made up for with a heavenly medley of fast food, which was perfect for the city. It did kebabs, fried chicken, fish and chips, salt beef, Chinese and so on. It did them so well that sometimes its own local variety superseded the original.

The Darkness Inside

In Martha's eyes, people didn't understand quality meats or quality ingredients; to Londoners a tomato had to look red and be large but taste did not matter and certainly wasn't worth paying for. Potatoes had to come super clean, without dirt, but to her dirt indicated freshness and vitality. Londoners knew next to nothing about shopping locally. They didn't understand that some of the stuff they were eating was from a place called Battipaglia, a few kilometres from Eboli; that it had been harvested by some poor migrant from Mali. London simply didn't understand food the way Naples did.

Naples was resplendent in its tradition – you could go to three different places in Campagna and the mozzarella would taste different in each one. You could have a caprese in the summer, just mozzarella, tomatoes, olive oil, salt and pepper with a bit of bread, and it was outstanding. What mattered was the ingredients; if they were good, everything was good. Martha looked for quality, local produce and bought things fresh every day. In London, Tesco delivered everything for the whole week and it tasted awful. That was why she loved to eat pizza in a restaurant on Exmouth Market called Santores. The whole place smacked of Naples; some of the waiters even pronounced the 's' like a 'sh'. They brought their stuff over from Italy and they made a wonderful pizza and parmigiana.

Martha had invited Gardener to meet her there for Sunday lunch. She was sitting outside, enjoying the spring sun and drinking a glass of Lacryma Christi, when he arrived looking, as always, sharp and somewhat out of place. He was wearing a tweed jacket, jeans, brogues and a red scarf. She got up and pecked him on the cheek. They

The Darkness Inside

ordered two pizzas: for her, a simple margherita and for him, a diavola. While they waited she poured him a glass of wine and made small talk.

Work for him was going well but he was contemplating a different direction in life. He figured he could sell his flat, buy a place up north, travel the world, and then come back and do something else.

'Mid-life crisis?' she asked. 'Has it come early?'

'No, not so much that. I am bored and I sometimes wonder what it is that these editors want. Remember when we were at university and we took that media and political communication course?'

She nodded.

'We,' said Gardener, 'are meant to be the fourth estate. We are meant to hold the various executives to account. We are meant to keep a sentient citizenry informed in the agora of the public debate so they can make informed decisions, aren't we? These days the director of the Beeb leaves for a job in Downing Street.'

He watched Martha roll her eyes as if to say, 'Does anyone believe in that stuff anymore?'

'I don't feel,' he continued, 'I am doing that anymore. I am under pressure from editors to give them juicier and juicier stuff. So people will click on it. Everything is a two- or three-minute read – it even says so on the article! Long reads are five minutes. Shit, people's tweets become news. Dog and cat videos become news, alongside Kardashian's magnificent bum. She's the Frankenstein of our age. You know humanity is in trouble when entertainers are in power and the media has been captured by the whims of the audience.

Where's the sentient citizenry that can distinguish between fake news and real news?'

'You are talking to someone from Italy,' Martha said, reeking of someone who has accepted that reality. 'Our TV is worse. It's all *Who Wants to be a Millionaire?*, salmon-lipped female football presenters and useless TV news. It's been captured already and the formula for keeping Italians docile is cheap entertainment while the politicians rob the country.'

She looked at Gardener and was almost disappointed in him. How could he be so square? So naive? Did people like that exist anymore?

'Why don't you come and work for me? Paul, although he's young, is a great editor, a real old-school journalist, used to work for the *Times*, you know. I need someone on the home bureau with Sid being out of action.'

'Not sure. What sort of stuff will I be working on?'

'Investigative stuff.'

'Like what?'

'Jihadis and the likes.'

'You mean the people who attacked Sid?'

'Yes.'

'How far have you gone?'

'I have stood up both of the killers with Anis' brother.'

'How?' He was amazed and started to listen more intently.

Martha smiled; she couldn't help her smugness. His amazement was acknowledgement that she may have a desk job but she still knew how to switch onto game mode – that ability to infiltrate and get at the information.

'I took a photo of them when the kingpin visited the car wash. Been recording our meetings too.'

The Darkness Inside

'Secretly?'

She smiled smugly and nodded.

'And your boss is cool with that?'

He looked concerned when she didn't respond with anything but her smugness. She was like a stubborn school kid getting away with something mischievous, but to him this wasn't a school prank.

'Is he?' His tone became increasingly impatient when he realised what was going on. 'So there was no backwatcher with you?'

'Okay, okay, I get it.'

'Martha, look at me. You are breaking every rule in the book. If Sid did that you would have kicked his ass. This is for real. Sid could have been killed by these guys. It's not just you who has game, you know. It's not hard to find out who you are. I mean it's not just investigative journalists who use Google, Facebook, Linkedin algorithms, you know. There's a reason why these criminals have survived for this long unnoticed. You don't think they couldn't find out who you are if they wanted to? If you search them on Facebook you will appear on their 'people you may know' list too.'

'Don't worry, they don't have my nom de plume.'

'It doesn't matter if you don't write under your real name Martha; you need to tell Paul to get you a backwatcher as soon as.'

'He will shut it down. He's super careful after the panel hearing. Won't even fart without checking with management now.'

'Wait, hold up, you mean to tell me he has no inkling? Who are you doing this with?'

'Just a bit of freelance work on the side.'

The Darkness Inside

'You haven't been doing freelance for years – that's a breach of contract, Martha. You're doing this with Sid aren't you? He's put you up to it hasn't he?' Gardener shook his head. 'That manipulative little cunt.'

'Don't patronise me. I can make my own choices.'

Gardener looked at her as if he didn't believe a single word.

'Yeah right.'

'What? It's true.'

'Come on, ever since uni you two have been as thick as thieves. Just admit it, this is the tail wagging the dog.'

'Che palle!' Martha said, exasperated by the lecture. 'Are you my dad?'

'No, I am your friend. I've got one in hospital and I don't want to see another one in a coffin. Is that too much to ask?'

'Then help me. Don't worry, these guys are illiterates. Total.'

'If they were stupid, they wouldn't be good at what they do.' He leaned back on his seat, tossing a tissue he had scrunched up on the table.

'How far have you gone?'

'I think I have one of them; I have been out with him a few times.'

'How many times?'

'Six, seven times now. He looks like a grizzly but he's a care bear at heart.'

'Seven times! It's fucked up, real fucked up. He'll maul you if you're not careful.'

She started singing the lines from 'Linger' by the Cranberries whilst twisting her locks with her finger.

The Darkness Inside

Gardener shook his head at her playfulness.

'I can't believe this.'

'Oh! You are so square. Anyway, listen, the other guy, Radio, he's the kingpin, he's a harder nut to crack. I don't quite know how to get to him. But if I can open up the grizzly bear, Abbas, then there's a chance. Now before you start don't ask me how – short of converting and marrying him I haven't figured that bit out yet, but I am working on it.'

'Martha, why are you doing this? You don't have to prove anything to Sid. You didn't do anything wrong.'

'Look, how many times have I told you, I'm not doing it for that!' Martha was defensive. 'This is a great story. I mean award-winning. Can't you see it?' Her eyes had a strange light to them.

'You are insane. I'm telling you.'

'Look,' she said, 'I just can't deal with the fact that people got hurt under my watch.'

'You don't feel guilty that a guy died because of Sid? He's a psychopath, Martha. You can't square the circle; you can't make this right.'

'I said I haven't figured out how but I'm going to try. I need Abbas to tell me that his boss killed Anis.'

Gardener stared at her in disbelief. She reminded him of Sid.

'You know smoking gun stories come along only once in a lifetime? He has to be an absolute moron to admit that.'

'Well,' replied Martha, 'I'm going to try, alright?'

There was steely determination in her blue eyes.

'So are you going to help me or are you just going to

carry on being my dad?'

'And if I don't?'

'Then I'm still going to do it. You know me.'

There was an awkward silence for a moment. Gardener gritted his teeth.

'Fucking hell, what do you need?'

It was as if she knew he would consent.

'Great, could you check whether these guys were known to the security services?'

Martha brought out a piece of paper and scribbled their names down. 'Just check on the off chance that they were aware of them. And check if lover boy, Abbas, had any significant criminal history. He's had a messed up childhood so he must have gone through the prison system.'

'I don't like it,' Gardener said, with the expression of a man who's being used. 'You can forget about me working for you though.'

The lunch didn't pan out very nicely afterwards. Conversation was thin. The only noise that Gardener made was the sound of his knife cutting the pizza and screeching against the ceramic plate. After finishing, he proffered an excuse to leave. He left her drinking her macchiato and headed towards London Bridge.

Gardener was in West Croydon within the hour and strode into Mayday Hospital on the London Road. He still hadn't formulated his ideas yet, what he would say, or how he would say it. But as his anger festered, for some odd reason he decided to buy Sid some chocolates, Quality Street. Why he brought him presents he didn't quite know. When Gardener wasn't working he was the sort of man who would insist on paying a barber who had

The Darkness Inside

cut his ears and torn up his face with a cut-throat razor, apologising about his rough face. Instead of striding in like those hard-boiled journalists in the movies, he knocked on Sid's door and waited patiently till he heard Sid's voice say: 'Come in!'

He entered. Sid was sat on a chair opposite Femi Johnson. Femi, sporting some fashionable threads, got up with a broad, warm smile and shook Gardener's hands.

'Hey man,' he said in a deep voice, 'how are you? It's been ages!'

Gardener was surprised to find an old university friend in the room, and not least to be hugged by him so affectionately. The anger ebbed away.

'Femi, well, what are you doing here? I thought you were in Africa.'

'No, I was in Dakar, Senegal.'

'Yes, that's what I mean.'

Femi laughed, shaking his head. Gardener didn't know what was so funny.

'What you doing here in Croydon?'

'Well, I was in London to see family and I heard about my man over here, and I thought, I have to see him. He's only down the road.'

'That's nice.'

'What about you? The broadsheets?'

'Yes, same old same old.'

'Anyway, I got to go. I'm here for a few days. Why don't we catch up?'

'Yes, for sure!' Gardener brought out his business card and handed it to him.

Femi handed his business card. Gardener looked at it –

editor of *DEEP* magazine, it said.

'Anyway,' said Femi, 'see you around. Sid, let's talk later.'

Femi left the two men. With Sid still sat down, Gardener stood there awkwardly holding his Quality Street sweets in his hands.

'Oh, I meant to give you this,' Gardener said and handed him the box of chocolates.

'Thanks,' Sid said, grabbing the chocolate box, and pointed to the empty chair.

Gardener took a seat next to him. It was nice to see his friend making a recovery, off the bed and actually sitting up.

'So I take it the physio is doing the trick,' said Gardener.

'Yes,' Sid replied and as an afterthought added, 'thank God.'

'What a blast from the past? Isn't it?'

'What?'

'Femi. What happened to him? After university he just disappeared.'

'No, he didn't.'

'Oh really?'

'Yeah, he worked for the *Voice*, until he became its editor. Then moved to Senegal doing all sorts of stuff working on the Dakar Biennale.'

'What's that?'

'An arts festival.'

'Nice, I didn't know that.'

'He's also done a lot of work for Al-Jaz.'

'Really? Al Jazeera?'

'Yes man, the guy got the Rory Peck Awards for covering Libya and Mali.'

'Wow. So what's this *DEEP* magazine?'

The Darkness Inside

'It's one of these start-up webzines, funded by some freethinking banker philanthropist in California. Wants to set up something like the *Intercept* but with less of an activist feel to it.'

'Less Julian Assange. Weird that, the bankers screw you and then they want to set up a magazine that helps to keep the agora of democracy open. But then we're in a world of contradictions.'

'Yep, without industry you'd never have Fleming inventing Penicillin and me and many other millions of souls would be dead. He's hoping the magazine will have its priorities right. You know, like Assange is in the Venezuelan embassy whilst Tony Blair walks free – that sort of priority.'

'Well, all power to him. Such a lovely chap.'

'Yes, exactly. You know he was the only guy that would share his contacts with me? I would be like man, this guy's mad but he'd always say that the rain will fall on every tin roof. Have a lot of love for him.'

There was a silence in the room. Gardener sat staring out the window into the grey light. It had started to rain and the raindrops fell with intermittent breaks of sunshine.

'Talking of contradictions, Sid,' Gardener added, 'what is going on with Martha?'

'What?'

'Why are you manipulating her?'

'Whoah! Hold on a minute.' Sid sat up rigid. 'What? I don't get your drift, come again?'

Gardener looked him straight in the eye.

'Why are you playing with her?'

'Come again?' Sid appeared not to get the thrust of the argument.

The Darkness Inside

'Why are you playing her, why are you making her secretly record these meetings? You know a lawyer has to make sure that it's warranted. What are you playing at?'

'What?!' Sid said. 'What if she just wants to do it of her own accord? She's a strong-willed woman you know.'

'Yeah, but not with you, ever since you took her under your wing at uni.'

'So did you mate.'

'Yes, but you pushed guys away who were trying to take advantage of her. You punched that Terry in the mouth when he wouldn't take no for an answer. You gave her your notes when she had a hangover.'

'You would have done the same. I'm telling you, this has nothing to do with me. She's the one who got me on board. Anyway, you know this is in the public interest?'

'Yes, but work gives you back-watchers who served in the Ulster Constabulary or something. What the hell are you playing at, Sid? Why are you making her do this? What do you gain from this?'

'How dare you? Maybe it's her, you thought about that? Maybe I got nothing to do with this! You ever thought maybe she is the one who is manipulating me? Man, when I was swimming around in the darkness, you know what I kept seeing?'

'Oh, here we go.'

'No, listen, I'm serious. Do you remember how she brought me in to the news desk as an assistant editor on a freelance shift at our first gig at AP? Do you know how grateful I was to her? Man, I worked like a dog. I was happy that she brought me in; she made it look like a promotion. Whenever I was invited to a leaving party,

The Darkness Inside

or Christmas party, the way she moved with all those journalists and editors who had only one thing in common – money. And I was there in some ragged clothes. It was this unspoken language. It didn't matter if she was Italian or not, she could spunk nine hundred pounds on a dress during break time and feel no way about it, drink her Prosecco, hobnob with them easily. She knew which knife to use with lobster and I was just happy that she took me with her. You know it was after a year that I got my first byline. She gave it to me. After a year of night shifts, she'd moved me to her bureau. You know why? She wanted to keep me to herself. I beavered away, people just thought I was some anonymous intern. I was so grateful to her for bringing me in and giving me that single byline; I forgot that it was her name that was credited for every story I had done that past year. When she went off to the *Loop* she took me with her. But here's the thing; when I was comatose I saw her wearing those beautiful dresses with Paul, with other editors, collecting awards for stories I'd worked on. I never got an invite to those parties. How comes? How comes Femi got recognition and I didn't for my work? I just about got bylines for those stories; Martha took credit for that. Do you remember that story about Whitehorse Academy? They even asked Michael Gove about it. That was my story. Martha got the circular email thanking her for her hard work. I don't blame her, you know. I don't think it's racism. You know what I call it? Protecting her 'game' – me. So who is manipulating who?'

'Is that what this is about? Is that how sad and lonely you are? I'd hoped you'd think about Jesus or something or see the light whilst you were conked out in the darkness.

The Darkness Inside

Even get motivated by revenge. But no, you wake up because you have this epiphany? You want me to buy that? Stop bullshitting me Sid. I know you better than that. You're playing her like you play all the chicks you want something from. And you know what, I'm not going to let you.'

'What,' Sid said, about to stand up, 'you think she can't play people? Mate, you fuck this up and you will never get together.'

'Is that what you think this is about?'

'Come on, Tom,' Sid said, smiling. 'Isn't that what it's about? You're trying to move to her.'

'You are so fucked up, Sid. After all these years that we've known each other?' Gardener said, shaking his head, disgusted. 'Maybe you should be like your sister and turn to the Quran to find some inner peace. But I'm not going to let you do this.'

'That's fine,' Sid said, 'you do what you have to do. But you are going to have to explain that to her. And if you do then you know what won't happen?' Sid took two fingers and made as if he was inserting them into a girl's vagina and gave him a lecherous grin. 'That won't happen.'

'Goodbye,' Gardener said, getting up to leave. 'Speak to Martha and call it all off or get Paul involved. I'll give you a few weeks to sort it out.'

'Don't fuck your chances up with her,' Sid said as he left the room. It was the last time Gardener would visit.

35. Snowflakes

'I swear down,' said Radio, 'if my boy was like that I'd bury him myself.' He stared grimly at a pale teenager with tattoos all over his body and face. There were slogans tattooed on the young man's face – he probably did not fully comprehend 'love and sex'. He had 'kiss me' written on his lips and ugly piercings came out of his nose. He walked around with girls, trainers with bright pink laces. 'This guy makes Justin Bieber look like Russell Crowe.' The young man was trying to bench press thirty kilograms and struggling to push it. 'I swear down,' Radio continued, shaking his head, 'back in the day man would be called a barbarian if you were without clothes and now you wear nothing, put on some women's clothes and you are called civilised? Wagwan? Beats, that is what they need, pure beats. That one over there, he needs bleach on his face and a brush. But you know what,' Radio said, putting another plate of twenty kilograms on the metal bar, 'it's already begun; my boy asked me what a paedo is while they were watching *Walking with Dinosaurs* and I was like: "No! No! No! No! Too early." I didn't know what to say or do. I swear down, never felt so helpless! The kid's only ten years old man! I can't show him a picture of Jimmy Savile or that dutty man? What's his name, Australian bloke, did all that business with kids?'

The Darkness Inside

'Rolf Harris?'

'Yes, that's the one.'

'So what did you tell him?'

'I told him to shut up, in case my girl started singing a nursery rhyme about paedos. Said I would tell him later.'

'That's no good,' said Abbas.

'Yeah? What would you do then?' Radio clenched his fist, then scratched his bare shoulder.

'I'd tell him it's a dinosaur from the Jurassic period – that would shut him up for another year or two at least.'

Radio shook his head. 'Please promise me you will never have kids, you're just setting my boy up to be touched up by some batty boi.'

Abbas grinned at that turn of phrase; he hadn't heard that for ages. Radio patted him on the shoulders and Abbas tucked his red vest into his tracksuit and lay down on the bench press. There were three plates of twenty on each side of the bar. The bar itself weighed twenty kilos.

'Come on,' said Radio, 'we are doing eight! Bismillah!'

Abbas roared into action and started to lift. Every part of his muscles was tensing and exerting itself.

Radio started to count. 'Eight... seven... six... five... four... three... two... one... come on! Just one more!'

In the end, Radio got ten pushes out of Abbas, which he did alone, without any help. Then he started to take off weights from the bar, shouting at Abbas to keep on pushing until all he was lifting was the barbell and nothing else, but even that was a struggle. And only then, once the pyramid was complete, did he let him off. Radio always knew how to get the best out of him. He knew just how much he needed to twist to get Abbas to push.

The Darkness Inside

Radio then went into the cross fit area and grabbed the battling ropes. He braced his core, held the ropes in front of his body and started to slam them hard on the floor so they moved like waves. He continued doing that for two minutes, took a minute's break in-between and then started the exercise again. Radio's gym was very different from Abbas' twenty-four-hour gym. It was in a rougher part of Croydon. The walls were coloured black and looked intimidating. It had more free weights and a large cross fit area. At the back lay a massive tractor wheel that he pushed up and down the hall. There was also a sledgehammer which he smashed against the wheels as if he was smashing skulls. Radio didn't pump as much iron as Abbas did – he was more into cross fit and calisthenics – but there was an explosiveness to him which Abbas lacked. And when it came to wrestling in the small cage fighting area, Radio could still get the better of Abbas despite his size and strength. But most of the time Abbas pinned him down, because he positively thrived on the fighting. He just came alive in the cage. It sparked off memories for both men – the discipline, the excitement of battle and all of those things most of us will never understand.

After the workout they went into the Whitgift Centre; Radio had to buy his kids some sports gear. They walked into Sports Direct and Radio started grumbling, holding up some luminous football boots. 'See, what I don't get,' he said, 'is why the hell do my kids need all of this shit? When I was growing up, a kid with a football was enough. You didn't need all this. It doesn't make you better. I guarantee you we could have twisted these kids up even with our shitty trainers.'

The Darkness Inside

'So why do you do it?'

'Because I am the man of the house – outside.' He grinned. 'You'll see, they just don't make women like they used to. They are spoilt and self-centred. That's why guys in this society don't even think about settling down. What's the point? Shit, you move to a girl and she gives you a feminist spiel and by the time she's finished your boner is non-existent or you're chasing batty.'

Abbas grinned. 'True.'

'Boy, I must be getting old. Hear this, you know Leeroy is carrying a borer?'

'What's he doing carrying a blade? He's only got a year left innit?'

'I went to see him a week back.'

'Where?'

'Long Lartin. He told me these yoot devils haven't been raised by mums and dads. The TV or their friends raised them, so they don't have any sense of order and they are just stabbing people left, right and centre. So he's forced to carry the knife so he can see out his time in peace.'

'Is that how they are going on? Times are changing.'

Radio nodded. 'No order. They don't understand it. Do you remember even amongst us they were the laziest spoilt shits you could have in the battalion. Gave you the ugliest screw face if you woke them up early.'

'This new generation, man,' Abbas added like he was Radio's echo chamber, 'they are either wild animals or they're gay. They get raised by mums and female teachers and they don't know how to be men, and then they ask how comes they are all faggots.'

'So anyway, what about this girl you're checking?'

The Darkness Inside

'Who?'

Radio did an impression of Martha, playing with his hair, twisting his fingers around his nipples, pushing them up, and grinning. It was comic to see this immensely muscular man doing a lurid impression of a woman. Abbas looked at him as if he didn't know what he was insinuating.

'Sorry,' Radio said, laughing, 'I mean you're educating her about Islam. Come on man, who you fooling.'

'What?'

'You really think she's going to convert?'

'That's in the hands of God.'

'Yes,' Radio said grinning, showing him his white teeth. He looked like a dog who wouldn't let go of a stick. 'Still, you're hoping, I know you are. But sorry to drop the bad news, that only happens in the movies.'

'Look, if she converts it's all good.'

'You really think she's into you or Islam? Sounds funny to me. The girls I know who convert to Islam have got some messed up history, mental problems or a Muslim boyfriend. But then again, the way you're looking now you do look like an animal, and some of these girls, that's all they want on top of them. All they want is a pounding.' He gave Abbas a dirty grin. 'You know I was married to a Syrian girl once with red hair. She had the nicest nipples ever, a beautiful hue of rose – her dad gave her to me because he couldn't support her so I married the girl. Every night! I had to tell her to take it easy. One day off, one day on. But she was having none of it.'

'So what happened?'

'Divorced her. Moved from Anadan so better to let her go, innit? If your girlfriend is an undercover fed, best keep an eye on her.'

The Darkness Inside

'She seems genuine though.'

'You been to her house?'

Abbas shook his head.

'You been to her workplace?'

Abbas shook his head.

'No? I wonder why?' said Radio. 'You guys have been talking for a long time. Usually girls these days, one date and their hands are already unzipping your flies.'

Abbas thought about that. 'But we're not together. And she's respectful.'

Radio raised his hands. 'Fair enough. I can tell you feel different about her. Better keep her close anyway. How comes she doesn't convert?'

'How would I know, she asks a hundred and one questions.'

'Like what?'

'Everything from women's rights to Jihad.'

'Jihad?'

'No, it's not what you think. She sees shit on YouTube like Islam is peace and is about defensive Jihad and I tell her the score.'

'Cool, cool, I wasn't saying anything. It's good to have this person close rather than far in any case. Slave girls are allowed in the house of war!' He grinned. 'Go and betake yourself a nice little Kafira!'

Abbas would have laughed with him but this time he didn't. He felt that he needed to respect her dignity even though she was not there and she was nothing to him in terms of his honour. Had she been his wife, things would have been different.

36. Shak

Whenever Gardener called over the phone Shak was always mysteriously vague about his role in the security services. Shak described his position as a 'liaison officer' or 'cultural attaché' but Gardener could never pin him down to what he actually was, for he struck him as a sort of unique intelligence operative more than a mere 'agent runner' or 'analyst'. On the phone he smacked of officialdom and used generic phrases which could be construed in so many ways that they were always deniable with the phrase, 'I didn't mean it that way.' Over the years, though, Gardener had managed to come to an understanding with Shak over what these phrases meant, and he had now built up a phrasebook of officialdom-speak which protected Shak as well as him.

But get Shak on his own, alone, away from other journalists and apparatchiks, face to face, and he was a completely different animal. Though it was not always possible to get him on his own. He was a man in high demand – it was not often that the services had a fluent Dari, Arabic and Urdu speaker at hand. Gardener had managed to convince him to meet.

They had agreed to meet in a Portuguese patisserie, Lisboa, after the noon prayer. Gardener found Shak already sitting down, having ordered several custard tarts and two coffees. He had chosen to sit outside the cafe to

The Darkness Inside

enjoy the spring sun and people watch whilst chomping on the custard tarts. His long beard still held drops of water from ablution and had a few flakes of the custard tarts stuck in there. He wore a Barbour jacket, a brown pair of corduroy trousers and a wool jumper; his hair was shiny and combed over, exuding metropolitanism.

'Thanks for seeing me,' Gardener said.

'Not at all, I love these,' Shak said in reply, scoffing the custard tarts and inviting him to savour them. 'The truth is I love coming here. After I am done I will eat at the Moroccan stall over there; they do amazing fish.' Gardener was always amazed at his ability to eat and never put on any weight.

'So it's me doing you a favour.'

'Afghan proverb, remember it: the cat doesn't chase the mouse for the sake of God. So what are you working on?'

'Returners.'

Shak rolled his eyes. 'Okay, what's new? By the way, you know this is all off record, agreed?'

Gardener nodded. 'Well there are a lot of groups saying that you are not allowing them back: the Turks are complaining that you don't want to see them back; the Kurds are complaining too.'

'What the fuck!' Shak said, exasperated.

The swearing was excellent news for Gardener because it meant that Shak was going to launch into a rant.

'Look, we are taking them in every day, if there's evidence to convict them we do, if not we allow them to return. We do distinguish between a girl who wanted a Jihadi boyfriend and a killer. Believe me we do.'

'Why don't you give the same treatment to foreign fighters returning from the front line as the Kurds? Is it a

The Darkness Inside

race thing?'

'Come on man! That's a bullshit, lazy question. The two things are very different; one group has local aims in the region and is not working against the interest of our country and, well, the other seeks to destroy our country. So the lawyers weigh those things up. The attorney general decides whether he should prosecute or not, and any right-thinking man would argue that the Kurds are very different from Jihadis – even Hezbollah and Taliban are different from these guys. Otherwise we'd see Hezbollah and Taliban blowing themselves up here, but they don't. Why? They certainly have the capability, so why? Because they aren't mad. They are rational actors with rational goals that contravene our interests, that is all. These guys are like Iran: a movement. That's a problem for us.'

'Does that justify us taking their nationality away?'

'See,' Shak said, taking a chomp on another custard tart, 'what I don't get? These fucking Jihadists are demanding these rights that they used to scorn back in the day. They were preaching sedition when we gave them refuge here. Fuck, they were going round these parts in the nineties, preaching against this country, raping and stealing, and then when they've fucked it up for everyone else they call me a sell out! How did I sell out? Because I work for the good of the country I was born in? These pricks cuss this country and talk about a police state – they haven't even seen what a police state is. You know what I don't get about these dickheads?' Shak was positively raging. 'Those fuckers were given safety, we let them say what they were saying, they were even raising money, we

The Darkness Inside

turned a blind eye. They were willing to put Muslim lives at risk for their fucking cause and for what? So I could get profiled in the airport when they did this shit in the nineties? They are banging on about Jihadi John; they were posting beheading videos when Jihadi John started growing a bit of bum fluff and had his first wet dream. And then the state thinks, okay, 9/11 has happened, we need a security strategy that targets Muslims, and they cry "it's unjust" and "human rights". Take it like a man.'

'What about foreign policy? This is what they point to.'

'What? A state has policies, some policies are wrong. But when they were doing their shit talk it was a mixed bag. See, to me Libya is a perfect example – when the Arab Spring happened and we helped the rebels they were thankful, cheering us. When it went pear-shaped, they blamed us. Now they want us to intervene in Syria when we are trying to do our best to stay out of Iraq coz we know we fucked up last time. So they blame us. Am I saying our foreign policy is good? No. But let me put it to you this way – I am a Muslim, not just a Muslim with a name but a five-times-a-day praying type, yeah? Now, for argument's sake let's say the West can throw me in Guantanamo, Russia and China can throw me in their fucking gulags or their 're-education facilities', yeah? Where do you think I can get a lawyer? Where do you think I can hold them to account? These dickheads ruined it for everyone else and they want to make Bin Laden the Muslim world's Bobby Sands? We got our heroes, their names are known. Spare me that leftist bullshit. You heard enough? They always look for black and white answers, for enemies. They think that the world is run by Jews when Arabs have equally massive shares in banking. I am doing my job, I am a servant, what the fuck are they? I prayed, I served my community, respected my elders and everything else whilst they were spreading this shit and denouncing everyone else as infidels. To me they are scum who destroy everything but have no answers to anything. They can be demagogues too, they are poisoning the people. They make my religion look ugly when I know that it is graceful, elegant and deep. Fuck, we had Muslims serving Genghis Khan! And they lecture me about selling out – they sold out. They should learn a bit of statecraft before they talk.'

Gardener looked at the empty plate Shak had just decimated. It was clear that he was in an imaginary court trying to answer and respond to his accusers.

'Look,' said Gardener, gently steering him back to the objective, 'I am trying to find out who Abdul Rahman and Abbas Rizwan are. Could you find out if they were known to the services?'

'Is this for you?' Shak said.

'No.'

'*Daily Mail*?' said Shak, frowning. 'I don't do anything for them.'

'Come on, have you ever seen me ask on their behalf?'

'So who?'

'A colleague who works for the *Loop*.'

'The *Loop*? On the internet?'

Gardener nodded. 'We're talking two million readers last year in Europe alone.'

'Okay, lemme see what I can do. Listen, I need to meet the director and pray the Asr prayer at Al-Manaar Mosque

The Darkness Inside

so I need to go.' Shak left Gardener at the cafe.

A few days later Shak called him regarding his query. He said that they could neither confirm nor deny whether the men were known to the security services. This standard response, which many security liaison officers gave, sounded strange considering that Gardener had cultivated a longstanding relationship with Shak. He wouldn't be drawn as to why such a response was given, adding that this was 'beyond his pay grade'. Gardener related it back to Martha, who didn't quite understand his disquiet. 'I thought,' said Gardener, 'we were beyond that. He's not given me such a response in years.'

Martha didn't pursue this mystery either; she just plowed on.

37. Ayman

All Ayman was going to do was just complete his bird. Prison was not unfamiliar to him and he figured that he would do what many of his friends did when they were inside: just read, read and read during lock up. When he got a chance he would work towards a qualification and hopefully, if God so willed, he'd come out of there on the eve of his thirtieth birthday. He might even try to memorise the whole Quran; one of his mates had memorised Francis Stillman's rhyming dictionary in prison and come out spitting so many bars that he became a successful grime artist and hit the big time. Unfortunately, he wrote some bars that got him killed.

But Ayman's plan had nothing to do with grime; it was all about learning a life skill, a trade like carpentry, plumbing or electronics and hopefully, with a bit of good behaviour, he might even convince the screws to work towards an industry standard qualification like the CORGI certificate. They might let him out once a week to go to further education college; there were many possibilities. The future, as he saw it, wasn't as bad as it might seem from the outside. In any case, in Syria bird could mean death, being bummed by some shabiha, or having two crocodile clips attached to your scrotum whilst an electric charge went through your balls, sterilising you forever. Bird in Feltham wasn't as bad as it looked. Even Belmarsh, though they called it the

The Darkness Inside

Guantanamo of the UK, was nothing like Guantanamo. He heard you could even get a pedicure there.

He had got his reading speed up to a level where he was finishing one book a week without a dictionary. In terms of privileges he had played it so that he was in the top tier. Ayman showed diligence in his work and he was well liked by the screws, if that was even possible. Some of the screws, he was certain, felt that he shouldn't even be inside. After all, you kill a man for killing your brother, that seems like a very human reaction. Everyone understood him; essentially he was a good man who had seen red. Shit like that happens even to the best. But you kill a man, you have to pay the price; even if it was diminished responsibility or manslaughter, you need to take it. And the way to deal with it for Ayman was to reduce his hopes to the absolute basics and work towards targets and goals that were achievable.

Even as he was getting transferred from Feltham he didn't have any issues about big man prison. In fact, in big man prison no one had anything to prove like they did in Feltham. There was no fronting; everyone just wanted to do their time and splurt. That was why he didn't mind being transferred to big man prison. There was no fear of the unknown.

In any case, the week before he got transferred he got into a silly argument with a weasel he worked with in the kitchen. Magdi was a skinny little Moroccan from Hanwell with a goatee. Everything hung off his wiry body, a proper Snoop Doggy Dogg lookalike in his younger years. But although he looked flimsy, rest assured he'd stab a man, kill a man even, and none of the screws would know it was him. Magdi wasn't stupid either. He'd taught himself how

The Darkness Inside

to read Arabic, as well as English and Spanish. If he hadn't been from such a messed up background he could have been the British version of Elon Musk, Ayman was sure of it. But like Musk there was something unhinged about him. The young man was inside for pulling up to his ex's boyfriend in a moped and throwing some acid in his face. The man had beaten up Magdi's autistic son after losing at Fortnite or FIFA or some other ridiculous computer game, and so Magdi was going to make sure that he would never ever do that to his son again and contrived an evil little plan in his mind. He was going to confine the boyfriend to the shadows forever by turning him into a monster. The problem with Magdi was that instead of attracting sympathy for what he did – many a father might go down the path of revenge – he was such a little shit that his cleverness just pissed people off. The jury felt little sympathy for the teenage dad as they sent him down.

Now usually Ayman kept Magdi at arm's length. They both worked in the kitchen, but knowing Magdi's connections and associations Ayman made sure their paths did not cross.

But that day, as Ayman worked in the prison kitchen Magdi made a comment that irked him. Ayman was wiping down the kitchen surfaces.

'So who is that redhead?' Magdi asked, leering as he came past him. He was brushing the floor lazily and stood next to him, stinking up the place with his body odour. 'Is she your persy?'

'What?'

'I hear you talking to her on the phone, so I was just askin'. I thought, is she something to you?' Magdi leaned on his broom as if he was going to have a long conversation, tugging at his little goatee. 'So is she your persy?' He gave him a dirty little smile.

'She's nothing to me; anyway, what's it to you?' Ayman said as he continued scouring the kitchen top. 'Why are you watching who visits me or talks to me?' Ayman was almost offended that Magdi should think of him as a fornicator or something.

'Nah blud, man's just sayin', y'get me? I thought it was your sister or somethin'.'

'If it was my sister why you watchin' her?'

The raised voice brought over several other inmates who started to follow the conversation.

'Blud, calm down! I'm just makin' conversation. Rah! Man can't even have a friendly conversation, y'get me.'

'Ey, Magdi, you must think I'm a fool. Just mind your own business.'

'Alright blud, rasclat, yoot these days! Man's just trying to pass the time.'

'You fuck with my women and I will fuck you up.'

'Bredrin,' Magdi said, facing him, 'people don't just bowl up to Magdi and threaten man, y'get me?'

'And people don't just come up to me and ask me about the women who visit me and look at them and me as dishonourable people. I ain't taking that sort of talk.' He stepped up to Magdi just to emphasise his threat.

By the time Ayman had finished with Magdi the kitchen staff had gathered around them and were laughing at Magdi. Magdi had humiliation writ large on his face and he knew that Ayman could use him to scour the kitchen tops, so he let it go.

Since that little verbal tussle, Ayman had noticed how

The Darkness Inside

Magdi had watched him slyly the whole week. He didn't think he'd be stabbed for it, but then again that evil little look in the weasel's face meant he was planning something and the look didn't go away. That's why he was relieved to go to big man prison. In big man prison everyone just wanted to do their time and leave.

But Ayman miscalculated. Magdi was a crook who had first seen the inside of prison walls at the age of sixteen. In Hanwell he had moved with bigger men, older men, well-connected men. He knew people everywhere. When Ayman entered Long Lartin he expected the problem to have gone away, and didn't expect the whack he felt in the rib as he went into the communal kitchen area. Now, you can have as much muscle as you want but no muscle can protect the ribs, and he felt the sharp pain as he went down. The next minute he felt a pile of bodies and voices grab hold of him. There was a sticky solution on his face. He screamed and tried to remove the hot, sticky syrup with his hands but it burned them like it burned his face. All he could do was scream with all his might. As he lay there screaming a hand grabbed his head and someone whispered in his ear: 'Yo! Magdi said you should lay off the redhead, y'hear me?' The hand let go and his head hit the cold floor. He felt the burning sensation on his chest. His body was flung on a rolling bed and rushed through the doors. He saw the bright lights pass him like a blur. He heard words like 'burns' and 'dermis' and descriptions like 'deep tissue charring'. Whilst he was sedated and seemingly asleep he heard doctors describe him as having napalm-like burn injuries. He couldn't move. His face was burning and burned for many months.

The Darkness Inside

When the prison wardens tried to speak to Ayman they could not figure out whether he had lost the ability to speak or whether he simply refused to identify the group of prisoners who had poured the hot sugar syrup on his face. The wardens had found the electric kettle where they had caramelised the sugar and mixed it with bleach and other stuff before pouring it on his face as he entered the kitchen. They even had a culprit, Leeroy, who only had a year left on his sentence. But Ayman was silent, he didn't want to speak; all he wanted to do was live in the shadows for the rest of his life. They put him on twenty-four-hour suicide watch. The Governor felt that it was better that he moved to another prison and no further action was taken against the suspected culprits.

When Martha didn't receive any replies from Ayman through phone or letter she decided to call on his family. His mother opened the door this time. Her grey eyes were hard. Martha softened her eyes and claimed yet again to be Sid's fidanzata, but the claim didn't magically lead to an invitation to come in. Instead she received an abrupt message: 'We don't want anything to do with this mess anymore. We just want to be left alone.'

'But Sid – Anis...'

'Some things are bigger than you or me,' the old woman told her. 'It's time you accepted that.' Her voice was sad. 'You need to learn when to leave things to God. Only He will give me justice.'

'But your son,' Martha pressed her, 'wants to bring the killers to justice.'

The Darkness Inside

'Not anymore. Leave us alone now.' She closed the door on Martha, saying, 'Don't try to come back here again when my daughter is here. I speak for her too.'

She closed the door with such certitude that Martha did not even bother writing a note trying to explain. Neither would she return and try to put her face in front of the daughter to find out what had happened to Ayman. The matter had been discarded. In fact, as she returned to the car she decided that it was no use bothering them. She had what she needed. Their son had stood up the pictures which she had shown him. She had her notes and his letters so there would be no doubt about it when she presented it to the lawyers. Sometimes the gut knows how much you can squeeze a source before they snap. That point had been reached with Ayman's family and so she pressed on towards her goal.

38. Closing down

Martha thought it was an April fool's when she received a phone call from Paul, but April was nearly at its end. He wanted to see her in the office. 'Now,' he said. The 'now' had such finality to it that she stopped writing her email and got up to go. Was this the moment she would be told that they couldn't afford her because they were soon leaving the European Union? But surely Paul wouldn't tell her that way? Whatever it was, it had to be serious. She made a prayer to Jesus, grabbed her pad and pen and headed to his office. The back wall of Paul's office was adorned with awards and pictures of staff, past and present in various states of inebriation. On his desk were pictures of his family and a pile of letters and reports.

Usually when she entered his office Paul would be reading one of these letters or reports. This time he was already waiting for her. Martha had never seen him this way. His expression was stern and angry. It wasn't the sort of anger he had meted out when Daniels had got into a live Twitter spat with a troll and he had told the troll to fuck off. That wasn't a dressing down; that was mere pretence. There hadn't been any real anger in Paul's voice. In fact, he had been doing impressions of Daniels after he'd left. But this time, as she entered the office she saw him sitting there, his lips tightly pursed like a Neapolitan guappo. He sat unnaturally rigid; his blue tie was knotted

The Darkness Inside

when usually it was loose and his top button was done up. This, then, was to be a formal affair. Hardcastle stood next to him, dressed immaculately. He should have looked lawyer-like – cufflinks, light blue shirt, watch with leather strap, burgundy tie and expensive designer spectacles – but he didn't. Curiously, Hardcastle's dress and posture reminded her of some sort of consiglieri from *The Godfather*; he looked serious and yet at the same time like he was there to temper the rage. Martha felt her heart pumping. This was serious. More serious than the panel.

'Sit down please, Martha,' said Paul with great formality.

She sat down, feeling that the offer was an instruction to be obeyed.

'I'm going to keep this short,' Paul said. 'I cannot tell you how disappointed I am with you, Martha. I nearly lost one of my best fucking reporters and now you are doing the same thing behind my back?!'

Martha was stunned; how did he know? She looked at Hardcastle, but he was a blank wall – there was no indication that he had told Paul.

'What are you talking about?' Martha said. 'Sid wasn't working.'

'Come on, Martha! You and I both know he was. Martha, how could you, after I backed you? I have to find out from my sources that you are working on this story.'

'Paul, I can explain.'

'Explain what? That you're working on the same story that nearly got Sid killed?'

'I was doing this on my own time.'

'Don't fuck around, Martha. You think I haven't done a beat? You think I am fucking stupid!' Paul banged the

The Darkness Inside

table. 'Do you think I'm fucking stupid?'

Hardcastle touched his shoulder as if to curtail his rage. He was always aware of the legal implications, even in the most emotive of situations.

'No, John, she has to hear this; that's why you are the witness. I am not going to travel to Italy to tell her dad that his daughter died under my watch. Fuck that. Fuck that. I go to Italy for a holiday, not for that. Fuck that.'

'It's best,' reminded Hardcastle, consciously aware that this could be construed as bullying in an employment tribunal, 'if we avoid intemperate language.'

Martha had never heard Paul swear, nor had she ever heard him get so angry. But for some reason she knew it was the same anger that a brother, sister, father or mother might have for someone they loved or deeply admired. There was love in that anger and so she didn't blame him. 'This is what you are going to do. You are going to give this story up.'

'What?' Martha said exasperated, and started to fight back. 'Your reporter was nearly killed and you are just going to let the story go?'

'Yes.'

'Just like that? What sort of editor are you?'

'How dare you?' Paul got up looking hurt and wounded.

'If I may... ' Hardcastle interjected trying to calm the situation down.

'No, you may not!' Paul said. 'Are you serious about exposing these guys?'

Martha nodded, staring directly at him. 'Of course I am.'

'Then how about we give the information to the police?

The Darkness Inside

We can always run it as an exclusive later.'

'No, no, this is mine.'

'Oh, okay, its about the scoop then, isn't it? The byline, the award.'

'Come on Paul,' said Martha, 'both of us are beyond that.'

'I think, Paul,' said Hardcastle, 'this story has some personal resonance.'

'I don't care.'

'Then give me a backwatcher!'

'Too late. You betrayed my trust. This is what I want: an email from you with Hardcastle CCed in saying that you are going to desist from this story or a resignation letter. The ball is in your court.'

The words were a punch in the stomach. For the whole afternoon she could not focus on her work. She went to Hardcastle, who was working diligently in his office, begging him to give her a backwatcher and to persuade Paul to rethink his position. But all he could say was, 'Martha, this doesn't come from me. I think you are onto something but this one you need to let go. I don't want to lose you.'

At four thirty she wrote that email. It was curt and professional. She wasn't handing in her resignation. She would desist from pursuing the investigation. Paul replied that should she pursue this story she would be promptly fired. She replied that she understood the consequences of her actions. The matter was laid to rest.

After work, Martha went straight to Mayday Hospital. As she was walking towards Sid's room she saw a man she hadn't seen in ages, in fact since university. He walked coolly down the hallway, clasping a file, wearing a captain's coat and denims.

The Darkness Inside

'Femi!' Martha said, recognising her old classmate and grabbing him by the forearm to stop him from walking past her. 'What are you doing here?'

Femi gave her a warm smile and a hug. 'Oh my God, Martha? I can't believe it's you. Wow! You look great after all these years! Not changed a bit.'

'Stop it. What are you doing here, mister?'

'Just visiting Sid. Heard about what happened to him so I'm doing my duty – that's all. He's getting better though!'

'Yes. Of course. So what about you, what are you doing with yourself these days?'

'Oh you know, this and that.'

'Freelancing?'

'You could say that.'

'Well look, we could get you in on shifts at the *Loop*. We need people to look into knife crime and youth crime. Also to give their thoughts on Windrush, Grenfell and immigration issues with regards to Brexit. There's bits and bobs that need doing on Africa too. Maybe get you on a sports gig if that takes your fancy.'

'How about art and culture?'

Martha looked at him for a moment as if he was strange. 'Yeah, well if that's what you want. But why? It's a boring gig.'

Femi laughed when he saw her expression. He shook his head with a knowing smile. 'You got a card?'

She handed him one, and he studied it.

'Impressive,' he said, almost to himself. 'I need to go. Look after Sid, he's a rough diamond. I'll call you, okay?'

'For sure.' Martha watched the tall figure leave, thinking that Femi's attitude was strange and that his presence

The Darkness Inside

might upset the equilibrium at the office. In any case, the way he walked away from her suggested that he wouldn't be making that call. She headed into Sid's room and found him leaning on the windowsill, looking out onto the car park. He looked trapped, like an animal in London Zoo.

He turned and saw her, smiled. 'What a ray of sunshine on such a shitty day,' he said. He hobbled towards her, wearing a brace that made him look like an android, pecked her on the cheek and bade her sit. There was some juice on the coffee table and he poured her some in a glass. She accepted it gratefully. 'So,' he said, 'what brings you here?'

'I don't know how or by who, but I've been rumbled.'

'What do you mean?'

'Paul pulled me into the office today and told me he knows what I am working on. That he wanted a letter telling him I have dropped it.'

'What did you do?'

'I wrote the letter.'

'Good girl.'

'Who do you think told him?'

'Oh, don't you know?'

'No.'

Sid looked at the floor awkwardly, as if he didn't want to tell her.

'Tell me,' insisted Martha. She was leaning forward as if she would get it out of him come what may.

'It's obvious,' said Sid calmly. 'It's Tom.'

'Tom? Tom?!' Martha said in disbelief. 'Why?'

'Come on, can't you see it?'

'See what?'

The Darkness Inside

'He's been into you ever since uni. You are his damsel.' Sid emphasised the word 'damsel', seeing what it would do.

'Damsel?' Martha said. 'Damsel? Into me?'

'Yes, he's always loved you. Why do you think he told Paul? He thinks I put you up to it. But I told him that you made that choice. That there's a reason why you are the editor and me a grunt. He doesn't believe it. The guy is super jealous. Reckons I'm pushing you to it, that I got you twisted around my finger. That you have no agency.'

'Pushing me?! Fuck him.'

'Take it easy,' Sid said. 'He's a good man and well intentioned.'

'Aren't you a good man?'

'That's irrelevant in our business. All I want is the truth.'

Martha reached for her phone but Sid reached over and put his hand over it.

'Don't, Martha, come on, not worth burning any bridges. You might need him in the future. You're the one who taught me that. Just get even. People do crazy things when they are in love.'

'The bastard. Sometimes you just need to push through to get to the ceiling.'

'Exactly! Move on. Forgive him, he's in love. He's the sort of man you want in your corner when the shit hits the fan; he'll drop everything for you. If I had a daughter that's the sort of man I wouldn't mind my girl bringing home. Trust me.'

'He's not my dad.'

'Point taken. So what do you want to do now?'

'Well,' she said, 'let's keep this away from all parties concerned. And just carry on as before.'

The Darkness Inside

'Sounds like a plan. This story is going to be epic. Look, it's all filed, transcribed and organised.' He pointed to a thick file on the windowsill. It was all there.

39. Abbó

'Abbó! Where have you been?' Martha said, stepping into the dark portakabin. 'You avoiding me?'

Abbas stood up from his desk. The place was messy and disorganised and despite the bright sun outside the blinds were down. Martha thought he glared at her for a moment.

'Oh, Martha, how are you? Uh, sorry, I have been so busy.'

She walked up to him, pointed her index finger at him accusingly and dug it into his chest. 'Where have you been? Hope you aren't ignoring my calls?' she said playfully.

'No, I just have a lot of work. Radio's abroad so I am kind of running the ship.'

'Where's he gone off to?'

'Dubai, for the Easter holidays.'

'That's funny, you don't seem to enjoy those holidays.'

'What do you mean?'

'Well, seems to me you do all his work and he's jetsetting around the world.'

'Maybe, but I live well, rent-free, and he looks after me. I make decent money considering I don't have any qualifications or anything. Better than stacking shelves in Tesco.'

'I don't know,' she said, trying to squirrel out a bit of resentment that she could work with, 'sounds like exploitation to me.'

The Darkness Inside

'What do you mean?' Abbas said, furrowing his brow.

'Well,' said Martha tentatively, watching his reaction, 'how comes you can't meet a nice girl, settle down, have children with her, go for nice walks and the like?' She looked at him as if that girl was her, as if she was proposing something that was unthinkable in Abbas' imagination. 'Abbó, this is what everyone does and hopes to do, how comes you don't? How comes Radio is allowed two wives and you hesitate to even go out for a meal with someone who cares for you, frightened that she will eat you alive? Those feelings are normal feelings that a man or woman experiences.'

'Okay! Who said I am afraid?' Abbas replied; he looked disturbed by her questioning. 'Just let me finish off the tasks and call you.'

'You know what,' said Martha, pulling back, 'I think I have learnt enough about Islam.' She walked out of that portakabin feeling his eyes on her. By the time she had stepped into the car she heard what she was waiting for.

'Wait! Marth! Wait!'

But she was already pulling out of the car wash, trying to contain her smile.

She answered his call in the evening. He had called fifteen times and sent her many WhatsApp messages. In comparison to other men there was no subterfuge in his messages. They were honest, predictable and to the point. She felt almost cruel.

'What do you want?' Martha said in a tone that was cold and uncaring.

'Marth,' he said apologetically, 'do you want to meet up?'

'No, I am busy.'

The Darkness Inside

'Doing what?'

She had seen it done on TV and she wondered if it would work on someone like him, so she used the hackneyed line from *Friends*: 'I am washing my hair.'

'Oh, okay. I'm sorry to disturb you, I'll call you another time,' Abbas said and was about to put the phone down.

Martha realised that he didn't understand these intricate dating rituals. She had overextended herself. 'Anyway,' she said, 'what did you have in mind?'

'Oh, well I was thinking we'd go out to get some real Syrian food in Shepherd's Bush? You ever tried Syrian?'

Martha's ears pricked up. 'Go on.'

'Well they do an amazing shakiriyeh.'

'Shakiriyeh? What is it?'

'You will find out; it is delicious.'

'Only if you explain why you behave the way you do?'

'Deal. Should I pick you up?'

'No, no, let's meet there. Ping me over the address.'

'Okay, see you there.'

He was already there in the corner when she entered the Syrian restaurant, Damasgate. It had Syrians queuing up outside wearing their white headscarves as if they were still in Syria. She squeezed past them, saying that someone was already waiting for her. As she entered she was introduced to the magical waft of Syrian cooking. The restaurant had scenes of Old Damascus and Aleppo on its walls. It was as if the owner was trying his best to conjure up an idyllic place, nay, a blessed place that he couldn't return to, and he dreamt of it every day. She found Abbas to be a different animal in the restaurant. He laughed so much you could see his molars. He cracked jokes with the waiter

The Darkness Inside

and high-fived him like they were from the same village. It was so lovely to see him so relaxed that Martha did not let him know of her presence. She just wanted to see him in his natural habitat, how he was when he wasn't afraid or had no inhibitions. He seemed like a fun guy to be with.

She had expected him to stop and change his behaviour once he spotted her but he did not. He looked at her, and looked at the waiter.

'Here she is, habibi,' Abbas said to the waiter, 'can you bring me the menu?'

'I didn't know you spoke Arabic,' Martha said in front of the waiter.

'Not just Arabic,' added the waiter, 'he speaks it like he's from Aleppo.'

'Really?'

'Believe me. I had to call my friends to let them listen to the accent. He's a linguist!'

'Sit down, let's eat and I'll tell you all about it.'

Abbas basically took over the ordering and chose a selection of hot and cold starters, the best of which was the kebbe, cracked bulgur wheat and mince. For himself he chose kebse, a biryani-type dish, and for her shakiriyeh, a lamb shank cooked in a rich yoghurt sauce infused with cloves, cinnamon and bay leaves. Martha loved the dish. It was so different from her own culinary heritage. As they ate, Abbas told her that one of the things he missed the most about Syria was the colourful pickled vegetables, mukhallal, especially the beetroot. 'Don't ask me why,' he said, waving his fork at her, 'but mukhallal is what I miss the most.'

'You never told me you were in Syria.'

The Darkness Inside

'It's not something that you declare these days, is it? Shit,' he added, 'even your doctor might rat you out.'

'So when did you live there?'

'During the war.'

'Oh my God! What were you doing there? Aid work?'

Abbas studied her for a moment, perhaps even with a pang of suspicion. 'I am a fighting man, Marth, so I did what came naturally.'

'I see.' She held his gaze as if she understood him now. 'That explains a lot, Abbó. How many years were you there?'

'I was there for about four years. Did a lot of fighting.'

'Let me guess,' said Martha. 'Radio was there too.'

Abbas nodded. 'We fought together; he put his life on the line for me plenty of times. That's why. He went beyond loyalty. He's proved himself in ways few people would do but fighting men. When a man does that for you he becomes your brother. So you hurt me when you said those things about him.'

'I am sorry,' Martha said. She saw the wounded wolf in this grizzled man whose neck muscles tensed every time he talked. 'I didn't realise. I'm sorry.'

'Khalas, it's past now, don't worry about it.'

'So you never told me how you two met.'

'That's a long story.'

Martha leaned forward as if they were sharing a secret. 'I would love to hear it. Thanks for trusting me.'

'I hope you'll keep it quiet.'

She crossed herself. 'Hope to die.'

He frowned as if pained by her crossing herself.

'Okay, I am not going to get into why I started to practise

The Darkness Inside

Islam but I have always been a fighting man, don't know why, but look at me, I'm built like an ox. So people have always found me useful. I started doing doors early, licensed or not. In the nineties you didn't need licences, just crews that provided the services to the clubs. I was one of those guys that did the doors. I used to do them in North London, mostly keeping them Cypriot Turks and Greeks away from each other, even though they looked pretty much the same to me. Just one was called Zaim and the other one Stavros or something. A lot of my mates did coke, astaghfirullah, when they did the doors; me, I just loved it. Course, with the crew came other things, drugs, women and all that, but I was eighteen or nineteen at the time having the time of my life. No commitments, all I had to do was make sure that I put a bit of change on my mum's table, did the shopping and she's kissing me on my forehead thinking I am her little angel. But on one of those club nights I must have bashed a guy good with a cosh and next thing you know I am sitting inside a cell looking at a GBH or attempted murder charge. Now prisons are nothing if you ask me – nothing compared to the prisons that Radio has been to, places where they use drills to extract a confession. For me remand was all about quiet time, to think where I was going in life. Funnily enough that's where I met Radio for the first time. Never told me what he was in for but he was alright, always hitting the praying mat. He was the guy who gave me this tape that just changed my life. In the nineties it was all about that famous tape by Khalid Yasin, "What is the purpose of life?". You can still hear it on YouTube now. I listened to it on my walkman and it just got me thinking. This guy

The Darkness Inside

just laid it out so clearly – your eyes, ears, mouth, stomach have a purpose, so why don't you have a purpose? Now one thing you have in prison is time, and I used it to think a lot about what my purpose was. And course I bumped into Radio too, and he was always a bro. He showed me how to pray, how to wash before prayer, so I owe him big time. Now here's the thing, I actually got off the charge and next thing you know I am back on the doors again and also working for the Asef brothers. They were some Turkish gangsters up in Edmonton ends and whatnot. My life was back to normal and my mum thought I was an angel. So I tried to forget about it all, but it played on my mind. On one of those days I had to do some protection work, and I was up in a snooker hall working for one of the brothers when a massive fight broke out between Asef and some other gangster – all hell broke loose. I am telling you it was like something out of *Braveheart* or *Goodfellas*. These guys brought out choppers and we were cracking heads with snooker cues, knuckle dusters, anything we could get our hands on. It was amazing. Then at one point I felt something lodge itself into the back of my head or neck, I don't know what. But from what my mum told me, the surgeon comes out of the operating room screaming, saying that this shouldn't be, that it's impossible, that I should be dead, and for a moment I was clinically dead. Look at the scar, look! Anyways, when I came to, the surgeon came up to me and said, "Somebody is looking after you mate." And that's what did it for me. I just thought, this is a second chance for me. So the thing that I did was just give up that job. Somehow I managed to talk my way into working in the men's concessions for Mulberry in Selfridges, thinking

The Darkness Inside

that at least I was living a clean life. In some ways I was, in other ways I wasn't, but you know how it is. By sheer coincidence, I bumped into Radio again in the Boxing Day sales and we hugged like long lost brothers. I told him what had happened and how I'd ended up there. He was so happy for me, but I told him, frankly speaking, how bored shitless I was. On top of that I didn't get some of the stuff these people were talking about. I swear down I went to a mosque once in Cricklewood and some Sudanese man was jumping up and down swinging from left to right like it was a jungle rave and shouting: "hooo, hooo!" I was like, what's going on? Is this Islam? What the hell is this? Another time I was going to another talk and they were talking about ahad Hadith and mutawatir Hadith and how one group is a deviant and the other isn't. On top of that, I had to be careful of grave worshippers, people who blindly followed the four madhabs, because I was reading pamphlets handed out to me after Friday prayer. It was confusing. Now it's different. I have studied a bit now, but then I didn't even have any GCSEs, let alone understand all of this stuff going on in every mosque. So when I saw him again I thanked Allah and he took time out to just explain everything.

'"Don't worry",' he told me, "take my number and come and see me."

'And since then he has always been there for me. Radio was like a Prophet, all he thought about was Islam. He had all the answers because he read – he had so many books at home. We'd go to this mosque raising money for this cause, go to that mosque giving out *Al-Ansar* magazine. He'd highlight the plight of our brothers in Afghanistan,

The Darkness Inside

Algeria, Bosnia, Somalia, Chechnya; you name it, he'd highlight it. And what was more, God always provided money; sometimes we were rolling in it.

'And we were always preparing ourselves, if God called us, to answer his call. We did everything from paintballing, hiking and trekking, to circles and self-defence classes in Finsbury Park Mosque. And on top of that, I was there when he basically made these evolutionary scientists bang the tables in protest in a lecture hall in Queen Mary and Westfield University like pathetic children. I remember him standing there and challenging them: "What is it to be, huh? Gould doesn't agree with Dawkins! Where are the fossil records for these intermediary species? Even GCSE science teaches us that mutations are always bad, so why are you teaching the exact opposite with evolution? Out with it!" And then he quoted a verse saying that God created everything in the heavens and the earth and I saw the Muslim students elated and these scientists just banging their fists on the table like kids. Talk about intellectuals, eh? That was the first time I saw what a force he could be. He was a fearless legend, spoke out against oppression, went to Abu Muntasir's JIMAS, took brothers to Tooting, Abu Hamza, you name it. And then 9/11 happened and everything changed; the honeymoon was over. Here's the thing, the brother who used to teach us martial arts was ex-military; he died suddenly. But we knew he'd been gripped by special branch. Then he turns up on the river Thames and people claimed it was suicide. No one bought that. Muslims just don't commit suicide. It's haraam. Brothers were getting arrested left, right and centre. Even boxing clubs in mosques like al-Muntada closed their doors. They

The Darkness Inside

hadn't done anything wrong but they shut down for fear of being accused of terrorism. Scholars were being thrown into prison for speaking the truth and nothing else. And then one day Radio was just gone. Didn't even say goodbye. I swear I was in tears for days, it was like my life had fallen apart. And then after two years he was back as if nothing had happened, except that he intensified the call.'

They finished dinner with a dollop of Syrian ice cream and pushed through the massive crowd waiting to get in even though it was eleven thirty. Abbas led the way past the crowd, shaking the hands of the Syrian waiters and thanking them. Clearly, Martha thought, the awkwardness was only with her and not the others. As she walked next to him, she tried to walk closer to him. But he made sure to maintain a respectful distance that indicated that they were together but not close enough for another Muslim to tarnish his honour and reputation as a God-fearing man.

'Let me drop you home,' Abbas said.

'It's okay, I got my car parked up.'

'Well let me take you there then?' Abbas said.

Martha noticed how he clenched his hands and unclenched them as if he was trying to get the cold out of them.

'Really,' she smiled delicately, 'there's no need.'

'Don't be silly,' Abbas said abruptly. So he walked beside her as she took one of the side streets towards her car. Suddenly a nervousness began to seize her. He had a steady step, and a determined look as they walked. He didn't say much either as the happy mood changed into

The Darkness Inside

the dark mood of Shepherd's Bush at night.

Martha watched him clench and unclench his fist, and wondered whether he had done the same thing when he walked alongside Sid as they crossed the road in Horley. In one of their meetings Sid had told her that it must have been Abbas who had sliced up Anis; he was the most logical candidate. Radio would never do such dirty work. In any case, it was obvious. Abbas would have done it so clinically, just like a butcher would, and probably would have put the knife back in the shop thinking that otherwise he might have committed the sin of 'theft'.

But she remained chatty, unnaturally so, as if she wanted desperately to keep that mood of relaxed happiness and nostalgia alive. She walked along the street where she was parked, looking for the lights coming out of the houses. She looked for people who might come out but apart from an Uber Eats rider on a moped going super fast over a traffic hump there was no one. It would only take a moment for a big man like him to snap her neck. Finally, they came to her red Fiat Punto nestled under a tree. There was no lamp post and the place appeared darker than the rest of the street.

'Well,' Martha said, 'here we are. Thank you for dinner.'

Abbas grabbed her hand suddenly; she jumped. He had never touched her hand and for a moment he caught her panic. 'Thank you,' Abbas said.

'For what?' Martha stuttered, desperately trying to compose herself.

'Well, I've never told anyone about this.'

She felt his hands; they were hairy, calloused and textured like rock. 'I am privileged.' She moved closer to him and

The Darkness Inside

hugged him. He didn't resist. In fact, if she looked at his face she would have found his eyes closed, breathing her in. He imagined himself waking up to her every day; he imagined how their children might look, how it would be to grow old with her. He imagined a whole lifetime with her, even felt how an eternity might feel woven into those strands of red hair.

'Well,' she said, extracting herself from his arms, 'I really need to go.'

'Oh, I am sorry,' he laughed, 'it has been a long time since I received a hug from a lady.'

She laughed too, as if she was laughing at her own foolishness. 'It's okay. I've never been hugged by a bear either.' She got into the car, gave him a wave and returned home, shaking nervously. God, she had pushed the limits this time. This was the first time Abbas had admitted to fighting in Syria and Radio's role in it! And, what's more, she had it all on tape. A little bit of work and maybe she might reveal more about the dastardly activities of his boss.

Abbas returned home to the Cronx and had such wild dreams that in the morning when he woke up to perform the Fajr prayer he needed to have a ritual shower due to the sticky semen discharge in his pyjamas.

40. Shak

Martha didn't care whether the government would fall, she really didn't. She didn't care that another boatload of wretched and desperate people had landed in Dover and a middle-aged Mr Smith was upset about it. It was the same language she heard in Italy, but Salvini knew as well as the British Prime Minister that without immigrants those vegetable fields in Battipaglia would be unpicked and left to rot. Fact. Why Paul wanted to run with it she couldn't understand, but he wanted to increase the website's revenue and the only way they could do that was through more clicks. As a result he'd recruited some useless uninformed little journalists who had no training whatsoever apart from vlogging, Snapchatting and micro-blogging, otherwise known as tweeting. They had mastered analytics and knew that the best time to tweet was between twelve and five. They knew when to use a hashtag and when not to. They felt comfortable talking about the most intimate topics without batting an eyelid. These nouveau-journalistes were self-centred, self-righteous and easily offended. On their shoulders rested the future of the fourth estate and they had to produce in-depth, catchy videos that summed things up in thirty seconds. Not only would this create more clicks but it would create intellectual dwarfs with the attention spans of children. Martha wondered how they would explain complex issues in thirty seconds. She was

The Darkness Inside

already disturbed by how low journalism had fallen. Her pet hates were the *Independent* articles which had top lines like 'Procrastination is a sign of intelligence', 'Watching trashy movies is a sign of intelligence', 'Sleeping in is a sign of intelligence', 'Flatulence is a sign... '. As always, these articles, peppered with modal verbs such as 'may' and 'could', didn't benefit anyone. They vindicated all of mankind's vices that ancient man used to fight against and gave modern man an inflated sense of his own abilities. It horrified her that such trash was beginning to appear on their website too. She was upset that the introduction of these digital journalists was harming the company. She wanted to bring it up with Paul but after their stormy meeting, she felt she could no longer raise those issues anymore. The meeting had put distance between them, not because he had changed but perhaps because she knew that she was being duplicitous, and felt that somehow his gaze would reveal that darkness. So she preferred to lurk in the shadows and chug along, acting as if everything was normal even though she loathed the presence of these journalists in the team. But then again, maybe she was getting old. The *Loop* was a website, it depended on clicks and advertising revenue, so these youngsters kept her in a well-paid job.

But she was not too bothered by those considerations anymore. The truth was, her real work began after she left Shoreditch. She had become part of the darkness. She didn't care that some lazy bum journalist on her watch was depriving society of sentient citizens by writing an article that suggested: promiscuity was a sign of intelligence or something to that effect.

The Darkness Inside

This Friday she was going to do the same thing as usual. She left her workplace hoping to grab a quick bite before she went home to prepare for the next day. As she turned the corner and headed towards Brick Lane a voice, a London voice, called her name.

'Miss Fillippo!'

She turned around and there was a man with gold-rimmed spectacles, black hair gelled back with a crisp parting showing, and a long beard which on account of his brownness indicated his religiosity and devotion to Islam. Had he been white it would have condemned him to hipsterhood. He wore a nicely turned out jacket of the black variety and khaki trousers and boots. Could have been anyone, but definitely a person of success.

'Yes?' she said, slightly taken aback by a stranger calling her name. She was also troubled by his formality; there was officialdom in the way he said her surname. It was a name he pronounced perfectly, as if he knew it. He had digested it. He had said that name before to himself, maybe, perhaps even to his superiors, but he knew it for sure.

'Do you have a moment?'

'Well,' she replied, 'depends on who you are.'

'I am Tom Gardener's friend.'

Martha relaxed slightly. 'Who?'

'Well I think that's a bit irrelevant,' he said. 'I think you asked me to do you a favour once. So I hope you could repay the favour and hear me out.'

'At least gimme a name I can call you by.'

'Tom calls me Shak.'

They were at the top of Brick Lane on the Bethnal Green end and started to walk towards Whitechapel. Shak had

The Darkness Inside

this meandering way of walking, as if he was pondering a topic close to his heart. He had a forward-leaning gait which suggested he was thinking about something deeply. 'I want to apologise to you in advance, I fucking swear a lot. I don't mean anything by it. It's just that I've been in the army. We swear a lot. And I can't shake the habit off.'

'Okay,' replied Martha, unsure of where this conversation was going. 'So what do you want to tell me?'

'Well, you know that story you are working on? I just don't think it's going to end well. Trust me.'

'What do you mean? I hope you are not threatening a journalist?'

'No, heavens no! I am just saying that I don't want this story to run its course. There's too much at stake. If you get my drift.'

'No, I don't.'

'Too many fucking plates are in the air spinning, and something's going to give and it's not going to be Radio. I hope that's fucking clear.'

'Sorry?'

'This scoop isn't worth it. We have too many people that will suffer from it.'

'And what if I don't stop?'

'Then, I don't think I can stop the direction of play. It might be too late. You might lose more than just your job.'

Martha started to shake, her face full of rage. 'How dare you tell me what story I can and cannot do? I am the home editor of the *Loop*.'

'I am not. You are free to choose your actions. It's just once you have made your choice, you will also suffer the consequences, like Sid.'

The Darkness Inside

'You despicable bastard,' she said.

'Yes, I know,' he said nonchalantly, walking past the brewery, 'everyone feels the way you feel. Doesn't feel right. In fact, it feels wrong. But we have bigger concerns.'

'Sid wasn't given a warning.'

Shak nodded. 'Believe me it was a slip-up, but you are being given that chance.'

'I am surprised,' she said disgusted, 'that out of all people, you are doing the dirty work of the state.'

'Out of all people?' he said, adjusting his glasses and focusing his gaze on her. 'What is wrong with the state? Why is everyone obsessed with revolution?'

'Well, the crap your community have to go through, and now you do this.'

'Do what?'

'You are trying to shut me down.'

'You talk as if you have more rights than me. Remember, I'm not the foreigner here, you are. As far as I am concerned this is my country, isn't it? My grandfather came here in 1933 as a sailor at the age of twelve.'

She was silent for a moment. In what way was she the natural defender of people and not him? He kept on walking. 'You see these restaurants over there? Those were built by my people; some of them are my uncles. My old grandfather was here during the war, in the days of empire, working as a cloth merchant sleeping seven in a room, some sleeping while some were in the docks, God have mercy on them. And then with that graft he brought over his uncles. He put money away, went back, got married and brought my father here and he did the same. He put more money away so we could have an education. I never saw

The Darkness Inside

him when I was growing up. But he built that mosque, he got us married, he sorted out disputes, he paid his taxes, he helped old aunties with their immigration letters right here in the East End and he built businesses all over the country and back home. This is his country and this is my country. I am not saying the state, this country, hasn't done despicable things; look at the Bengal famine, millions died. Old man said they bloody raped my ancestral home. It's fucking true, and I hate them for it. But do I want to stop thinking in English? Do I want to have grown up in Bangladesh instead of here? I am not so sure. It's like having a bastard of a dad who you may have hated but still he's part of you. There is a tie that you can't sever. He's your father whether you like it or not. And now that he's old you have a duty to care for him the way God has instructed us to. So why shouldn't I join and serve instead of letting some fuckers ruin things for us?'

'But what happened to Sid needs justice. You should have stopped it.'

'Look, sometimes the choice is only between a bad choice and a worse choice. That's it. And you make your choice and you live with the consequences. Sometimes there are other considerations. You see, when a man says that he will kill fifty men unless you select one man to die from them, the right answer is to let him be responsible for the murder and if he kills them all, then you are blameless in the eyes of God. He is responsible for their deaths; he will be accountable. For the state, though, the moral choice is to select one of them to die to save the majority of its citizenry. The state thinks differently and operates on a different plane of morality. Whilst the state made an

The Darkness Inside

immoral choice and you a moral one, the men of state sleep soundly whilst you have insomnia.'

'And you? How do you sleep?'

'Like a baby, Martha,' he said smiling, using her first name for the first time. 'Walk away from this one.' He gave her his card; it just said 'Shak' and there was a number on it. 'Call me anytime.'

She took it. He began strolling away like he didn't have a care in the world. 'There's a great little Bengali restaurant behind the mosque where you can eat with your hands; it's delicious. You should try it.'

Martha had lost her appetite. She watched this strange figure walk away from her.

'Listen!' she shouted. Shak stopped. 'I am not sure I can walk away.'

He didn't look back, just raised his hand and made the sign of a telephone. 'Think about it,' he said, 'and let me know. Still not too late.'

He left her on Brick Lane deeply perturbed by the encounter and instead of going home she headed to West Croydon. Sid not only calmed her nervousness but also took the whole account down word for word and took a snap of Shak's calling card.

41. Radio Pakistan

Abdul Rahman sat in the barren room; the dark green paint was flaking off the wall and its cruelty became apparent. The call of the hoopoe outside made him look to the window. He could not see the crested bird but he could envy it. He imagined it taking a dust bath in the courtyard, undisturbed by the inmates inside. He looked up and could see the bright sun rays coming in through the window bars and falling on the table and his arm. The heat's intensity was nice in the coolness of the room he was sitting in. A fly buzzed around him and sat on his sweaty forehead, uncurling its long tongue on his salty brow, and he brought his cuffed hands up to discourage it from licking him. But it really didn't make a difference. He began to have murderous designs on the fly – there was really nothing else to do, so why not?

The steel door was opened and the governor, a grim fellow with a classic Pakistani mustachio wearing a crisp uniform, entered. He spoke perfect English, albeit with a Pakistani accent. They had already clashed before; he was a proper fucker. The governor was determined to put the Pakistani back into him by hook or by crook.

'Butt Saab,' Abdul Rahman said in an exaggerated version of a Pakistani accent that you might hear in Peshawar or Lahore. It annoyed the prison governor no end. He knew that although 'Butt' was a very common Pakistani surname the addition of 'Saab', a term of respect, had been by way

The Darkness Inside

of the accent turned into one which punned on the English 'butt' and therefore took aim at his character. To his mind the prisoner was implying that he was not an authority but a mere peasant. In other words, he was a country bumpkin arsehole; Mr Bum, as it were. And the governor knew it, as did the prisoner. If the governor tried to pin it on him for insubordination, the prisoner could always plead ignorance and deny it. That was the beauty of it.

The question had always been what to do with the prisoner. When the prisoner had been seized he had continued to fight even as he had the muzzle of a gun stuck into him. In here, he insisted on seeing a lawyer, declaring that he was a British citizen. He demanded consular services. So the governor was in a fix. Was he British? And if he was, what would the British response be if he was maltreated? In his experience, sometimes they cared and sometimes they turned a blind eye. He tried various things to beat the 'Pakistani' back into him. Initially, he thought he was acting. Pakistanis knew and understood hierarchy – a woman was either a wife or a sister, mother, aunty and so forth. A man was a brother, uncle, father, grandfather, sheikh. Respect and honour were given according to age and place in society. It was beautiful – the governor thought it was the way God had ordered the world. As long as one remembered that every pauper had a king in his lineage and every king had a pauper in his, one could remain humble. Thus when he dealt with Pakistani prisoners they gave him his due and if not he could beat it into them real quick: pop! pop! pop! with a lollipop stick and that was it; order was restored. But this one did not understand these universal concepts and it confounded him. He had applied so many strategies that

The Darkness Inside

he became convinced that maybe, just maybe, he should get in touch with the British consulate to check whether he actually was British.

Governor Butt had used the classic drill tactic; he had placed the prisoner next to a room where he could hear the drill whirring and the screaming – that wild screaming that one could not simply act out or recreate. He had told the prisoner that right now, Islam Khan was using a Black+Decker and causing a lifetime of damage to a man's rectum. No response. That bearded bastard just stuck to his story. He recited verses from the Quran and repeated the refrain: 'I am British. I want a lawyer.'

The wardens, all wiry fellows, were not keen on administering any beatings because the pain they would suffer in order to inflict them would not be worth their while. So they were reluctant to go into his cell. He could see it in their faces; it was as if they were going into a cage with a bear totally unprepared.

Once they had pounced on him in his bare cell thinking he was asleep but the animal woke up like a werewolf and mauled them; one of them was hospitalised and it looked like the inmate had bitten off his nose. Every time he walked past the guard he'd rub his stomach as if to say that his nose was delicious, that it had nourished his thick arms. To keep them on their toes, he would do his martial arts on the walls, every day banging away on them just to let them know that he was always alert. It meant that even paying some big inmates to attack him was not worth it; sometimes, he'd walk around the courtyard in his vest, his big arms swinging from side to side as if he was strutting or grandstanding to everyone. He'd barge one of the prisoners, and see if they would dare to say anything to him. The scars of cuts on his neck, the tattoos, it was all there for them to see. They had seen the Bollywood movies – the inmate seemed to fit all of that. Soon enough he was grandstanding with a crew, some of whom knew who he was by his reputation, and some of whom became mesmerised by his brutal charisma. The governor was in a dilemma – if he asked for outside help from his colleagues, he would be a laughing stock.

'To submit an ox,' they would say, 'you have to beat him till he's black and blue and then he will say he is Bin Laden's sister if you order him to.'

It wasn't as simple as that. Somehow the bastard had contrived, perhaps with his visitors, to get the governor's brother kidnapped. People in Peshawar, Sialkot, Jhelum knew the reputation of his family, and so to kidnap his brother so blatantly must have been achieved with tribal sanction. So when Governor Butt walked in to confront the prisoner, the latter just raised his hands innocently and told him to get in touch with the Kharroti tribe to facilitate his brother's release.

There was the same insolent refrain, 'I am a British citizen,' then a grin would follow and he'd add the word 'mate'. Not 'sir' as was expected. It was as if they were equals. The governor would be fuming in the office whilst his teary sister-in-law demanded that her husband be released and told him that it was all his fault. He would go home, and the women would start, and then the elders would be banging on his door and he would have no peace. No peace. So he called the consulate and explained the situation. They called him back.

The Darkness Inside

'Mr Butt,' the man said, 'is it possible that we can visit him?'

'Certainly.'

'When?'

'Tuesday.'

The governor then moved the prisoner to a better cell and instructed his wardens to treat him well.

And now here they were. It was Tuesday and he stood in front of the smug bastard, who looked at him as if to say: 'I told you so.'

The consular staff, both English-English, presented themselves in front of Abdul Rahman. One of them, Ms Ophelia, was a lady in her early forties; she was slightly podgy and clearly didn't enjoy the humid climate his country offered. The second was Mr Tyson. He wasn't much of a talker, and preferred to sit at the back, as it were, merely to observe the drama.

'Hello, Mr Khan, I am Margaret and this here is Mr Tyson,' Ms Ophelia said apologetically. Just why she was apologetic only she knew. 'We got here as soon as we found out. I hope you have been treated well?'

'Not at all,' said Abdul Rahman, his inflections, his intonations imperceptibly mimicking hers. 'I have been treated atrociously. I have been placed in solitary confinement, tortured, beaten and threatened. All my human rights have been violated and I have constantly asked for consular assistance, stating that I am a British citizen. Nothing more, nothing less.'

'I will certainly pass on your and indeed our concerns to the Pakistani government. Human rights are a cornerstone of our country.'

The Darkness Inside

'If you will allow me,' intervened the governor, 'I wouldn't believe a terrorist, if I were you. As we speak my brother has been kidnapped by his gang.'

Abdul Rahman laughed. 'Madam, my family ancestors are Pathaans from the Kharroti tribe; belonging to a tribe is like belonging to a large extended family. So when these people took me unlawfully and the elders gathered in a jirga council to see how they could help, they decided to mete out justice that way. Unfortunately, since I am stuck here I could do nothing about it.'

'I see,' said Ms Ophelia. 'Considering the circumstances that we are in, and this particularly tempestuous period in the region, Mr Khan, what exactly are you doing here?'

'Well I am a businessman and my uncles told me that there was business to be done here. You know especially as we are bombing the country there's lots of business to be had in the construction trade. Especially in Kabul.'

There was a barely perceptible smirk on Tyson's face. This was the first time the man with the silver hair had shown any sort of emotion at all. Abdul Rahman had just assumed he was a security detail but the smirk suggested otherwise.

'What's so funny?' Abdul Rahman asked, turning to the man. 'It's Tyson right? There are not many Tysons around in the UK, are there?'

'That's right,' said Tyson, 'not many of us at all.' He had a South London cockney-ish accent, and the way he carried himself suggested he was ex-army or ex-para, but Abdul Rahman couldn't be sure.

'So what is so funny then?' Abdul Rahman's intonation began to subtly mimic Tyson.

The Darkness Inside

'Well, can I talk freely, sir?'

Abdul Rahman nodded his assent.

Tyson turned to Ms Ophelia, 'Ms Ophelia, would you give us a moment alone?'

'Yes, certainly,' replied Ms Ophelia; she got up and left the interrogation room. Tyson turned to the governor. 'Mr Butt, could I have a moment alone with Mr Khan?'

'Certainly, sir,' the Governor said and left the room.

Tyson's hard face studied Abdul Rahman for a moment. 'Right mate, truth is I don't believe you. I just don't. Next minute you are going to tell me that you went over to Kabul because the naan breads over there are excellent. I can tell you for a fact that the naans of Peshawar beat them any day of the week. Smells like good old bullshit to me. What my old man would describe as a cock and bull story. If you ask me, you look like you're in deep fucking shit. I reckon you're a bog standard Jihadist who listened to Bin Laden's call to come and fight the Americans in Afghanistan.'

'Hang on a minute, just hang on a minute,' replied Abdul Rahman in a mock-surprised tone, mimicking his interrogator's cockney accent, 'me? Al-Qaeda? Me a global Jihadist? Are you having a laugh?! I don't know what you're on about. Good job no one is asking you isn't it?'

'Oh, but they do ask me. You might not know it yet, but you are what I say you are.' Tyson raised his hands up in mock innocence like one of those wise cockneys who still flogged his fruit and veg in Canning Town or Bermondsey. 'So why don't you help your country get rid of this scum, eh? What's wrong with that, eh?'

'All I want is to get back to finishing up my business

The Darkness Inside

contracts. That is all I want to do.'

'Suit yourself,' said Tyson, 'consular assistance takes a long time in Pakistan.' He got up and went to the door. The governor was waiting outside; he was so close to the door it looked as if he was eavesdropping. 'Mr Butt,' said Tyson, 'we're finished here, do convince him to cooperate with us. Take care, though, not to hurt him, he's a handsome feller.'

'Where I'm from, the only guys that call other guys handsome are fruitcakes,' said Abdul Rahman.

Tyson laughed. 'Ha! Good one! I like that! Proper cockney saying that, my old man uses that word! You might be British after all. Take care now. We'll be in touch.'

Abdul Rahman was no longer mistreated by Governor Butt. In theory this was a Pakistani version of remand – he was charged with 'visa violations' and all sorts of other charges they were cooking up against him. But clearly possessing the red passport helped in the way he was being treated. There were others in his situation but they were not getting the same five-star deluxe treatment. Still, it did not mean that he gave up on his tactics; he continued practising martial arts, pumping weights and doing crunches, press ups and exercises because he would be out soon and he wanted to look his best.

After a month, there still hadn't been any movement on his release. Ms Ophelia still visited him to check that his human rights were not being violated but she did not have any answers.

'Why am I still here?' he said, puzzled. 'I am a British citizen.'

'They are still working on your case.'

The Darkness Inside

The governor, of course, would make his visits and check up on the inmate. He had this British officer strut about him as he came down the corridor past his cell. There would be this faint smile underneath that impeccable mustachio.

Two months passed, and then three and four, and as the months went by Abdul Rahman realised that for some odd reason, any friends or human relationships he had cultivated were moved or transferred. Any new relationship he started, that person too would be moved to another prison. So if Abdul Rahman liked someone he would purposefully keep away from him, so he could at least see him from afar. Now he walked on his own and sat away from the rest. If the prisoners wanted to make friends he pushed them away. In fact, it came to a point when he preferred to sit alone. The prisoners thought he was a sulky bastard, and believed it was because he was British.

'What's the matter? Pakistani prison not good enough for him?' they would say behind his back. 'What does he expect? The Hilton? These Britishers are arrogant you know.'

Then for some reason there were wild rumours going around that he was an Indian spy from Kashmir; that he was in here for insulting the Prophet. That was not good news for him, for Pakistani criminals may have been scum but they also took pride in their country and they loved their Prophet. So Abdul Rahman had to make sure he was constantly on his guard against people who called themselves the Pakistani Defence League.

'They are plotting to kill me here,' he said to Ms Ophelia.

'How do you know? Are you being treated well?'

'Yes. But it's the rumours, they're turning the prisoners

against me.'

'Try to ignore them, that's what I would do.'

'Yes, but you are not here! It's been six months now and I have not even seen what the case against me is. What I am being charged with? I'm British! I'm British. I want to see someone above you.'

'I'll see what I can do.'

After a week Mr Taffazul and Mr Tyson came up to Peshawar from Islamabad. Mr Taffazul wore round, gold-rimmed spectacles and Mr Tyson, as always, wore his game face.

'Mr Khan, I am terribly sorry,' said Mr Taffazul, leaning forward; there was no sign of apology on his face. 'There are just a lot of issues we are trying to deal with so we can get you out of here as soon as possible.'

'What are they, exactly?'

'Well, it's the Americans.'

'What about the fucking Americans?'

'Calm down. Rest assured we are trying our best.'

'Well your best doesn't seem to be good enough. So what exactly is the problem?'

'Tyse,' said Mr Taffazul, 'have you got the file?'

'Certainly, sir.' Mr Tyson brought out a file from his briefcase and handed it over.

'Thank you.' Mr Taffazul looked at Abdul Rahman quietly. 'Look, it's not looking good for you, if I am honest.'

'Why, Mr Taffazul?'

'Please call me Shak,' said Mr Taffazul. 'Right now, the FBI has matched your fingerprints to several IEDs that killed some of their servicemen in Qargha reservoir near Kabul.'

The Darkness Inside

'Bullshit!'

'No, no, the evidence is all here. It's compelling enough. See, the Yanks have got a centre set up specifically for that – lessons learnt from their War on Terror in Iraq. So if they come across a cache or a house or even fragments that killed their men wherever they were fighting, they send it back to the labs and they have about three thousand six hundred government staff and forensics all over it.'

'They want to give the message,' interrupted Tyson, 'that US justice reaches everywhere. Your boys in Iraq were killing so many of their boys that in 2006 one of their generals, Abizaid, requested that a centre be set up to deal with just that. So now here we are nearing 2009 and the American military machine is working overtime to go after every fucker that kills one of their own. You've got to love the Americans for that – they always look after their own.' Tyson studied Abdul Rahman's reaction. He looked immovable. But beyond the stone-wall face, Tyson knew that this nugget of information had penetrated him. He gave Abdul Rahman a malevolent smile. Slowly but surely the moment of realisation would come.

'So,' said Shak, 'what we are saying, Mr Khan, is that the Americans are fighting to get you over to the States.'

'They want to put you on the chair and fry your brains out,' Tyson said with a morbid sneer.

'That's quite enough, Tyse,' Shak said, reining him in. He didn't want this to turn into some sadistic mental game, where the interrogator was metaphorically pulling the suspect's limbs apart one by one. This job had to be clinical and no pleasure should be had from cracking his skull open.

The Darkness Inside

'Well,' said Abdul Rahman, 'they can't do that can they?'

'Well, they are our allies. Of course we wouldn't extradite any of our citizens to another country if they faced the death penalty. But you fall under Pakistani jurisdiction and they might bypass us and ask Islamabad to extradite you. To put it lightly, we have a diplomatic shit storm. So we are trying to work with the Pakistanis on how to just keep you here.'

'What, forever?'

'Well, the Pakistani government has to consider who they are willing to upset: handing you over to us and upsetting Washington or handing you over to them and upsetting us. The British lion doesn't roar as loudly these days so you know what choice they are likely to make. But one hopes they will consider the impact this will have on our bilateral relations. My guess is that they will hand you over eventually when no one is looking. So we are trying desperately to keep you here. Hence the delay.'

'So you are saying that I won't be able to see my wife and kids?'

'No,' said Tyson, smiling like he loved his job. 'They can always visit, can't they?'

'There is, if I may, Mr Khan, another option,' said Shak. 'Look, you are clearly a very experienced, clever and useful man. You speak what, five languages? Is that right? You have a lot of field experience. If we and our US partners could benefit from your knowledge and you turned your skills to assisting us and saving a lot of lives, then I think you could go back to your wife and children. I think repentance and making amends would be viewed favourably by them.'

The Darkness Inside

'You mean come over to the empire, to the dark side?'

'Look, there isn't really a light and dark side in this world, is there? The cat doesn't chase the mouse for the sake of God. In this case, however, I believe that this is a good cause. Otherwise I wouldn't do what I am doing.'

'So give up living like a lion?'

'I wouldn't put it like that; rather you could help keep the wolves at bay and be a good shepherd. That's service.'

'Well I'm not sure I could do that.'

'Well, let me give you my card, and you think about it. You could be back with your wife and child in no time.' Shak handed over his card. 'And I will personally look after you. You have my word on that.'

Mr Tyson got up and gave him a leer. 'You know, your missus is a beautiful woman still – imagine her wasting away. When was the last time you was with her?'

Abdul Rahman got up, about to go for him.

'You can't do that. I am British.'

'Mate,' said Tyson, bored, 'you sound like a radio.'

That night, as Abdul Rahman lay in his cell, he found himself making love to his wife. It was incredible and felt so real. So real that when he woke up he turned onto his side, to hold her, and not finding her there thought that she was in the other room feeding their daughter. But when he called her she was absent. He lay there realising where he was; he started to cry. Would she wait for him? He felt in between his legs and he was sticky. Didn't they have those desires as well? What about his daughter? He got up, brushing the thought out of his mind. He was about to start his training in his cell, the press ups, the push ups, the wall-punching, all of it. But then, he wondered whether there was any point to it. He knew that the governor wouldn't do anything to him now. And so he sat down and went back to bed and slept.

When the governor came around over the following weeks and inquired chirpily, 'Mr Radio, would you like to see Ms Ophelia today?' Abdul Rahman shook his head. The name that the governor had introduced somehow made the rounds amongst the inmates and the wardens and they used it so often that in the end Abdul Rahman started to answer to it. By the end of the year, he had ballooned to eighteen stone and would only answer to the name of Radio since there were many Abdul Rahmans in prison. It was only when he received a letter from his wife with a picture of her in all her resplendent, fecund and beautiful glory with their little daughter, and he caught a reflection of himself, a fat, ugly slob, that he requested to see Mr Shaker Taffazul in Islamabad.

42. La Proposizione

Martha and Abbas met again at the Syrian restaurant in Shepherd's Bush and it was as though he was back in the streets of Aleppo again, smiling and bantering with the waiters. He had smartened up, wearing a blazer and a suit jacket made of worsted wool. Admittedly, the boots and jeans needed work but it was a start. He had even tidied up his beard and had a haircut. He could just about pass for handsome when he looked after himself. It was funny, she thought, how someone so harsh could be so relaxed. Even though he said that one should get used to the rough life, because luxury didn't last forever, he introduced her to fetteh, a combination of chickpeas, sesame, walnuts, oil and bread; the dish was perhaps one of the simplest but tastiest foods she had ever tried. He probably wouldn't admit it but he was a bonafide buongustaio – a food connoisseur.

'Fetteh,' he said lovingly, 'used to keep us warm during the winter. We were always cold.' He shuddered with the memory of the Syrian winter.

'I'm surprised that you, for all your talk of not liking luxury, relish it.'

'Who doesn't?' Abbas replied. 'I just don't want to get used to it. You know we used to have showers in ice-cold rivers in Syria and now I can't even stick my toes in if it's not warm. See what luxury does? Makes you soft. Makes you too attached to the world so you can't let go.'

The Darkness Inside

Martha noticed this strange nervousness, an affected nonchalance about him, like tonight was all or nothing. Everything she asked, he had an answer to. 'How comes you never told me about your family?'

'What is there to tell? We were poor.'

'Tell me about your mum.'

'Why? Do you want to meet her?' he replied, followed by nervous laughter which had a serious edge to it. She could feel it. In the end it became tiring and she looked at her watch and she made an excuse.

'I need to go back home. I have an important meeting tomorrow.'

'Me too.'

He took care of the bill. She expected him to accompany her to the car but this time she wasn't nervous at all. The night was warmer and had that spring feel to it. She had also made sure she was parked in Westfield Shopping Centre; it was well-lit, there were cameras everywhere and, moreover, there were plenty of security guards about. So she walked towards Shepherd's Bush Green without fear, chatting away with him.

When they reached the underground car park Abbas told her, 'You know, I am going away soon.'

'I see. That's a bit unusual and sudden, isn't it? How long for? Where are you going?'

'Well,' said Abbas nervously, 'that sort of depends on you.'

'How?'

'Well, I would like to introduce you to my mum.'

'I see.' She pretended not to understand his meaning but she knew exactly what he meant. In her culture, introducing someone to your parents meant that marriage was on the

The Darkness Inside

cards – that the person was special. 'How lovely,' she replied, feigning ignorance. 'Me too, I would love to meet her!'

'No, I don't think you understand, Martha. I want to be your husband. I don't know if this thing you're playing with me is real or not. So I need to know.'

'Of course this is real,' said Martha, drawing closer.

He allowed her to come closer. He didn't push her away.

'I know where you work. I know what you do.'

'Oh, I see,' said Martha, taken slightly aback. The game was up. 'Do you know where I live?'

He nodded.

'You see, I'd like to believe that you're not a cold, calculating bitch, Martha.' There was menace in his voice. 'Maybe you started with one intention but then you got to know me and your intention changed. I don't know.'

It felt as if Abbas was throwing her a lifeline. He refused to believe that he had been played; he could not believe that this was just acting – her eyes didn't seem to lie. Her heart seemed so pure. He wanted to believe that she really did love him and instead of inflicting violence upon her like he would have done to any other spy, he made her this perverse offer. As if it was the only way for her to prove her loyalty, to avert accusations of betrayal, disloyalty and treachery. This was pure witch-dunking. Only marriage would wipe the slate clean. It would prove that she loved him. Otherwise he would just cut her, slice her and dice her and he'd feel no way about it.

In reality it was something she could not refuse, slavery as practised by the ancients; the conqueror won all the women and children and those that refused submission were put to the sword.

The Darkness Inside

She did not want to contemplate what would happen to her if she said 'no'. Those hard hands were clenching and unclenching – a sure sign of his nervousness.

'I am praying you will say "yes" because this thing is beyond my control,' Abbas said. There was a look on his face which had steel and sorrow written on it. 'That's why you shouldn't be attached to too many things.'

'What do you mean this thing is beyond your control?'

'I mean just that. Radio loves and respects me and he's given me a bit of time. He'd feel no way about running people over and leaving them for dead. So I'm praying that you'll say "yes".'

'I – do love you,' Martha said, her mind making thousands of calculations. 'But Islam is the biggest obstacle for me. I'm not the sort of woman who will obey her husband, which is your right in return for providing for and protecting me.'

His face lit up.

'Really? You would?' He nearly punched the air as if Liverpool had scored just because she was even considering it. 'Don't worry about it. You know I've been praying for this every night, since I found out.'

'And,' she added, 'I can't share you with another woman, like Radio's wives.' She grimaced. 'Italians are very jealous; how can I be with you after you have been with someone else? Yuck!'

'I promise, you will be the only one.' He willed her to say yes, moving forward now without the menace and gravitas, but with a longing for her.

'Look, I don't know,' she said, nervously stepping back. 'Just give me a few days?'

'Why?' he said. 'Either you know or you don't?'

The Darkness Inside

'It's a big step for a girl.'

'I see,' Abbas replied. She was right; marriage was a big step. 'Your friend, Tom, does he know about us?'

'A little bit.' She wanted to kick herself. 'Will you give me a few days?' She touched his hands and rubbed them. He looked towards the ground for a moment, thinking hard, and nodded.

'Show me what we have is real,' he said, 'and not an illusion – not just a game – and all will be good. I promise you.'

She kissed him on the cheek, smelt his sickly cheap aftershave and stepped into the Punto.

'It's all real, darling, believe me.' She flashed him a smile and a wave and drove off. Had Abbas sat next to her at that moment, he would have realised how hard she was breathing. She tried her best to stop herself shaking by gripping the steering wheel tightly as she drove. Once she was out of the Shepherd's Bush roundabout she took the first exit towards Notting Hill Gate, turned down the nearest side road and pulled in and stopped the car. She broke down in tears. She knew she could not run. He would find her, he would find Gardener and Sid, and Sid couldn't run from him. He'd probably chase her all the way back to Italy if need be – the sick bastard. She reached for her bag, brought out her cigarettes and lit one. She started to think clearly once the nicotine flowed through her. She needed more than a few days to settle her affairs here too; there was work, the mortgage and everything else. She couldn't just drop everything and run off, could she? If she rang the police, that would be another disaster; he would know. And if he knew, she would be in permanent fear of him – this murderer. The police, in her experience, permanently messed things up and usually sent you a letter with a 'no further action' statement, conveniently adding that if you had been a victim of crime you could call the victim support number below. They would kill her and they wouldn't even know about it till after the inquest. She sat there for a moment, wracking her brains trying to think of all the options that were available to her. She messaged Sid, staring at the screen, willing him to respond. But no response was forthcoming. She called him but he did not pick up.

She started the car up again and drove around London aimlessly, hoping that she would find the answers on its streets. She worried about returning home – perhaps there was someone waiting for her there. She worried about going to Gardener's house – perhaps he would be there watching her go in. It was around half past ten, when she drove past Vauxhall Bridge and the MI5 building, that Sid replied.

'Hey. What's up? You okay?'

She pulled up on a side road on the Embankment, put the hazard lights on and called him, not caring that she was parked on a double yellow. He picked up.

'Hey.'

'Sid, I need to see you.'

'Oh, you okay?' Sid replied. 'It's kinda late. Can't it wait till tomorrow?'

'Sid, I'm not messing with you. It's an emergency. Speak to the fucking nurse.'

'Okay,' Sid replied, 'come over. I'll speak to Rosa.'

She drove across Westminster Bridge and within forty

The Darkness Inside

minutes found herself in Mayday Hospital. She drove in, making sure that her car was parked in full view of the CCTV cameras. Entering the hospital, she found the nurse in Sid's ward expecting her. The nurse escorted her to Sid's room.

Sid was lying on the bed.

'Hey, Marth, what's going on?'

'Get your phone, I want this down, in case something happens to me.'

'Okay.' His eyes lit up. With some discomfort he hauled himself off the bed, reached for his phone, checked that it had enough juice in it and sat down on the chair opposite Martha.

Martha told him what had happened. She brought out the Marantz recorder from her jacket and handed him the SD card.

'It's all there, we need to break this story now,' she said. 'Expose this and run for the hills.'

'What? What are you talking about?'

'Look, we need to expose him now.'

'Marth, listen to yourself. We're not there yet.'

'What do you mean?' she said impatiently. 'You transcribed all the SD cards, right? You have been standing the stories up? We have enough, and today he more or less gave me the closest thing there is to a confession!'

He nodded. 'We still haven't had a legal team on this. We'd be sued if we were wrong. Only the lawyer can determine if this will amount to a smoking gun yet. Anyway, as soon as you break the story you are finished; Paul will fire you immediately. And not only that, you might just end up in a ditch. Marth, this story isn't worth it. It's not. Look at me.

The Darkness Inside

No story is worth it. I can live with this happening to me but not to you. I'm calling it a day.'

Martha's shoulders slumped, more out of relief than anything. She was worried that he would egg her on, just push things that one extra notch, but somehow he was different since the accident. More grown up, more calculating even. He didn't make her feel guilty any more.

'So what do we do now?'

'Call him.'

'Who?'

'Shak.'

Martha reached for her bag and looked for Shak's card. She found his number and called it. No one picked up. She saved the number, wrote a message on WhatsApp and sat there waiting for the two grey ticks to turn blue.

They talked about old times at uni and the things they had done together to pass the time. By the time the messages had turned blue she had called him twenty-five times; it was two in the morning. Shak called her and kept it brief.

'So you are letting this thing go?'

'Yes,' she replied.

'Promise? And I don't mean the sort of promise you made to your editor.'

'A serious promise. A Catholic promise.'

Shak laughed. 'Okay, that's good enough for me. Leave it to me. Stay at a friend's house, and you'll know when the problem has been solved.'

'You sure? What will you do about Abbas?'

'Leave him to me. Stay at a friend's house. Gardener's is fine.'

'Gardener's? You sure? How will I know?'

The Darkness Inside

'You'll know, don't worry about it.'

Martha put the phone down. 'That's it,' she said with finality.

'That was easy,' said Sid, stopping the recorder. 'Now let's do what he told you to do.'

Gardener was one of the few people they knew who had a landline. If he hadn't possessed one Martha would probably not have gone through with it and would have ended up sleeping on Sid's chair that night.

'How dare you call me at this time of night?' said his groggy voice, about to have a go at the person on the other end. Most of the calls he received those days on the landline were either from the AA or from a salesman trying to find out whether he had taken out a payment protection plan. He didn't expect Martha to be on the end, and he sensed a quiver of fear in her voice when she asked if she could stay over for a few days at his place. He told her to come over.

By the time she got to him, Martha found him in pyjamas with two mugs of hot chocolate, waiting for her. Over a mug she told him everything, and he listened. He didn't say anything more about it except that it was over and that she must be tired. And she was; it was dawn by the time they finished. Like a gentleman he slept in the living room while she slept in his bed. He had even changed the bedsheets for her. As she went to bed, he kissed her on the forehead.

'You can stay here for as long as you need.'

Over the following week she went into work as normal, always conscious that she might be watched. She asked Gardener if he could go back to her flat to fetch some clothes and toiletries. He obliged and was very

The Darkness Inside

understanding about her predicament. Not once did he judge her or tell her off for her stupidity. She suspected it was because he thought she might leave and go back to her house. During the evening they played Burraco, which she introduced to him, and he in turn introduced her to a game he loved called Risk. She also cooked for him in return for his sleeping in the living room. She thought he would make a wonderful dad, as he sat with her in the living room with his reading glasses enjoying a book, saying nothing but just being there.

It was during the second week, on a sunny morning, when she received an email from Natasha, one of the journalists who monitored the news during the night. The email was a circular sent to all the editors to update them of the major events that they had to be aware of in the morning editorial. Natasha had noted that a man in his late thirties had been found with several or 'multiple' stab wounds that proved to be fatal. The body was found in a country lane in Horley. The police had named the victim as Mr Abbas Rizwan. 'Police,' Natasha wrote, 'are keeping an open mind, but are not ruling out that the killing might be gang-related. The victim had a criminal record.'

In the editorial meeting, one of the younger editors suggested that perhaps the story could be used as a peg to ask the bigger question about the state of knife crime in London. 'Perhaps,' he said, lighting up as if he could see it in his mind's eye, 'we could make a big splash on it. With infographics, incorporating text, video and interactive parts – you know we could really own this story, like the way the *New York Times* did with the shooting spree in Las Vegas! Amazing!'

The Darkness Inside

Martha watched him. He was young, hungry and willing to go with any story that would lead to accolades and glory.

'Perhaps we could ask whether Sadiq Khan or even the Home Office are on top of crime figures? We could doorstep the Mayor!'

The young editor was already seeing how many clicks and retweets and likes that would get.

But Martha shut the story and his ambitions down brutally.

'Look,' she said, 'we have nearly lost a member of the team over such stories so we need to think about our stakeholders. They are still sore about stories like these, let alone staff members who knew Sid. Let's not make too much out of this.'

Paul agreed with her assessment. Afterwards he pulled her aside to thank her for being so sensitive to staff morale and not reopening such a painful chapter in the *Loop*'s history.

The death of Abbas made a short print segment in the *Loop* which simply rehashed the police press release and left the story to die. But after the meeting Martha could no longer work that day, nor the next. She called in sick and stayed in bed all day. Gardener noticed. He had also seen the news of the latest knife crime victim of London.

He came face to face with the victim; a picture of him smiling with his friends was being circulated. There was the usual quote from one of the workers, Zia, in the car wash: 'He was the nicest guy in the world. Wouldn't harm a fly.' His mother was, of course, shocked and described him as her angel; the local MP was saddened by this 'tragic loss'; and so the news cycle ended. On Twitter someone blamed Brexit for his death, whilst another blamed Remainers, another the Elders of Zion, and so Abbas was forgotten with

The Darkness Inside

a gif, a meme and an emoji.

After two days of staying in bed, Gardener confronted Martha.

'What is going on? Martha? Why are you not going to work?'

'I can't.'

'Why?'

'Because I feel there's a darkness inside me that has grown and grown and is about to bloom, or maybe it has already bloomed. It is killing me inside. This need for the bright, bold and intense is consuming me. And I don't know what to do.'

'Well,' said Gardener, 'maybe it's time to get out?'

'You think?'

'Maybe. I know I would. I don't want to die a cynical bastard with no faith in humanity, feeling nothing for no one.'

'Maybe I should get out.'

'Maybe I should join you.'

He held her hand and squeezed it.

43. Mo Salah and Firmino

Sid and Femi were like the two Liverpool strikers Mo Salah and Firmino – totally unstoppable. They had smashed through, they were kings of Europe. After his resignation at the *Loop*, Femi got Sid moved from Mayday Hospital to the Radisson Blu, Covent Garden. Before they broke the story, they sat down and meticulously planned out the news strategy.

Then the team was briefed in detail on how they were going to break the story, who was going to be responsible for what and how to prepare themselves for the consequences. The news cycle would be gruelling.

'Give the wife and kids kisses and hugs because they aren't going to see you for a week or two.'

Sid had worked hard despite the thirst and hunger of Ramadan. They had asked the questions, they had stood up the facts, they had surveilled and watched their subjects. Femi had the calm confidence of a man who knew himself. He got Middle East specialists to locate witnesses who had participated in the Battle of Aleppo Hospital and the massacre that followed. Some of them were now living in Istanbul selling tissues or working as day labourers or smugglers close to the Turkish-Syrian border. Femi sent these journalists to meet them in Antakya, Gaziantep, Reyhanli and Urfa to stand up the account, and many were able to identify the likes of Abbas Rizwan and Radio. They

The Darkness Inside

had also located people in Atmah, not just Syrians but also Médecins sans Frontières doctors who confirmed what had occurred on the day Anis' friend Khaled was killed. In fact, a hungry trainee had even found a YouTube video of Radio listening to a Najdi fighter reciting poetry. He was clapping along and joined in when the chorus came in. They had also turned Martha into an anonymous source; Sid was confident that she would not contest or challenge them. If she did, they could always pay her a day rate. Likely she wouldn't want anything to do with the story. That, along with Ayman's testimony and his own, meant that when they presented the material, from the secret recordings to the videos, the whole lot, they were confident that the lawyers would allow it to go to print. Still, they took their time scrutinising the evidence. What was to their advantage was that both Sami and Abbas were dead, and so could not pursue them for libel in the courts. But Radio could, of course, so the lawyers had to discuss each and every phrase that they could use in the articles.

The first story had a creative title: 'The Curious Incident of Anis Ferjani in the Night Time'. From there they dropped the bomb of a headline, direct and pugnacious: 'British Spies in League with Jihadists?' It was so sensational that all the papers and the broadcasters picked up on the story. It was a fantastic story on its own merit but Femi got the Public Relations team pushing hard to get it onto the agenda.

By the time the PR team had finished with the story it dominated the news cycle. Sid could just see every editorial meeting focused on bringing in new top lines, new questions, and editors barking at their reporters to bring something fresh to the table. It was like the Panama papers story breaking. He could see his ex-boss Paul pushing Daniels to get a new line. He pictured Daniels standing outside New Scotland Yard scrambling for a comment from Metropolitan Police Commissioner Cressida Dick or Neil Basu or some other counter-terror bigwig, whilst he would be sitting in a Radisson Blu working on the next piece and filing it.

The discomfort, the pain that shot through his body on occasion, was not even a thing as he worked. Sid had the news on constantly and watched his work from the hotel suite as *DEEP* Magazine dropped nugget after nugget every other day, making rival editors scramble and urge their reporters to get something new. They dropped the pictures. They dropped the names. They dropped the transcripts. They were so transparent that the police didn't even bother with a production order to get hold of the material. Usually the police slapped one of those on any terror-related story. Sometimes it was clear from the wording that they didn't want to do the legwork, that they were lazy shits and they saw fit to just take the hack's hard graft like a school bully. Other times it was just a fishing expedition; it was becoming increasingly clear that the production order was not being used for its intended purpose and it was causing journalists immense problems. Journos were having to shred, delete and get rid of material just before going to press and sometimes they killed the story in the cot knowing full well that the police would come after it and would want to know the source; they would have no leg to stand on. So much for free speech and Article 10 of the European Convention on Human Rights.

The Darkness Inside

Had they received a letter citing some counter-terror law or some obscure subsection of the law, they would have presented the police with neat indexed files with everything they needed to do their job effectively. But the production order never materialised. Sid scratched his head, wondering why they hadn't come after the material. He was even tempted to call them lazy.

'With all the heat on this case and the stink we've kicked up,' Femi explained, 'they're just playing it safe. Don't worry, we'll give them the files. It will give us more mileage on the story.'

'We can pick some little hungry DC and we'll own him forever.' Sid gave Femi a dirty little grin.

'They're feds, Sid, not journos.'

'So? That doesn't make them incorruptible.'

Then it became more personal. Sid penned his story: 'How I was left for dead by a former al-Qaeda operative.' This was followed up by a big feature: 'The Unit: An extrajudicial killing: the death of Abbas Rizwan.' In it, Sid showed in meticulous detail how this unit had taken him out when he had become a liability; and moreover, he made another allegation that it was Abbas Rizwan who was Anis' killer. He had sliced him by the neck with a butcher's knife as easily as he would cut a topside or slit the throat of a lamb. All these stories were dropped and the security services did not once rebut them. In fact, Sid suspected that this may have been a covert unit gone rogue, but he could not be sure. But then again, British spy chiefs had been in league with dictators in the past, so why not?

Soon ministers were being asked about what they knew and what they did not know. Labour was putting the Home

The Darkness Inside

Secretary on the spot during Prime Minister's Question Time. The Prime Minister looked even more haggard than usual. The Home Secretary's bald head was even shinier, glistening with nervous perspiration. His counterpart, Diane Abbott, asked him whether British security services were complicit in such acts and what protocol had been followed. He did not have satisfactory answers.

There were reviews and more reviews in Portcullis House. Comment was sought. A BBC correspondent located Ms Ophelia and Mr Tyson. Mr Taffazul found himself opening his door ambushed by a hungry press asking him whether he was the handler for Mr Abdul Rahman Khan and responsible for Anis' death. There were anonymous interviews done by *DEEP* Magazine with Anis' sister.

Video emerged of armed police making several arrests including Yasser Balkhi, the former employer of Abbas Rizwan, and Radio. Whilst many of the men and women covered their faces, there was none of that hiding or skulking from Radio. He walked into the police van, calm, handcuffed as if he was a political prisoner, even giving those filming the V for the victory sign, calling it police harassment and Islamophobia. He acted as though he was Julian Assange. Both Yasser and Radio were held at Paddington high security police station where special branch officers were itching to ask them about everything mentioned in the articles, from Anis' disability and Radio's role in Khaled's death to Anis trying to expose Radio's business activities because he wanted revenge for his friend's death in Syria. They wanted to ask him about Sid's accident, the killing of Abbas Rizwan and, of course, his links to the security services. They had a lot of questions to

The Darkness Inside

ask. All of them were met with a 'no comment'.

In the end there were ministerial firings. To Sid's satisfaction, before he even started his new job as *DEEP* magazine's investigations editor, he had already dropped one of the biggest stories of the year. He was getting phone calls and job offers from all the international papers, from the *New York Times*; to the *Washington Post* to the *Economist* to Al Jazeera. He finally got his blue-tick verification.

He watched his Twitter timeline. There were competitors and colleagues who had seventeen thousand followers, then some with as many as seventy thousand followers, and he was somewhere in between. He frowned at that. But having so many followers and newfound friends also had its price. He had to be careful what he said and how he behaved. Whilst he had many new online friends and followers, he had also lost a few.

Tom and Martha left for Italy pretty soon after the story broke – it made sense. Sid guessed that Tom would have to work hard to reestablish trust in his line of business and would probably spend the rest of his days chugging out dull court reports for the broadsheets. Tom had betrayed a source, and if he could betray his source then who else could he betray? He hadn't called since the day they had argued. But Sid knew he had done him a favour – Tom had her now. He was sure he'd give up his job for that any day of the week.

Martha, though, did call. But he didn't reply. So she wrote him a whole bunch of expletives: bastard, traitor, duplicitous cunt and other Italian swear words that he had to Google to fully understand. Rompicazzo was probably

The Darkness Inside

his favourite. He didn't blame her. She got sacked as soon as the story broke. Paul had clocked on immediately and told her to clear her desk.

After all, how could an invalid in hospital have broken such a big story if it wasn't for her? It all came out; she had broken every single code in the company rule book and she had to go that same day. Paul was right; if she behaved like that at the magazine Sid would fire her himself, but even so, she had found Tom. So it was all good. No real harm done. Perhaps he could rekindle the relationship when they'd had a bunch of kids together and they would thank him for pushing through.

It was only his sister who went all sanctimonious on him; how could he live with betraying them?

Easy. What she didn't understand was that everyone was an oppressor in someone else's story – that's life. It just can't be helped.

'You need to push through,' he had said, 'to get to the next level. They were holding me back.'

'I take it Ramadan did your heart no good.'

'Well at least Anis' mum prayed for me for nailing her killers.'

'That's a start,' she replied sarcastically.

'Yeah, that is a start.'

Printed in Great Britain
by Amazon